MR. GREX OF MONTE CARLO

She leaned across and with trembling fingers backed number
fourteen *en plein*. FRONTISPIECE. *See page 257.*

THE WORKS OF

E. PHILLIPS OPPENHEIM

MR. GREX OF MONTE CARLO

THE REVIEW OF REVIEWS CORPORATION
PUBLISHERS   ::   ::   ::   NEW YORK

Published by arrangement with Little, Brown & Co.

Printed in the U.S.A.

MR. GREX OF MONTE CARLO

CHAPTER I

AN UNEXPECTED MEETING

The eyes of the man who had looked in upon
a scene inordinately, fantastically brilliant, under-
went, after those first few moments of comparative
indifference, a curious transformation. He was con-
templating one of the sights of the world. Crowded
around the two roulette tables, promenading or
lounging on the heavily cushioned divans against the
wall, he took note of a conglomeration of people
representing, perhaps, every grade of society, every
nationality of importance, yet with a curious common likeness by reason of their tribute paid to
fashion. He glanced unmoved at a beautiful Englishwoman who was a duchess but looked otherwise;
at an equally beautiful Frenchwoman, who looked
like a duchess but was — otherwise. On every side
of him were women gowned by the great artists of
the day, women like flowers, all perfume and soft-
ness and colour. His eyes passed them over almost
carelessly. A little tired with many weeks' travel
in countries where the luxuries of life were few, his
senses were dulled to the magnificence of the scene,
his pulses as yet had not responded to its charm

and wonder. And then the change came. He saw
a woman standing almost exactly opposite to him
at the nearest roulette table, and he gave a notice-
able start. For a moment his pale, expressionless
face was transformed, his secret was at any one's
mercy. That, however, was the affair of an instant
only. He was used to shocks and he survived this
one. He moved a little on one side from his prominent place in the centre of the wide-flung doorway.
He stood by one of the divans and watched.

She was tall and fair and slight. She wore a
high-necked gown of shimmering grey, a black hat,
under which her many coils of hair shone like gold,
and a necklace of pearls around her throat, pearls
on which his eyes had rested with a curious expression. She played, unlike many of her neighbours,
with restraint, yet with interest, almost enthusiasm.
There was none of the strain of the gambler about
her smooth, beautiful face. Her delicately curved
lips were free from the grim lines of concentrated
acquisitiveness. She was thirty-two years old but
she looked much younger as she stood there, her lips
a little parted in a pleased smile of anticipation.
She was leaning a little over the table and her eyes
were fixed with humorous intentness upon the spin-
ning wheel. Even amongst that crowd of beautiful
women she possessed a certain individual distinction.
She not only looked what she was — an Englishwoman of good birth — but there was a certain delicate aloofness about her expression and bearing
which gave an added charm to a personality which
seemed to combine the two extremes of provocative-
ness and reserve. One would have hesitated to ad-

dress to her even the chance remarks which pass so easily between strangers around the tables.

"Violet here!" the man murmured under his breath. "Violet!"

There was tragedy in the whisper, a gleam of something like tragedy, too, in the look which passed between the man and the woman a few moments later. With her hands full of plaques which she had just won, she raised her eyes at last from the board. The smile upon her lips was the delighted smile of a girl. And then, as she was in the act of sweeping her winnings into her gold bag, she saw the man opposite. The smile seemed to die from her lips; it appeared, indeed, to pass with all else of expression from her face. The plaques dropped one by one through her fingers, into the satchel. Her eyes remained fixed upon him as though she were looking upon a ghost. The seconds seemed drawn out into a grim hiatus of time. The croupier's voice, the muttered imprecation of a loser by her side, the necessity of making some slight movement in order to allow the passage of an arm from some one in search of change — some such trifle at last brought her back from the shadows. Her expression became at once more normal. She did not remove her eyes but she very slightly inclined her head towards the man. He, in return, bowed very gravely and without a smile.

The table in front of her was cleared now. People were beginning to consider their next coup. The voice of the croupier, with his parrot-like cry, travelled down the board.

"*Faites vos jeux, mesdames et messieurs.*"

The woman made no effort to stake. After a

moment's hesitation she yielded up her place, and moving backwards, seated herself upon an empty divan. Rapidly the thoughts began to form themselves in her mind. Her delicate eyebrows drew closer together in a distinct frown. After that first shock, that queer turmoil of feeling, beyond analysis, yet having within it some entirely unexpected constituent, she found herself disposed to be angry. The sensation had not subsided when a moment or two later she was conscious that the man whose coming had proved so disturbing was standing before her.

"Good afternoon," he said, a little stiffly.

She raised her eyes. The frown was still upon her forehead, although to a certain extent it was contradicted by a slight tremulousness of the lips.

"Good afternoon, Henry!"

For some reason or other, further speech seemed to him a difficult matter. He moved towards the vacant place.

"If you have no objection," he observed, as he seated himself.

She unfurled her fan — an ancient but wonderful weapon of defence. It gave her a brief respite. Then she looked at him calmly.

"Of all places in the world," she murmured, "to meet you here!"

"Is it so extraordinary?"

"I find it so," she admitted. "You don't at all fit in, you know. A scene like this," she added, glancing around, "would scarcely ever be likely to attract you for its own sake, would it?"

"It doesn't particularly," he admitted.

"Then why have you come?"

He remained silent. The frown upon her forehead deepened.

"Perhaps," she went on coldly, "I can help you with your reply. You have come because you are not satisfied with the reports of the private detective whom you have engaged to watch me. You have come to supplement them by your own investigation."

His frown matched hers. The coldness of his tone was rendered even more bitter by its note of anger.

"I am surprised that you should have thought me capable of such an action," he declared. "All I can say is that it is thoroughly in keeping with your other suspicions of me, and that I find it absolutely unworthy."

She laughed a little incredulously, not altogether naturally.

"My dear Henry," she protested, "I cannot flatter myself that there is any other person in the world sufficiently interested in my movements to have me watched."

"Are you really under the impression that that is the case?" he enquired grimly.

"It isn't a matter of impression at all," she retorted. "It is the truth. I was followed from London, I was watched at Cannes, I am watched here day by day — by a little man in a brown suit and a Homburg hat, and with a habit of lounging. He lounges under my windows, he is probably lounging across the way now. He has lounged within fifty yards of me for the last three weeks, and to tell you the truth I am tired of him. Couldn't I have a

week's holiday? I'll keep a diary and tell you all
that you want to know."

" Is it sufficient," he asked, " for me to assure you,
upon my word of honour, that I know nothing of
this? "

She was somewhat startled. She turned and
looked at him. His tone was convincing. He had
not the face of a man whose word of honour was a
negligible thing.

" But, Henry," she protested, " I tell you that
there is no doubt about the matter. I am watched
day and night — I, an insignificant person whose
doings can be of no possible interest save to you and
you only."

The man did not at once reply. His thoughts
seemed to have wandered off for a moment. When
he spoke again, his tone had lost its note of resentment.

" I do not blame you for your suspicion," he said
calmly, " although I can assure you that I have
never had any idea of having you watched. It is
not a course which could possibly have suggested
itself to me, even in my most unhappy moments."

She was puzzled — at once puzzled and interested.

" I am so glad to hear this," she said, " and of
course I believe you, but there the fact is. I think
that you will agree with me that it is curious."

" Isn't it possible," he ventured to suggest, " that
it is your companions who are the object of this
man's vigilance? You are not, I presume, alone
here? "

She eyed him a little defiantly.

" I am here," she announced, " with Mr. and Mrs. Draconmeyer."

He heard her without any change of expression, but somehow or other it was easy to see that her news, although more than half expected, had stung him.

" Mr. and Mrs. Draconmeyer," he repeated, with slight emphasis on the latter portion of the sentence.

" Certainly! I am sorry," she went on, a moment late, " that my companions do not meet with your approval. That, however, I could scarcely expect, considering—"

" Considering what? " he insisted, watching her steadfastly.

" Considering all things," she replied, after a moment's pause.

" Mrs. Draconmeyer is still an invalid? "

" She is still an invalid."

The slightly satirical note in his question seemed to provoke a certain defiance in her manner as she turned a little sideways towards him. She moved her fan slowly backwards and forwards, her head was thrown back, her manner was almost belligerent. He took up the challenge. He asked her in plain words the question which his eyes had already demanded.

" I find myself constrained to ask you," he said, in a studiously measured tone, " by what means you became possessed of the pearls you are wearing? I do not seem to remember them as your property."

Her eyes flashed.

" Don't you think," she returned, " that you are a little outstepping your privileges? "

"Not in the least," he declared. "You are my wife, and although you have defied me in a certain matter, you are still subject to my authority. I see you wearing jewels in public of which you were certainly not possessed a few months ago, and which neither your fortune nor mine —"

"Let me set your mind at rest," she interrupted icily. "The pearls are not mine. They belong to Mrs. Draconmeyer."

"Mrs. Draconmeyer!"

"I am wearing them," she continued, "at Linda's special request. She is too unwell to appear in public and she is very seldom able to wear any of her wonderful jewelry. It gives her pleasure to see them sometimes upon other people."

He remained quite silent for several moments. He was, in reality, passionately angry. Self-restraint, however, had become such a habit of his that there were no indications of his condition save in the slight twitchings of his long fingers and a tightening at the corners of his lips. She, however, recognised the symptoms without difficulty.

"Since you defy my authority," he said, "may I ask whether my wishes have any weight with you?"

"That depends," she replied.

"It is my earnest wish," he went on, "that you do not wear another woman's jewelry, either in public or privately."

She appeared to reflect for a moment. In effect she was struggling against a conviction that his request was reasonable.

"I am sorry," she said at last. "I see no harm

whatever in my doing so in this particular instance. It gives great pleasure to poor Mrs. Draconmeyer to see her jewels and admire them, even if she is unable to wear them herself. It gives me an intense joy which even a normal man could scarcely be expected to understand; certainly not you. I am sorry that I cannot humour you."

He leaned towards her.

" Not if I beg you? "

She looked at him fixedly, looked at him as though she searched for something in his face, or was pondering over something in his tone. It was a moment which might have meant much. If she could have seen into his heart and understood the fierce jealousy which prompted his words, it might have meant a very great deal. As it was, her contemplation appeared to be unsatisfactory.

" I am sorry that you should lay so much stress upon so small a thing," she said. " You were always unreasonable. Your present request is another instance of it. I was enjoying myself very much indeed until you came, and now you wish to deprive me of one of my chief pleasures. I cannot humour you."

He turned away. Even then chance might have intervened. The moment her words had been spoken she realised a certain injustice in them, realised a little, perhaps, the point of view of this man who was still her husband. She watched him almost eagerly, hoping to find some sign in his face that it was not only his stubborn pride which spoke. She failed, however. He was one of those men who know too well how to wear the mask.

"May I ask where you are staying here?" he enquired presently.

"At the Hotel de Paris."

"It is unfortunate," he observed. "I will move my quarters to-morrow."

She shrugged her shoulders.

"Monte Carlo is full of hotels," she remarked, "but it seems a pity that you should move. The place is large enough for both of us."

"It is not long," he retorted, "since you found London itself too small. I should be very sorry to spoil your holiday."

Her eyes seemed to dwell for a moment upon the Spanish dancer who sat at the table opposite them, a woman whose name had once been a household word, dethroned now, yet still insistent for notice and homage; commanding them, even, with the wreck of her beauty and the splendour of her clothes.

"It seems a queer place, this," she observed, "for domestic disagreements. Let us try to avoid disputable subjects. Shall I be too inquisitive if I ask you once more what in the name of all that is unsuitable brought you to such a place as Monte Carlo?"

He fenced with her question. Perhaps he resented the slightly ironical note in her tone. Perhaps there were other reasons.

"Why should I not come to Monte Carlo?" he enquired. "Parliament is not particularly amusing when one is in opposition, and I do not hunt. The whole world amuses itself here."

"But not you," she replied quickly. "I know you better than that, my dear Henry. There is nothing here or in this atmosphere which could possibly attract you for long. There is no work for you to do — work, the very breath of your body; work, the one thing you live for and were made for; work, you man of sawdust and red tape."

" Am I as bad as all that? " he asked quietly.

She fingered her pearls for a moment.

" Perhaps I haven't the right to complain," she acknowledged. " I have gone my own way always. But if one is permitted to look for a moment into the past, can you tell me a single hour when work was not the prominent thought in your brain, the idol before which you worshipped? Why, even our honeymoon was spent canvassing!"

" The election was an unexpected one," he reminded her.

" It would have been the same thing," she declared. " The only literature which you really understand is a Blue Book, and the only music you hear is the chiming of Big Ben."

" You speak," he remarked, " as though you resented these things. Yet you knew before you married me that I had ambitions, that I did not propose to lead an idle life."

" Oh, yes, I knew! " she assented drily. " But we are wandering from the point. I am still wondering what has brought you here. Have you come direct from England? "

He shook his head.

" I came to-day from Bordighera."

" More and more mysterious," she murmured. " Bordighera, indeed! I thought you once told me that you hated the Riviera."

" So I do," he agreed.

" And yet you are here? "

" Yet I am here."

" And you have not come to look after me," she went on, " and the mystery of the little brown man who watches me is still unexplained."

" I know nothing about that person," he asserted, " and I had no idea that you were here."

" Or you would not have come? " she challenged him.

" Your presence," he retorted, nettled into forgetting himself for a moment, " would not have altered my plans in the slightest."

" Then you have a reason for coming! " she exclaimed quickly.

He gave no sign of annoyance but his lips were firmly closed. She watched him steadfastly.

" I wonder at myself no longer," she continued. " I do not think that any woman in the world could ever live with a man to whom secrecy is as great a necessity as the very air he breathes. No wonder, my dear Henry, the politicians speak so well of you, and so confidently of your brilliant future! "

" I am not aware," he observed calmly, " that I have ever been unduly secretive so far as you are concerned. During the last few months, however, of our life together, you must remember that you chose to receive on terms of friendship a person whom I regard —"

Her eyes suddenly flashed him a warning. He dropped his voice almost to a whisper. A man was approaching them.

" As an enemy," he concluded, under his breath.

CHAPTER II

BY ACCIDENT OR DESIGN

The newcomer, who had presented himself now before Hunterleys and his wife, was a man of somewhat unusual appearance. He was tall, thickly-built, his black beard and closely-cropped hair were streaked with grey, he wore gold-rimmed spectacles, and he carried his head a little thrust forward, as though, even with the aid of his glasses, he was still short-sighted. He had the air of a foreigner, although his tone, when he spoke, was without accent. He held out his hand a little tentatively, an action, however, which Hunterleys appeared to ignore.

"My dear Sir Henry!" he exclaimed. "This is a surprise, indeed! Monte Carlo is absolutely the last place in the world in which I should have expected to come across you. The Sporting Club, too! Well, well, well!"

Hunterleys, standing easily with his hands behind his back, raised his eyebrows. The two men were of curiously contrasting types. Hunterleys, slim and distinguished, had still the frame of an athlete, notwithstanding his colourless cheeks and the worn lines about his eyes. He was dressed with extreme simplicity. His deep-set eyes and sensitive mouth were in marked contrast to the other's coarser mould of features and rather full lips. Yet there was about both men an air of strength, strength developed, perhaps, in a different manner, but still an appreciable quality.

"They say that the whole world is here," Hunterleys remarked. "Why may not I form a harmless unit of it?"

"Why not, indeed?" Draconmeyer assented heartily. "The most serious of us must have our frivolous moments. I hope that you will dine with us to-night? We shall be quite alone."

Hunterleys shook his head.

"Thank you," he said, "I have another engagement pending."

Mr. Draconmeyer was filled with polite regrets, but he did not renew the invitation.

"When did you arrive?" he asked.

"A few hours ago," Hunterleys replied.

"By the Luxe? How strange! I went down to meet it."

"I came from the other side."

"Ah!"

Mr. Draconmeyer's ejaculation was interrogative, Hunterleys hesitated for a moment. Then he continued with a little shrug of the shoulders.

"I have been staying at San Remo and Bordighera."

Mr. Draconmeyer was much interested.

"So that is where you have been burying yourself," he remarked. "I saw from the papers that you had accepted a six months' pair. Surely, though, you don't find the Italian Riviera very amusing?"

"I am abroad for a rest," Hunterleys replied.

Mr. Draconmeyer smiled curiously.

"A rest?" he repeated. "That rather belies your reputation, you know. They say that you are tireless, even when you are out of office."

Hunterleys turned from the speaker towards his wife.

"I have not tempted fortune myself yet," he observed. "I think that I shall have a look into the baccarat room. Do you care to stroll that way?"

Lady Hunterleys rose at once to her feet. Mr. Draconmeyer, however, intervened. He laid his fingers upon Hunterleys' arm.

"Sir Henry," he begged, "our meeting has been quite unexpected, but in a sense it is opportune. Will you be good enough to give me five minutes' conversation?"

"With pleasure," Hunterleys replied. "My time is quite at your disposal, if you have anything to say."

Draconmeyer led the way out of the crowded room, along the passage and into the little bar. They found a quiet corner and two easy-chairs. Draconmeyer gave an order to a waiter. For a few moments their conversation was conventional.

"I trust that you think your wife looking better for the change?" Draconmeyer began. "Her companionship is a source of great pleasure and relief to my poor wife."

"Does the conversation you wish to have with me refer to Lady Hunterleys?" her husband asked quietly. "If so, I should like to say a few preliminary words which would, I hope, place the matter at once beyond the possibility of any misunderstanding."

Draconmeyer moved a little uneasily in his place.

"I have other things to say," he declared, "yet I would gladly hear what is in your mind at the present moment. You do not, I fear, approve of this friendship between my wife and Lady Hunterleys."

Hunterleys was uncompromising, almost curt.

"I do not," he agreed. "It is probably no secret to you that my wife and I are temporarily estranged," he continued. "The chief reason for that estrangement is that I forbade her your house or your acquaintance."

Draconmeyer was a little taken back. Such extreme directness of speech was difficult to deal with.

"My dear Sir Henry," he protested, "you distress me. I do not understand your attitude in this matter at all."

"There is no necessity for you to understand it," Hunterleys retorted coolly. "I claim the right to regulate my wife's visiting list. She denies that right."

"Apart from the question of marital control," Mr. Draconmeyer persisted, "will you tell me why you consider my wife and myself unfit persons to find a place amongst Lady Hunterleys' acquaintances?"

"No man is bound to give the reason for his dislikes," Hunterleys replied. "Of your wife I know nothing. Nobody does. I have every sympathy with her unfortunate condition, and that is all. You personally I dislike. I dislike my wife to be seen with you, I dislike having her name associated with yours in any manner whatsoever. I dislike sitting with you here myself. I only hope that the five minutes' conversation which you have asked for will not be exceeded."

Mr. Draconmeyer had the air of a benevolent person who is deeply pained.

"Sir Henry," he sighed, "it is not possible for me to disregard such plain speaking. Forgive me if I am a little taken aback by it. You are known to be a very skilful diplomatist and you have many weapons in your armoury. One scarcely expected, however — one's breath is a little taken away by such candour."

"I am not aware," Hunterleys said calmly, "that the question of diplomacy need come in when one's only idea is to regulate the personal acquaintances of oneself and one's wife."

Mr. Draconmeyer sat quite still for a moment, stroking his black beard. His eyes were fixed upon the carpet. He seemed to be struggling with a problem.

"You have taken the ground from beneath my feet," he declared. "Your opinion of me is such that I hesitate to proceed at all in the matter which I desired to discuss with you."

"That," Hunterleys replied, "is entirely for you to decide. I am perfectly willing to listen to anything you have to say — all the more ready because now there can be no possibility of any misunderstanding between us."

"Very well," Mr. Draconmeyer assented, "I will proceed. After all, I am not sure that the personal element enters into what I was about to say. I was

going to propose not exactly an alliance — that, of
course, would not be possible — but I was certainly
going to suggest that you and I might be of some
service to one another."

" In what way? "

" I call myself an Englishman," Mr. Draconmeyer
went on. " I have made large sums of money in
England, I have grown to love England and English
ways. Yet I came, as you know, from Berlin. The
position which I hold in your city is still the position
of president of the greatest German bank in the
world. It is German finance which I have directed,
and with German money I have made my fortune.
To be frank with you, however, after these many
years in London I have grown to feel myself very
much of an Englishman."

Hunterleys was sitting perfectly still. His face
was rigid but expressionless. He was listening intently.

" On the other hand," Mr. Draconmeyer proceeded
slowly, " I wish to be wholly frank with you. At
heart I must remain always a German. The interests of my country must always be paramount. But
listen. In Germany there are, as you know, two
parties, and year by year they are drawing further
apart. I will not allude to factions. I will speak
broadly. There is the war party and there is the
peace party. I belong to the peace party. I belong to it as a German, and I belong to it as a
devoted friend of England, and if the threatened
conflict between the two should come, I should take
my stand as a peace-loving German-cum-English-
man against the war party even of my own country."

Hunterleys still made no sign. Yet for one who knew him it was easy to realise that he was listening and thinking with absorbed interest.

"So far," Draconmeyer pointed out, "I have laid my cards on the table. I have told you the solemn truth. I regret that it did not occur to me to do so many months ago in London. Now to proceed. I ask you to emulate my frankness, and in return I will give you information which should enable us to work hand in hand for the peace which we both desire."

"You ask me," Hunterleys said thoughtfully, "to be perfectly frank with you. In what respect? What is it that you wish from me?"

"Not political information," Mr. Draconmeyer declared, his eyes blinking behind his glasses. "For that I certainly should not come to you. I only wish to ask you a question, and I must ask it so that we may meet on a common ground of confidence. Are you here in Monte Carlo to look after your wife, or in search of change of air and scene? Is that your honest motive for being here? Or is there any other reason in the world which has prompted you to come to Monte Carlo during this particular month — I might almost say this particular week?"

Hunterleys' attitude was that of a man who holds in his hand a puzzle and is doubtful where to commence in his efforts to solve it.

"Are you not a little mysterious this afternoon, Mr. Draconmeyer?" he asked coldly. "Or are you trying to incite a supposititious curiosity? I really cannot see the drift of your question."

"Answer it," Mr. Draconmeyer insisted.

Hunterleys took a cigarette from his case, tapped it upon the table and lit it in leisurely fashion.

" If you have any idea," he said, " that I came here to confront my wife, or to interfere in any way with her movements, let me assure you that you are mistaken. I had no idea that Lady Hunterleys was in Monte Carlo. I am here because I have a six months' holiday, and a holiday for the average Englishman between January and April generally means, as you must be aware, the Riviera. I have tried Bordighera and San Remo. I have found them, as I no doubt shall find this place, wearisome. In the end I suppose I shall drift back to London."

Mr. Draconmeyer frowned.

" You left London," he remarked tersely, " on December first. It is to-day February twentieth. Do you wish me to understand that you have been at Bordighera and San Remo all that time? "

" How did you know when I left London? " Hunterleys demanded.

Mr. Draconmeyer pursed his lips.

" I heard of your departure from London entirely by accident," he said.   " Your wife, for some reason or other, declined to discuss your movements. I imagine that she was acting in accordance with your wishes."

" I see," Hunterleys observed coolly.   " And your present anxiety is to know where I spent the intervening time, and why I am here in Monte Carlo? Frankly, Mr. Draconmeyer, I look upon this close interest in my movements as an impertinence. My travels have been of no importance, but they concern myself only. I have no confidence to offer respecting them. If I had, it would not be to you that I should unburden myself."

" You suspect me, then? You doubt my integrity? "

" Not at all," Hunterleys assured his questioner. " For anything I know to the contrary, you are, outside the world of finance, one of the dullest and most harmless men existing. My own position is simply as I explained it during the first few sentences we exchanged. I do not like you, I detest my wife's name being associated with yours, and for that reason, the less I see of you the better I am pleased."

Mr. Draconmeyer nodded thoughtfully. He was, to all appearance, studying the pattern of the carpet. For once in his life he was genuinely puzzled. Was this man by his side merely a jealous husband, or had he any idea of the greater game which was being played around them? Had he, by any chance, arrived to take part in it? Was it wise, in any case, to pursue the subject further? Yet if he abandoned it at this juncture, it must be with a sense of failure, and failure was a thing to which he was not accustomed.

" Your frankness," he admitted grimly, " is almost exhilarating. Our personal relations being so clearly defined, I am inclined to go further even than I had intended. We cannot now possibly misunderstand one another. Supposing I were to tell you that your arrival in Monte Carlo, accidental though it may be, is in a sense opportune; that you may, in a short time meet here one or two politicians, friends of mine, with whom an interchange of views might be agreeable? Supposing I were to offer my services as an intermediary? You would like to bring about better relations with my country, would you not, Sir Henry? You are admittedly a statesman and an influential man in your Party. I am only a banker, it is true, but I have been taken into the confidence of those who direct the destinies of my country."

Hunterleys' face reflected none of the other's earnestness. He seemed, indeed, a little bored, and he answered almost irritably.

" I am much obliged to you," he said, " but Monte Carlo seems scarcely the place to me for political discussions, added to which I have no official position. I could not receive or exchange confidences. While my Party is out of power, there is nothing left for us but to mark time. I dare say you mean well, Mr. Draconmeyer," he added, rising to his feet, " but I am here to forget politics altogether, if I can. If you will excuse me, I think I will look in at the baccarat rooms."

He was on the point of departure when through the open doorway which communicated with the baccarat rooms beyond came a man of sufficiently arresting personality, a man remarkably fat, with close-cropped grey hair which stuck up like bristles all over his head; a huge, clean-shaven face which seemed concentrated at that moment in one tremendous smile of overwhelming good-humour. He held by the hand a little French girl, dark, small, looking almost like a marionette in her slim tailor-made costume. He recognised Draconmeyer with enthusiasm.

"My friend Draconmeyer," he exclaimed, in stentorian tones, "baccarat is the greatest game in the world. I have won — I, who know nothing about it, have won a hundred louis. It is amazing! There is no place like this in the world. We are here to drink a bottle of wine together, mademoiselle and I, mademoiselle who was at once my instructress and my mascot. Afterwards we go to the jeweler's. Why not? A fair division of the spoils — fifty louis for myself, fifty louis for a bracelet for mademoiselle. And then —"

He broke off suddenly. His gesture was almost dramatic.

"I am forgotten!" he cried, holding out his hand to Hunterleys,—"forgotten already! Sir Henry, there are many who forget me as a humble Minister of my master, but there are few who forget me physically. I am Selingman. We met in Berlin, six years ago. You came with your great Foreign Secretary."

"I remember you perfectly," Hunterleys assured him, as he submitted to the newcomer's vigorous handshake. "We shall meet again, I trust."

Selingman thrust his arm through Hunterleys' as though to prevent his departure.

"You shall not run away!" he declared. "I introduce both of you — Mr. Draconmeyer, the great Anglo-German banker; Sir Henry Hunterleys, the English politician — to Mademoiselle Estelle Nipon, of the Opera House. Now we all know one another. We shall be good friends. We will share that bottle of champagne."

"One bottle between four!" mademoiselle laughed,

poutingly. " And I am parched! I have taught
monsieur baccarat. I am exhausted."

" A magnum!" Selingman ordered in a voice of
thunder, shaking his fist at the startled waiter.
" We seat ourselves here at the round table.
Mademoiselle, we will drink champagne together
until the eyes of all of us sparkle as yours do. We
will drink champagne until we do not believe that
there is such a thing as losing at games or in life.
We will drink champagne until we all four believe
that we have been brought up together, that we are
bosom friends of a lifetime. See, this is how we will
place ourselves. Mademoiselle, if the others make
love to you, take no notice. It is I who have put
fifty louis in one pocket for that bracelet. Do not
trust Sir Henry there; he has a reputation."

As usual, the overpowering Selingman had his
way. 'Neither Draconmeyer nor Hunterleys at-
tempted to escape. They took their places at the
table. They drank champagne and they listened to
Selingman. All the time he talked, save when
mademoiselle interrupted him. Seated upon a chair
which seemed absurdly inadequate, his great stomach
with its vast expanse of white waistcoat in full view,
his short legs doubled up beneath him, he beamed
upon them all with a smile which never failed.

" It is a wonderful place," he declared, as he lifted
his glass for the fifth time. " We will drink to it,
this Monte Carlo. It is here that they come from
all quarters of the world — the ladies who charm
away our hearts," he added, bowing to mademoiselle,
" the financiers whose word can shake the money-
markets of the world, and the politicians who un-

this wonderful air, every time our feet touch the buoyant ground. Believe me, little one, the other things are of no account. The true philosophy of life and living is here in Monte Carlo. You and I will solve it."

CHAPTER III

A WARNING

Hunterleys dined alone at a small round table, set in a remote corner of the great restaurant attached to the Hotel de Paris. The scene around him was full of colour and interest. A scarlet-coated band made wonderful music. The toilettes of the women who kept passing backwards and forwards, on their way to the various tables, were marvellous; in their way unique. The lights and flowers of the room, its appointments and adornments, all represented the last word in luxury. Everywhere was colour, everywhere an almost strained attempt to impress upon the passerby the fact that this was no ordinary holiday resort but the giant pleasure-ground of all in the world who had money to throw away and the capacity for enjoyment. Only once a more somber note seemed struck when Mrs. Draconmeyer, leaning on her husband's arm and accompanied by a nurse and Lady Hunterleys, passed to their table. Hunterleys' eyes followed the little party until they had reached their destination and taken their places. His wife was wearing black and she had discarded the pearls which had hung around her neck during the afternoon. She wore only a collar of diamonds, his gift. Her hair was far less elaborately coiffured and her toilette less magnificent than the

toilettes of the women by whom she was surrounded.
Yet as he looked from his corner across the room at
her, Hunterleys realised as he had realised instantly
twelve years ago when he had first met her, that she
was incomparable. There was no other woman in the
whole of that great restaurant with her air of quiet
elegance; no other woman so faultless in the smaller
details of her toilette and person. Hunterleys
watched with expressionless face but with anger
growing in his heart, as he saw Draconmeyer bend-
ing towards her, accepting her suggestions about the
dinner, laughing when she laughed, watching almost
humbly for her pleasure or displeasure. It was a
cursed mischance which had brought him to Monte
Carlo!

Hunterleys hurried over his dinner, and without
even going to his room for a hat or coat, walked
across the square in the soft twilight of an unusually
warm February evening and took a table outside the
Café de Paris, where he ordered coffee. Around him
was a far more cosmopolitan crowd, increasing every
moment in volume. Every language was being
spoken, mostly German. As a rule, such a gathering
of people was, in its way, interesting to Hunterleys.
To-night his thoughts were truant. He forgot his
strenuous life of the last three months, the dangers
and discomforts through which he had passed, the
curious sequence of events which had brought him,
full of anticipation, nerved for a crisis, to Monte
Carlo of all places in the world. He forgot that he
was in the midst of great events, himself likely to
take a hand in them. His thoughts took, rarely
enough for him, a purely personal and sentimental

turn. He thought of the earliest days of his marriage, when he and his wife had wandered about the gardens of his old home in Wiltshire on spring evenings such as these, and had talked sometimes lightly, sometimes seriously, of the future. Almost as he sat there in the midst of that noisy crowd, he could catch the faint perfume of hyacinths from the borders along which they had passed and the trimly-cut flower-beds which fringed the deep green lawn. Almost he could hear the chiming of the old stable clock, the clear note of a thrush singing. A puff of wind brought them a waft of fainter odour from the wild violets which carpeted the woods. Then the darkness crept around them, a star came out. Hand in hand they turned towards the house and into the library, where a wood fire was burning on the grate. His thoughts travelled on. A wave of tenderness had assailed him. Then he was awakened by the waiter's voice at his elbow.

" Le café, monsieur."

He sat up in his chair. His dreaming moments were few and this one had passed. He set his heel upon that tide of weakening memories, sipped his coffee and looked out upon the crowd. Three or four times he glanced at his watch impatiently. Precisely at nine o'clock, a man moved from somewhere in the throng behind and took the vacant chair by his side.

" If one could trouble monsieur for a match! "

Hunterleys turned towards the newcomer as he handed his matchbox. He was a young man of medium height, with sandy complexion, a little freckled, and with a straggling fair moustache. He had keen

grey eyes and the faintest trace of a Scotch accent.
He edged his chair a little nearer to Hunterleys.

"Much obliged," he said. "Wonderful evening,
isn't it?"

Hunterleys nodded.

"Have you anything to tell me, David?" he asked.

"We are right in the thick of it," the other replied, his tone a little lowered. "There is more to
tell than I like."

"Shall we stroll along the Terrace?" Hunterleys
suggested.

"Don't move from your seat," the young man en-
joined. "You are watched here, and so am I, in a
way, although it's more my news they want to cen-
sor than anything personal. This crowd of Germans around us, without a single vacant chair, is the
best barrier we can have. Listen. Selingman is
here."

"I saw him this afternoon at the Sporting Club,"
Hunterleys murmured.

"Douaille will be here the day after to-morrow, if
he has not already arrived," the newcomer continued.
"It was given out in Paris that he was going down to
Marseilles and from there to Toulon, to spend three
days with the fleet. They sent a paragraph into
our office there. As a matter of fact, he's coming
straight on here. I can't learn how, exactly, but I
fancy by motor-car."

"You're sure that Douaille is coming himself?"
Hunterleys asked anxiously.

"Absolutely! His wife and family have been bus-
tled down to Mentone, so as to afford a pretext for
his presence here if the papers get hold of it. I have

found out for certain that they came at a moment's
notice and were not expecting to leave home at all.
Douaille will have full powers, and the conference will
take place at the Villa Mimosa. That will be the
headquarters of the whole thing. . . . Look out, Sir
Henry. They've got their eyes on us. The little
fellow in brown, close behind, is hand in glove with
the police. They tried to get me into a row last
night. It's only my journalism they suspect, but
they'd shove me over the frontier at the least excuse.
They're certain to try something of the sort with
you, if they get any idea that we are on the scent.
Sit tight, sir, and watch. I'm off. You know where
to find me."

The young man raised his hat and left Hunterleys
with the polite farewell of a stranger. His seat was
almost immediately seized by a small man dressed in
brown, a man with a black imperial and moustache
curled upwards. As Hunterleys glanced towards
him, he raised his Homburg hat politely and smiled.

" Monsieur's friend has departed? " he enquired.
" This seat is disengaged? "

" As you see," Hunterleys replied.

The little man smiled his thanks, seated himself
with a sigh of content and ordered coffee from a passing waiter.

" Monsieur is doubtless a stranger to Monte
Carlo? "

" It is my second visit only," Hunterleys admitted.

" For myself I am an habitué," the little man continued, " I might almost say a resident. Therefore,
all faces soon become familiar to me. Directly I saw
monsieur, I knew that he was not a frequenter."

Hunterleys turned a little in his chair and surveyed his neighbour curiously. The man was neatly dressed and he spoke English with scarcely any accent. His shoulders and upturned moustache gave him a military appearance.

" There is nothing I envy any one so much in life," he proceeded, " as coming to Monte Carlo for the first or second time. There is so much to know, to see, to understand."

Hunterleys made no effort to discourage his companion's obvious attempts to be friendly. The latter talked with spirit for some time.

" If it would not be regarded as a liberty," he said at last, as Hunterleys rose to move off, " may I be permitted to present myself? My name is Hugot? I am half English, half French. Years ago my health broke down and I accepted a position in a bank here. Since then I have come in to money. If I have a hobby in life, it is to show my beloved Monte Carlo to strangers. If monsieur would do me the honour to spare me a few hours to-night, later on, I would endeavour to see that he was amused."

Hunterleys shook his head. He remained, however, perfectly courteous. He had a conviction that this was the man who had been watching his wife.

" You are very kind, sir," he replied. " I am here only for a few days and for the benefit of my health. I dare not risk late hours. We shall meet again, I trust."

He strolled off and as he hesitated upon the steps of the Casino he glanced across towards the Hotel de Paris. At that moment a woman came out, a light cloak over her evening gown. She was followed

by an attendant. Hunterleys recognised his wife
and watched them with a curious little thrill. They
turned towards the Terrace. Very slowly he, too,
moved in the same direction. They passed through
the gardens of the Hotel de Paris, and Hunterleys,
keeping to the left, met them upon the Terrace
as they emerged. As they came near he accosted
them.

"Violet," he began.

She started.

"I beg your pardon," she said. "I did not recognise you."

"Haven't you been told," he asked stiffly, "that
the Terrace is unsafe for women after twilight?"

"Very often," she assented, with that little smile
at the corners of her lips which once he had found so
charming and which now half maddened him. "Unfortunately, I have a propensity for doing things
which are dangerous. Besides, I have my maid."

"Another woman is no protection," he declared.

"Susanne can shriek," Lady Hunterleys assured
him. "She has wonderful lungs and she loves to use
them. She would shriek at the least provocation."

"And meanwhile," Hunterleys observed drily,
"while she is indulging in her vocal exercises, things
happen. If you wish to promenade here, permit me
to be your escort."

She hesitated for a moment, frowning. Then she
continued her walk.

"You are very kind," she assented. "Perhaps
you are like me, though, and feel the restfulness of a
quiet place after these throngs and throngs of people."

They passed slowly down the broad promenade,
deserted now save for one or two loungers like themselves, and a few other furtive, hurrying figures.
In front of them stretched an arc of glittering lights
— the wonderful Bay of Mentone, with Bordighera
on the distant sea-board; higher up, the twinkling
lights from the villas built on the rocky hills. And
at their feet the sea, calm, deep, blue, lapping the
narrow belt of hard sand, scintillating with the re-
flection of a thousand lights; on the horizon a blood-
red moon, only half emerged from the sea.

"Since we have met, Henry," Lady Hunterleys
said at last, "there is something which I should like
to say to you."

"Certainly!"

She glanced behind. Susanne had fallen dis-
creetly into the rear. She was a new importation
and she had no idea as to the identity of the tall,
severe-looking Englishman who walked by her mistress's side.

"There is something going on in Monte Carlo,"
Lady Hunterleys went on, "which I cannot understand. Mr. Draconmeyer knows about it, I believe,
although he is not personally concerned in it. But
he will tell me nothing. I only know that for some
reason or other your presence here seems to be an
annoyance to certain people. Why it should be I
don't know, but I want to ask you about it. Will
you tell me the truth? Are you sure that you did
not come here to spy upon me?"

"I certainly did not," Hunterleys answered firmly.
"I had no idea that you were near the place. If I
had —"

She turned her head. The smile was there once more and a queer, soft light in her eyes.

" If you had? " she murmured.

" My visit here, under the present circumstances, would have been more distasteful than it is," Hunterleys replied stiffly.

She bit her lip and turned away. When she resumed the conversation, her tone was completely changed.

" I speak to you now," she said, " in your own interests. Mr. Draconmeyer is, of course, not personally connected with this affair, whatever it may be, but he is a wonderful man and he hears many things. To-night, before dinner, he gave me a few words of warning. He did not tell me to pass them on to you but I feel sure that he hoped I would. You would not listen to them from him because you do not like him. I am afraid that you will take very little more heed of what I say, but at least you will believe that I speak in your own interests. Mr. Draconmeyer believes that your presence here is misunderstood. A person whom he describes as being utterly without principle and of great power is incensed by it. To speak plainly, you are in danger."

" I am flattered," Hunterleys remarked, " by this interest on my behalf."

She turned her head and looked at him. His face, in this cold light before the moon came up, was almost like the face of some marble statue, lifeless, set, of almost stonelike severity. She knew the look so well and she sighed.

" You need not be," she replied bitterly. " Mine is merely the ordinary feeling of one human creature for another. In a sense it seems absurd, I suppose, to speak to you as I am doing. Yet I do know that this place which looks so beautiful has strange undercurrents. People pass away here in the most orthodox fashion in the world, outwardly, but their real ending is often never known at all. Everything is possible here, and Mr. Draconmeyer honestly believes that you are in danger."

They had reached the end of the Terrace and they turned back.

"I thank you very much, Violet," Hunterleys said earnestly. "In return, may I say something to you? If there is any danger threatening me or those interests which I guard, the man whom you have chosen to make your intimate friend is more deeply concerned in it than you think. I told you once before that Draconmeyer was something more than the great banker, the king of commerce, as he calls himself. He is ambitious beyond your imaginings, a schemer in ways you know nothing of, and his residence in London during the last fifteen years has been the worst thing that ever happened for England. To me it is a bitter thing that you should have ignored my warning and accepted his friendship —"

"It is not Mr. Draconmeyer who is my friend, Henry," she interrupted. "You continually ignore that fact. It is Mrs. Draconmeyer whom I cannot desert. I knew her long before I did her husband. We were at school together, and there was a time before her last illness when we were inseparable."

"That may have been so at first," Hunterleys agreed, "but how about since then? You cannot deny, Violet, that this man Draconmeyer has in some

way impressed or fascinated you. You admire him.
You find great pleasure in his society. Isn't that the
truth, now, honestly?"

Her face was a little troubled.

" I do certainly find pleasure in his society," she
admitted. " I cannot conceive any one who would
not. He is a brilliant, a wonderful musician, a delightful talker, a generous host and companion. He
has treated me always with the most scrupulous regard, and I feel that I am entirely reasonable in re-
senting your mistrust of him."

" You do resent it still, then?"

" I do," she asserted emphatically.

" And if I told you," Hunterleys went on, " that
the man was in love with you. What then?"

" I should say that you were a fool!"

Hunterleys shrugged his shoulders.

" There is no more to be said," he declared, " only,
for a clever woman, Violet, you are sometimes woe-
fully or wilfully blind. I tell you that I know the
type. Sooner or later — before very long, I should
think — you will have the usual scene. I warn you
of it now. If you are wise, you will go back to England."

" Absurd!" she scoffed. " Why, we have only
just come! I want to win some money — not that
your allowance isn't liberal enough," she added hastily, " but there is a fascination in winning, you
know. And besides, I could not possibly desert Mrs.
Draconmeyer. She would not have come at all if I
had not joined them."

" You are the mistress of your own ways," Hunterleys said. " According to my promise, I shall at-

tempt to exercise no authority over you in any way, but I tell you that Draconmeyer is my enemy, and the enemy of all the things I represent, and I tell you, too, that he is in love with you. When you realise that these things are firmly established in my brain, you can perhaps understand how thoroughly distasteful I find your association with him here. It is all very well to talk about Mrs. Draconmeyer, but she goes nowhere. The consequence is that he is your escort on every occasion. I am quite aware that a great many people in society accept him. I personally am not disposed to. I look upon him as an unfit companion for my wife and I resent your appearance with him in public."

"We will discuss this subject no further," she decided. "From the moment of our first disagreement, it has been your object to break off my friendship with the Draconmeyers. Until I have something more than words to go by, I shall continue to give him my confidence."

They crossed the stone flags in front of the Opera together, and turned up towards the Rooms.

"I think, perhaps, then," he said, "that we may consider the subject closed. Only," he added, "you will forgive me if I still —"

He hesitated. She turned her head quickly. Her eyes sought his but unfortunately he was looking straight ahead and seeing gloomy things. If he had happened to turn at that moment, he might have concluded his speech differently.

"If I still exhibit some interest in your doings."

"I shall always think it most kind of you," she replied, her face suddenly hardening. "Have I not done my best to reciprocate? I have even passed on to you a word of warning, which I think you are very unwise to ignore."

They were outside the hotel. Hunterleys paused.

"I have nothing to fear from the mysterious source you have spoken of," he assured her. "The only enemy I have in Monte Carlo is Draconmeyer himself."

"Enemy!" she repeated scornfully. "Mr. Draconmeyer is much too wrapped up in his finance, and too big a man, in his way, to have enemies. Oh, Henry, if only you could get rid of a few of your prejudices, how much more civilised a human being you would be!"

He raised his hat. His expression was a little grim.

"The man without prejudices, my dear Violet," he retorted, "is a man without instincts. . . . I wish you luck."

She ran lightly up the steps and waved her hand. He watched her pass through the doors into the hotel.

CHAPTER IV

ENTER THE AMERICAN

Lady Weybourne was lunching on the terrace of Ciro's restaurant with her brother. She was small, dark, vivacious. Her friends, of whom she had thousands, all called her Flossie, and she was probably the most popular American woman who had ever married into the English peerage. Her brother, Richard Lane, on the other hand, was tall, very broad-shouldered, with a strong, clean-shaven face, inclined by disposition to be taciturn. On this particular morning he had less even than usual to say, and although Lady Weybourne, who was a great chatterbox, was content as a rule to do most of the talking for herself, his inattention became at last a little too obvious. He glanced up eagerly as every newcomer appeared, and his answers to his sister's criticisms were sometimes almost at random.

" Dicky, I'm not at all sure that I'm liking you this morning," she observed finally, looking across at him with a critically questioning smile. " A certain amount of non-responsiveness to my advances I can put up with — from a brother — but this morning you are positively inattentive. Tell me your troubles at once. Has Harris been bothering you, or did you lose a lot of money last night? "

Considering that the young man's income was derived from an exceedingly well-invested capital of nine million dollars, and that Harris was the all too perfect captain of his yacht lying then in the harbour, whose worst complaint was that he had never enough work to do, Lady Weybourne's enquiries might have been considered as merely tentative. Richard shook his head a little gloomily.

" Those things aren't likely to trouble me," he remarked. " Harris is all right, and I've promised him we'll make up a little party and go over to Cannes in a day or two."

" What a ripping idea!" Lady Weybourne declared, breaking up her thin toast between her fingers. " I'd love it, and so would Harry. We could easily get together a delightful party. The Pelhams are here and simply dying for a change, and there's Captain Gardner and Frank Clowes, and lots of nice girls. Couldn't we fix a date, Dick? "

" Not just yet," her brother replied.

" And why not? "

" I am waiting," he told her, " until I can ask the girl I want to go."

" And why can't you now? " she demanded, with upraised eyebrows. " I'll be hostess and chaperone all in one."

" I can't ask her because I don't know her yet," the young man explained doggedly.

Lady Weybourne leaned back in her chair and laughed.

" So that's it! " she exclaimed. " Now I know why you're sitting there like an owl this morning! In love with a fair unknown, are you, Dick? Be careful. Monte Carlo is full of young ladies whom it would be just as well to know a little about before you thought of taking them yachting."

" This one isn't that sort," the young man said.

" How do you know that? " she asked, leaning across the table, her head resting on her clasped hands.

He looked at her almost contemptuously.

" How do I know! " he repeated. " There are just one or two things that happen in this world which a man can be utterly and entirely sure of. She is one of them. Say, Flossie," he added, the enthusiasm creeping at last into his tone, " you never saw any one quite like her in all your life! "

" Do I know her, I wonder? " Lady Weybourne enquired.

" That's just what I've asked you here to find out," her brother replied ingenuously. " I heard her tell the man she was with this morning — her father, I believe — about an hour ago, that she would be at Ciro's at half-past one. It's twenty minutes to two now."

Lady Weybourne laughed heartily.

" So that's why you dragged me out of bed and made me come to lunch with you! Dick, what a fraud you are! I was thinking what a dear, affectionate brother you were, and all the time you were just making use of me."

" Sorry," the young man said briskly, " but, after all, we needn't stand on ceremony, need we? I've always been your pal; gave you a leg up with the old man, you know, when he wasn't keen on the British alliance."

She nodded.

"Oh, I'll do what I can for you," she promised. "If she is any one in particular I expect I shall know her. What's happening, Dick?"

The young man's face was almost transformed. His eyes were bright and very fixed. His lips had come together in a firm, straight line, as though he were renewing some promise to himself. Lady Weybourne followed the direction of his gaze. A man and a girl had reached the entrance to the restaurant and were looking around them as though to select a table. The chief maître d'hôtel had hastened out to receive them. They were, without doubt, people of importance. The man was of medium height, with iron-grey hair and moustache, and a small imperial. He wore light clothes of perfect cut; patent shoes with white linen gaiters; a black tie fastened with a pin of opals. He carried himself with an air which was unmistakable and convincing. The girl by his side was beautiful. She was simply dressed in a tailor-made gown of white serge. Her black hat was a miracle of smartness. Her hair was of a very light shade of golden-brown, her complexion wonderfully fair. Lady Weybourne glanced at her shoes and gloves, at the bag which she was carrying, and the handle of her parasol. Then she nodded approvingly.

"You don't know her?" Richard asked, in a disappointed whisper.

She shook her head.

"Sorry," she admitted, "but I don't. They've probably only just arrived."

With great ceremony the newcomers were conducted to the best table upon the terrace. The man was evidently an habitué. He had scarcely taken his seat before, with a very low bow, the sommelier brought him a small wine-glass filled with what seemed to be vermouth. While he sipped it he smoked a Russian cigarette and with a gold pencil wrote out the menu of his luncheon. In a few minutes the manager himself came hurrying out from the restaurant. His salute was almost reverential. When, after a few moments' conversation, he departed, he did so with the air of one taking leave of royalty. Lady Weybourne, who was an inquisitive little person, was puzzled.

"I don't know who they are, Dick," she confessed, "but I know the ways of this place well, and I can tell you one thing — they are people of importance. You can tell that by the way they are received. These restaurant people don't make mistakes."

"Of course they are people of importance," the young man declared. "Any one can see that by a glance at the girl. I am sorry you don't know them," he went on, "but you've got to find out who they are, and pretty quickly, too. Look here, Flossie. I am a bit useful to you now and then, aren't I?"

"Without you, my dear Dick," she murmured, "I should never be able to manage those awful trustees. You are invaluable, a perfect jewel of a brother."

"Well, I'll give you that little electric coupé you were so keen on last time we were in London, if you'll get me an introduction to that girl within twenty-four hours."

Lady Weybourne gasped.

"What a whirlwind!" she exclaimed. "Dicky, are you, by any chance, in earnest?"

"In earnest for the first time in my life," he assured her. "Something has got hold of me which I'm not going to part with."

She considered him reflectively. He was twenty-seven years of age, and notwithstanding the boundless opportunities of his youth and great wealth he had so far shown an almost singular indifference to the whole of the opposite sex, from the fascinating chorus girls of London and New York to the no less enterprising young women of his own order. As she sat there studying his features, she felt a sensation almost of awe. There was something entirely different, something stronger in his face. She thought for a moment of their father as she had known him in her childhood, the founder of their fortunes, a man who had risen from a moderate position to immense wealth through sheer force of will, of pertinacity. For the first time she saw the same look upon her brother's face.

"Well," she sighed, "I shall do my best to earn it. I only hope, Dick, that she is —"

"She is what?" he demanded, looking at her steadfastly.

"Oh! not engaged or anything, I mean," Lady Weybourne explained hastily. "I must admit, Dick, although I don't suppose any sister is particularly keen upon her brother's young women, that I think you've shown excellent taste. She is absolutely the best style of any one I've seen in Monte Carlo."

"How are you going to manage that introduction?" he asked bluntly. "Have you made any plans?"

"I don't suppose it will be difficult," she assured him, lighting a cigarette and shaking her head at the tray of liqueurs which the sommelier was offering. "Get me some cream for my coffee, Dick. Now I'll tell you," she continued, as the waiter disappeared. "You will have to call that under-maître d'hôtel. You had better give him a substantial tip and ask him quietly for their names. Then I'll see about the rest."

"That seems sensible enough," he admitted.

"And look here, Dick," she went on, "I know how impetuous you are. Don't do anything foolish. Remember this isn't an ordinary adventure. If you go rushing in upon it you'll come to grief."

"I know," he answered shortly. "I was fool enough to hang about the flower shops and that milliner's this morning. I couldn't help it. I don't know whether she noticed. I believe she did. Once our eyes did meet, and although I'll swear she never changed her expression, I felt that the whole world didn't hold so small a creature as I. Here comes Charles. I'll ask him."

He beckoned to the maître d'hôtel and talked for a moment about the luncheon. Then he ordered a table for the next day, and slipping a louis into the man's hand, leaned over and whispered in his ear.

"I want you to tell me the name of the gentleman and young lady who are sitting over there at the corner table?"

The maître d'hôtel glanced covertly in the direction indicated. He did not at once reply. His face was perplexed, almost troubled.

" I am very sorry, sir," he said hesitatingly, " but our orders are very strict. Monsieur Ciro does not like anything in the way of gossip about our clients, and the gentleman is a very honoured patron. The young lady is his daughter."

" Quite right," the young man agreed bluntly. " This isn't an ordinary case, Charles. You go over to the desk there, write me down the name and bring it, and there's a hundred franc note waiting here for you. No need for the name to pass your lips."

The man bowed and retreated. In a few minutes he came back again and laid a small card upon the table.

" Monsieur will pardon my reminding him," he begged earnestly, " but if he will be so good as to never mention this little matter —"

Richard nodded and waved him away.

" Sure ! " he promised.

He drew the card towards him and looked at it in a puzzled manner. Then he passed it to his sister. Her expression, too, was blank.

" Who in the name of mischief," he exclaimed softly, " is Mr. Grex ! "

CHAPTER V

" WHO IS MR. GREX? "

Lady Weybourne insisted, after a reasonable amount of time spent over their coffee, that her brother should pay the bill and leave the restaurant. They walked slowly across the square.

" What are you going to do about it? " he asked.

" There is only one thing to be done," she replied. " I shall speak to every one I meet this afternoon — I shall be, in fact, most sociable — and sooner or later in our conversation I shall ask every one if they know Mr. Grex and his daughter. When I arrive at some one who does, that will be the first step, won't it? "

" I wonder whether we shall see some one soon! " he grumbled, looking around. " Where are all the people to-day! "

She laughed softly.

" Just a little impetuous, aren't you? "

" I should say so," he admitted. " I'd like to be introduced to her before four o'clock, propose to her this evening, and — and —"

" And what? "

" Never mind," he concluded, marching on with his head turned towards the clouds. " Let's go and sit down upon the Terrace and talk about her."

" But, my dear Dicky," his sister protested, " I

don't want to sit upon the Terrace. I am going to my dressmaker's across the way there, and afterwards to Lucie's to try on some hats. Then I am going back to the hotel for an hour's rest and to prink, and afterwards into the Sporting Club at four o'clock. That's my programme. I shall be doing what I can the whole of the time. I shall make discreet enquiries of my dressmaker, who knows everybody, and I sha'n't let a single acquaintance go by. You will have to amuse yourself till four o'clock, at any rate. There's Sir Henry Hunterleys over there, having coffee. Go and talk to him. He may put you out of your misery. Thanks ever so much for my luncheon, and au revoir!"

She turned away with a little nod. Her brother, after a moment's hesitation, approached the table where Hunterleys was sitting alone.

"How do you do, Sir Henry?"

Hunterleys returned his greeting, a little blankly at first. Then he remembered the young man and held out his hand.

"Of course! You are Richard Lane, aren't you? Sit down and have some coffee. What are you doing here?"

"I've got a little boat in the harbour," Richard replied, as he drew up a chair. "I've been at Algiers for a time with some friends, and I've brought them on here. Just been lunching with my sister. Are you alone?"

Hunterleys hesitated.

"Yes, I am alone."

"Wonderful place," the young man went on. "Wonderful crowd of people here, too. I suppose you know everybody?" he added, warming up as he approached his subject.

"On the contrary," Hunterleys answered, "I am almost a stranger here. I have been staying further down the coast."

"Happen to know any one of the name of Grex?" Lane asked, with elaborate carelessness.

Hunterleys made no immediate reply. He seemed to be considering the name.

"Grex," he repeated, knocking the ash from his cigarette. "Rather an uncommon name, isn't it? Why do you ask?"

"Oh, I've seen an elderly man and a young lady about once or twice," Lane explained. "Very interesting-looking people. Some one told me that their name was Grex."

"There is a person living under that name, I think," Hunterleys said, "who has taken the Villa Mimosa for the season."

"Do you know him personally?" the young man asked eagerly.

"Personally? No, I can scarcely say that I do."

Richard Lane sighed. It was disappointment number one. For some reason or other, too, Hunterleys seemed disposed to change the conversation.

"The young lady who is always with him," Richard persisted, "would that be his daughter?"

Hunterleys turned a little in his seat and surveyed his questioner. He had met Lane once or twice and rather liked him.

"Look here, young fellow," he said, good humouredly, "let me ask you a question for a change. What is the nature of these enquiries of yours?"

Lane hesitated. Something in Hunterleys' face and manner induced him to tell the truth.

" I have fallen head over heels in love with the young lady," he confessed. " Don't think I am a confounded jackass. I am not in the habit of doing such things. I'm twenty-seven and I have never gone out of my way to meet a girl yet. This is something — different. I want to find out about them and get an introduction."

Hunterleys shook his head regretfully.

" I am afraid," he said, " that I can be of no use to you — no practical use, that is. I can only give you one little piece of advice."

" Well, what is it? " Richard asked eagerly.

" If you are in earnest," Hunterleys continued, " and I will do you the credit to believe that you are, you had better pack up your things, return to your yacht and take a cruise somewhere."

" Take a cruise somewhere! "

Hunterleys nodded.

" Get out of Monte Carlo as quickly as you can, and, above all, don't think anything more of that young lady. Get the idea out of your head as quickly as you can."

The young man was sitting upright in his chair. His manner was half minatory.

" Say, what do you mean by this? " he demanded.

" Exactly what I said just now," Hunterleys rejoined. " If you are in earnest, and I have no doubt that you are, I should clear out."

" What is it you are trying to make me understand? " Richard asked bluntly.

" That you have about as much chance with that

young lady," Hunterleys assured him, " as with that very graceful statue in the square yonder."

Richard sat for a moment with knitted brows.

" Then you know who she is, any way? "

" Whether I do or whether I do not," the older man said gravely, " so far as I am concerned, the subject is exhausted. I have given you the best advice you ever had in your life. It's up to you to follow it."

Richard looked at him blankly.

" Well, you've got me puzzled," he confessed.

Hunterleys rose to his feet, and, summoning a waiter, paid his bill.

" You'll excuse me, won't you? " he begged. " I have an appointment in a few minutes. If you are wise, young man," he added, patting him on the shoulder as he turned to go, " you will take my advice."

Left to himself, Richard Lane strolled around the place towards the Terrace. He had no fancy for the Rooms and he found a seat as far removed as possible from the Tir du Pigeons. He sat there with folded arms, looking out across the sun-dappled sea. His matter-of-fact brain offered him but one explanation as to the meaning of Hunterleys' words, and against that explanation his whole being was in passionate revolt. He represented a type of young man who possesses morals by reason of a certain unsuspected idealism, mingled with perfect physical sanity. It seemed to him, as he sat there, that he had been waiting for this day for years. The old nights in New York and Paris and London floated before his memory. He pushed them on one side with a shiver, and yet with a curious feeling of exultation. He recalled a certain sensation which had been drawn through his life like a thin golden thread, a sensation which had a habit of especially asserting itself in the midst of these youthful orgies, a curious sense of waiting for something to happen, a sensation which had been responsible very often for what his friends had looked upon as eccentricity. He knew now that this thing had arrived, and everything else in life seemed to pale by the side of it. Hunterleys' words had thrown him temporarily into a strange turmoil. Solitude for a few moments he had felt to be entirely necessary. Yet directly he was alone, directly he was free to listen to his convictions, he could have laughed at that first mad surging of his blood, the fierce, instinctive rebellion against the conclusion to which Hunterleys' words seemed to point. Now that he was alone, he was not even angry. No one else could possibly understand!

Before long he was once more upon his feet, starting out upon his quest with renewed energy. He had scarcely taken a dozen steps, however, when he came face to face with Lady Hunterleys and Mr. Draconmeyer. Quite oblivious of the fact that they seemed inclined to avoid him, he greeted them both with unusual warmth.

"Saw your husband just now, Lady Hunterleys," he remarked, a little puzzled. "I fancied he said he was alone here."

She smiled.

"We did not come together," she explained; "in fact, our meeting was almost accidental. Henry

had been at Bordighera and San Remo and I came
out with Mr. and Mrs. Draconmeyer."

The young man nodded and turned towards Draconmeyer, who was standing a little on one side as
though anxious to proceed.

"Mr. Draconmeyer doesn't remember me, perhaps. I met him at my sister's, Lady Weybourne's,
just before Christmas."

"I remember you perfectly," Mr. Draconmeyer
assured him courteously. "We have all been
admiring your beautiful yacht in the harbour
there."

"I was thinking of getting up a little cruise before long," Richard continued. "If so, I hope
you'll all join us. Flossie is going to be hostess,
and the Montressors are passengers already."

They murmured something non-committal. Lady
Hunterleys seemed as though about to pass on but
Lane blocked the way.

"I only arrived the other day from Algiers," he
went on, making frantic efforts to continue the conversation. "I brought Freddy Montressor and his
sister, and Fothergill."

"Mr. Montressor has come to the Hotel de Paris,"
Lady Hunterleys remarked. "What sort of weather
did you have in Algiers?"

"Ripping!" the young man replied absently, entirely oblivious of the fact that they had been driven
away by incessant rain. "This place is much more
fun, though," he added, with sudden inspiration.
"Crowds of interesting people. I suppose you know
every one?"

Lady Hunterleys shook her head.

"Indeed I do not.   Mr. Draconmeyer here is my
guide.   He is as good as a walking directory."

"I wonder if either of you know some people
named Grex?" Richard asked, with studious indifference.

Mr. Draconmeyer for the first time showed some
signs of interest.   He looked at their questioner
steadfastly.

"Grex," he repeated.   "A very uncommon
name."

"Very uncommon-looking people," Richard declared.   "The man is elderly, and looks as though
he took great care of himself — awfully well turned
out and all that.   The daughter is — good-looking."

Mr. Draconmeyer took off his gold-rimmed spectacles and rubbed them with his handkerchief.

"Why do you ask?" he enquired.   "Is this just
curiosity?"

"Rather more than that," Richard said boldly.
"It's interest."

Mr. Draconmeyer readjusted his spectacles.

"Mr. Grex," he announced, "is a gentleman of
great wealth and illustrious birth, who has taken a
very magnificent villa and desires for a time to lead a
life of seclusion.   That is as much as I or any one
else knows."

"What about the young lady?" Richard persisted.

"The young lady," Mr. Draconmeyer answered,
"is, as you surmised, his daughter. . . . Shall we
finish our promenade, Lady Hunterleys?"

Richard stood grudgingly a little on one side.

"Mr. Draconmeyer," he said desperately, "do you think there'd be any chance of my getting an introduction to the young lady?"

Mr. Draconmeyer at first smiled and then began to laugh, as though something in the idea tickled him. He looked at the young man and Richard hated him.

"Not the slightest in the world, I should think," he declared. "Good afternoon!"

Lady Hunterleys joined in her companion's amusement as they continued their promenade.

"Is the young man in love, do you suppose?" she enquired lightly.

"If so," her companion replied, "he has made a somewhat unfortunate choice. However, it really doesn't matter. Love at his age is nothing more than a mood. It will pass as all moods pass."

She turned and looked at him.

"Do you mean," she asked incredulously, "that youth is incapable of love?"

They had paused for a moment, looking out across the bay towards the glittering white front of Bordighera. Mr. Draconmeyer took off his hat. Somehow, without it, in that clear light, one realised, notwithstanding his spectacles, his grizzled black beard of unfashionable shape, his over-massive forehead and shaggy eyebrows, that his, too, was the face of one whose feet were not always upon the earth.

"Perhaps," he answered, "it is a matter of degree, yet I am almost tempted to answer your question absolutely. I do not believe that youth can love, because from the first it misapprehends the meaning of the term. I believe that the gift of loving comes only to those who have reached the hills."

She looked at him, a little surprised. Always thoughtful, always sympathetic, generally stimulating, it was very seldom that she had heard him speak with so much real feeling. Suddenly he turned his head from the sea. His eyes seemed to challenge hers.

"Your question," he continued, "touches upon one of the great tragedies of life. Upon those who are free from their youth there is a great tax levied. Nature has decreed that they should feel something which they call love. They marry, and in this small world of ours they give a hostage as heavy as a millstone of their chances of happiness. For it is only in later life, when a man has knowledge as well as passion, when unless he is fortunate it is too late, that he can know what love is."

She moved a little uneasily. She felt that something was coming which she desired to avoid, some confidence, something from which she must escape. The memory of her husband's warning was vividly present with her. She felt the magnetism of her companion's words, his compelling gaze.

"It is so with me," he went on, leaning a little towards her, "only in my case —"

Providence was intervening. Never had the swish of a woman's skirt sounded so sweet to her before.

"Here's Dolly Montressor," she interrupted, "coming up to speak to us."

CHAPTER VI

CAKES AND COUNSELS

The Sporting Club seemed to fill up that after-noon almost as soon as the doors were opened. At half-past four, people were standing two or three deep around the roulette tables. Selingman, very warm, and looking somewhat annoyed, withdrew himself from the front row of the lower table, and taking Mr. Grex and Draconmeyer by the arm, led them towards the tea-room.

"I have lost six louis!" he exclaimed, fretfully. "I have had the devil's own luck. I shall play no more for the present. We will have tea together."

They appropriated a round table in a distant corner of the restaurant.

"History," Selingman continued, heaping his plate with rich cakes, "has been made before now in strange places. Why not here? We sit here in close touch with one of the most interesting phases of modern life. We can even hear the voice of fate, the click of the little ball as it finishes its momentous journey and sinks to rest. Why should we, too, not speak of fateful things?"

Mr. Draconmeyer glanced around.

"For myself," he muttered, "I must say that I prefer a smaller room and a locked door."

Selingman demolished a chocolate éclair and shook his head vigorously.

"The public places for me," he declared. "Now look around. There is no one, as you will admit, within ear-shot. Very well. What will they say, those who suspect us, if they see us drinking tea and eating many cakes together? Certainly not that we conspire, that we make mischief here. On the other hand, they will say ' There are three great men at play, come to Monte Carlo to rest from their labours, to throw aside for a time the burden from their shoulders; to flirt, to play, to eat cakes.' It is a good place to talk, this, and I have something in my mind which must be said."

Mr. Grex sipped his pale, lemon-flavoured tea and toyed with his cigarette-case. He was eating nothing.

"Assuming you to be a man of sense, my dear Selingman," he remarked, "I think that what you have to say is easily surmised. The Englishman!"

Selingman agreed with ponderous emphasis.

"We have before us," he declared, "a task of unusual delicacy. Our friend from Paris may be here at any moment. How we shall fare with him, heaven only knows! But there is one thing very certain. At the sight of Hunterleys he will take alarm. He will be like a frightened bird, all ruffled feathers. He will never settle down to a serious discussion. Hunterleys knows this. That is why he presents himself without reserve in public, why he is surrounded with Secret Service men of his own country, all on the *qui vive* for the coming of Douaille."

"It appears tolerably certain," Mr. Draconmeyer

said calmly, " that we must get rid of Hunterleys."

Mr. Grex looked out of the window for a moment.

" To some extent," he observed, " I am a stranger here. I come as a guest to this conference, as our other friend from Paris comes, too. Any small task which may arise from the necessities of the situation, devolves, I think I may say without unfairness, upon you, my friend."

Selingman assented gloomily.

" That is true," he admitted, " but in Hunterleys we have to do with no ordinary man. He does not gamble. To the ordinary attractions of Monte Carlo he is indifferent. He is one of these thin-blooded men with principles. Cromwell would have made a lay preacher of him."

" You find difficulties? " Mr. Grex queried, with slightly uplifted eyebrows.

" Not difficulties," Selingman continued quickly. " Or if indeed we do call them difficulties, let us say at once that they are very minor ones. Only the thing must be done neatly and without ostentation, for the sake of our friend who comes."

" My own position," Mr. Draconmeyer intervened, " is, in a way, delicate. The unexplained disappearance of Sir Henry Hunterleys might, by some people, be connected with the great friendship which exists between my wife and his."

Mr. Grex polished his horn-rimmed eyeglass. Selingman nodded sympathetically. Neither of them looked at Draconmeyer. Finally Selingman heaved a sigh and brushed the crumbs from his waistcoat.

" If one were assured," he murmured thoughtfully,

" that Hunterleys' presence here had a real significance —"

Draconmeyer pushed his chair forward and leaned across the table. The heads of the three men were close together. His tone was stealthily lowered.

" Let me tell you something, my friend Selingman, which I think should strengthen any half-formed intention you may have in your brain. Hunterleys is no ordinary sojourner here. You were quite right when you told me that his stay at Bordighera and San Remo was a matter of days only. Now I will tell you something. Three weeks ago he was at Bukharest. He spent two days with Novisko. From there he went to Sofia. He was heard of in Athens and Constantinople. My own agent wrote me that he was in Belgrade. Hunterleys is the bosom friend of the English Foreign Secretary. That I know for myself. You have your reports. You can read between the lines. I tell you that Hunterleys is the man who has paralysed our action amongst the Balkan States. He has played a neat little game out there. It is he who was the inspiration of Roumania. It is he who drafted the secret understanding with Turkey. The war which we hoped for will not take place. From there Hunterleys came in a gunboat and landed on the Italian coast. He lingered at Bordighera for appearances only. He is here, if he can, to break up our conference. I tell you that you none of you appreciate this man. Hunterleys is the most dangerous Englishman living —"

" One moment," Selingman interrupted. " To some extent I follow you, but when you speak of Hunterleys as a power in the present tense, doesn't it occur to you that his Party is not in office? He is simply a member of the Opposition. If his Party get in again at the next election, I grant you that he will be Foreign Minister and a dangerous one, but to-day he is simply a private person."

"It is not every one," Mr. Draconmeyer said slowly, "who bows his knee to the shibboleth of party politics. Remember that I come to you from London and I have information of which few others are possessed. Hunterleys is of the stuff of which patriots are made. Party is no concern of his. He and the present Foreign Secretary are the greatest of personal friends. I know for a fact that Hunterleys has actually been consulted and has helped in one or two recent crises. The very circumstance that he is not of the ruling Party makes a free lance of him. When his people are in power, he will have to take office and wear the shackles. To-day, with every quality which would make him the greatest Foreign Minister England has ever had since Disraeli, he is nothing more nor less than a roving diplomatist, Emperor of his country's Secret Service, if you like to put it so. Furthermore, look a little into that future of which I have spoken. The present English Government will last, at the most, another two years. I tell you that when they go out of power, whoever comes in, Hunterleys will go to the Foreign Office. We shall have to deal with a man who knows, a man —"

"I am not wholly satisfied with these éclairs," Selingman interrupted, gazing into the dish. "Maître d'hôtel, come and listen to an awful complaint," he went on, and, addressing one of the head-

waiters. "Your éclairs are too small, your cream-
cakes too irresistible. I eat too much here. How,
I ask you in the name of common sense, can a man
dine who takes tea here! Bring the bill."

The man, smiling, hastened away. Not a word
had passed between the three, yet the other two
understood the situation perfectly. Hunterleys and
Richard Lane had entered the room together and
were seated at an adjoining table. Selingman
plunged into a fresh tirade, pointing to the half-
demolished plateful of cakes.

"I will eat one more," he declared. "We will
bilk the management. The bill is made out. I shall
not be observed. Our friend," he continued, under
his breath, " has secured a valuable bodyguard, something very large and exceedingly powerful."

Draconmeyer hesitated for a moment. Then he
turned to Mr. Grex.

"You have perhaps observed," he said, " the
young man who is seated at the next table. It may
amuse you to hear of a very extraordinary piece
of impertinence of which, only this afternoon, he
was guilty. He accosted me upon the Terrace —
he is a young American whom I have met in London — and asked me for information respecting a
Mr. and Miss Grex."

Mr. Grex looked slowly towards the speaker.
There was very little change in his face, yet Draconmeyer seemed in some way confused.

"You will understand, I am sure, sir," he continued, a little hastily, " that I was in no way to
blame for the question which the young man addressed to me. He had the presumption to enquire

whether I could procure for him an introduction to the young lady whom he knew as Miss Grex. Even at this moment," Draconmeyer went on, lowering his voice, " he is trying to persuade Hunterleys to let him come over to us."

" The young man," Mr. Grex said deliberately, " is ignorant. If necessary, he must be taught his lesson."

Selingman intervened. He breathed a heavy sigh.

" Well," he observed, " I perceive that the task at which we have hinted is to fall upon my shoulders. We must do what we can. I am a tender-hearted man, and if extremes can be avoided, I shall like my task better. . . . And now I have changed my mind. The loss of that six louis weighs upon me. I shall endeavour to regain it. Let us go."

They rose and passed out into the roulette rooms. Richard Lane, who remained in his seat with an effort, watched them pass with a frown upon his face.

" Say, Sir Henry," he complained, " I don't quite understand this. Why, I'd only got to go over to Draconmeyer there and stand and talk for a moment, and he must have introduced me."

Hunterleys shook his head.

" Let me assure you," he said, " that Draconmeyer would have done nothing of the sort. For one thing, we don't introduce over here as a matter of course, as you do in America. And for another — well, I won't trouble you with the other reason. . . . Look here, Lane, take my advice, there's a sensible fellow. I am a man of the world, you know, and there are certain situations in which one can make no mistake.

If you are as hard hit as you say you are, go for a cruise and get over it. Don't hang around here. No good will come of it."

The young man set his teeth. He was looking very determined indeed.

"There isn't anything in this world, short of a bomb," he declared, "which is going to blow me out of Monte Carlo before I have made the acquaintance of Miss Grex!"

CHAPTER VII

THE EFFRONTERY OF RICHARD

Hunterleys took leave of his companion as soon as they arrived at the roulette rooms.

"Take my advice, Lane," he said seriously. "Find something to occupy your thoughts. Throw a few hundred thousand of your dollars away at the tables, if you must do something foolish. You'll get into far less trouble."

Richard made no direct reply. He watched Hunterleys depart and took up his place opposite the door to await his sister's arrival. It was a quarter to five before she appeared and found him waiting for her in the door-way.

"Say, you're late, Flossie!" he grumbled. "I thought you were going to be here soon after four."

She glanced at the little watch upon her wrist. "How the time does slip away!" she sighed. "But really, Dicky, I am late in your interests as much as anything. I have been paying a few calls. I went out to the Villa Rosa to see some people who almost live here, and then I met Lady Crawley and she made me go in and have some tea."

"Well?" he asked impatiently. "Well?"

She laid her fingers upon his arm and drew him into a less crowded part of the room.

"Dicky," she confessed, "I don't seem to have

had a bit of luck. The Comtesse d'Hausson, who lives at the Villa Rosa, knows them and showed me from the window the Villa Mimosa, where they live, but she would tell me absolutely nothing about them. The villa is the finest in Monte Carlo, and has always been taken before by some one of note. She declares that they do not mix in the society of the place, but she admits that she has heard a rumour that Grex is only an assumed name."

" I begin to believe that myself," he said doggedly. " Hunterleys knows who they are and won't tell me. So does that fellow Draconmeyer."

" Sir Henry and Mr. Draconmeyer! " she repeated, raising her eyes. " My dear Dick, that doesn't sound very reasonable, does it? "

" I tell you that they do," he persisted. " They as good as told me so. Hunterleys, especially, left me here only half-an-hour ago, and his last words were advising me to chuck it. He's a sensible chap enough but he won't even tell me why. I've had enough of it. I've a good mind to take the bull by the horns myself. Mr. Grex is here now, somewhere about. He was sitting with Mr. Draconmeyer and a fat old German a few minutes ago, at the next table to ours. If I had been alone I should have gone up and chanced being introduced, but Hunterleys wouldn't let me."

" Well, so far," Lady Weybourne admitted, " I fear that I haven't done much towards that electric coupé; but," she added, in a changed tone, looking across the tables, " there is just one thing, Dicky. Fate sometimes has a great deal to do with these little affairs. Look over there."

Richard left his sister precipitately, without even a word of farewell. She watched him cross the room, and smiled at the fury of a little Frenchman whom he nearly knocked over in his hurry to get round to the other side of the table. A moment later he was standing a few feet away from the girl who had taken so strange a hold upon his affections. He himself was conscious of a curious and unfamiliar nervousness. Physically he felt as though he had been running hard. He set his teeth and tried to keep cool. He found some plaques in his pocket and began to stake. Then he became aware that the girl was holding in her hand a note and endeavouring to attract the attention of the man who was giving change.

" *Petite monnaie, s'il vous plaît,*" he heard her say, stretching out the note.

The man took no notice. Richard held out his hand.

" Will you allow me to get it changed for you? " he asked.

Her first impulse at the sound of his voice was evidently one of resentment. She seemed, indeed, in the act of returning some chilling reply. Then she glanced half carelessly towards him and her eyes rested upon his face. Richard was good-looking enough, but the chief characteristic of his face was a certain honesty, which seemed accentuated at that moment by his undoubted earnestness. The type was perhaps strange to her. She was almost startled by what she saw. Scarcely knowing what she did, she allowed him to take the note from her fingers.

" Thank you very much," she murmured.

Richard procured the change. He would have lifted every one out of the way if she had been in a hurry. Then he turned round and counted it very slowly into her hands. From the left one she had removed the glove and he saw, to his relief, that there was no engagement ring there. He counted so slowly that towards the end she seemed to become a little impatient.

"That is quite all right," she said. "It was very kind of you to trouble."

She spoke very correct English with the slightest of foreign accents. He looked once more into her eyes.

"It was a pleasure," he declared.

She smiled faintly, an act of graciousness which absolutely turned his head. With her hand full of plaques, she moved away and found a place a little lower down the table. Richard fought with his first instinct and conquered it. He remained where he was, and when he moved it was in another direction. He went into the bar and ordered a whisky and soda. He was as excited as he had been in the old days when he had rowed stroke in a winning race for his college boat. He felt, somehow or other, that the first step had been a success. She had been inclined at first to resent his offer. She had looked at him and changed her mind. Even when she had turned away, she had smiled. It was ridiculous, but he felt as though he had taken a great step. Presently Lady Weybourne, on her way to the baccarat rooms, saw him sitting there and looked in.

"Well, Dicky," she exclaimed, "what luck?"

"Sit down, Flossie," he begged. "I've spoken to her."

"You don't mean,—" she began, horrified.

"Oh, no, no! Nothing of that sort!" he interrupted. "Don't think I'm such a blundering ass. She was trying to get change and couldn't reach. I took the note from her, got the change and gave it to her. She said, 'Thank you.' When she went away, she smiled."

Lady Weybourne flopped down upon the divan and screamed with laughter.

"Dicky," she murmured, wiping her eyes, "tell me, is that why you are sitting there, looking as though you could see right into Heaven? Do you know that your face was one great beam when I came in?"

"Can't help it," he answered contentedly. "I've spoken to her and she smiled."

Lady Weybourne opened her gold bag and produced a card.

"Well," she said, "here is another chance for you. Of course, I don't know that it will come to anything, but you may as well try your luck."

"What is it?" he asked.

She thrust a square of gilt-edged cardboard into his hand.

"It's an invitation," she told him, "from the directors, to attend a dinner at La Turbie Golf Clubhouse, up in the mountains, to-night. It isn't entirely a joke, I can tell you. It takes at least an hour to get there, climbing all the way, and the place is as likely as not to be wrapped in clouds, but a great many of the important people are going,

and as I happened to see Mr. Grex's name amongst
the list of members, the other night, there is always
a chance that they may be there. If not, you see,
you can soon come back."

" I'm on," Richard decided. " Give me the ticket.
I am awfully obliged to you, Flossie."

" If she is there," Lady Weybourne declared,
rising, " I shall consider that it is equivalent to one
wheel of the coupé."

" Have a cocktail instead," he suggested.

She shook her head.

" Too early. If we meet later on, I'll have one.
What are you going to do? "

" Same as I've been doing ever since lunch," he
answered,—" hang around and see if I can meet any
one who knows them."

She laughed and hurried off into the baccarat
room, and Richard presently returned to the table
at which the girl was still playing. He took particular care not to approach her, but he found a
place on the opposite side of the room, from which
he could watch her unobserved. She was still standing and apparently she was losing her money. Once,
with a little petulant frown, she turned away and
moved a few yards lower down the room. The first
time she staked in her new position, she won, and a
smile which it seemed to him was the most brilliant he
had ever seen, parted her lips. He stood there looking at her, and in the midst of a scene where money
seemed god of all things, he realised all manner of
strange and pleasant sensations. The fact that he
had twenty thousand francs in his pocket to play
with, scarcely occurred to him. He was watching a

little wisp of golden hair by her ear, watching her slightly wrinkled forehead as she leaned over the table, her little grimace as she lost and her stake was swept away. She seemed indifferent to all by-standers. It was obvious that she had very few acquaintances. Where he stood it was not likely that she would notice him, and he abandoned him-self wholly to the luxury of gazing at her. Then some instinct caused him to turn his head. He felt that he in his turn was being watched. He glanced towards the divan set against the wall, by the side of which he was standing. Mr. Grex was seated there, only a few feet away, smoking a cigarette. Their eyes met and Richard was conscious of a sudden embarrassment. He felt like a detected thief, and he acted at that moment as he often did — en-tirely on impulse. He leaned down and resolutely addressed Mr. Grex.

"I should be glad, sir, if you would allow me to speak to you for a moment."

Mr. Grex's expression was one of cold surprise, unmixed with any curiosity.

"Do you address me?" he asked.

His tone was vastly discouraging but it was too late to draw back.

"I should like to speak to you, if I may," Richard continued.

"I am not aware," Mr. Grex said, "that I have the privilege of your acquaintance."

"You haven't," Richard admitted, "but all the same I want to speak to you, if I may."

"Since you have gone so far," Mr. Grex conceded, "you had better finish, but you must allow me to tell you in advance that I look upon any address from a perfect stranger as an impertinence."

"You'll think worse of me before I've finished, then," Richard declared desperately. "You don't mind if I sit down?"

"These seats," Mr. Grex replied coldly, "are free to all."

The young man took his place upon the divan with a sinking heart. There was something in Mr. Grex's tone which seemed to destroy all his confidence, a note of something almost alien in the measured contempt of his speech.

"I am sorry to give you any offence," Richard began. "I happened to notice that you were watching me. I was looking at your daughter — staring at her. I am afraid you thought me impertinent."

"Your perspicuity," Mr. Grex observed, "seems to be of a higher order than your manners. You are, perhaps, a stranger to civilised society?"

"I don't know about that," Richard went on doggedly. "I have been to college and mixed with the usual sort of people. My birth isn't much to speak of, perhaps, if you count that for anything."

Something which was almost like the ghost of a smile, devoid of any trace of humour, parted Mr. Grex's lips.

"If I count that for anything!" he repeated, half closing his eyes for a moment. "Pray proceed, young man."

"I am an American," Richard continued. "My name is Richard Lane. My father was very wealthy and I am his heir. My sister is Lady Weybourne. I was lunching with her at Ciro's to-day when I saw you and your daughter. I think I can say that I am a respectable person. I have a great many friends to whom I can refer you."

"I am not thinking of engaging anybody, that I know of," Mr. Grex murmured.

"I want to marry your daughter," Richard declared desperately, feeling that any further form of explanation would only lead him into greater trouble.

Mr. Grex knocked the ash from his cigarette.

"Is your keeper anywhere in the vicinity?" he asked.

"I am perfectly sane," Richard assured him. "I know that it sounds foolish but it isn't really. I am twenty-seven years old and I have never asked a girl to marry me yet. I have been waiting until —"

The words died away upon his lips. It was impossible for him to continue, the cold enmity of this man was too chilling.

"I am absolutely in earnest," he insisted. "I have been endeavouring all day to find some mutual friend to introduce me to your daughter. Will you do so? Will you give me a chance?"

"I will not," Mr. Grex replied firmly.

"Why not? Please tell me why not?" Richard begged. "I am not asking for anything more now than just an opportunity to talk with her."

"It is not a matter which admits of discussion," Mr. Grex pronounced. "I have permitted you to say what you wished, notwithstanding the colossal, the unimaginable impertinence of your suggestion. I request you to leave me now and I advise you most heartily to indulge no more in the most preposterous and idiotic idea which ever entered into the head of an apparently sane young man."

Richard rose slowly to his feet.

"Very well, sir," he replied, "I'll go. All the same, what you have said doesn't make any difference."

"Does not make any difference?" Mr. Grex repeated, with arched eyebrows.

"None at all," Richard declared. "I don't know what your objection to me is, but I hope you'll get over it some day. I'd like to make friends with you. Perhaps, later on, you may look at the matter differently."

"Later on?" Mr. Grex murmured.

"When I have married your daughter," Richard concluded, marching defiantly away.

Mr. Grex watched the young man until he had disappeared in the crowd. Then he leaned back amongst the cushions of the divan with folded arms. Little lines had become visible around his eyes, there was a slight twitching at the corners of his lips. He looked like a man who was inwardly enjoying some huge joke.

CHAPTER VIII

UP THE MOUNTAIN

Richard, passing the Hotel de Paris that evening in his wicked-looking grey racing car, saw Hunterleys standing on the steps and pulled up.

" Not going up to La Turbie, by any chance? " he enquired.

Hunterleys nodded.

" I'm going up to the dinner," he replied. " The hotel motor is starting from here in a few minutes."

" Come with me," Richard invited.

Hunterleys looked a little doubtfully at the long, low machine.

" Are you going to shoot up? " he asked. " It's rather a dangerous road."

" I'll take care of you," the young man promised. " That hotel 'bus will be crammed."

They glided through the streets on to the broad, hard road, and crept upwards with scarcely a sound, through the blue-black twilight. Around and in front of them little lights shone out from the villas and small houses dotted away in the mountains. Almost imperceptibly they passed into a different atmosphere. The air became cold and exhilarating. The flavour of the mountain snows gave life to the breeze. Hunterleys buttoned up his coat but bared his head.

"My young friend," he said, "this is wonderful."

"It's a great climb," Richard assented, "and doesn't she just eat it up!"

They paused for a moment at La Turbie. Below them was a chain of glittering lights fringing the Bay of Mentone, and at their feet the lights of the Casino and Monte Carlo flared up through the scented darkness. Once more they swung upwards. The road now had become narrower and the turnings more frequent. They were up above the region of villas and farmhouses, in a country which seemed to consist only of bleak hillside, open to the winds, wrapped in shadows. Now and then they heard the tinkling of a goat bell; far below they saw the twin lights of other ascending cars. They reached the plateau at last and drew up before the clubhouse, ablaze with cheerful lights.

"I'll just leave the car under the trees," Richard declared. "No one will be staying late."

Hunterleys unwound his scarf and handed his coat and hat to a page-boy. Then he stood suddenly rigid. He bit his lip. His wife had just issued from the cloak-room and was drawing on her gloves. She saw him and hesitated. She, too, turned a little paler. Slowly Hunterleys approached her.

"An unexpected pleasure," he murmured.

"I am here with Mr. Draconmeyer," she told him, almost bluntly.

Hunterleys bowed.

"And a party?" he enquired.

"No," she replied. "I really did not want to come. Mr. Draconmeyer had promised Monsieur

Pericot, the director here, to come and bring Mrs. Draconmeyer. At the last moment, however, she was not well enough, and he almost insisted upon my taking her place."

" Is it necessary to explain? " Hunterleys asked quietly. " You know very well how I regard this friendship of yours."

" I am sorry," she said. " If I had known that we were likely to meet — well, I would not have come here to-night."

" You were at least considerate," he remarked bitterly. " May I be permitted to compliment you upon your toilette? "

" As you pay for my frocks," she answered, " there is certainly no reason why you shouldn't admire them."

He bit his lip. There was a certain challenge in her expression which made him, for a moment, feel weak. She was a very beautiful woman and she was looking her best. He spoke quickly on another subject.

" Are you still," he asked, " troubled by the attentions of the person you spoke to me about? "

" I am still watched," she replied drily.

" I have made some enquiries," Hunterleys continued, " and I have come to the conclusion that you are right."

" And you still tell me that you have nothing to do with it? "

" I assure you, upon my honour, that I have nothing whatever to do with it."

It was obvious that she was puzzled, but at that moment Mr. Draconmeyer presented himself. The newcomer simply bowed to Hunterleys and addressed some remark about the room to Violet. Then Richard came up and they all passed on into the reception room, where two or three very fussy but very suave and charming Frenchmen were receiving the guests. A few minutes afterwards dinner was announced. A black frown was upon Richard's forehead.

"She isn't coming!" he muttered. "I say, Sir Henry, you won't mind if we leave early?"

"I shall be jolly glad to get away," Hunterleys assented heartily.

Then he suddenly felt a grip of iron upon his arm.

"She's come!" Richard murmured ecstatically. "Look at her, all in white! Just look at the colour of her hair! There she is, going into the reception room. Jove! I'm glad we are here, after all!"

Hunterleys smiled a little wearily. They passed on into the *salle à manger*. The seats at the long dining-tables were not reserved, and they found a little table for two in a corner, which they annexed. Hunterleys was in a grim humour, but his companion was in the wildest spirits. Considering that he was placed where he could see Mr. Grex and his daughter nearly the whole of the time, he really did contrive to keep his eyes away from them to a wonderful extent, but he talked of her unceasingly.

"Say, I'm sorry for you, Sir Henry!" he declared. "It's just your bad luck, being here with me while I've got this fit on, but I've got to talk to some one, so you may as well make up your mind to it. There never was anything like that girl upon the earth. There never was anything like the feeling you get," he went on, " when you're absolutely and entirely convinced, when you know — that there's just one girl who counts for you in the whole universe. Gee whiz! It does get hold of you! I suppose you've been through it all, though."

" Yes, I've been through it!" Hunterleys admitted, with a sigh.

The young man bit his lip. The story of Hunterleys' matrimonial differences was already being whispered about. Richard talked polo vigorously for the next quarter of an hour. It was not until the coffee and liqueurs arrived that they returned to the subject of Miss Grex. Then it was Hunterleys himself who introduced it. He was beginning to rather like this big, self-confident young man, so full of his simple love affair, so absolutely honest in his purpose, in his outlook upon life.

" Lane," he said, " I have given you several hints during the day, haven't I? "

" That's so," Richard agreed. " You've done your best to head me off. So did my future father-in-law. Sort of hopeless task, I can assure you."

Hunterleys shook his head.

" Honestly," he continued, " I wouldn't let myself think too much about her, Lane. I don't want to explain exactly what I mean. There's no real reason why I shouldn't tell you what I know about Mr. Grex, but for a good many people's sakes, it's just as well that those few of us who know keep quiet. I am sure you trust me, and it's just the same, therefore, if I tell you straight, as man to man, that you're only laying up for yourself a store of unhappiness by fixing your thoughts so entirely upon that young woman."

Richard, for all his sublime confidence, was a little staggered by the other's earnestness.

"Look here," he said, "the girl isn't married, to start with?"

"Not that I know of," Hunterleys confessed.

"And she's not engaged because I've seen her left hand," Richard proceeded. "I'm not one of those Americans who go shouting all over the world that because I've got a few million dollars I am the equal of anybody, but honestly, Sir Henry, there are a good many prejudices over this side that you fellows lay too much store by. Grex may be a nobleman in disguise. I don't care. I am a man. I can give her everything she needs in life and I am not going to admit, even if she is an aristocrat, that you croakers are right when you shake your heads and advise me to give her up. I don't care who she is, Hunterleys. I am going to marry her."

Hunterleys helped himself to a liqueur.

"Young man," he said, "in a sense I admire your independence. In another, I think you've got all the conceit a man needs for this world. Let us presume, for a moment, that she is, as you surmise, the daughter of a nobleman. When it suits her father to throw off his incognito, she is probably in touch with young men in the highest circles of many countries. Why should you suppose that you can come along and cut them all out?"

"Because I love her," the young man answered simply. "They don't."

"You must remember," Hunterleys resumed,

" that all foreign noblemen are not what they are
represented to be in your comic papers. Austrian
and Russian men of high rank are most of them very
highly cultivated, very accomplished, and very good-
looking. You don't know much of the world, do
you? It's a pretty formidable enterprise to come
from a New York office, with only Harvard behind
you, and a year or so's travel as a tourist, and enter
the list against men who have had twice your opportunities. I am talking to you like this, young fellow, for your good. I hope you realise that.
You're used to getting what you want. That's because you've been brought up in a country where
money can do almost anything. I am behind the
scenes here and I can assure you that your money
won't count for much with Mr. Grex."

" I never thought it would," Richard admitted.
" I think when I talk to her she'll understand that I
care more than any of the others. If you want to
know the reason, that's why I'm so hopeful."

Monsieur le Directeur had risen to his feet. Some
one had proposed his health and he made a graceful little speech of acknowledgment. He remained
standing for a few minutes after the cheers which had
greeted his neat oratorical display had died away.
The conclusion of his remarks came as rather a surprise to his guests.

" I have to ask you, ladies and gentlemen," he
announced, " with many, many regrets, and begging
you to forgive my apparent inhospitality, to make
your arrangements for leaving us as speedily as
may be possible. Our magnificent situation, with
which I believe that most of you are familiar, has

but one drawback. We are subject to very dense mountain mists, and alas! I have to tell you that one of these has come on most unexpectedly and the descent must be made with the utmost care. Believe me, there is no risk or any danger," he went on earnestly, " so long as you instruct your chauffeurs to proceed with all possible caution. At the same time, as there is very little chance of the mist becoming absolutely dispelled before daylight, in your own interests I would suggest that a start be made as soon as possible."

Every one rose at once, Richard and Hunterleys amongst them.

" This will test your skill to-night, young man," Hunterleys remarked. " How's the nerve, eh? "

Richard smiled almost beatifically. For once he had allowed his eyes to wander and he was watching the girl with golden hair who was at that moment receiving the respectful homage of the director.

" Lunatics, and men who are head over heels in love," he declared, " never come to any harm. You'll be perfectly safe with me."

CHAPTER IX

IN THE MISTS

Their first glimpse of the night, as Hunterleys and Lane passed out through the grudgingly opened door, was sufficiently disconcerting. A little murmur of dismay broke from the assembled crowd. Nothing was to be seen but a dense bank of white mist, through which shone the brilliant lights of the automobiles waiting at the door. Monsieur le Directeur hastened about, doing his best to reassure everybody.

"If I thought it was of the slightest use," he declared, "I would ask you all to stay, but when the clouds once stoop like this, there is not likely to be any change for twenty-four hours, and we have not, alas! sleeping accommodation. If the cars are slowly driven and kept to the inside, it is only a matter of a mile or two before you will drop below the level of the clouds."

Hunterleys and Lane made their way out to the front, and with their coat collars turned up, groped their way to the turf on the other side of the avenue. From where they stood, looking downwards, the whole world seemed wrapped in mysterious and somber silence. There was nothing to be seen but the grey, driving clouds. In less than a minute their hair and eyebrows were dripping. A slight breeze had sprung up, the cold was intense.

"Cheerful sort of place, this," Lane remarked gloomily. "Shall we make a start?"

Hunterleys hesitated.

"Not just yet. Look!"

He pointed downwards. For a moment the clouds had parted. Thousands of feet below, like little pinpricks of red fire, they saw the lights of Monte Carlo. Almost as they looked, the clouds closed up again. It was as though they had peered into another world.

"Jove, that was queer!" Lane muttered. "Look! What's that?"

A long ray of sickly yellow light shone for a moment and was then suddenly blotted out by a rolling mass of vapour. The clouds had closed in again once more. The obscurity was denser than ever.

"The lighthouse," Hunterleys replied. "Do you think it's any use waiting?"

"We'll go inside and put on our coats," Lane suggested. "My car is by the side of the avenue there. I covered it over and left it."

They found their coats in the hall, wrapped themselves up and lit cigarettes. Already many of the cars had started and vanished cautiously into obscurity. Every now and then one could hear the tooting of their horns from far away below. The chief steward was directing the departures and insisting upon an interval of three minutes between each. The two men stood on one side and watched him. He was holding open the door of a large, exceptionally handsome car. On the other side was a servant in white livery. Lane gripped his companion's arm.

" There she goes! " he exclaimed.

The girl, followed by Mr. Grex, stepped into the landaulette, which was brilliantly illuminated inside with electric light. Almost immediately the car glided noiselessly off. The two men watched it until it disappeared. Then they crossed the road.

" Now then, Sir Henry," Richard observed grimly, as he turned the handle of the car and they took their places in the little well-shaped space, " better say your prayers. I'm going to drive slowly enough but it's an awful job, this, crawling down the side of a mountain in the dark, with nothing between you and eternity but your brakes."

They crept off. As far as the first turn the lights from the club-house helped them. Immediately afterwards, however, the obscurity was enveloping. Their faces were wet and shiny with moisture. Even the fingers of Lane's gloves which gripped the wheel were sodden. He proceeded at a snail's pace, keeping always on the inside of the road and only a few inches from the wall or bank. Once he lost his way and his front wheel struck a small stump, but they were going too slowly for disaster. Another time he failed to follow the turn of the road and found himself in a rough cart track. They backed with difficulty and got right once more. At the fourth turn they came suddenly upon a huge car which had left the road as they had done and was standing amongst the pine trees, its lights flaring through the mist.

" Hullo ! " Lane called out, coming to a standstill.
" You've missed the turn."

" My master is going to stay here all night," the
chauffeur shouted back.

A man put his head from the window and began
to talk in rapid French.

" It is inconceivable," he exclaimed, " that any one
should attempt the descent!   We have rugs, my wife
and I.   We stay here till the clouds pass."

" Good night, then! " Lane cried cheerfully.

" Not sure that you're not wise," Hunterleys
added, with a shiver.

Twice they stopped while Lane rubbed the moisture from his gloves and lit a fresh cigarette.

" This is a test for your nerve, young fellow,"
Hunterleys remarked.   " Are you feeling it ? "

" Not in the least," Lane replied.   " I can't make
out, though, why that steward made us all start at
intervals of three minutes.   Seems to me we should
have been better going together at this pace.   Save
any one from getting lost, anyhow."

They crawled on for another twenty minutes.
The routine was always the same — a hundred yards
or perhaps two, an abrupt turn and then a similar
distance the other way.   They had one or two slight
misadventures   but   they   made   progress.   Once,
through a rift, they caught a momentary vision of a
carpet of lights at a giddy distance below.

" We'll make it all right," Lane declared, crawling
around another corner.   " Gee! but this is the tough-
est thing in driving I've ever known!   I can do
ninety with this car easier than I can do this three.
Hullo, some one else in trouble! "

Before them, in the middle of the road, a light was being slowly swung backwards and forwards. Lane brought the car to a standstill. He had scarcely done so when they were conscious of the sound of footsteps all around them. The arms of both men were seized from behind. They were addressed in guttural French.

" Messieurs will be pleased to descend."

" What the — what's wrong? " Lane demanded.

" Descend at once," was the prompt order.

By the light of the lantern which the speaker was holding, they caught a glimpse of a dozen white faces and the dull gleam of metal from the firearms which his companions were carrying. Hunterleys stepped out. An escort of two men was at once formed on either side of him.

" Tell us what it's all about, anyhow? " he asked coolly.

" Nothing serious," the same guttural voice answered,— " a little affair which will be settled in a few minutes. As for you, monsieur," the man continued, turning to Lane, " you will drive your car slowly to the next turn, and leave it there. Afterwards you will return with me."

Richard set his teeth and leaned over his wheel. Then it suddenly flashed into his mind that Mr. Grex and his daughter were already amongst the captured. He quickly abandoned his first instinct.

" With pleasure, monsieur," he assented. " Tell me when to stop."

He drove the car a few yards round the corner, past a line of others. Their lights were all extinguished and the chauffeurs absent.

" This is a pleasant sort of picnic!" he grumbled, as he brought his car to a standstill. " Now what do I do, monsieur? "

" You return with me, if you please," was the reply.

Richard stood, for a moment, irresolute. The idea of giving in without a struggle was most distasteful to this self-reliant young American. Then he realised that not only was his captor armed but that there were men behind him and one on either side.

" Lead the way," he decided tersely.

They marched him up the hill, a little way across some short turf and round the back of a rock to a long building which he remembered to have noticed on his way up. His guide threw open the door and Richard looked in upon a curious scene. Ranged up against the further wall were about a dozen of the guests who had preceded him in his departure from the Club-house. One man only had his hands tied behind him. The others, apparently, were considered harmless. Mr. Grex was the one man, and there was a little blood dripping from his right hand. The girl stood by his side. She was no paler than usual — she showed, indeed, no signs of terror at all — but her eyes were bright with indignation. One man was busy stripping the jewels from the women and throwing them into a bag. In the far corner the little group of chauffeurs was being watched by two more men, also carrying firearms. Lane looked down the line of faces. Lady Hunterleys was there, and by her side Draconmeyer. Hunterleys was a little apart from the others. Freddy

Montressor, who was leaning against the wall, chuckled as Lane came in.

" So they've got you, too, Dicky, have they? " he remarked. " It's a hold-up — a bully one, too. Makes one feel quite homesick, eh? How much have you got on you? "

" Precious little, thank heavens! " Richard muttered.

His eyes were fixed upon the brigand who was collecting the jewels, and who was now approaching Miss Grex. He felt something tingling in his blood. One of the guests began to talk excitedly. The man who was apparently the leader, and who was standing at the door with an electric torch in one hand and a revolver in the other, stepped a little forward.

" Ladies and gentlemen," he said, " once more I beg you not to be alarmed. So long as you part with your valuables peaceably, you will be at liberty to depart as soon as every one has been dealt with. If there is no resistance, there will be no trouble. We do not wish to hurt any one."

The collector of jewels had arrived in front of the girl. She unfastened her necklace and handed it to him.

" The little pendant around my neck," she remarked calmly, " is valueless. I desire to keep it."

" Impossible! " the man replied. " Off with it."

" But I insist! " she exclaimed. " It is an heirloom."

The man laughed brutally. His filthy hand was raised to her neck. Even as he touched her, Lane, with a roar of anger, sent one of his guards flying on to the floor of the barn, and, snatching the gun from his hand, sprang forward.

"Come on, you fellows!" he shouted, bringing it down suddenly upon the hand of the robber. "These things aren't loaded. There's only one of these blackguards with a revolver."

"And I've got him!" Hunterleys, who had been watching Lane closely, cried, suddenly swinging his arm around the man's neck and knocking his revolver up.

There was a yell of pain from the man with the jewels, whose wrist Lane had broken, a howl of dismay from the others — pandemonium.

"At 'em, Freddy!" Lane shouted, seizing the nearest of his assailants by the neck and throwing him out into the darkness. "To hell with you!" he added, just escaping a murderous blow and driving his fist into the face of the man who had aimed it. "Good for you, Hunterleys! There isn't one of those old guns of theirs that'll go off. They aren't even loaded."

The barn seemed suddenly to become half empty. Into the darkness the little band of brigands crept away like rats. In less than half a minute they had all fled, excepting the one who lay on the ground unconscious from the effects of Richard's blow, and the leader of the gang, whom Hunterleys still held by the throat. Richard, with a clasp-knife which he had drawn from his pocket, cut the cord which they had tied around Mr. Grex's wrists. His action, however, was altogether mechanical. He scarcely glanced at what he was doing. Somehow or other, he found the girl's hands in his.

"That brute — didn't touch you, did he?" he asked.

She looked at him. Whether the clouds were still outside or not, Lane felt that he had passed into Heaven.

"He did not, thanks to you," she murmured. "But do you mean really that those guns all the time weren't loaded?"

"I don't believe they were," Richard declared stoutly. "That chap kept on playing about with the lock of his old musket and I felt sure that it was of no use, loaded or not. Anyway, when I saw that brute try to handle you — well —"

He stopped, with an awkward little laugh. Mr. Grex tapped a cigarette upon his case and lit it.

"I am sure, my young friend, we are all very much indebted to you. The methods which sometimes are scarcely politic in the ordinary affairs of life," he continued drily, "are admirable enough in a case like this. We will just help Hunterleys tie up the leader of the gang. A very plucky stroke, that of his."

He crossed the barn. One of the women had fainted, others were busy collecting their jewelry. The chauffeurs had hurried off to relight the lamps of the cars.

"I must tell you this," Richard said, drawing a a little nearer to the girl. "Please don't be angry with me. I went to your father this afternoon. I made an idiot of myself — I couldn't help it. I was staring at you and he noticed it. I didn't want him to think that I was such an ill-mannered brute as I seemed. I tried to make him understand but

he wouldn't listen to me.   I'd like to tell you now —
now that I have the opportunity — that I think
you're just —"

She smiled very faintly.

" What is it that you wish to tell me? " she asked
patiently.

" That I love you," he wound up abruptly.

There was a moment's silence, a silence with a
background of strange noises.   People were talking,
almost shouting to one another with excitement.
Newcomers were being told the news.   The man
whom Hunterleys had captured was shrieking and
cursing.   From beyond came the tooting of motor-
horns as the cars returned.   Lane heard nothing.
He saw nothing but the white face of the girl as she
stood in the shadows of the barn, with its walls of
roughly threaded pine trunks.

" But I have scarcely ever spoken to you in my
life! " she protested, looking at him in astonishment.

" It doesn't make any difference," he replied.
" You know I am speaking the truth.   I think, in
your heart, that you, too, know that these things
don't matter, now and then.   Of course, you don't
— you couldn't feel anything of what I feel, but
with me it's there now and for always, and I want to
have a chance, just a chance to make you understand.   I'm not really mad.   I'm just — in love
with you."

She smiled at him, still in a friendly manner, but
her face had clouded.   There was a look in her eyes
almost of trouble, perhaps of regret.

" I am so sorry," she murmured.   " It is only a
sudden feeling on your part, isn't it?   You have

been so splendid to-night that I can do no more than
thank you very, very much. And as for what you
have told me, I think it is an honour, but I wish you
to forget it. It is not wise for you to think of me
in that way. I fear that I cannot even offer you my
friendship."

Again there was a brief silence. The clamour of
exclamations from the little groups of people still
filled the air outside. They could hear cars coming
and going. The man whom Hunterleys and Mr.
Grex were tying up was still groaning and cursing.

"Are you married?" Richard asked abruptly.

She shook her head.

"Engaged?"

"No!"

"Do you care very much for any one else?"

"No!" she told him softly.

He drew her away.

"Come outside for one moment," he begged. "I
hate to see you in the place where that beast tried to
lay hands upon you. Here is your necklace."

He picked it up from her feet and she followed him
obediently outside. People were standing about,
shadowy figures in little groups. Some of the cars
had already left, others were being prepared for a
start. Below, once more the clouds had parted and
the lights twinkled like fireflies through the trees.
This time they could even see the lights from the vil-
lage of La Turbie, less brilliant but almost at their
feet. Richard glanced upwards. There was a star
clearly visible.

"The clouds are lifting," he said. "Listen. If
there is no one else, tell me, why there shouldn't be

the slightest chance for me? I am not clever, I am nobody of any account, but I care for you so wonderfully. I love you, I always shall love you, more than any one else could. I never understood before, but I understand now. Just this caring means so much."

She stood close to his side. Her manner at the same time seemed to depress him and yet to fill him with hope.

"What is your name?" she enquired.

"Richard Lane," he told her. "I am an American."

"Then, Mr. Richard Lane," she continued softly, "I shall always think of you and think of to-night and think of what you have said, and perhaps I shall be a little sorry that what you have asked me cannot be."

"Cannot?" he muttered.

She shook her head almost sadly.

"Some day," she went on, "as soon as our stay in Monte Carlo is finished, if you like, I will write and tell you the real reason, in case you do not find it out before."

He was silent, looking downwards to where the gathering wind was driving the clouds before it, to where the lights grew clearer and clearer at every moment.

"Does it matter," he asked abruptly, "that I am rich — very rich?"

"It does not matter at all," she answered.

"Doesn't it matter," he demanded, turning suddenly upon her and speaking with a new passion, almost a passion of resentment, "doesn't it matter that without you life doesn't exist for me any longer? Doesn't it matter that a man has given you his whole heart, however slight a thing it may seem to you? What am I to do if you send me away? There isn't anything left in life."

" There is what you have always found in it," she reminded him.

" There isn't," he replied fiercely. " That's just what there isn't. I should go back to a world that was like a dead city."

He suddenly felt her hand upon his.

" Dear Mr. Lane," she begged, " wait for a little time before you nurse these sad thoughts, and when you know how impossible what you ask is, it will seem easier. But if you really care to hear something, if it would really please you sometimes to think of it when you are alone and you remember this little foolishness of yours, let me tell you, if I may, that I am sorry — I am very sorry."

His hand was suddenly pressed, and then, before he could stop her, she had glided away. He moved a step to follow her and almost at once he was surrounded. Lady Hunterleys patted him on the shoulder.

" Really," she exclaimed, " you and Henry were our salvation. I haven't felt so thrilled for ages. I only wish," she added, dropping her voice a little, " that it might bring you the luck you deserve."

He answered vaguely. She turned back to Hunterleys. She was busy tearing up her handkerchief.

" I am going to tie up your head," she said. " Please stoop down."

He obeyed at once. The side of his forehead was bleeding where a bullet from the revolver of the man he had captured had grazed his temple.

" Too bad to trouble you," he muttered.

" It's the least we can do," she declared, laughing nervously. " Forgive me if my fingers tremble. It is the excitement of the last few minutes."

Hunterleys stood quite still. Words seemed difficult to him just then.

" You were very brave, Henry," she said quietly. " Whom — whom are you going down with? "

" I am with Richard Lane," he answered, " in his two-seated racer."

She bit her lip.

" I did not mean to come alone with Mr. Draconmeyer, really," she explained. " He thought, up to the last moment, that his wife would be well enough to come."

" Did he really believe so, do you think? " Hunterleys asked.

A voice intervened. Mr. Draconmeyer was standing by their side.

" Well," he said, " we might as well resume our journey. We all look and feel, I think, as though we had been taking part in a scene from some opéra bouffe."

Lady Hunterleys shivered. She had drawn a little closer to her husband. Her coat was unfastened. Hunterleys leaned towards her and buttoned it with strong fingers up to her throat.

" Thank you," she whispered. " You wouldn't — you couldn't drive down with us, could you? "

" Have you plenty of room? " he enquired.

"Plenty," she declared eagerly. "Mr. Dracon-meyer and I are alone."

For a moment Hunterleys hesitated. Then he caught the smile upon the face of the man he detested.

"Thank you," he said, "I don't think I can desert Lane."

She stiffened at once. Her good night was almost formal. Hunterleys stepped into the car which Richard had brought up. There was just a slight mist around them, but the whole country below, though chaotic, was visible, and the lights on the hill-side, from La Turbie down to the sea-board, were in plain sight.

"Our troubles," Hunterleys remarked, as they glided off, "seem to be over."

"Maybe," Lane replied grimly. "Mine seem to be only just beginning!"

CHAPTER X

At ten o'clock the next morning, Hunterleys crossed the sunlit gardens towards the English bank, to receive what was, perhaps, the greatest shock of his life. A few minutes later he stood before the mahogany counter, his eyes fixed upon the half sheet of notepaper which the manager had laid before him. The words were few enough and simple enough, yet they constituted for him a message written in the very ink of tragedy. The notepaper was the notepaper of the Hotel de Paris, the date the night before, the words few and unmistakable:

To the Manager of the English Bank.
    Please hand my letters to bearer.
                        HENRY HUNTERLEYS.

He read it over, letter by letter, word by word. Then at last he looked up. His voice sounded, even to himself, unnatural.

"You were quite right," he said. "This order is a forgery."

The manager was greatly disturbed. He threw open the door of his private office.

"Come and sit down for a moment, will you, Sir Henry?" he invited. "This is a very serious matter, and I should like to discuss it with you."

They passed behind into the comfortable little sitting-room, smelling of morocco leather and roses, with its single high window, its broad writing-table, its carefully placed easy-chairs. Men had pleaded in here with all the eloquence at their command, men of every rank and walk in life, thieves, nobles, ruined men and pseudo-millionaires, always with the same cry — money; money for the great pleasure-mill which day and night drew in its own. Hunterleys sank heavily into a chair. The manager seated himself in an official attitude before his desk.

"I am sorry to have distressed you with this letter, Sir Henry," he said. "However, you must admit that things might have been worse. It is fortunately our invariable custom, when letters are addressed to one of our clients in our care, to deliver them to no one else under any circumstances. If you had been ill, for instance, I should have brought you your correspondence across to the hotel, but I should not have delivered it to your own secretary. That, as I say, is our invariable rule, and we find that it has saved many of our clients from inconvenience. In your case," the manager concluded impressively, "your communications being, in a sense, official, any such attempt as has been made would not stand the slightest chance of success. We should be even more particular than in any ordinary case to see that by no possible chance could any correspondence addressed to you, fall into other hands."

Hunterleys began to recover himself a little. He drew towards himself the heap of letters which the manager had laid by his side.

" Please make yourself quite comfortable here,"
the latter begged. " Read your letters and answer
them, if you like, before you go out. I always call
this," he added, with a smile, " the one inviolable
sanctuary of Monte Carlo."

" You are very kind," Hunterleys replied. " Are
you sure that I am not detaining you? "

" Not in the least. Personally, I am not at all
busy. Three-quarters of our business, you see, is
merely a matter of routine. I was just going to
shut myself up here and read the *Times*. Have a
cigarette? Here's an envelope opener and a waste-
paper basket. Make yourself comfortable."

Hunterleys glanced through his correspondence,
rapidly reading and destroying the greater portion
of it. He came at last to two parchment envelopes
marked " On His Majesty's Service." These he
opened and read their contents slowly and with great
care. When he had finished, he produced a pair of
scissors from his waistcoat pocket and cut the letters
into minute fragments. He drew a little sigh of relief when at last their final destruction was assured,
and rose shortly afterwards to his feet.

" I shall have to go on to the telegraph office," he
said, " to send these few messages. Thank you very
much, Mr. Harrison, for your kindness. If you do
not mind, I should like to take this forged order
away with me."

The manager hesitated.

" I am not sure that I ought to part with it," he
observed doubtfully.

" Could you recognise the person who presented
it — you or your clerk? "

The manager shook his head.

"Not a chance," he replied. "It was brought in, unfortunately, before I arrived. Young Parsons, who was the only one in the bank, explained that letters were never delivered to an order, and turned away to attend to some one else who was in a hurry. He simply remembers that it was a man, and that is all."

"Then the document is useless to you," Hunterleys pointed out. "You could never do anything in the matter without evidence of identification, and that being so, if you don't mind I should like to have it."

Mr. Harrison yielded it up.

"As you wish," he agreed. "It is interesting, if only as a curiosity. The imitation of your signature is almost perfect."

Hunterleys took up his hat. Then for a moment, with his hand upon the door, he hesitated.

"Mr. Harrison," he said, "I am engaged just now, as you have doubtless surmised, in certain investigations on behalf of the usual third party whom we need not name. Those investigations have reached a pitch which might possibly lead me into a position of some — well, I might almost say danger. You and I both know that there are weapons in this place which can be made use of by persons wholly without scruples, which are scarcely available at home. I want you to keep your eyes open. I have very few friends here whom I can wholly trust. It is my purpose to call in here every morning at ten o'clock for my letters, and if I fail to arrive within half-an-hour of that time without having given you

verbal notice, something will have happened to me.
You understand what I mean? "

" You mean that you are threatened with assas-
sination? " the manager asked gravely.

" Practically it amounts to that," Hunterleys
admitted. " I received a warning letter this morning. There is a very important matter on foot here,
Mr. Harrison, a matter so important that to bring
it to a successful conclusion I fancy that those who
are engaged in it would not hesitate to face any risk.
I have wired to England for help. If anything happens that it comes too late, I want you, when you find
that I have disappeared, even if my disappearance
is only a temporary matter, to let them know in London — you know how — at once."

The manager nodded.

" I will do so," he promised. " I trust, however,"
he went on, " that you are exaggerating the danger.
Mr. Billson lived here for many years without any
trouble."

Hunterleys smiled slightly.

" I am not a Secret Service man," he explained.
" Billson's successor lives here now, of course, and
is working with me, under the usual guise of newspaper correspondent. I don't think that he will
come to any harm. But I am here in a somewhat
different position, and my negotiations in the east,
during the last few weeks, have made me exceedingly
unpopular with some very powerful people. However, it is only an outside chance, of course, that I
wish to guard against. I rely upon you, if I should
fail to come to the bank any one morning without
giving you notice, to do as I have asked."

Hunterleys left the bank and walked out once more into the sunlight. He first of all made his way down to the Post Office, where he rapidly dispatched several cablegrams which he had coded and written out in Mr. Harrison's private office. Afterwards he went on to the Terrace, and finding a retired seat at the further end, sat down. Then he drew the forged order once more from his pocket. Word by word, line by line, he studied it, and the more he studied it, the more hopeless the whole thing seemed. The handwriting, with the exception of the signature, which was a wonderful imitation of his own, was the handwriting of his wife. She had done this thing at Draconmeyer's instigation, done this thing against her husband, taken sides absolutely with the man whom he had come to look upon as his enemy. What inference was he to draw? He sat there, looking out over the Mediterranean, soft and blue, glittering with sunlight, breaking upon the yellow stretch of sand in little foam-flecked waves no higher than his hand. He watched the sunlight glitter on the white houses which fringed the bay. He looked idly up at the trim little vineyards on the brown hill-side. It was the beauty spot of the world. There was no object upon which his eyes could rest, which was not beautiful. The whole place was like a feast of colour and form and sunshine. Yet for him the light seemed suddenly to have faded from life. Danger had only stimulated him, had helped him to cope with the dull pain which he had carried about with him during the last few months. He was face to face now with something else. It was worse, this, than anything he had dreamed. Somehow or other, notwithstanding the growing estrangement with his wife which had ended in their virtual separation, he had still believed in her, still had faith in her, still had hope of an ultimate reconciliation. And behind it all, he had loved her. It seemed at that moment that a nightmare was being formed around him. A new horror was creeping into his thoughts. He had felt from the first a bitter dislike of Draconmeyer. Now, however, he realised that this feeling had developed into an actual and harrowing jealousy. He realised that the man was no passive agent. It was Draconmeyer who, with subtle purpose, was drawing his wife away! Hunterleys sprang to his feet and walked angrily backwards and forwards along the few yards of Terrace, which happened at that moment to be almost deserted. Vague plans of instant revenge upon Draconmeyer floated into his mind. It was simple enough to take the law into his own hands, to thrash him publicly, to make Monte Carlo impossible for him. And then, suddenly, he remembered his duty. They were trusting him in Downing Street. Chance had put into his hands so many threads of this diabolical plot. It was for him to checkmate it. He was the only person who could checkmate it. This was no time for him to think of personal revenge, no time for him to brood over his own broken life. There was work still to be done — his country's work. . . .

He felt the need of change of scene. The sight of the place with its placid, enervating beauty, its constant appeal to the senses, was beginning to have a curious effect upon his nerves. He turned back upon the Terrace, and by means of the least frequented streets he passed through the town and up towards the hills. He walked steadily, reckless of time or direction. He had lunch at a small inn high above the road from Cannes, and it was past three o'clock when he turned homewards. He had found his way into the main road now and he trudged along heedless of the dust with which the constant procession of automobiles covered him all the while. The exercise had done him good. He was able to keep his thoughts focussed upon his mission. So far, at any rate, he had held his own. His dispatches to London had been clear and vivid. He had told them exactly what he had feared, he had shown them the inside of this scheme as instinct had revealed it to him, and he had begged for aid. One man alone, surrounded by enemies, and in a country where all things were possible, was in a parlous position if once the extent of his knowledge were surmised. So far, the plot had not yet matured. So far, though the clouds had gathered and the thunder was muttering, the storm had not broken. The reason for that he knew — the one person needed, the one person for whose coming all these plans had been made, had not yet arrived. There was no telling, however, how long the respite might last. At any moment might commence this conference, whose avowed purpose was to break at a single blow, a single treacherous but deadly blow, the Empire whose downfall Selingman had once publicly declared was the one great necessity involved by his country's expansion. . . .

Hunterleys quenched his thirst at a roadside café, sitting out upon the pavement and drinking coarse

red wine and soda-water. Then he bought a packet
of black cigarettes and continued his journey. He
was within sight of Monte Carlo when for the twentieth time he had to step to the far side of the path-
way to avoid being smothered in dust by an advanc-
ing automobile. This time, by some chance, he
glanced around, attracted by the piercing character
of its long-distance whistle. A high-powered grey
touring car came by, travelling at a great pace.
Hunterleys stood perfectly rigid, one hand grasping
the wall by the side of which he stood. Notwithstanding his spectacles and the thick coating of dust
upon his clothes, the solitary passenger of the car
was familiar enough to him. It was the man for
whom this plot had been prepared. It was Paul
Douaille, the great Foreign Minister into whose
hands even the most cautious of Premiers had declared himself willing to place the destinies of his
country!

Hunterleys pursued the road no longer. He took
a ticket at the next station and hurried back to
Monte Carlo. He went first to his room, bathed and
changed, and, passing along the private passage,
made his way into the Sporting Club. The first
person whom he saw, seated in her accustomed place
at her favourite table, was his wife. She beckoned
him to come over to her. There was a vacant chair
by her side to which she pointed.

"Thank you," he said, "I won't sit down. I
don't think that I care to play just now. You are
fortunate this afternoon, I trust?"

Something in his face and tone checked that rush
of altered feeling of which she had been more than

once passionately conscious since the night before.

"I am hideously out of luck," she confessed slowly. "I have been losing all day. I think that I shall give it up."

She rose wearily to her feet and he felt a sudden compassion for her. She was certainly looking tired. Her eyes were weary, she had the air of an unhappy woman. After all, perhaps she too sometimes knew what loneliness was.

"I should like some tea so much," she added, a little piteously.

He opened his lips to invite her to pass through into the restaurant with him. Then the memory of that forged order still in his pocket, flashed into his mind. He hesitated. A cold, familiar voice at his elbow intervened.

"Are you quite ready for tea, Lady Hunterleys? I have been in and taken a table near the window."

Hunterleys moved at once on one side. Draconmeyer bowed pleasantly.

"Cheerful time we had last night, hadn't we?" he remarked. "Glad to see your knock didn't lay you up."

Hunterleys disregarded his wife's glance. He was suddenly furious.

"All Monte Carlo seems to be gossiping about that little contretemps," Draconmeyer continued. "It was a crude sort of hold-up for a neighbourhood of criminals, but it very nearly came off. Will you have some tea with us?"

"Do, Henry," his wife begged.

Once again he hesitated. Somehow or other, he

felt that the moment was critical. Then a hand was laid quietly upon his arm, a man's voice whispered in his ear.

"Monsieur will be so kind as to step this way for a moment — a little matter of business."

"Who are you?" Hunterleys demanded.

"The Commissioner of Police, at monsieur's service."

CHAPTER XI

Hunterleys, in accordance with his request, followed the Commissioner downstairs into one of the small private rooms on the ground floor. The latter was very polite but very official.

"Now what is it that you want?" Hunterleys asked, a little brusquely, as soon as they were alone.

The representative of the law was distinctly mysterious. He had a brown moustache which he continually twirled, and he was all the time dropping his voice to a whisper.

"My first introduction to you should explain my mission, Sir Henry," he said. "I hold a high position in the police here. My business with you, however, is on behalf of a person whom I will not name, but whose identity you will doubtless guess."

"Very well," Hunterleys replied. "Now what is the nature of this mission, please? In plain words, what do you want with me?"

"I am here with reference to the affair of last night," the other declared.

"The affair of last night?" Hunterleys repeated, frowning. "Well, we all have to appear or be represented before the magistrates to-morrow morning. I shall send a lawyer."

"Quite so! Quite so! But in the meantime, something has transpired. You and the young American, Mr. Richard Lane, were the only two who offered any resistance. It was owing to you two, in fact, that the plot was frustrated. I am quite sure, Sir Henry, that every one agrees with me in appreciating your courage and presence of mind."

"Thank you," Hunterleys replied. "Is that what you came to say?"

The other shook his head.

"Unfortunately, no, monsieur! I am here to bring you certain information. The chief of the gang, Armand Martin, the man whom you attacked, became suddenly worse a few hours ago. The doctors suspect internal injuries, injuries inflicted during his struggle with you."

"I am very sorry to hear it," Hunterleys said coolly. "On the other hand, he asked for anything he got."

"Unfortunately," the Commissioner continued, "the law of the State is curiously framed in such matters. If the man should die, as seems more than likely, your legal position, Sir Henry, would be most uncomfortable. Your arrest would be a necessity, and there is no law granting what I believe you call bail to a person directly or indirectly responsible for the death of another. I am here, therefore, to give you what I may term an official warning. Your absence as a witness to-morrow morning will not be commented upon — events of importance have called you back to England. You will thereby be saved a very large amount of annoyance, and the authorities here will be spared the most regrettable necessity of having to deal with you in a manner unbefitting your rank."

Hunterleys became at once thoughtful. The whole matter was becoming clear to him.

" I see," he observed. " This is a warning to me to take my departure. Is that so? "

The Commissioner beamed and nodded many times.

" You have a quick understanding, Sir Henry," he declared. " Your departure to-night, or early to-morrow morning, would save a good deal of unpleasantness. I have fulfilled my mission, and I trust that you will reflect seriously upon the matter. It is the wish of the high personage whom I represent, that no inconvenience whatever should befall so distinguished a visitor to the Principality. Good day, monsieur! "

The official took his leave with a sweep of the hat and many bows. Hunterleys, after a brief hesitation, walked out into the sun-dappled street. It was the most fashionable hour of the afternoon. Up in the square a band was playing. Outside, two or three smart automobiles were discharging their freight of wonderfully-dressed women and debonair men from the villas outside. Suddenly a hand fell upon his arm. It was Richard Lane who greeted him.

" Say, where are you off to, Sir Henry? " he inquired.

Hunterleys laughed a little shortly.

" Really, I scarcely know," he replied. " Back to London, if I am wise, I suppose."

" Come into the Club," Richard begged.

" I have just left," Hunterleys told him. " Besides, I hate the place."

" Did you happen to notice whether Mr. Grex was in there? " Richard enquired.

" I didn't see him," Hunterleys answered. " Neither," he added significantly, " did I see Miss Grex."

" Well, I am going in to have a look round, anyway," Richard decided. " You might come along. There's nothing else to do in this place until dinnertime."

Hunterleys suffered himself to be persuaded and remounted the steps.

" Tell me, Lane," he asked curiously, " have you heard anything about any of the victims of our little struggle last night — I mean the two men we tackled? "

Richard shook his head.

" I hear that mine has a broken wrist," he said. " Can't say I am feeling very badly about that! "

" I've just been told that mine is going to die," Hunterleys continued.

The young man laughed incredulously.

" Why, I went over the prison this morning," he declared. " I never saw such a healthy lot of ruffians in my life. That chap whom you tackled — the one with the revolver — was smoking cigarettes and using language — well, I couldn't understand it all, but what I did understand was enough to melt the bars of his prison."

" That's odd," Hunterleys remarked drily. " According to the police commissioner who has just left me, the man is on his deathbed, and my only chance

of escaping serious trouble is to get out of Monte
Carlo to-night."

" Are you going? "

Hunterleys shook his head.

" It would take a great deal more than that to
move me just now," he said, " even if I had not suspected from the first that the man was lying."

Richard glanced at his companion a little curiously.

" I shouldn't have said that you were having such
a good time, Sir Henry," he observed; " in fact I
should have thought you would have been rather
glad of an opportunity to slip away."

Hunterleys looked around them. They had
reached the top of the staircase and were in sight
of the dense crowd in the rooms.

" Come and have a drink," he suggested. " A
great many of these people will have cleared off presently."

" I'll have a drink, with pleasure," Richard answered, " but I still can't see why you're stuck on
this place."

They strolled into the bar and found two vacant
places.

" My dear young friend," Hunterleys said, as he
ordered their drinks, " if you were an Englishman
instead of an American, I think that I would give
you a hint as to the reason why I do not wish to
leave Monte Carlo just at present."

" Can't see what difference that makes," Richard
declared. " You know I'm all for the old country."

" I wonder whether you are," Hunterleys remarked
thoughtfully. " I tell you frankly that if I thought

you meant it, I should probably come to you before long for a little help."

"If ever you do, I'm your man," Richard assured him heartily. "Any more scraps going?"

Hunterleys sipped his whisky and soda thoughtfully. There had been an exodus from the room to watch some heavy gambling at *Trente et Quarante*, and for a moment they were almost alone.

"Lane," he said, "I am going to take you a little into my confidence. In a way I suppose it is foolish, but to tell you the truth, I am almost driven to it. You know that I am a Member of Parliament, and you may have heard that if our Party hadn't gone out a few years ago, I was to have been Foreign Minister."

"I've heard that often enough," Lane assented. "I've heard you quoted, too, as an example of the curse of party politics. Just because you are forced to call yourself a member of one Party you are debarred from serving your country in any capacity until that Party is in power."

"That's quite true," Hunterleys admitted, "and to tell you the truth, ridiculous though it seems, I don't see how you're to get away from it in a practical manner. Anyhow, when my people came out I made up my mind that I wasn't going to just sit still in Opposition and find fault all the time, especially as we've a real good man at the Foreign Office. I was quite content to leave things in his hands, but then, you see, politically that meant that there was nothing for me to do. I thought matters over and eventually I paired for six months and was supposed to go off for the benefit of my health. As a matter of fact, I have been in the Balkan States since Christmas," he added, dropping his voice a little.

"What the dickens have you been doing there?"

"I can't tell you that exactly," Hunterleys replied. "Unfortunately, my enemies are suspicious and they have taken to watching me closely. They pretty well know what I am going to tell you — that I have been out there at the urgent request of the Secret Service Department of the present Government. I have been in Greece and Servia and Roumania, and, although I don't think there's a soul in the world knows, I have also been in St. Petersburg."

"But what's it all about?" Richard persisted. "What have you been doing in all these places?"

"I can only answer you broadly," Hunterleys went on. "There is a perfectly devilish scheme afloat, directed against the old country. I have been doing what I can to counteract it. At the last moment, just as I was leaving Sofia for London, by the merest chance I discovered that the scene for the culmination of this little plot was to be Monte Carlo, so I made my way round by Trieste, stayed at Bordighera and San Remo for a few days to put people off, and finally turned up here."

"Well, I'm jiggered!" Lane muttered. "And I thought you were just hanging about for your health or because your wife was here, and were bored to death for want of something to do."

"On the contrary," Hunterleys assured him, "I was up all night sending reports home — very interesting reports, too. I got them away all right, but there's no denying the fact that there are certain people in Monte Carlo at the present moment who suspect my presence here, and who would go to any lengths whatever to get rid of me. It isn't the actual harm I might do, but they have to deal with a very delicate problem and to make a bargain with a very sensitive person, and they are terribly afraid that my presence here, and a meeting between me and that person, might render all their schemes abortive."

Richard's face was a study in astonishment.

"Well," he exclaimed, "this beats everything! I've read of such things, of course, but one only half believes them. Right under our very noses, too! Say, what are you going to do about it, Sir Henry?"

"There is only one thing I can do," Hunterleys replied grimly. "I am bound to keep my place here. They'll drive me out if they can. I am convinced that the polite warning I have received to leave Monaco this afternoon because of last night's affair, is part of the conspiracy. In plain words, I've got to stick it out."

"But what good are you doing here, anyway?"

Hunterleys smiled and glanced carefully around the room. They were still free from any risk of being overheard.

"Well," he said, "perhaps you will understand my meaning more clearly if I tell you that I am the brains of a counterplot. The English Secret Service has a permanent agent here under the guise of a newspaper correspondent, who is in daily touch with me, and he in his turn has several spies at work. I am, however, the dangerous person. The others are only servants. They make their reports, but they don't understand their true significance. If these people could remove me before any one else could arrive to take my place, their chances of bringing off their coup here would be immensely improved."

" I suppose it's useless for me to ask if there's anything I can do to help? " Richard enquired.

" You've helped already," Hunterleys replied. " I have been nearly three months without being able to open my lips to a soul. People call me secretive, but I feel very human sometimes. I know that not a word of what I have said will pass your lips."

" Not a chance of it," Richard promised earnestly. " But look here, can't I do something? If I am not an Englishman, I'm all for the Anglo-Saxons. I hate these foreigners — that is to say the men," he corrected himself hastily.

Hunterleys smiled.

" Well, I was coming to that," he said. " I do feel hideously alone here, and what I would like you to do is just this. I would like you to call at my room at the Hotel de Paris, number 189, every morning at a certain fixed hour — say half-past ten. Just shake hands with me — that's all. Nothing shall prevent my being visible to you at that hour. Under no consideration whatever will I leave any message that I am engaged or have gone out. If I am not to be seen when you make your call, something has happened to me."

" And what am I to do then? "

" That is the point," Hunterleys continued. " I don't want to bring you too deeply into this matter. All that you need do is to make your way to the English Bank, see Mr. Harrison, the manager, and tell him of your fruitless visit to me. He will give you a letter to my wife and will know what other steps to take."

" Is that all? " Richard asked, a little disappointed. " You don't anticipate any scrapping, or anything of that sort? "

" I don't know what to anticipate," Hunterleys confessed, a little wearily. " Things are moving fast now towards the climax. I promise I'll come to you for help if I need it. You can but refuse."

" No fear of my refusing," Richard declared heartily. " Not on your life, sir! "

Hunterleys rose to his feet with an appreciative little nod. It was astonishing how cordially he had come to feel towards this young man, during the last few hours.

" I'll let you off now," he said. " I know you want to look around the tables and see if any of our friends of last night are to be found. I, too, have a little affair which I ought to have treated differently a few minutes ago. We'll meet later."

Hunterleys strolled back into the rooms. He came almost at once face to face with Draconmeyer, whom he was passing with unseeing eyes. Draconmeyer, however, detained him.

" I was looking for you, Sir Henry! " he exclaimed. " Can you spare me one moment? "

They stood a little on one side, out of the way of the moving throng of people. Draconmeyer was fingering nervously his tie of somewhat vivid purple. His manner was important.

" Do you happen, Sir Henry," he asked, " to have had any word from the prison authorities to-day? "

Hunterleys nodded.

" I have just received a message," he replied. " I understand that the man with whom I had a struggle last night has received some internal injuries and is likely to die."

Draconmeyer's manner became more mysterious. He glanced around the room as though to be sure that they were not overheard.

" I trust, Sir Henry," he said, " that you will not think me in any way presumptuous if I speak to you intimately. I have never had the privilege of your friendship, and in this unfortunate disagreement between your wife and yourself I have been compelled to accept your wife's point of view, owing to the friendship between Mrs. Draconmeyer and herself. I trust you will believe, however, that I have no feelings of hostility towards you."

" You are very kind," Hunterleys murmured.

His face seemed set in graven lines. For all the effect the other's words had upon him, he might have been wearing a mask.

" The law here in some respects is very curious," Draconmeyer continued. " Some of the statutes have been unaltered for a thousand years. I have been given to understand by a person who knows, that if this man should die, notwithstanding the circumstances of the case, you might find yourself in an exceedingly awkward position. If I might venture, therefore, to give you a word of disinterested advice, I would suggest that you return to England at once, if only for a week or so."

His eyes had narrowed. Through his spectacles he was watching intently for the effect of his words.

Hunterleys, however, only nodded thoughtfully, as though to some extent impressed by the advice he had received.

"Very likely you are right," he admitted. "I will discuss the matter with my wife."

"She is playing over there," Draconmeyer pointed out. "And while we are talking in a more or less friendly fashion," he went on earnestly, "might I give you just one more word of counsel? For the sake of the friendship which exists between our wives, I feel sure you will believe that I am disinterested."

He paused. Hunterleys' expression was now one of polite interest. He waited, however, for the other to continue.

"I wish that you could persuade Lady Hunterleys to play for somewhat lower stakes."

Hunterleys was genuinely startled for a moment.

"Do you mean that my wife is gambling beyond her means?" he asked.

Draconmeyer shrugged his shoulders.

"How can I tell that? I don't know what her means are, or yours. I only know that she changes mille notes more often than I change louis, and it seems to me that her luck is invariably bad. I think, perhaps, just a word or two from you, who have the right to speak, might be of service."

"I am very much obliged to you for the hint," Hunterleys said smoothly. "I will certainly mention the matter to her."

"And if I don't see you again," Draconmeyer concluded, watching him closely, "good-bye!"

Hunterleys did not appear to notice the tentative movement of the other's hand. He was already on his way to the spot where his wife was sitting. Draconmeyer watched his progress with inscrutable face. Selingman, who had been sitting near, rose and joined him.

" Will he go? " he whispered. " Will our friend take this very reasonable hint and depart? "

Draconmeyer's eyes were still fixed upon Hunterleys' slim, self-possessed figure. His forehead was contorted into a frown. Somehow or other, he felt that during their brief interview he had failed to score; he had felt a subtle, underlying note of contempt in Hunterleys' manner, in his whole attitude.

" I do not know," he replied grimly. " I only hope that if he stays, we shall find the means to make him regret it! "

CHAPTER XII

" I CANNOT GO ! "

Hunterleys stood for several minutes, watching his wife's play from a new point of view. She was certainly playing high and with continued ill-fortune. For the first time, too, he noticed symptoms which disturbed him. She sat quite motionless, but there was an unfamiliar glitter in her eyes and a hardness about her mouth. It was not until he had stood within a few feet of her for nearly a quarter of an hour, that she chanced to see him.

" Did you want me? " she asked, with a little start.

" There is no hurry," he replied. " If you could spare me a few moments later, I should be glad."

She rose at once, thrusting her notes and gold into the satchel which she was carrying, and stood by his side. She was very elegantly dressed in black and white, but she was pale, and, watching her with a new intentness, he discovered faint violet lines under her eyes, as though she had been sleeping ill.

" I am rather glad you came," she said. " I was having an abominable run of bad luck, and yet I hated to give up my seat without an excuse. What did you want, Henry? "

" I should like," he explained, " to talk to you for a quarter of an hour. This place is rather crowded and it is getting on my nerves. We seem to live here, night and day. Would you object to driving with me — say as far as Mentone and back? "

" I will come if you wish it," she answered, looking a little surprised. " Wait while I get my cloak."

Hunterleys hired an automobile below and they drove off. As soon as they were out of the main street, he thrust his hand into the breast-pocket of his coat and smoothed out that half-sheet of note-paper upon his knee.

" Violet," he said, " please read that."

She read the few lines instructing the English Bank to hand over Sir Henry Hunterleys' letters to the bearer. Then she looked up at him with a puzzled frown.

" I don't understand."

" Did you write that? " he enquired.

She looked at him indignantly.

" What an absurd question! " she exclaimed. " Your correspondence has no interest for me."

Her denial, so natural, so obviously truthful, was a surprise to him. He felt a sudden impulse of joy, mingled with shame. Perhaps, after all, he had been altogether too censorious. Once more he directed her attention to the sheet of paper. There was a marked change in his voice and manner.

" Violet," he begged, " please look at it. Accepting without hesitation your word that you did not write it, doesn't it occur to you that the body of the letter is a distinct imitation of your handwriting, and the signature a very clever forgery of mine? "

" It is rather like my handwriting," she admitted,

" and as for the signature, do you mean to say really that that is not yours? "

" Certainly not," he assured her. " The whole thing is a forgery."

" But who in the world should want to get your letters? " she asked incredulously. " And why should you have them addressed to the bank? "

He folded up the paper then and put it in his pocket.

" Violet," he said earnestly, " for the disagreements which have resulted in our separation I may myself have been to some extent responsible, but we have promised one another not to refer to them again and I will not break our compact. All I can say is that there is much in my life which you know little of, and for which you do not, therefore, make sufficient allowance."

" Then you might have treated me," she declared, " with more confidence."

" It was not possible," he reminded her, " so long as you chose to make an intimate friend of a man whose every interest in life is in direct antagonism to mine."

" Mr. Draconmeyer? "

" Mr. Draconmeyer," he assented.

She smiled contemptuously.

" You misunderstand Mr. Draconmeyer completely," she insisted. " He is your well-wisher and he is more than half an Englishman. It was he who started the league between English and German commercial men for the propagation of peace. He formed one of the deputation who went over to see the Emperor. He has done more, both by his speeches and letters to the newspaper, to promote a good understanding between Germany and England, than any other person. You are very much mistaken about Mr. Draconmeyer, Henry. Why you cannot realise that he is simply an ordinary commercial man of high intelligence and most agreeable manners, I cannot imagine."

"The fact remains, my dear Violet," Hunterleys said emphatically, "that it is not possible for me to treat you with the confidence I might otherwise have done, on account of your friendship with Mr. Draconmeyer."

"You are incorrigible!" she exclaimed. "Can we change the subject, please? I want to know why you showed me that forged letter?"

"I am coming to that," he told her. "Please be patient. I want to remind you of something else. So far as I remember, my only request, when I gave you your liberty and half my income, was that your friendship with the Draconmeyers should decrease. Almost the first persons I see on my arrival in Monte Carlo are you and Mr. Draconmeyer. I learn that you came out with them and that you are staying at the same hotel."

"Your wish was an unreasonable one," she protested. "Linda and I were school-girls together. She is my dearest friend and she is a hopeless invalid. I think that if I were to desert her she would die."

"I have every sympathy with Mrs. Draconmeyer," he said slowly, "but you are my wife. I am going to make one more effort — please don't be uneasy — not to re-establish any relationship between us, but to

open your eyes as to the truth concerning Mr. Draconmeyer. You asked me a moment ago why I had
shown you that forged letter. I will tell you now.
It was Draconmeyer who was the forger."

She leaned back in her seat. She was looking at
him incredulously.

"You mean to say that Mr. Draconmeyer wrote
that order — that he wanted to get possession of
your letters?"

"Not only that," Hunterleys continued, "but he
carried out the business in such a devilish manner
as to make me for a moment believe that it was you
who had helped him. You are wrong about Draconmeyer. The man is a great schemer, who under
the pretence of occupying an important commercial
position in the City of London, is all the time a secret agent of Germany. He is there in her interests. He studies the public opinion of the country.
He dissects our weaknesses. He is there to point
out the best methods and the opportune time for the
inevitable struggle. He is the worst enemy to-day
England has. You think that he is here in Monte
Carlo on a visit of pleasure — for the sake of his
wife, perhaps. Nothing of the sort! He is here at
this moment associated with an iniquitous scheme,
the particulars of which I can tell you nothing of.
Furthermore, I repeat what I told you on our first
meeting here — that in his still, cold way he is in
love with you."

"Henry!" she cried.

"I cannot see how you can remain so wilfully
blind," Hunterleys continued. "I know the man inside out. I warned you against him in London, I

warn you against him now. This forged letter was designed to draw us further apart. The little brown man who has dogged your footsteps is a spy employed by him to make you believe that I was having you watched. You are free still to act as you will, Violet, but if you have a spark of regard for me or yourself, you will go back to London at once and drop this odious friendship."

She leaned back in the car. They had turned round now and were on the way back to Monte Carlo by the higher road. She sat with her eyes fixed upon the mountains. Her heart, in a way, had been touched, her imagination stirred by her husband's words. She felt a return of that glow of admiration which had thrilled her on the previous night, when he and Richard Lane alone amongst that motley company had played the part of men. A curious, almost pathetic wistfulness crept into her heart. If only he would lean towards her at that moment, if she could see once more the light in his eyes that had shone there during the days of their courtship! If only he could remember that it was still his part to play the lover! If he could be a little less grave, a little less hopelessly correct and fair! Despite her efforts to disbelieve, there was something convincing about his words. At any moment during that brief space of time, a single tremulous word, even a warm clasp of the hand, would have brought her into his arms. But so much of inspiration was denied him. He sat waiting for her decision with an eagerness of which he gave no sign. Nevertheless, the fates were fighting for him. She thought gratefully, even at that moment, yet with less enthusiasm than ever before, of the devout homage, the delightful care for her happiness and comfort, the atmosphere of security with which Draconmeyer seemed always to surround her. Yet all this was cold and unsatisfying, a poor substitute for the other things. Henry had been different once. Perhaps it was jealousy which had altered him. Perhaps his misconception of Draconmeyer's character had affected his whole outlook. She turned towards him, and her voice, when she spoke, was no longer querulous.

" Henry," she said, " I cannot admit the truth of all that you say concerning Mr. Draconmeyer, but tell me this. If I were willing to leave this place tonight —"

She paused. For some reason a sudden embarrassment had seized her. The words seemed to come with difficulty. She turned ever so slightly away from him. There was a tinge of colour at last in her pale cheeks. She seemed to him now, as she leaned a little forward in her seat, completely beautiful.

" If I make my excuses and leave Monte Carlo to-night," she went on, " will you come with me? "

He gave a little start. Something in his eyes flashed an answer into her face. And then the flood of memory came. There was his mission. He was tied hand and foot.

" It is good of you to offer that, Violet," he declared. " If I could — if only I could! "

Already her manner began to change. The fear of his refusal was hateful, her lips were trembling.

" You mean," she faltered, " that you will not come? Listen. Don't misunderstand me. I will order my boxes packed, I will catch the eight o'clock train either through to London or to Paris — anywhere. I will do that if you will come. There is my offer. That is my reply to all that you have said about Mr. Draconmeyer. I shall lose a friend who has been gentleness and kindness and consideration itself. I will risk that. What do you say? Will you come?"

"Violet, I cannot," he replied hoarsely. "No, don't turn away like that!" he begged. "Don't change so quickly, please! It isn't fair. Listen. I am not my own master."

"Not your own master?" she repeated incredulously. "What do you mean?"

"I mean that I am here in Monte Carlo not for my own pleasure. I mean that I have work, a purpose —"

"Absurd!" she interrupted him, almost harshly. "There is nobody who has any better claim upon you than I have. You are over-conscientious about other things. For once remember your duty as a husband."

He caught her wrist.

"You must trust me a little," he pleaded. "Believe me that I really appreciate your offer. If I were free to go, I should not hesitate for a single second. . . . Can't you trust me, Violet?" he implored, his voice softening.

The woman within her was fighting on his side. She stifled her wounded feelings, crushed down her disappointment that he had not taken her at once into his arms and answered her upon her lips.

"Trust me, then," she replied. "If you refuse

my offer, don't hint at things you have to do. Tell
me in plain words why. It is not enough for you
to say that you cannot leave Monte Carlo. Tell
me why you cannot. I have invited you to escort
me anywhere you will — I, your wife. . . . Shall we
go?"

The woman had wholly triumphed. Her voice had
dropped, the light was in her eyes. She swayed a
little towards him. His brain reeled. She was once
more the only woman in the world for him. Once
more he fancied that he could feel the clinging of her
arms, the touch of her lips. These things were
promised in her face.

"I tell you that I cannot go!" he cried sharply.
"Believe me — do believe me, Violet!"

She pulled down her veil suddenly. He caught at
her hand. It lay passively in his. He pleaded for
her confidence, but the moment of inspiration had
gone. She heard him with the air of one who listens
no longer. Presently she stopped him.

"Don't speak to me for several minutes, please,"
she begged. "Tell him to put me down at the hotel.
I can't go back to the Club just yet."

"You mustn't leave me like this," he insisted.

"Will you tell me why you refuse my offer?" she
asked.

"I have a trust!"

The automobile had come to a standstill. She
rose to her feet.

"I was once your trust," she reminded him, as she
passed into the hotel.

CHAPTER XIII

MISS GREX AT HOME

Richard Lane, as he made his way up the avenue towards the Villa Mimosa, wondered whether he was not indeed finding his way into fairyland. On either side of him were drooping mimosa trees, heavy with the snaky, orange-coloured blossom whose perfumes hung heavy upon the windless air. In the background, bordering the gardens which were themselves a maze of colour, were great clumps of glorious purple rhododendrons, drooping clusters of red and white roses. A sudden turn revealed a long pergola, smothered in pink blossoms and leading to the edge of the terrace which overhung the sea. The villa itself, which seemed, indeed, more like a palace, was covered with vivid purple clematis, and from the open door of the winter-garden, which was built out from the front of the place in a great curve, there came, as he drew near, a bewildering breath of exotic odours. The front-door was wide open, and before he could reach the bell a butler had appeared.

"Is Mr. Grex at home?" Richard enquired.

"Mr. Grex is not at home, sir," was the immediate reply.

"I should like to see Miss Grex, then," Richard proceeded.

The man's face was curiously expressionless, but a momentary silence perhaps betrayed as much surprise as he was capable of showing.

"Miss Grex is not at home, sir," he announced.

Richard hesitated and just then she came out from the winter-garden. She was wearing a pink linen morning gown and a floppy pink hat. She had a book under her arm and a parasol swinging from her fingers. When she saw Lane, she stared at him in amazement. He advanced a step or two towards her, his hat in his hand.

"I took the liberty of calling to see your father, Miss Grex," he explained. "As he was not at home, I ventured to enquire for you."

She was absolutely helpless. It was impossible to ignore his outstretched hand. Very hesitatingly she held out her fingers, which Richard grasped and seemed in no hurry at all to release.

"This is quite the most beautiful place I have seen anywhere near Monte Carlo," he remarked enthusiastically.

"I am glad," she murmured, "that you find it attractive."

He was standing by her side now, his hat under his arm. The butler had withdrawn a little into the background. She glanced around.

"Did my father ask you to call, Mr. Lane?" she enquired, dropping her voice a little.

"He did not," Richard confessed. "I must say that I gave him plenty of opportunities but he did not seem to be what I should call hospitably inclined. In any case, it really doesn't matter. I came to see you."

She bit her lip, struggling hard to repress a smile.

"But I did not ask you to call upon me either," she reminded him gravely.

"Well, that's true," Lane admitted, a little hesitatingly. "I don't quite know how things are done over here. Say, are you English, or French, or what?" he asked, point blank. "I have been puzzling about that ever since I saw you."

"I am not sure that my nationality matters," she observed.

"Well, over on the other side," he continued,— "I mean America, of course — if we make up our minds that we want to see something of a girl and there isn't any real reason why one shouldn't, then the initiative generally rests with the man. Of course, if you are an only daughter, I can quite understand your father being a bit particular, not caring for men callers and that sort of thing, but that can't go on for ever, you know, can it?"

"Can't it?" she murmured, a little dazed.

"I have a habit," he confided, "of making up my mind quickly, and when I decide about a thing, I am rather hard to turn. Well, I made up my mind about you the first moment we met."

"About me?" she repeated.

"About you."

She turned and looked at him almost wonderingly. He was very big and very confident; good to look upon, less because of his actual good looks than because of a certain honesty and tenacity of purpose in his expression; a strength of jaw, modified and rendered even pleasant by the kindness and humour of his clear grey eyes. He returned her gaze without embarrassment and he wondered less than ever at finding himself there. Her complexion in this clear light seemed more beautiful than ever. Her rich golden-brown hair was waved becomingly over her forehead. Her eyebrows were silky and delicately straight, her mouth delightful. Her figure was girlish, but unusually dignified for her years.

"You know," he said suddenly, "you look to me just like one of those beautiful plants you have in the conservatory there, just as though you'd stepped out of your little glass home and blossomed right here. I am almost afraid of you."

She laughed outright this time — a low, musical laugh which had in it something of foreign intonation.

"Well, really," she exclaimed, "I had not noticed your fear! I was just thinking that you were quite the boldest young man I have ever met."

"Come, that's something!" he declared. "Couldn't we sit down somewhere in these wonderful gardens of yours and talk?"

She shook her head.

"But have I not told you already," she protested, "that I do not receive callers? Neither does my father. Really, your coming here is quite unwarrantable. If he should return at this moment and find you here, he would be very angry indeed. I am afraid that he would even be rude, and I, too, should suffer for having allowed you to talk with me."

"Let's hope that he doesn't return just yet, then," Richard observed, smiling easily. "I am very good-tempered as a rule, but I do not like people to be rude to me."

"Fortunately, he cannot return for at least an hour —" she began.

"Then we'll sit down on that terrace, if you please, for just a quarter of that time," he begged.

She opened her lips and closed them again. He was certainly a very stubborn young man!

"Well," she sighed, "perhaps it will be the easiest way of getting rid of you."

She motioned him to follow her. The butler, from a discreet distance, watched her as though he were looking at a strange thing. Round the corner of the villa remote from the winter-garden, was a long stone terrace upon which many windows opened. Screened from the wind, the sun here was of almost midsummer strength. There was no sound. The great house seemed asleep. There was nothing but the droning of a few insects. Even the birds were songless. The walls were covered with drooping clematis and roses, roses that twined over the balustrades. Below them was a tangle of mimosa trees and rhododendrons, and further below still the blue Mediterranean. She sank into a chair.

"You may sit here," she said, "just long enough for me to convince you that your coming was a mistake. Indeed that is so. I do not wish to seem foolish or unkind, but my father and I are living here with one unbreakable rule, and that is that we make no acquaintances whatsoever."

"That sounds rather queer," he remarked. "Don't you find it dull?"

"If I do," she went on, "it is only for a little time. My father is here for a certain purpose, and as soon as that is accomplished we shall go away. For him to accomplish that purpose in a satisfactory manner, it is necessary that we should live as far apart as possible from the ordinary visitors here."

"Sounds like a riddle," he admitted. "Do you mind telling me of what nationality you are?"

"I see no reason why I should tell you anything."

"You speak such correct English," he continued, "but there is just a little touch of accent. You don't know how attractive it sounds. You don't know —"

He hesitated, suddenly losing some part of his immense confidence.

"What else is there that I do not know?" she asked, with a faintly amused smile.

"I have lost my courage," he confessed simply. "I do not want to offend you, I do not want you to think that I am hopelessly foolish, but you see I have the misfortune to be in love with you."

She laughed at him, leaning back in her chair with half-closed eyes.

"Do people talk like this to casual acquaintances in your country?" she asked.

"They speak sometimes a language which is common to all countries," he replied quickly. "The only thing that is peculiar to my people is that when we say it, it is the sober and the solemn truth."

She was silent for a moment. She had plucked one of the blossoms from the wall and was pulling to pieces its purple petals.

"Do you know," she said, "that no young man has ever dared to talk to me as you have done?"

"That is because no one yet has cared so much as I do," he assured her. "I can quite understand

their being frightened. I am terribly afraid of you
myself. I am afraid of the things I say to you, but
I have to say them because they are in my heart,
and if I am only to have a quarter of an hour with
you now, you see I must make the best use of my
time. I must tell you that there isn't any other girl
in the world I could ever look at again, and if you
won't promise to marry me some day, I shall be the
most wretched person on earth."

"I can never, never marry you," she told him
emphatically. "There is nothing which is so impossible as that."

"Well, that's a pretty bad start," he admitted.

"It is the end," she said firmly.

He shook his head. There was a terrible obsti-
nacy in his face. She frowned at him.

"You do not mean that you will persist after what
I have told you?"

He looked at her, almost surprised.

"There isn't anything else for me to do, that I
know of," he declared, "so long as you don't care
for any one else. Tell me again, you are sure that
there is no one?"

"Certainly not," she replied stiffly. "The subject has not yet been made acceptable to me. You
must forgive my adding that in my country it is not
usual for a girl to discuss these matters with a man
before her betrothal."

"Say, I don't understand that," he murmured,
looking at her thoughtfully. "She can't get engaged before she is asked."

"The preliminaries," she explained, "are always
arranged by one's parents."

He smiled pityingly.

" That sort of thing's no use," he asserted confidently. " You must be getting past that, in whatever corner of Europe you live. What you mean to say, then, is that your father has some one up his sleeve whom he'll trot out for you before long? "

" Without doubt, some arrangement will be proposed." she agreed.

" And you'll have to be amiable to some one you've never seen in your life before, I suppose? " he persisted.

" Not necessarily. It sometimes happens, in my position," she went on, raising her head, " that certain sacrifices are necessary."

"In your position," he repeated quickly. " What does that mean? You aren't a queen, are you, or anything of that sort? "

She laughed.

" No," she confessed, " I am not a queen, and yet —"

" And yet? "

" You must go back," she insisted, rising abruptly to her feet. " The quarter of an hour is up. I do not feel happy, sitting here talking with you. Really, if my father were to return he would be more angry with me than he has ever been in his life. This sort of thing is not done amongst my people."

" Little lady," he said, gently forcing her back into her place, " believe me, it's done all the world over, and there isn't any girl can come to any harm by being told that a man is fond of her when it's the truth, when he'd give his life for her willingly. It's just like that I feel about you. I've never felt it before. I could never feel it for any one else. And I am not going to give you up."

She was looking at him half fearfully. There was a little colour in her cheeks, her eyes were suddenly moist.

" I think," she murmured, " that you talk very nicely. I think I might even say that I like to hear you talk. But it is so useless. Won't you go now? Won't you please go now? "

" When may I come again? " he begged.

" Never," she replied firmly. " You must never come again. You must not even think of it. But indeed you would not be admitted. They will probably tell my father of your visit, as it is, and he will be very angry."

" Well, when can I see you, then, and where? " he demanded. " I hope you understand that I am not in the least disheartened by anything you have said."

" I think," she declared, " that you are the most persistent person I ever met."

" It is only," he whispered, leaning a little towards her, " because I care for you so much."

She was suddenly confused, conscious of a swift desire to get rid of him. It was as though some one were speaking a new language. All her old habits and prejudices seemed falling away.

" I cannot make appointments with you," she protested, her voice shaking. " I cannot encourage you in any way. It is really quite impossible."

" If I go now, will you be at the Club to-morrow afternoon? " he pleaded.

" I am not sure," she replied. " It is very likely that I may be there. I make no promise."

He took her hand abruptly, and, stooping down, forced her to look into his eyes.

"You will be there to-morrow afternoon, please," he begged, "and you will give me the rose from your waistband."

She laughed uneasily.

"If the rose will buy your departure —" she began.

"It may do that," he interrupted, as he drew it through his buttonhole, "but it will assuredly bring me back again."

Richard walked down the hill, whistling softly to himself and with a curious light in his eyes. As he reached the square in front of the Casino, he was accosted by a stranger who stood in the middle of the pavement and respectfully removed his hat.

"You are Mr. Richard Lane, is it not so, monsieur?"

"You've guessed it in one," Richard admitted. "Have I ever seen you before?"

"Never, monsieur, unless you happened to notice me on your visit to the prison. I have an official position in the Principality. I am commissioned to speak to you with respect to the little affair in which you were concerned at La Turbie."

"Well, I thought we'd thrashed all that out," Lane replied. "Anyway, Sir Henry Hunterleys and I have engaged a lawyer to look after our interests."

"Just so," the little man murmured. "A very clever man indeed is Monsieur Grisson. Still, there is a view of the matter," he continued, "which is perhaps hard for you Englishmen and Americans to

understand. Assault of any description is very severely punished here, especially when it results in
bodily injury. Theft of all sorts, on the other hand,
is very common indeed. The man whom you injured
is a native of Monte Carlo. To a certain extent, the
Principality is bound to protect him."

"Why, the fellow was engaged in a flagrant attempt at highway robbery!" Richard declared, genuinely astonished.

His companion stretched out his hands.

"Monsieur," he replied, "every one robs here,
whether they are shop-keepers, restaurant keepers
or loafers upon the streets. The people expect it.
At the adjourned trial next week there will be many
witnesses who are also natives of Monte Carlo. I
have been commissioned to warn monsieur. It would
be best, on the whole, if he left Monte Carlo by the
next train."

"Why in the name of mischief should I do that?"
Richard demanded.

"In the first place," the other pointed out, "because this man, whom you treated a little roughly,
has many friends and associates. They have sworn
revenge. You are even now being followed about,
and the police of the Principality have enough to do
without sparing an escort to protect you against vio-
lence. In the second place, I am not at all sure that
the finding of the court next week will be altogether
to your satisfaction."

"Do you mean this?" Richard asked incredulously.

"Without a doubt, monsieur."

"Then all I can say," Richard declared, "is that

your magistrate or judge, or whatever he calls himself, is a rotter, and your laws absurd. I sha'n't
budge."

" It is in your own interests, monsieur, this warning," the other persisted. " Even if you escape
these desperadoes, you still run some risk of dis-
covering what the inside of a prison in Monaco is
like."

" I think not," Lane answered grimly. " If
there's anything of that sort going about, I shall
board my yacht yonder and hoist the Stars and
Stripes. I shall take some getting into prison, I
can tell you, and if I once get there, you'll hear
about it."

" Monsieur will be much wiser to avoid trouble,"
the official advised.

Lane placed his hand upon the other's shoulder.

" My friend," he said, " not you or a dozen like
you could make me stir from this place until I am
ready, and just now I am very far from ready.
See? You can go and tell those who sent you, what
I say."

The emissary of the law shrugged his shoulders.
His manner was stiff but resigned.

" I have delivered my message, monsieur," he announced. " Monsieur naturally must decide for
himself."

He disappeared with a bow. Richard continued
on his way and a few minutes later ran into Hunterleys.

" Say, did you ever hear such cheek!" he exclaimed, passing his arm through the latter's. " A
little bounder stopped me in the street and has been

trying to frighten me into leaving Monte Carlo, just because I broke that robber's wrist. Same Johnny that came to you, I expect. What are they up to, anyway? What do they want to get rid of us for? They ought to be jolly grateful."

Hunterleys shook his head.

" So far as I am concerned," he said, " their reasons for wanting to get rid of me are fairly obvious, I am afraid, but I must say I don't know where you come in, unless —"

He stopped short.

" Well, unless what? " Richard interposed. " I should just like to know who it is trying to get me kicked out."

" Can't you guess? " Hunterleys asked. " There is one person who I think would be quite as well pleased to see the back of you."

" Here in Monte Carlo? "

" Absolutely! "

Richard was mystified.

" You are not very bright, I am afraid," Hunterleys observed. " What about your friend Mr. Grex? "

Richard whistled softly.

" Are you serious? "

" Of course I am," Hunterleys assured him.

" But has he any pull here, this Mr. Grex? "

Hunterleys' eyes twinkled for a moment.

" Yes," he replied, " I think that Mr. Grex has very considerable influence in this part of the world, and he is a man who, I should say, was rather used to having his own way."

" I gathered that I wasn't exactly popular with

him this afternoon," Richard remarked meditatively. " I've been out there to call."

Hunterleys stopped short upon the pavement.

" What? " he exclaimed.

" I have been out to call at the Villa Mimosa," Richard repeated. " I don't see anything extraordinary in that."

" Did you see — Miss Fedora? "

" Rather! And thank you for telling me her name, at any rate. We sat on the terrace and chatted for a quarter of an hour. She gave me to understand, though, that the old man was dead against me. It all seems very mysterious. Anyway, she gave me this rose I am wearing, and I think she'll be at the Club to-morrow afternoon."

Hunterleys was silent for a moment. He seemed much impressed.

" You know, Richard," he declared, " there is something akin to genius in your methods."

" That's all very well," the young man protested, " but can you give me a single solid reason why, considering I am in love with the girl, I shouldn't go and call upon her? Who is this Mr. Grex, anyway? "

" I've a good mind to tell you," Hunterleys said meditatively.

" I don't care whether you do or not," Lane pronounced firmly, as they parted. " I don't care whether Mr. Grex is the Sultan of Turkey or the Czar of Russia. I'm going to marry his daughter. That's settled."

CHAPTER XIV

DINNER FOR TWO

At a few minutes before eight o'clock that evening Lady Hunterleys descended the steps of the Casino and crossed the square towards the Hotel de Paris. She walked very slowly and she looked neither to the right nor to the left. She had the air of seeing no one. She acknowledged mechanically the low bow of the commissionaire who opened the door for her. A reception clerk who stood on one side to let her pass, she ignored altogether. She crossed the hall to the lift and pressed the bell. Draconmeyer, who had been lounging in an easy-chair waiting for her, watched her entrance and noticed her abstracted manner with kindling eyes. He threw away his newspaper and, hastily approaching her, touched her arm.

" You are late," he remarked.

She started.

" Yes, I am late."

" I did not see you at the Club."

" I have been to the Casino instead," she told him. " I thought that it might change my luck."

" Successful, I trust? "

She shook her head. Then she opened her gold satchel and showed him. It was empty.

" The luck must turn sometime," he reminded her soothingly. " How long will you be changing? "

" I am tired," she confessed. " I thought that to-night I would not dine. I will have something sent up to my room."

He was obviously disappointed.

" Couldn't you dine as you are? " he begged. " You could change later, if you wished to. It is always such a disappointment when you do not appear — and to-night," he added, " especially."

Violet hesitated. She was really longing only to be alone and to rest. She thought, however, of the poor invalid to whom their meeting at dinner-time was the one break of the day.

" Very well," she promised, " I will be down in ten minutes."

Draconmeyer, as the lift bore her upwards, strolled away. Although the custom was a strange one to him, he sought out the American bar and drank a cocktail. Then he lit a cigarette and made his way back into the lounge, moving restlessly about, his hands behind his back, his forehead knitted. In his way he had been a great schemer, and in the crowded hall of the hotel that night, surrounded by a wonderfully cosmopolitan throng of loungers and passers-by, he lived again through the birth and development of many of the schemes which his brain had conceived since he had left his mother-country. One and all they had been successful. He seemed, indeed, to have been imbued with the gift of success. He had floated immense loans where other men had failed; he had sustained the credit of his country on a high level through more than one serious financial crisis; he had pulled down or built up as his judgment or fancy had dictated; and all the time the man's relaxations, apart from the actual trend of great affairs, had been few and slight. Then had come his acquaintance with Linda's school-friend. He looked back through the years. At first he had scarcely noticed her visits. Gradually he had become conscious of a dim feeling of thankfulness to the woman who always seemed able to soothe his invalid wife. Then, scarcely more than a year or so ago, he had found himself watching her at unexpected moments, admiring the soft grace of her movements, the pleasant cadence of her voice, the turn of her head, the colour of her hair, the elegance of her clothes, her thin, fashionable figure. Gradually he had begun to look for her, to welcome her at his table — and from that, the rest. Finally the birth of this last scheme of his. He had very nearly made a fatal mistake at the very commencement, had pulled himself right again only with a supreme effort. His heart beat quicker even now as he thought of that moment. They had been alone together one evening. She had sat talking with him after Linda had gone to bed worse than usual, and in the dim light he had almost lost his head, he had almost said those words, let her see the things in his eyes for which the time was not yet ripe. She had kept away for a while after that. He had treated it as a mistake but he had been very careful not to err again. By degrees she forgot. The estrangement between husband and wife was part of his scheme, largely his doing. He was all the time working to make the breach wider. The visit to Monte Carlo, rather a difficult accomplishment, he had arranged. He had seen with delight the necessity for some form of excitement growing up in her, had watched her losses and only wished that they had been larger. He had encouraged her to play for higher stakes and found that she needed very little encouragement indeed. To-night he felt that a crisis was at hand. There was a new look upon her face. She had probably lost everything. He knew exactly how she would feel about asking her husband for help. His eyes grew brighter as he waited for the lift.

She came at last and they walked together into the dining-room. When she reached their accustomed table, it was empty, and only their two places were laid. She looked at him in surprise.

" But I thought you said that Linda would be so disappointed! " she reminded him.

He shook his head.

" I do not think that I mentioned Linda's name," he protested. " She went to bed soon after tea in an absolutely hopeless state. I am afraid that to-night I was selfish. I was thinking of myself. I have had nothing in the shape of companionship all day. I came and looked at the table, and the thought of dining alone wearied me. I have to spend a great deal of time alone, unfortunately. You and I are, perhaps, a little alike in that respect."

She seated herself after a moment's hesitation. He moved his chair a little closer to hers. The pink-shaded lamp seemed to shut them off from the rest of the room. A waiter poured wine into their glasses.

" I ordered champagne to-night," he remarked.

" You looked so tired when you came in. Drink a glass at once."

She obeyed him, smiling faintly. She was, as a matter of fact, craving for something of the sort.

" It was thoughtful of you," she declared. " I am tired. I have been losing all day, and altogether I have had a most depressing time."

" It is not as it should be, that," he observed, smiling. " This is a city of pleasure. One was meant to leave one's cares behind here. If any one in this world," he added, " should be without them, it should be you."

He looked at her respectfully yet with an admiration which he made no effort to conceal. There was nothing in the look over-personal. She accepted it with gratitude.

" You are always kind," she murmured.

" This reminds me of some of our evenings in London," he went on, " when we used to talk music before we went to the Opera. I always found those evenings so restful and pleasant. Won't you try and forget that you have lost a few pennies; forget, also, your other worries, whatever they may be? I have had a letter to-day from the one great writer whom we both admire. I shall read it to you. And I have a list of the operas for next week. I see that your husband's little protégée, Felicia Roche, is here."

" My husband's protégée? " she repeated. " I don't quite understand."

He seemed, for a moment, embarrassed.

" I am sorry," he said. " I had no idea. But your husband will tell you if you ask him. It was he who paid for her singing education, and her triumph is his. But the name must be known to you."

"I have never heard it in connection with my husband," she declared, frowning slightly. "Henry does not always take me into his confidence."

"Then I am sorry," he continued penitently, "that I mentioned the matter. It was clumsy of me. I had an idea that he must have told you all about her. . . . Another glass of wine, please, and you will find your appetite comes. Jules has prepared that salmon trout specially. I'll read you the letter from Maurice, if you like, and afterwards there is a story I must tell you."

The earlier stages of dinner slipped pleasantly away. Draconmeyer was a born conversationalist, — a good talker and a keen tactician. The food and the wine, too, did their part. Presently Violet lifted her head, the colour came back to her cheeks, she too began to talk and laugh. All the time he was careful not to press home his advantage. He remembered that one night in the library at Grosvenor Square, when she had turned her head and looked at him for a moment before leaving. She must be different now, he told himself fiercely. It was impossible that she could continue to love a husband who neglected her, a man whose mistaken sense of dignity kept him away from her!

"I want you," he begged, as they drew towards the close of the meal, "to treat me, if you will, just a little more confidentially."

She glanced up at him quickly, almost suspiciously.

"What do you mean?"

"You have troubles of which you do not speak," he went on. "If my friendship is worth anything, it ought to enable me to share those troubles with you. You have had a little further disagreement with your husband, I think, and bad luck at the tables. You ought not to let either of these things depress you too much. Tell me, do you think that I could help with Sir Henry?"

"No one could help," she replied, her tone unconsciously hardening. "Henry is obstinate, and it is my firm conviction that he has ceased to care for me at all. This afternoon — this very afternoon," she went on, leaning across the table, her voice trembling a little, her eyes very bright, "I offered to go away with him."

"To leave Monte Carlo?"

"Yes! He refused. He said that he must stay here, for some mysterious reason. I begged him to tell me what that reason was, and he was silent. It was the end. He gives me no confidence. He has refused the one effort I made at reconciliation. I am convinced that it is useless. We have parted finally."

Draconmeyer tried hard to keep the light from his eyes as he leaned towards her.

"Dear lady," he said, "if I do not admit that I am sorry — well, there are reasons. Your husband did well to be mysterious. I can tell you the reason why he will not leave Monte Carlo. It is because Felicia Roche makes her début at the Opera House to-morrow night. There! I didn't mean to tell you but the whole world knows it. Even now I would not have told you but for other things. It is best that you know the truth. It is my firm belief that your husband does not deserve your interest, much more your affection. If only I dared —"

He paused for a moment. Every word he was compelled to measure.

"Sometimes," he continued, "your condition reminds me so much of my own. I think that there is no one so lonely in life as I am. For the last few years Linda has been fading away, physically and mentally. I touch her fingers at morning and night, we speak of the slight happenings of the day. She has no longer any mind or any power of sympathy. Her lips are as cold as her understanding. For that I know she is not to blame, yet it has left me very lonely. If I had had a child," he went on, "even if there were one single soul of whom I was fond, to whom I might look for sympathy; even if you, my dear friend — you see, I am bold, and I venture to call you my dear friend — could be a little kinder sometimes, it would make all the difference in the world."

She turned her head and looked at him. His teeth came together hastily. It seemed to him that already she was on her guard.

"You have something more to say, haven't you?" she asked.

He hesitated. Her tone was non-committal. It was a moment when he might have risked everything, but he feared to make a mistake.

"This is what I mean," he declared, with the appearance of great frankness. "I am going to speak to you upon the absurd question of money. I have an income of which, even if I were boundlessly ex-

travagant, I could not hope to spend half. A specu-
lation, the week before I left England, brought me a
profit of a million marks. But for the banking interests of my country and the feeling that I am the
trustee for thousands of other people, it would weary
me to look for investments. And you — you came
in to-night, looking worn out just because you had
lost a handful or so of those wretched plaques.
There, you see it is coming now. I should like permission to do more than call myself your friend. I
should like permission to be also your banker."

She looked at him quietly and searchingly. His
heart began to beat faster. At least she was in
doubt. He had not wholly lost. His chance, even,
was good.

" My friend," she said, " I believe that you are
honest. I do indeed recognise your point of view.
The thing is an absurdity, but, you know, all conven-
tions, even the most foolish, have some human and
natural right beneath them. I think that the convention which forbids a woman accepting money
from a man, however close a friend, is like that.
Frankly, my first impulse, a few minutes ago, was to
ask you to lend me a thousand pounds. Now I know
that I cannot do it."

" Do you really mean that? " he asked, in a tone
of deep disappointment. " If you do, I am hurt.
It proves that the friendship which to me is so dear,
is to you a very slight thing."

" You mustn't think that," she pleaded. " And
please, Mr. Draconmeyer, don't think that I don't
appreciate all your kindness. Short of accepting
your money, I would do anything to prove it."

"There need be no question of a gift," he reminded her, in a low tone. "If I were a perfect stranger, I might still be your banker. You must have money from somewhere. Are you going to ask your husband?"

She bit her lip for a moment. If indeed he had known her actual position, his hopes would have been higher still.

"I cannot possibly ask Henry for anything," she confessed. "I had made up my mind to ask him to authorise the lawyers to advance me my next quarter's allowance. After — what has passed between us, though, and — considering everything, I don't feel that I can do it."

"Then may I ask how you really mean to get more money?" he went on gently.

She looked at him a little piteously.

"Honestly, I don't know," she admitted. "I will be quite frank with you. Henry allows me two thousand, five hundred a year. I brought nine hundred pounds out with me, and I have nothing more to come until June."

"And how much have you left of the nine hundred pounds?" he asked.

"Not enough to pay my hotel bill," she groaned.

He smiled.

"Circumstances are too strong for you," he declared. "You must go to a banker. I claim the right of being that banker. I shall draw up a promissory note — no, we needn't do that — two or three cheques, perhaps, dated June, August and October. I shall charge you five per cent. interest and I shall lend you a thousand pounds."

Her eyes sparkled. The thought of the money was wonderful to her. A thousand pounds in mille notes that very night! She thought it all over rapidly. She would never run such risks again. She would play for small amounts each day — just enough to amuse herself. Then, if she were lucky, she would plunge, only she would choose the right moment. Very likely she would be able to pay the whole amount back in a day or two. If Henry minded, well, it was his own fault. He should have been different.

" You put it so kindly," she said gratefully, " that I am afraid I cannot refuse. You are very, very considerate, Mr. Draconmeyer. It certainly will be nicer to owe you the money than a stranger."

" I am only glad that you are going to be reasonable," he remarked,— " glad, really, for both our sakes. And remember," he went on cheerfully, " that one isn't young and at Monte Carlo too many times in one's life. Make up your mind to enjoy yourself. If the luck goes against you for a little longer, come again. You are bound to win in the end. Now, if you like, we'll have our coffee outside. I'll go and fetch the money and you shall make out your cheques."

He scribbled hastily on a piece of paper for a moment.

" These are the amounts," he pointed out. " I have charged you five per cent. per annum interest. As I can deal with money at something under four, I shall make quite a respectable profit — more than enough," he added good-naturedly, " to pay for our dinner ! "

She seemed suddenly years younger. The prospect of the evening before her was enchanting.

"You really are delightful!" she exclaimed. "You can't think how differently I shall feel when I go into the Club to-night. I am perfectly certain that it's having plenty of money that helps one to win."

He smiled.

"And plenty of courage," he added. "Don't waste your time trifling with small stakes. Bid up for the big things. It is the only way in gambling and in life."

He rose to his feet and their eyes met for a moment. Once more she felt vaguely troubled. She put that disturbing thought away from her, however. It was foolish to think of drawing back now. If he admired her — well, so did most men!

CHAPTER XV

The Villa Mimosa flamed with lights from the top story to the ground-floor. The entrance gates stood wide-open. All along the drive, lamps flashed from unsuspected places beneath the yellow-flowering trees. One room only seemed shrouded in darkness and mystery, and around that one room was concentrated the tense life of the villa. Thick curtains had been drawn with careful hands. The heavy door had been securely closed. The French-windows which led out on to the balcony had been almost barricaded. The four men who were seated around the oval table had certainly secured for themselves what seemed to be a complete and absolute isolation. Yet there was, nevertheless, a sense of uneasiness, an indescribable air of tension in the atmosphere. The quartette had somehow the appearance of conspirators who had not settled down to their work. It was the last arrival, the man who sat at Mr. Grex's right hand, who was responsible for the general unrest.

Mr. Grex moved a little nervously in the chair which he had just drawn up to the table. He looked towards Draconmeyer as he opened the proceedings.

"Monsieur Douaille," he said, "has come to see us his evening at my own urgent request. Before

we commence any sort of discussion, he has asked me
to make it distinctly understood to you both — to
you, Mr. Draconmeyer, and to you, Herr Selingman
— that this is not in any sense of the word a formal
meeting or convention. We are all here, as it happens, by accident. Our friend Selingman, for instance, who is a past master in the arts of pleasant
living, has not missed a season here for many years.
Draconmeyer is also an habitué. I myself, it is
true, have spent my winters elsewhere, for various
reasons, and am comparatively a stranger, but my
visit here was arranged many months ago. You
yourself, Monsieur Douaille, are a good Parisian,
and no good Parisian should miss his yearly pilgrim-
ages to the Mecca of the pleasure-seeker. We meet
together this evening, therefore, purely as friends
who have a common interest at heart."

The man from whom this atmosphere of nervousness radiated — a man of medium height, inclined
towards corpulence, with small grey imperial, a thin
red ribbon in his buttonhole, and slightly prominent
features — promptly intervened. He had the air
of a man wholly ill-at-ease. All the time Mr. Grex
had been speaking, he had been drumming upon the
table with his forefinger.

"Precisely! Precisely!" he exclaimed. "Above
all things, that must be understood. Ours is a
chance meeting. My visit in these parts is in no
way connected with the correspondence I have had
with one of our friends here. Further," Monsieur
Douaille continued impressively, " it must be distinctly understood that any word I may be disposed
to utter, either in the way of statement or criticism,

is wholly and entirely unofficial. I do not even know what the subject of our discussion is to be. I approach it with the more hesitation because I gather, from some slight hint which has fallen from our friend here, that it deals with a scheme which, if ever it should be carried into effect, is to the disadvantage of a nation with whom we are at present on terms of the greatest friendship. My presence here, except on the terms I have stated," he concluded, his voice shaking a little, " would be an unpardonable offence to that country."

Monsieur Douaille's somewhat laboured explanation did little to lighten the atmosphere. It was the genius of Herr Selingman which intervened. He leaned back in his chair and he patted his waistcoat thoughtfully.

" I have things to say," he declared, " but I cannot say them. I have nothing to smoke — no cigarette, no cigar. I arrive here choked with dust. As yet, the circumstance seems to have escaped our host's notice. Ah! what is that I see? " he added, rising suddenly to his feet. " My host, you are acquitted. I look around the table here at which I am invited to seat myself, and I perceive nothing but a few stumpy pens and unappetising blotting-paper. By chance I lift my eyes. I see the parting of the curtains yonder, and behold! "

He rose and crossed the room, throwing back a curtain at the further end. In the recess stood a sideboard, laden with all manner of liqueurs and wines, glasses of every size and shape, sandwiches, pasties, and fruit. Herr Selingman stood on one side with outstretched hand, in the manner of a

showman. He himself was wrapped for a moment
in admiration.

"For you others I cannot speak," he observed,
surveying the label upon a bottle of hock. "For
myself, here is nectar."

With careful fingers he drew the cork. At a murmured word of invitation from Mr. Grex, the others
rose from their places and also helped themselves
from the sideboard. Selingman took up his position in the centre of the hearthrug, with a long tumbler of yellow wine in one hand and a sandwich in
the other.

"For myself," he continued, taking a huge bite,
"I wage war against all formality. I have been
through this sort of thing in Berlin. I have been
through it in Vienna, I have been through it in
Rome. I have sat at long tables with politicians,
have drawn little pictures upon the blotting-paper
and been bored to death. In wearisome fashion we
have drafted agreements, we have quarrelled and
bickered, we have yawned and made of ourselves men
of parchment. But to-night," he added, taking another huge bite from his sandwich, "to-night nothing of that sort is intended. Draconmeyer and I
have an idea. Mr. Grex is favourably inclined towards it. That idea isn't a bit of good to ourselves or any one else unless Monsieur Douaille here
shares our point of view. Here we are, then, all met
together — let us hope for a week or two's enjoyment. Little by little we must try and see what we
can do towards instilling that idea into the mind of
Monsieur Douaille. We may succeed, we may fail,
but let us always remember that our conversations

are the conversations of four friends, met together upon what is nothing more or less than a holiday. I hate the sight of those sheets of blotting-paper and clean pens. Who wants to make notes, especially of what we are going to talk about! The man who cannot carry notes in his head is no statesman."

Monsieur Douaille, who had chosen champagne and was smoking a cigarette, beamed approval. Much of his nervousness had departed.

"I agree," he declared, "I like well the attitude of our friend Selingman. There is something much too formal about this table. I am not here to talk treaties or to upset them. To exchange views, if you will — no more. Meanwhile, I appreciate this very excellent champagne, the cigarettes are delicious, and I remove myself to this easy-chair. If any one would talk world politics, I am ready. Why not? Why should we pretend that there is any more interesting subject to men like ourselves, in whom is placed the trust of our country?"

Mr. Grex nodded his head in assent.

"The fault is mine," he declared, "but, believe me, it was not intentional. It was never my wish to give too formal an air to our little meeting — in fact I never intended to do more than dwell on the outside edge of great subjects to-night. Unfortunately, Monsieur Douaille, neither you nor I, whatever our power or influence may be, are directly responsible for the foreign affairs of our countries. We can, therefore, speak with entire frankness. Our countries — your country and mine — are to-day bound together by an alliance. You have some-

thing which almost approaches an alliance with another country. I am going to tell you in plain
words what I think you have been given to understand indirectly many times during the last few
years — that understanding is not approved of in
St. Petersburg."

Monsieur Douaille knocked the ash from his cigarette. He gazed thoughtfully into the fire of pine
logs which was burning upon the open hearth.

" Mr. Grex," he said, " that is plainer speaking
than we have ever received from any official source."

" I admit it," Mr. Grex replied. " Such a statement on my part may sound a little startling, but I
make it advisedly. I know the feeling — you will
grant that my position entitles me to know the feeling — of the men who count for anything in Russian politics. Perhaps I do not mean the titular
heads of my Government. There are others who
have even more responsibilities, who count for more.
I honestly and truthfully assure you that I speak
for the powers that are behind the Government of
Russia when I tell you that the English dream of a
triple alliance between Russia, England, and France
will never be accepted by my country."

Monsieur Douaille sipped his champagne.

" This is candour," he remarked, " absolute candour. One speaks quite plainly, I imagine, before
our friend the enemy?" he added, smiling towards
Selingman.

" Why not?" Selingman demanded. " Why not,
indeed? We are not fools here."

" Then I would ask you, Mr. Grex," Monsieur
Douaille continued, " where in the name of all that is

equitable are you to find an alliance more likely to preserve the status quo in Europe? Both logically and geographically it absolutely dovetails. Russia is in a position to absorb the whole attention of Austria and even to invade the north coast of Germany. The hundred thousand troops or so upon which we could rely from Great Britain, would be invaluable for many reasons — first, because a mixture of blood is always good; secondly, because the regular army which perforce they would have to send us, is of very fine fighting material; and thirdly, because they could land, to give away a very open secret to you, my friend Selingman, in a westerly position, and would very likely succeed thereby in making an outflanking movement towards the north. I presume that at present the German fleet would not come out to battle, in which case the English would certainly be able to do great execution upon the northern coast of Germany. All this, of course, has been discussed and written about, and the next war been mapped out in a dozen different ways. I must confess, however, that taking every known consideration into account, I can find no other distribution of powers so reasonable or so favourable to my country."

Mr. Grex nodded.

" I find no fault with any word of what you have said," he declared, " except that yours is simply the superficial and obvious idea of the man in the street as to the course of the next probable war. Now let us go a little further. I grant all the points which you urge in favour of your suggested triple alliance. I will even admit that your forecast of a war taking place under such conditions, is a fairly faithful one. We proceed, then. The war, if it came to pass, could never be decisive. An immense amount of blood would be shed, treasure recklessly poured out, Europe be rendered desolate, for the sake most largely of whom? — of Japan and America. That is the weakness of the whole thing. A war carried out on the lines you suggest would be playing the game of these two countries. Even the victors would be placed at a huge disadvantage with them, to say nothing of the losers, who must see slipping away from them forever their place under the sun. It is my opinion — and I have studied this matter most scientifically and with the help of the Secret Service of every country, not excepting your own, Herr Selingman — it is my opinion that this war must be indecisive. The German fleet would be crippled and not destroyed. The English fleet would retain its proportionate strength. No French advance into Germany would be successful, no German advance into France is likely. The war would languish for lack of funds, through sheer inanition it would flicker out, and the money of the world would flow into the treasuries of America. Russia would not be fighting for her living. With her it could be at best but a half-hearted war. She would do her duty to the alliance. Nothing more could be hoped from her. You could not expect, for instance, that she would call up all her reserves, leave the whole of her eastern frontier unprotected, and throw into mid-Europe such a force as would in time subjugate Germany. This could be done but it will not be done. We all know that."

Monsieur Douaille smoked thoughtfully for several moments.

"Very well," he pronounced at last, "I am rather inclined to agree with all that you have said. Yet it seems to me that you evade the great point. The status quo is what we desire, peace is what the world wants. If, before such a war as you have spoken of is begun, people realise what the end of it must be, don't you think that that itself is the greatest help towards peace? My own opinion is, I tell you frankly, that for many years to come, at any rate, there will be no war."

Herr Selingman set down his glass and turned slowly around.

"Then let me tell you that you are mistaken," he declared solemnly. "Listen to me, my friend Douaille — my friend, mind, and not the statesman Douaille. I am a German citizen and you are a French one, and I tell you that if in three years' time your country does not make up its mind to strike a blow for Alsace and Lorraine, then in three years' time Germany will declare war upon you."

Monsieur Douaille had the expression of a man who doubts. Selingman frowned. He was suddenly immensely serious. He struck the palm of one hand a great blow with his clenched fist.

"Why is it that no one in the world understands," he cried, "what Germany wants? I tell you, Monsieur Douaille, that we don't hate your country. We love it. We crowd to Paris. We expand there. It is the holiday place of every good German. Who wants a ruined France? Not we! Yet, unless there is a change in the international situation, we shall

go to war with you and I will tell you why. There
are no secrets about this sort of thing. Every politician who is worth his salt knows them. The only
difficulty is to know when a country is in earnest,
and how far it will go. That is the value of our
meeting. That is what I am here to say. We shall
go to war with you, Monsieur Douaille, to get Calais,
and when we've got Calais — oh, my God!" Selingman almost reverently concluded, " then our solemn
task will be begun."

"England!" Monsieur Douaille murmured.

There was a brief pause. Selingman had seemed,
for a moment, to have passed into the clouds.
There was a sort of gloomy rapture upon his face.
He caught up Douaille's last word and repeated it.

"England! England, and through her . . . "

He moved to the sideboard and filled his tumbler
with wine. When he came back to his place, his expression had lightened.

" Ah, well! dear Monsieur Douaille," he exclaimed,
patting the other's shoulder in friendly fashion, " to-
night we merely chatter. To-night we are here to
make friends, to gain each the confidence of the
other. To ourselves let us pretend that we are little boys, playing the game of our nation — France,
Germany, and Russia. Germany and Russia, to be
frank with you, are waiting for one last word from
Germany's father, something splendid and definite
to offer. What we would like France to do, while
France loses its money at roulette and flirts with the
pretty ladies at Ciro's, is to try and accustom itself
not to an alliance with Germany — no! Nothing
so utopian as that. The lion and the lamb may re-

main apart. They may agree to be friends, they may even wave paws at one another, but I do not suggest that they march side by side. What we ask of France is that she looks the other way. It is very easy to look the other way. She might look, for instance — towards Egypt."

There was a sudden glitter in the eyes of Monsieur Douaille. Selingman saw it and pressed on.

" There are laurels to be won which will never fade," he continued, setting down his empty tumbler, " laurels to be won by that statesman of your country, the little boy France, who is big enough and strong enough to stand with his feet upon the earth and proclaim —' I am for France and my own people, and my own people only, and I will make them great through all the centuries by seeing the truth and leading them towards it, single-purposed, single-minded.' . . . But these things are not to be disposed of so readily as this wonderful Berncastler — I beg its pardon, Berncastler Doctor — of our host. For to-night I have said my say. I have whims, perhaps, but with me serious affairs are finished for the night. I go to the Sporting Club. Mademoiselle keeps my place at the baccarat table. I feel in the vein. It is a small place, Monte Carlo. Let us make no appointments. We shall drift together. And, monsieur," he concluded, laying his hand for a moment upon Douaille's shoulder, " let the thought sink into your brain. Wipe out that geographical and logical map of Europe from your mind; see things, if you can, in the new daylight. Then, when the idea has been there for just a little time — well, we speak again. . . . Come, Draconmeyer. I am

relying upon your car to get me into Monte Carlo.
My bounteous host, Mr. Grex, good night! I touch
your hand with reverence. The man who possesses
such wine and offers it to his friends, is indeed a
prince."

Mr. Grex rose a little unwillingly from his chair.
"It is of no use to protest," he remarked, smiling.
"Our friend Selingman will have his way. Besides,
as he reminded us, there is one last word to arrive.
Come and breathe the odours of the Riviera, Monsieur Douaille. This is when I realise that I am not
at my villa on the Black Sea."

They passed out into the hall and stood on the
terrace while the cars drew up. The light outside
seemed faintly violet. The perfume of mimosa and
roses and oleander came to him in long waves, subtle
and yet invigorating. Below, the lights of Monte
Carlo, clear and brilliant, with no northern fog or
mist to dull their radiance, shone like gems in the
mantle of night. Selingman sighed as he stepped
into the automobile.

"We are men who deserve well from history," he
declared, "who, in the midst of a present so wonderful, can spare time to plan for the generations to
come!"

CHAPTER XVI

A BARGAIN WITH JEAN COULOIS

Selingman drew out his watch and held it underneath the electric light set in the back of the automobile.

"Good!" he declared. "It is not yet half-past eleven."

"Too early for the Austria," Draconmeyer murmured, a little absently.

Selingman returned the watch to his pocket.

"By no means," he objected. "Mademoiselle is doubtless amusing herself well enough, but if I go now and leave in an hour, she will be peevish. She might want to accompany us. To-night it would not be convenient. Tell your chauffeur, Draconmeyer, to take us direct to the rendezvous. We can at least watch the people there. One is always amused. We will forget our nervous friend. These little touches, Draconmeyer, my man, they mark the man of genius, mind you. Did you notice how his eyes lit up when I whispered that one word 'Egypt'? It is a great game when you bait your hook with men and fish for empires!"

Draconmeyer gave an instruction to his chauffeur and leaned back.

"If we succeed,—" he began.

"Succeed?" Selingman interrupted. "Why,

man alive, he is on our hooks already! Be at rest, my friend. The affair is half arranged. It remains only with us to deal with one man."

Draconmeyer's eyes sparkled beneath his spectacles. A slow smile crept over his white face.

"You are right," he agreed. "That man is best out of the way. If he and Douaille should meet —"

"They shall not meet," Selingman thundered. "I, Selingman, declare it. We are here already. Good! The aspect of the place pleases me."

The two men, arriving so early, received the distinguished consideration of a bowing maître d'hôtel as they entered the Austria. They were ushered at once to a round table in a favourable position. Selingman surrendered his hat and coat to the obsequious vestiaire, pulled down his waistcoat with a familiar gesture, spread his pudgy hands upon the table and looked around him with a smile of benevolent approval.

"I shall amuse myself here," he declared confidently. "Pass the menu to me, Draconmeyer. You have no more idea how to eat than a rabbit. That is why you suffer from indigestion. At this hour — why, it is not midnight yet — one needs sustenance — sustenance, mark you, intelligently selected, something nourishing yet not heavy. A sheet of paper, waiter. You see, I like to write out my dishes. It saves trouble and there are no disappointments, nothing is forgotten. As to the wine, show me the vintage champagnes. . . . So! You need not hurry with the meal. We shall spend some time here."

Draconmeyer arrested the much impressed maître d'hôtel as he was hurrying away.

"Is there dancing here to-night?" he enquired.

"But certainly, monsieur," the man replied. "A Spanish lady, altogether ravishing, the equal of Otéro at her best — Signorina Melita."

"She dances alone?"

"By no means. There is the young Frenchman, Jean Coulois, who is engaged for the season. A wonderful pair, indeed! When May comes, they go to the music-halls in Paris and London."

Draconmeyer nodded approval.

"Coulois was the name," he whispered to Selingman, as the man moved away.

The place filled up slowly. Presently the supper was served. Selingman ate with appetite, Draconmeyer only sparingly. The latter, however, drank more freely than usual. The wine had, nevertheless, curiously little effect upon him, save for a slight additional brightness of the eyes. His cheeks remained pale, his manner distrait. He watched the people enter and pass to their places, without any apparent interest. Selingman, on the other hand, easily absorbed the spirit of his surroundings. As the night wore on he drank healths with his neighbours, beamed upon the pretty little Frenchwoman who was selling flowers, ate and drank what was set before him with obvious enjoyment. Both men, however, showed at least an equal interest when Mademoiselle Melita, in Spanish costume, accompanied by a slim, dark-visaged man, began to dance. Draconmeyer was no longer restless. He sat with folded arms, watching the performance with a strangely absorbed air. One thing, however, was singular. Although Selingman was confessedly a ladies' man, his eyes, after her first few movements, scarcely rested for a moment upon the girl. Both Draconmeyer and he watched her companion steadfastly. When the dance was over they applauded with spirit. Selingman sat up in his place, a champagne bottle in his hand. He beckoned to the man, who, with a little deprecating shrug of the shoulders, swaggered up to their table with some show of condescension.

"A chair for Monsieur Jean Coulois, the great dancer," Selingman ordered, "a glass, and another bottle of wine. Monsieur Jean, my congratulations! But a word in your ear. Her steps do not match yours. It is you who make the dance. She has no initiative. She can do nothing but imitate," he added.

The dancer looked at his host a little curiously. He was slightly built and without an atom of colour. His black hair was closely cropped, his eyes of sombre darkness, his demeanour almost sullen. At Selingman's words, however, he nodded rapidly and seated himself more firmly upon his chair. It was apparent that although his face remained expressionless, he was gratified.

"They notice nothing, these others," he remarked, with a little wave of the hand. "It is always the woman who counts. You are right, monsieur. She dances like a stick. She has good calves and she rolls her eyes. The *canaille* applaud. It is always like that. Your health, monsieur!"

He drank his wine without apparent enjoyment,

but he drank it like water. Selingman leaned across the table.

"Coulois," he whispered, "the wolves bay loudest at night, is it not so?"

The man sat quite still. If such a thing had been possible, he might have grown a shade paler. His eyes glittered. He looked steadfastly at Selingman.

"Who are you?" he muttered.

"The wolves sleep in the daytime," Selingman replied.

The dancer shrugged his shoulders. He held out his glass to be replenished. The double password had reassured him.

"Pardon, monsieur," he said, "these have been anxious hours."

"The little affair at La Turbie?" Selingman suggested.

Coulois set down his glass for the first time half finished. His mouth had taken an evil turn. He leaned across the table.

"See you," he exclaimed in a hoarse whisper, "what happened, happened justly! Martin is responsible. The whole thing was conducted in the spirit of a pantomime, a great joke. Who are we, the Wolves, to brandish empty firearms, to shrink from letting a little blood! Bah!"

He finished his wine. Selingman nodded approvingly as he refilled his glass.

"My friend and I," he confided, "were amongst those who were held up. Imagine it! We stood against the wall like a row of dummies. Such treasure as I have never before seen was poured into that sack. Jewels, my friend, such as only the women of

Monte Carlo wear! Packet after packet of mille notes! Wealth immeasurable! Oh, Coulois, Coulois, it was an opportunity lost!"

"Lost!" the dancer echoed fiercely. "It was thrown into the gutter! It was madness! It was hellish, such ill-fortune! Yet what could I do? If I had been absent from here — I, Coulois, whom men know of — even the police would have had no excuse. So it was Martin who must lead. Our armoury had never been fuller. There were revolvers for every one, ammunition for a thousand. . . . Pardon, monsieur, but I cannot talk of this affair. The anger rises so hot in my heart that I fear to betray myself to those who may be listening. And besides, you have not come here to talk with me of it."

"It is true," Selingman confessed.

There was a brief silence. The dancer was studying them both. There was uneasiness in his expression.

"I do not understand," he enquired hoarsely, "how you came by the passwords?"

"Make yourself wholly at ease, my young friend," Selingman begged him reassuringly. "We are men of the world, my friend and I. We seek our own ends in life and we have often to make use of the nearest and the best means for the purpose of securing them. Martin has served me before. A week ago I should have gone to him. To-night, as you know, he lies in prison."

"Martin, indeed!" the dancer jeered. "You would have gone, then, to a man of sawdust, a chicken-livered bungler! What is it that you want done? Speak to me. I am a man."

The leader of the orchestra was essaying upon his violin the tentative strains of a popular air. The girl had reappeared and was poising herself upon her toes. The leader of the orchestra summoned Coulois.

" I must dance," he announced. " Afterwards I will return."

He leapt lightly to his feet and swung into the room with extended arms. Draconmeyer looked down at his plate.

" It is a risk, this, we are running," he muttered. " I do not see, Selingman, why you could not have hired this fellow through Allen or one of the others."

Selingman shook his head.

" See here, Draconmeyer," he explained, " this is one of the cases where agents are dangerous. For Allen to have been seen with Jean Coulois here would have been the same as though I had been seen with him myself. I cannot, alas! in this place, with my personality, keep my identity concealed. They know that I am Selingman. They know well that wherever I move, I have with me men of my Secret Service. I cannot use them against Hunterleys. Too many are in the know. Here we are simply two visitors who talk to a dancer. We depart. We do not see him again until afterwards. Besides, this is where fate is with us. What more natural than that the Wolves should revenge themselves upon the man who captured one of their leaders? It was the young American, Richard Lane, who really started the débacle, but it was Hunterleys who seized Martin. What more natural than revenge? These fellows hang by one another always."

Draconmeyer nodded with grim approval.

"It was devilish work he did in Sofia," he said softly. "But for him, much of this would have been unnecessary."

The dance was over. Both men joined enthusiastically in the applause. Coulois, with an insolent nod to his admirers, returned to his seat. He threw himself back in his chair, crossed his legs and held out his empty glass. Though he had been dancing furiously, there was not a single bead of perspiration upon his forehead.

"You are in good condition, my friend," Selingman observed admiringly.

"I need to be for my work," Coulois replied. "Let us get to business. There is no need to mince words. What do you want with me? Who is the quarry?"

"The man who ruined your little affair at La Turbie and captured your comrade Martin," Selingman whispered. "You see, you have every provocation to start with."

Coulois' eyes glittered.

"He was an Englishman," he muttered.

"Quite true," Selingman assented. "His name is Hunterleys — Sir Henry Hunterleys. He lives at the Hotel de Paris. His room is number 189. He spends his time upon the Terrace, at the Café de Paris, and in the Sporting Club. Every morning he goes to the English Bank for his letters, deals with them in his room, calls at the post-office and takes a walk, often up into the hills."

"Come, come, this is not so bad!" Coulois exclaimed. "They laugh at us in the cafés and down

in the wine shops of Monaco, those who know," he
went on, frowning. "They say that the Wolves
have become sheep. We shall see! It is an affair,
this, worth considering. What do you pay, Monsieur
le Gros, and for how long do you wish him out
of the way?"

"The pay," Selingman announced, "is two hundred
louis, and the man must be in hospital for at
least a fortnight."

Draconmeyer leaned suddenly forward. His eyes
were bright, his hands gripped the table.

"Listen!" he whispered in Coulois' ear. "Are
the Wolves sheep, indeed, that they can do no more
than twist ankles and break heads? That two hundred
shall be five hundred, Jean Coulois, but it must
be a cemetery to which they take him, and not a
hospital!"

There was a moment's silence. Selingman sat
back in his place. He was staring at his companion
with wide-open eyes. Jean Coulois was moistening
his lips with his tongue, his eyes were brilliant.

"Five hundred louis!" he repeated under his
breath.

"Is it not enough?" Draconmeyer asked coldly.
"I do not believe in half measures. The man who
is wounded may be well before he is welcome. If five
hundred louis is not enough, name your price,
but let there be no doubt. Let me see what the
Wolves can do when it is their leader who handles the
knife!"

The face of the dancer was curiously impassive.
He lifted his glass and drained it.

"An affair of death!" he exclaimed softly. "We

Wolves — we bite, we wound, we rob. But death —
ugh! There are ugly things to be thought of."

"And pleasant ones," Draconmeyer reminded him.
"Five hundred louis is not enough. It shall be six
hundred. A man may do much with six hundred
golden louis."

Selingman sat forward once more in his place.

"Look here," he intervened, "you go too far, my
friend. You never spoke to me of this. What have
you against Hunterleys?"

"His nationality," Draconmeyer answered coolly.
"I hate all Englishmen!"

The gaiety had left Selingman's face. He gazed
at his companion with a curious expression.

"My friend," he murmured, "I fear that you are
vindictive."

"Perhaps," Draconmeyer replied quietly. "In
these matters I like to be on the safe side."

Jean Coulois struck the table lightly with his
small, feminine hand. He showed all his teeth as
though he had been listening to an excellent joke.

"It is to be done," he decided. "There is no
more to be said."

Some visitors had taken the next table. Coulois
drew his chair a little closer to Draconmeyer.

"I accept the engagement," he continued. "We
will talk no more. Monsieur desires my address?
It is here,"— scribbling on a piece of paper. "But
monsieur may be warned," he added, with a light-
ning-like flash in his eyes as he became conscious of
the observation of some passers-by. "I will not
dance in England. I will not leave Monte Carlo before May. Half that sum — three hundred louis,

mind — must come to me on trust; the other three hundred afterwards. Never fear but that I will give satisfaction. Keep your part of the bargain," he added, under his breath, " and the Wolves' fangs are already in this man's throat."

He danced again. The two men watched him. Draconmeyer's face was as still and colourless as ever. In Selingman's there was a shade of something almost like repulsion. He poured himself out a glass of champagne.

" Draconmeyer," he exclaimed, " you are a cold-blooded fish, indeed! You can sit there without blinking and think of this thing which we have done. Now as for me, I have a heart. I can never see the passing out of the game of even a bitter opponent, without a shiver. Talk philosophy to me, Draconmeyer. My nerves are shaken."

Draconmeyer turned his head. He, too, raised his wine to his lips and drank deliberately.

" My friend," he said, " there is no philosophy save one. A child cries for the star he may not have; the weak man comforts himself in privation by repeating to himself the dry-as-dust axioms conceived in an alien brain, and weaving from them the miserable comfort of empty words. The man who knows life and has found wisdom, pays the price for the thing he desires, and obtains it!"

CHAPTER XVII

DUTY INTERFERES AGAIN

Hunterleys sat that night alone in a seat at the Opera for a time and lost himself in a maze of recollections. He seemed to find himself growing younger as he listened to the music. The days of a more vivid and ardent sentimentality seemed to reassert themselves. He thought of the hours when he had sat side by side with his wife, the only woman to whom he had ever given a thought; of the thrill which even the touch of her fingers had given him, of the drive home together, the little confidences and endearments, the glamour which seemed to have been thrown over life before those unhappy misunderstandings. He remembered so well the beginning of them all — the terrible pressure of work which was thrown upon his shoulders, his engrossed days, his disturbed nights; her patience at first, her subsequent petulance, her final anger. He was engaged often in departmental work which he could not even explain. She had taken up with unhappy facility the rôle of a neglected wife. She declared that he had ceased to care for the lighter ways. There had certainly been a time when her complaints had been apparently justified, when the Opera had been banned, theatres were impossible, when she could not even rely upon his escort to a dinner or to a reception. He had argued with her very patiently at first, but very unsuccessfully. It was then that her friendship with Linda Draconmeyer had been so vigorously renewed, a friendship which seemed from the first to have threatened his happiness. Had it been his fault? he wondered. Had he really been too much engrossed in his work? His country had made large demands upon him in those days. Had he ever explained the matter fully and carefully enough to her? Perhaps not. At any rate, he was the sufferer. He realised more than ever, as the throbbing of the music stole into his blood, the loneliness of his life. And yet it seemed so hopeless. Supposing he threw up his work and let things take their course? The bare thought chilled him. He recognised it as unworthy. The great song of mortification from the broken hero rang in his ears. Must every woman bring to every man the curse of Delilah! . . .

He passed out of the building into the cool, starlit night. People were strolling about in evening clothes, hatless, the women in white opera cloaks and filmy gowns, their silk-stockinged feet very much in evidence, resembling almost some strange kind of tropical birds with their little shrill laughter and graceful movements, as they made their way towards the Club or round to the Rooms, or to one of the restaurants for supper. Whilst Hunterleys hesitated, there was a touch upon his arm. He glanced around.

" Hullo, David! " he exclaimed. " Were you waiting for me? "

The young man fell into step by his side.

" I have been to the hotel," he said, in a low tone.

" They thought you might be here. Can you come up later — say at one o'clock? "

" Certainly," Hunterleys answered. " Where's Sidney? "

" He's working now. He'll be home by half-past twelve unless anything goes wrong. He thinks he'll have something to tell you."

" I'll come," Hunterleys agreed. " How's Felicia? "

" All right, but working herself to death," the young man replied. " She is getting anxious, too. Give her a word of encouragement if you see her to-night. She was hoping you might have been up to see her."

" I won't forget," Hunterleys promised.

The young man drifted silently away, and Hunterleys, after a moment's hesitation and a glance at his watch, turned towards the Club. He climbed the broad staircase, surrendered his hat and turned in at the roulette room. The magic of the music was still in his veins, and he looked around him almost eagerly. There was no sign of Violet. He strolled into the baccarat room but she was not there. Perhaps she, too, had been at the Opera. In the bar he found Richard Lane, sitting moodily alone. The young man greeted him warmly.

" Come and have a drink, Sir Henry," he begged. " I've got the hump."

Hunterleys sat down by his side.

" Whiskey and apollinaris," he ordered. " What's the matter with you, Richard? "

" She isn't here," the young man declared. " I've been to the Rooms and she isn't there either."

"What about the Opera?" Hunterleys asked.

"I started at the Opera," Lane confessed, "took a box so as to be able to see the whole house. I sat through the first act but there wasn't a sign of her. Then I took a spin out and had another look at the villa. It was all lit up as though there were a party. I very nearly marched in."

"Just as well you didn't, I think," Hunterleys remarked, smiling. "I see you're feeling just the same about it."

The young man did not even vouchsafe an answer.

"Then you're not going to take advantage of your little warning and clear out?" Hunterleys continued.

"Don't you think I'm big enough to take care of myself?" Lane asked, with a little laugh. "Besides, there's an American Consul here, and plenty of English witnesses who saw the whole thing. Can't think why they're trying on such a silly game."

"Mr. Grex may have influence," Hunterleys suggested.

"Who the mischief is my prospective father-in-law?" Richard demanded, almost testily. "There's an atmosphere about that house and the servants I can't understand a bit."

"You wouldn't," Hunterleys observed drily. "Well, in a day or two I'll tell you who Mr. Grex is. I'd rather not to-night."

"By the way," Lane continued, "your wife was asking if you were here, a few minutes ago."

Hunterleys rose quickly to his feet.

"Where is she?"

"She was at her usual place at the top roulette table, but she gave it up just as I passed, said she was going to walk about," the young man replied. "I don't think she has left yet."

Hunterleys excused himself hastily. In the little space between the restaurant and the roulette rooms he came suddenly upon Violet. She was leaning back in an obscure corner, with her hands clasped helplessly in her lap before her. She was sitting quite still and his heart sank when he saw her. The lines under her eyes were unmistakable now; her cheeks, too, seemed to have grown hollow. Her first look at him almost made him forget all their differences. There was something piteous in the tremble of her lips. He drew a chair to her side.

"Richard told me that you wished to speak to me," he began, as lightly as he could.

"I asked if he had seen you, a few minutes ago," she admitted. "I am afraid that my interest was rather mercenary."

"You want to borrow some money?" he enquired, taking out his pocket-book.

She looked at it, and though her eyes at first were listless, they still seemed fascinated.

"I don't think I can play any more to-night," she sighed.

"You have been losing?"

"Yes!"

"Come and have something," he invited. "You look tired."

She rose willingly enough. They passed out, side by side, into the little bar.

"Some champagne?" he suggested.

She shook her head quickly. The memory of the champagne at dinner-time came back to her with a sudden sickening insistence. She thought of the loan, she thought of Draconmeyer with a new uneasiness. It was as though she had admitted some new complication into her life.

" Could I have some tea? " she begged.

He ordered some and sat with her while she drank it.

" You know," he declared, " if I might be permitted to say so, I think you are taking the gaming here a little too seriously. If you have been unlucky, it is very easy to arrange an advance for you. Would you like some money? If so, I will see to it when I go to the bank to-morrow. I can let you have a hundred pounds at once, if you like."

A hundred pounds! If only she dared tell him that she had lost a thousand within the last two hours! Once more he was fingering his pocket-book.

" Come," he went on pleasantly, " you had better have a hundred from me, for luck."

He counted out the notes. Her fingers began to shake.

" I didn't mean to play any more to-night," she faltered, irresolutely.

" Nor should I," he agreed. " Take my advice, Violet, and go home now. This will do for you to-morrow."

She took the money and dropped it into her jewelled bag.

" Very well," she said, " I won't play any more, but I don't want to go home yet. It is early, and I can never sleep here if I go to bed. Sit with me for

half-an-hour, and then perhaps you could give me
some supper?"

He shook his head.

"I am so sorry," he answered, "but at one o'clock
I have an appointment."

"An appointment?"

"Such bad luck," he continued. "It would have
given me very great pleasure to have had supper
with you, Violet."

"An appointment at one o'clock," she repeated
slowly. "Isn't that just a little — unusual?"

"Perhaps so," he assented. "I can assure you
that I am very sorry."

She leaned suddenly towards him. The aloofness
had gone from her manner. The barrier seemed for
a moment to have fallen down. Once more she was
the Violet he remembered. She smiled into his face,
and smiled with her eyes as well as her lips, just the
smile he had been thinking of an hour ago in the
Opera House.

"Don't go, please," she begged. "I am feeling lonely to-night and I am so tired of everybody
and everything. Take me to supper at the Café de
Paris. Then, if you like, we might come back here
for half-an-hour. Or —"

She hesitated.

"I am horribly sorry," he declared, in a tone
which was full of real regret. "Indeed, Violet, I
am. But I have an appointment which I must keep,
and I can't tell exactly how long it may take me."

The very fact that the nature of that appointment
concerned things which from the first he had made
up his mind must be kept entirely secret, stiffened

his tone. Her manner changed instantly. She had drawn herself a little away. She considered for a moment.

"Are you inclined to tell me with whom your appointment is, and for what purpose?" she asked coldly. "I don't want to be exacting, but after the request I have made, and your refusal —"

"I cannot tell you," he interrupted. "I can only ask you to take my word for it that it is one which I must keep."

She rose suddenly to her feet.

"I forgot!" she exclaimed. "I haven't the slightest right to your confidence. Besides, when I come to think of it, I don't believe that I am hungry at all. I shall try my luck with your money?"

"Violet! —"

She swept away with a little farewell nod, half insolent, half angry. Hunterleys watched her take her place at the table. For several moments he stood by her side. She neither looked up nor addressed him. Then he turned and left the place.

CHAPTER XVIII

Hunterleys remained in the hotel only long enough to change his straw hat for a cap, put on a long, light overcoat and take an ash stick from his wardrobe. He left the place by an unfrequented entrance and commenced at once to climb to the back part of the town. Once or twice he paused and looked around, to be sure that he was not followed. When he had arrived as far as the Hotel de Prince de Galles, he crossed the road. From here he walked very quickly and took three turns in rapid succession. Finally he pushed open a little gate and passed up a tiled walk which led between a little border of rose trees to a small white villa, covered with creepers. A slim, girlish figure came suddenly out from the porch and danced towards him with outstretched hands.

" At last! " she exclaimed. " At last! Tell me, my co-guardian, how you are going to excuse yourself? "

He took her outstretched hands and looked down into her face. She was very small and dark, with lustrous brown eyes and a very sensitive mouth, which just now was quivering with excitement.

" All the excuses have gone out of my head, Fe-

licia," he declared. " You look such a little elf in
the moonlight that I can't do more than say that I
am sorry. But I have been busy."

She was suddenly serious. She clasped his arm
with both her hands and turned towards the house.

" Of course you have," she sighed. " It seems too
bad, though, in Monte Carlo. Sidney and David are
like ghouls. I don't ask what it is all about — I
know better — but I wish it were all over, whatever
it is."

" Is Sidney back? " Hunterleys asked eagerly.

She nodded.

" He came in half-an-hour ago, looking like a
tramp. David is writing as though he hadn't a moment to spare in life. They are both waiting for
you, I think."

" And you? " he enquired. " How do the rehearsals go? "

" The rehearsals are all right," she admitted, looking up at him almost pathetically. " It's the night
itself that seems so awful. I know every word, I
know every note, and yet I can't feel sure. I can't
sleep for thinking about it. Only last night I had
a nightmare. I saw all those rows and rows of faces,
and the lights, and my voice went, my tongue was dry
and hard, not a word would come. And you were
there — and the others! "

He laughed at her.

" Little girl," he said solemnly, " I shall have to
speak to Sidney. One of those two young men must
take you out for a day in the country to-morrow."

" They seem so busy," she complained. " They
don't seem to have time to think of me. I suppose I

had better let you go in.   They'd be furious if they thought I was keeping you."

They passed into the villa, and with a farewell pat of the hand Hunterleys left her and opened a door on the left-hand side of the hall.   The young man who had met him coming out of the Opera was standing with his hands in his pockets, upon the hearthrug of an exceedingly untidy-looking apartment. There was a table covered with papers, another piled with newspapers.   There were books upon the floor, pipes and tobacco laid about haphazard.   A space had been swept clear upon the larger table for a typewriter, a telephone instrument stood against the wall. A man whose likeness to Felicia was at once apparent, swung round in his chair as Hunterleys entered.   He had taken off his coat and waistcoat and his trousers seemed smothered with dust.

" Regular newspaper correspondent's den," Hunterleys remarked, as he looked around him.   " I never saw such a mess in my life.   I wonder Felicia allows it."

" We don't let her come in," her brother chuckled. " Is the door closed? "

" Fast," Hunterleys replied, moving away from it.

" Things are moving," the other went on.   " 1 took the small car out to-day on the road to Cannes and I expect I was the first to see Douaille."

" I saw him myself," Hunterleys announced.   " I was out on that road, walking."

" Douaille," Roche continued, " went direct to the Villa Mimosa.   Grex was there, waiting for him. Draconmeyer and Selingman both kept out of the way."

Hunterleys nodded.

"Reasonable enough, that. Grex was the man to pave the way. Well?"

"At ten o'clock, Draconmeyer and Selingman arrived. The Villa Mimosa gets more difficult every day. I have only one friend in the house, although it is filled with servants. Three-quarters of them only speak Russian. My man's reliable but he is in a terrible minority. The conference took place in the library. It lasted about an hour and a half. Selingman and Draconmeyer came out looking fairly well satisfied. Half-an-hour later Douaille went on to Mentone, to the Hotel Splendide, where his wife and daughters are staying. No writing at all was done in the room."

"The conference has really begun, then," Hunterleys observed moodily.

"Without a doubt," Roche declared. "I imagine, though, that the meeting this evening was devoted to preliminaries. I am hoping next time," he went on, "to be able to pass on a little of what is said."

"If we could only get the barest idea as to the nature of the proposals," Hunterleys said earnestly. "Of course, one can surmise. Our people are already warned as to the long conferences which have taken place between Grex and Selingman. They mean something — there's no doubt about that. And then this invitation to Douaille, and his coming here so furtively. Everything points the same way, but a few spoken words are better than all the surmises in the world. It isn't that they are unreasonable at home, but they must be convinced."

"It's the devil's own risk," Roche sighed, "but I am hard at it. I was about the place yesterday as much as I dared. My plans are all ready now but things looked pretty awkward at the villa to-night. If they are going to have the grounds patrolled by servants every time they meet, I'm done. I've cut a pane of glass out of the dome over the library, and I've got a window-cleaning apparatus round at the back, and a ladder. The passage along the roof is quite easy and there's a good deal of cover amongst the chimneys, but if they get a hint, it will be touch and go."

Hunterleys nodded. He was busy now, going through the long sheets of writing which the other young man had silently passed across to him. For half-an-hour he read, making pencil notes now and then in the margin. When at last he had finished, he returned them and, sitting down at the table, drew a packet of press cable sheets towards him and wrote for some time steadily. When he had finished, he read through the result of his labours and leaned back thoughtfully in his chair.

"You will send this off from Cannes with your own, Briston?" he asked.

The young man assented.

"The car will be here at three," he announced. "They'll be on their way by eight."

"Press message, mind, to the *Daily Post*. If the operator wants to know what 'Number 1' means after '*Daily Post*,' you can tell him that it simply indicates to which editorial room the message is to be delivered."

"That's a clever idea," Roche mused. "Code dispatches to Downing Street might cause a little comment."

"They wouldn't do from here," Hunterleys declared. "They might be safe enough from Cannes but it's better to run no risks. These will be passed on to Downing Street, unopened. Be careful tomorrow, Sidney."

"I can't see that they can do anything but throw me out, Sir Henry," Roche remarked. "I have my *Daily Post* authority in my pocket, and my passport. Besides, I got the man here to announce in the *Monte Carlo News* that I was the accredited correspondent for the district, and that David Briston had been appointed by a syndicate of illustrated papers to represent them out here. That's in case we get a chance of taking photographs. I had some idea of going out to interview Monsieur Douaille."

Hunterleys shook his head.

"I shouldn't. The man's as nervous as he can be now, I am pretty sure of that. Don't do anything that might put him on his guard. Mind, for all we know he may be an honest man. To listen to what these fellows have to say doesn't mean that he's prepared to fall in with their schemes. By the by, you've nothing about the place, I suppose, if you should be raided?"

"Not a thing," was the confident reply. "We are two English newspaper correspondents, and there isn't a thing to be found anywhere that's not in keeping, except my rather large make-up outfit and my somewhat mixed wardrobe. I am not the only newspaper correspondent who goes in for that, though. Then there's Felicia. They all know who she is and

they all know that she's my sister. Anyhow, even
if I do get into trouble up at the Villa Mimosa, I
can't see that I shall be looked upon as anything
more than a prying newspaper correspondent. They
can't hang me for that."

Hunterleys accepted a cigarette and lit it.

" I needn't tell you fellows," he said gravely, " that
this place is a little unlike any other in Europe.
You may think you're safe enough, but all the same
I wouldn't trust a living soul. By-the-by, I saw Felicia as I came in. You don't want her to break
down, do you? "

" Good heavens, no! " her brother exclaimed.

" Break down? " David repeated. " Don't suggest such a thing! "

" It struck me that she was rather nervy," Hunterleys told them. " One of you ought to look after
her for an hour or two to-morrow."

" I can't spare a moment," her brother sighed.

" I'll take her out," Briston declared eagerly.
" There's nothing for me to do to-morrow till Sidney gets back."

" Well, between you, keep an eye on her," Hunterleys advised. " And, Sidney, I don't want to make a
coward of you, and you and I both know that if
there's danger ahead it's our job to face it, but have
a care up at the Villa Mimosa. I don't fancy the
law of this Principality would see you out of any
trouble if they got an idea that you were an English
Secret Service man."

Roche laughed shortly.

" Exactly my own idea," he admitted. " However, we've got to see it through. I sha'n't consider

I've done my work unless I hear something of what Grex and the others have to say to Douaille the next time they meet."

Hunterleys found Felicia waiting for him outside. He shook his head reproachfully.

" A future prima donna," he said, " should go to bed at ten o'clock."

She opened the door for him and walked down the path, her hands clasped in his arm.

" A future prima donna," she retorted, " can't do always what she likes. If I go to bed too early I cannot sleep. To-night I am excited and nervous. There isn't anything likely to bring trouble upon — them, is there? "

" Certainly not," he replied promptly. " Your brother is full of enterprise, as you know. He runs a certain amount of risk in his eagerness to acquire news, but I never knew a man so well able to take care of himself."

" And — and Mr. Briston? "

" Oh, he's all right, anyway," Hunterleys assured her. " His is the smaller part."

She breathed a little sigh of relief. They had reached the gate. She still had something to say. Below them flared the lights of Monte Carlo. She looked down at them almost wistfully.

" Very soon," she murmured, " I shall know my fate. Sir Henry," she added suddenly, " did I see Lady Hunterleys to-day on the Terrace? "

" Lady Hunterleys is here," he replied.

" Am I — ought I to go and see her? " she enquired. " You see, you have done so much for me, I should like to do what you thought best."

"Just as you like, child," he replied, a little carelessly.

She clung to his arm. She seemed unwilling to let him go.

"Dear co-guardian," she murmured, "to-night I felt for a little time so happy, as though all the good things in life were close at hand. Then I watched you come up, and your step seemed so heavy, and you stooped as though you had a load on your shoulders."

He patted her hand.

"Little girl," he advised, "run away in and take care of your throat. Remember that everything depends upon the next few hours. As for me, perhaps I am getting a little old."

"Oh, la, la!" she laughed. "That's what Sidney says when I tease him. I know I am only the mouse, but I could gnaw through very strong cords. Look!"

Her teeth gleamed white in the moonlight. He swung open the gate.

"Sing your way into the hearts of all these strange people," he bade her, smiling. "Sing the envy and malice away from them. Sing so that they believe that England, after all, is the one desirable country."

"But I am going to sing in French," she pouted.

"Your name," he reminded her, "that is English. 'The little English prima donna,' that is what they will be calling you."

She kissed his hands suddenly as he parted from her and swung off down the hill. Then she stood at the gate, looking down at the glittering lights.

Would they shine as brightly for her, she wondered, in twenty-four hours' time? It was so much to strive for, much to lose, so wonderfully much to gain. Slowly her eyes travelled upwards. The symbolism of those higher lights calmed her fear. She drew a great sigh of happiness.

" Felicia ! "

She turned around with a soft little laugh.

" David ! "

CHAPTER XIX

" TAKE ME AWAY ! "

Richard presented himself the next morning at the Hotel de Paris.

" Cheero ! " he exclaimed, on being shown into Hunterleys' sitting-room. " All right up to date, I see."

Hunterleys nodded. He had just come in from the bank and held his letters in his hand. Richard seated himself on the edge of the table.

" I slept out on the yacht last night," he said. " Got up at six o'clock and had a swim. What about a round of golf at La Turbie? We can get down again by luncheon-time, before the people are about."

" Afraid I can't," Hunterleys replied. " I have rather an important letter to go through carefully, and a reply to think out."

" You're a queer chap, you know," Richard went on. " You always seem to have something on but I'm hanged if I can see how you pass your time here in Monte Carlo. This political business, even if you do have to put in a bit of time at it now and then, can't be going on all the while. Monte Carlo, too! So far as the women are concerned, they might as well be off the face of the earth, and I don't think I've ever seen you make a bet at the tables. How did your wife do last night? I thought she seemed to be dropping it rather."

"I think that she lost," Hunterleys replied indifferently. "Her gambling, however, is like mine, I imagine, on a fairly negligible scale."

Richard whistled softly.

"Well, I don't know," he observed. "I saw her going for maximums yesterday pretty steadily. A few thousands doesn't last very long at that little game."

Hunterleys smiled.

"A few thousands!" he repeated. "I don't suppose Violet has ever lost or won a hundred pounds in her life."

Richard abandoned the subject quickly. He was obliged to tell himself that it was not his business to interfere between husband and wife.

"Say, Hunterleys," he suggested, "do you think I could do something for the crowd on my little boat — a luncheon party or a cruise, eh?"

"I should think every one would enjoy it immensely," Hunterleys answered.

"I can count on you, of course, if I arrange anything?"

"I am afraid not," Hunterleys regretted. "I am too much engrossed now to make any arrangements."

"I'm hanged if you don't get more mysterious every moment!" Richard exclaimed vigorously. "What's it all about? Can't you even be safe in your room for five minutes without keeping one of those little articles under your newspaper while you read your letters?" he added, lifting with his stick the sheet which Hunterleys had hastily thrown over a small revolver. " What's it all about, eh? Are you plotting to dethrone the Prince of Monaco and take his place? "

" Not exactly that," Hunterleys replied, a little wearily. " Lane, old fellow, you're much better off not to know too much. I have told you that there's a kind of international conference going on about here and I've sort of been pitchforked into the affair. Over in your country you don't know much about this sort of thing, but since I've been out of harness I've done a good deal of what really amounts to Secret Service work. One must serve one's country somehow or other, you know, if one gets the chance."

Richard was impressed.

" Gee! " he exclaimed. " The sort of thing that one reads about, eh, and only half believes. Who's the French Johnny who arrived last night? "

" Douaille. He's the coming President, they say. I'm thinking of paying him a visit of ceremony this afternoon."

There was a knock at the door. A waiter entered with a note upon a salver.

" From Madame, monsieur," he announced, presenting it to Hunterleys.

The latter tore it open and read the few lines hastily:

Dear Henry,

If you could spare a few minutes, I should be glad if you would come round to my apartment.

Yours,

VIOLET.

Hunterleys twisted the note up in his fingers.

" Tell Lady Hunterleys that I will be round in a few moments," he instructed the servant.

Richard took up his stick and hat.

" If you have an opportunity," he said, " ask Lady Hunterleys what she thinks about a little party on the yacht. If one could get the proper people together —"

" I'll tell her," Hunterleys promised. " You'd better wait till I get back."

He made his way to the other wing of the hotel. For the first time since he had been staying there, he knocked at the door of his wife's apartments. Her maid admitted him with a smile. He found Violet sitting in the little salon before a writing-table. The apartment was luxuriously furnished and filled with roses. Somehow or other, their odour irritated him. She rose from her place and hastened towards him.

" How nice of you to come so promptly!" she exclaimed. " You're sure it didn't inconvenience you?"

" Not in the least," he replied. " I was only talking to Richard Lane."

" You seem to have taken a great fancy to that young man all at once," she remarked.

Hunterleys was sitting upon the arm of an easy-chair. He had picked up one of Violet's slippers and was balancing it in his hand.

" Oh, I don't know. He is rather refreshing after some of these people. He still has enthusiasms, and his love affair is quite a poem. Aren't you up rather early this morning?"

" I couldn't sleep," she sighed. " I think it has

come to me in the night that I am sick of this place. I wondered —"

She hesitated. He bent the slipper slowly back, waiting for her to proceed.

"The Draconmeyers don't want to go," she went on. "They are here for another month, at least. Linda would miss me terribly, I suppose, but I have really given her a lot of my time. I have spent several hours with her every day since we arrived, and I don't know what it is — perhaps my bad luck, for one thing — but I have suddenly taken a dislike to the place. I wondered —"

She had picked up one of the roses from a vase close at hand, and was twirling it between her fingers. For some reason or other she seemed ill at ease. Hunterleys watched her silently. She was very pale, but since his coming a slight tinge of pink colour had stolen into her cheeks. She had received him in a very fascinating garment of blue silk, which was really only a dressing-gown. It seemed to him a long time since he had seen her in so intimate a fashion.

"I wondered," she concluded at last, almost abruptly, "whether you would care to take me away."

He was, for a moment, bereft of words. Somehow or other, he had been so certain that she had sent to him to ask for more money, that he had never even considered any other eventuality.

"Take you away," he repeated. "Do you really mean take you back to London, Violet?"

"Just anywhere you like," she replied. "I am sick of this place and of everything. I am weary to death of trying to keep Linda cheerful — you don't

realise how depressing it is to be with her; and —
and every one seems to have got a little on my nerves.
Mr. Draconmeyer," she added, a little defiantly, raising her eyes to his, " has been most kind and delightful, but — somehow I want to get away."

He sat down on the edge of a couch. She seated
herself at the further end of it.

"Violet," he said, " you have taken me rather by
surprise."

"Well, you don't mind being taken by surprise
once in a while, do you? " she asked, a little petu-
lantly. "You know I am capricious — you have
told me so often enough. Here is a proof of it.
Take me back to London or to Paris, or wherever you
like."

He was almost overwhelmed. It was unfortunate
that she had chosen that moment to look away and
could not see, therefore, the light which glowed in his
eyes.

"Violet," he assured her earnestly, " there is nothing in the world I should like so much. I would beg
you to have your trunks packed this morning, but
unfortunately I cannot leave Monte Carlo just now."

"Cannot leave Monte Carlo? " she repeated de-
risively. "Why, my dear man, you are a fish out of
water here! You don't gamble, you do nothing but
moon about and go to the Opera and worry about
your silly politics. What on earth do you mean
when you say that you cannot leave Monte Carlo? "

"I mean just what I say," he replied. "I cannot
leave Monte Carlo for several days, at any rate."

She looked at him blankly, a little incredulously.

"You have talked like this before, Henry," she

said, " and it is all too absurd. You must tell me
the truth now. You can have no business here. You
are travelling for pleasure. You can surely leave
a place or not at your own will? "

" It happens," he sighed, " that I cannot. Will
you please be very kind, Violet, and not ask me too
much about this? If there is anything else I can
do," he went on, hesitatingly, " if you will give me
a little more of your time, if you will wait with me
for a few days longer —"

" Can't you understand," she interrupted impatiently, " that it is just this very moment, this instant, that I want to get away? Something has
gone wrong. I want to leave Monte Carlo. I am
not sure that I ever want to see it again. And I
want you to take me. . . . Please! "

She held out her hands, swaying a little towards
him. He gripped them in his. She yielded to their
pressure until their lips almost met.

" You'll take me away this morning? " she whispered.

" I cannot do that," he replied, " but, Violet —"

She snatched herself away from him. An ungov-
ernable fit of fury seemed to have seized her. She
stood in the centre of the room and stamped her
foot.

" You cannot! " she repeated. " And you will not
give me a reason? Very well, I have done my best,
I have made my appeal. I will stay in Monte Carlo,
then. I will —"

There was a knock at the door.

" Come in," she cried. " Who is it? "

The door was softly opened. Draconmeyer stood

upon the threshold. He looked from one to the other in some surprise.

"I am sorry," he murmured. "Please excuse me."

"Come in, Mr. Draconmeyer," she called out to his retreating figure. "Come in, please. How is Linda this morning?"

Draconmeyer smiled a little ruefully as he returned.

"Complaining," he replied, "as usual. I am afraid that she has had rather a bad night. She is going to try and sleep for an hour or two. I came to see if you felt disposed for a motor ride this morning?"

"I should love it," she assented. "I should like to start as soon as possible. Henry was just going, weren't you?" she added, turning to her husband.

He stood his ground.

"There was something else I wished to say," he declared, glancing at Draconmeyer.

The latter moved at once towards the door but Violet stopped him.

"Not now," she begged. "If there is really anything else, Henry, you can send up a note, or I dare say we shall meet at the Club to-night. Now, please, both of you go away. I must change my clothes for motoring. In half an hour, Mr. Draconmeyer."

"The car will be ready," he answered.

Hunterleys hesitated. He looked for a moment at Violet. She returned his glance of appeal with a hard, fixed stare. Then she turned away.

"Susanne," she called to her maid, who was in the inner room, "I am dressing at once. I will show you what to put out."

She disappeared, closing the connecting door behind her. The two men walked out to the lift in silence. Draconmeyer rang the bell.

" You are not leaving Monte Carlo at present, then, Sir Henry? " he remarked.

" Not at present," Hunterleys replied calmly.

They parted without further speech. Hunterleys returned to his room, where Richard was still waiting.

" Say, have you got a valet here with you? " the young man enquired.

Hunterleys shook his head.

" Never possessed such a luxury in my life," he declared.

" Chap came in here directly you were gone — mumbled something about doing something for you. I didn't altogether like the look of him, so I sat on the table and watched. He hung around for a moment, and then, when he saw that I was sticking it out, he went off."

" Was he wearing the hotel livery? " Hunterleys asked quickly.

" Plain black clothes," Richard replied. " He looked the valet, right enough."

Hunterleys rang the bell. It was answered by a servant in grey livery.

" Are you the valet on this floor? " Hunterleys enquired.

" Yes, sir! "

" There was a man in here just now, said he was my valet or something of the sort, hung around for a minute or two and then went away. Who was he? "

The servant shook his head. He was apparently a German, and stupid.

"There are no valets on this floor except myself," he declared.

"Then who could this person have been?" Hunterleys demanded.

"A tailor, perhaps," the man suggested, "but he would not come unless you had ordered him. I have been on duty all the time. I have seen no one about."

"Very well," Hunterleys said, "I'll report the matter in the office."

"Some hotel thief, I suppose," Lane remarked, as soon as the door was closed. "He didn't look like it exactly, though."

Hunterleys frowned.

"Not much here to satisfy any one's curiosity," he observed. "Just as well you were in the room, though."

"Surrounded by mysteries, aren't you, old chap?" Richard yawned, lighting a cigarette.

"I don't know exactly about that," Hunterleys replied, "but I'll tell you one thing, Lane. There are things going on in Monte Carlo at the present moment which would bring out the black headlines on the halfpenny papers if they had an inkling of them. There are people here who are trying to draw up a new map of Europe, a new map of the world."

Richard shook his head.

"I can't get interested in anything, Hunterleys," he declared. "You could tell me the most amazing things in the world and they'd pass in at one ear and out at the other. Kind of a blithering idiot, eh? You know what I did last night after dinner.

If you'll believe me, when I got to the villa, I found the place patrolled as though they were afraid of dynamiters. I skulked round to the back, got on the beach, and climbed a little way up towards the rock garden. I hid there and waited to see if she'd come out on the terrace. She never came, but I caught a glimpse of her passing from one room to another, and I tell you I'm such a poor sort of an idiot that I felt repaid for waiting there all that time. I shall go there again to-night. The boys wanted me to dine — Eddy Lanchester and Montressor and that lot — a jolly party, too. I sha'n't do it. I shall have a mouthful alone somewhere and spend the rest of the evening on those rocks. Something's got to come of this, Hunterleys."

"Let's go into the lounge for a few moments," Hunterleys suggested. "I may as well hear all about it."

They made their way downstairs, and sat there talking, or rather Hunterleys listened while Richard talked. Then Draconmeyer strolled across the hall and waited by the lift. Presently he returned with Violet by his side, followed by her maid, carrying rugs. As they approached, Hunterleys rose slowly to his feet. Violet was looking up into her companion's face, talking and laughing. She either did not see Hunterleys, or affected not to. He stood, for a moment, irresolute. Then, as she passed, she glanced at him quite blankly and waved her hand to Richard. The two disappeared. Hunterleys resumed his seat. He had, somehow or other, the depressing feeling of a man who has lost a great opportunity.

"Lady Hunterleys looks well this morning," Lane

remarked, absolutely unconscious of anything un-usual.

Hunterleys watched the car drive off before he answered.

"She looks very well," he assented gloomily.

CHAPTER XX

They had skirted the wonderful bay and climbed the mountainous hill to the frontier before Violet spoke. All the time Draconmeyer leaned back by her side, perfectly content. A man of varied subtleties, he understood and fully appreciated the intrinsic value of silence. Whilst the Customs officer, however, was making out the deposit note for the car, she turned to him.

" Will you tell me something, Mr. Draconmeyer? "

" Of course! "

" It is about my husband," she went on. " Henry isn't your friend — you dislike one another, I know. You men seem to have a sort of freemasonry which compels you to tell falsehoods about one another, but in this case I am going to remind you that I have the greater claim, and I am going to ask you for the sober truth. Henry has once or twice, during the last few days, hinted to me that his presence in Monte Carlo just now has some sort of political significance. He is very vague about it all, but he evidently wants me to believe that he is staying here against his own inclinations. Now I want to ask you a plain question. Is it likely that he could have any business whatever to transact for the Government in Monte Carlo? What I mean is, could there possibly be anything to keep him in this place which for political reasons he couldn't tell me about?"

"I can answer your question finally so far as regards any Government business," Mr. Draconmeyer assured her. "Your husband's Party is in Opposition. As a keen politician, he would not be likely to interest himself in the work of his rival."

"You are quite sure," she persisted, "you are quite sure that he could not have a mission of any sort? — that there isn't any meeting of diplomatists here in which he might be interested?"

Mr. Draconmeyer smiled with the air of one listening to a child's prattle.

"If I were not sure that you are in earnest — !" he began. "However, I will just answer your question. Nothing of the sort is possible. Besides, people don't come to Monte Carlo for serious affairs, you know."

Her face hardened a little.

"I suppose," she said, "that you are quite sure of what you told me the other evening about this young singer — Felicia Roche?"

"I should not allude to a matter of that sort," he declared, "unless I had satisfied myself as to the facts. It is true that I owe nothing to your husband and everything to you, or I should have probably remained silent. As it is, all that I know is at your service. Felicia Roche is to make her début at the Opera House to-night. Your husband has been seen with her repeatedly. He was at her villa at one o'clock this morning. I have heard it said that he is a little infatuated."

"Thank you," she murmured, "that is quite enough."

The formalities were concluded and the car drove on. They paused at the last turn to gaze downward at the wonderful view — the gorgeous Bay of Mentone, a thousand feet below, with its wealth of mimosa-embosomed villas; Monte Carlo glittering on the seaboard; the sweep of Monaco, red-roofed, picturesque. And behind, the mountains, further away still, the dim, snow-capped heights. Violet looked, as she was bidden, but her eyes seemed incapable of appreciation. When the car moved on, she leaned back in her seat and dropped her veil. She was paler even than when they had started.

"I am going to talk to you very little," he said gravely. "I want you just to rest and breathe this wonderful air. If my reply to your question troubles you, I am sorry, but you had to know it some day. It is a wrench, of course, but you must have guessed it. Your husband is a man of peculiar temperament, but no man could have refused such an offer as you made him, unless there had been some special reason for it — no man in the world."

There was a little tremble in his tone, artistic and not overdone. Somehow, she felt that his admiration ministered to her self-respect. She permitted his hand to remain upon hers. The touch of her fingers very nearly brought the torrent from his lips. He crushed the words down, however. It was too great a risk. Very soon things would be different; he could afford to wait.

They drove on to San Remo and turned into the hotel.

"You are better away from Monte Carlo for a few hours," he decided. "We will lunch here and drive back afterwards. You will feel greatly refreshed."

She accepted his suggestion without enthusiasm and with very little show of pleasure. They found a table on the terrace in a retired corner, surrounded with flowering cactus plants and drooping mimosa, and overhung by a giant oleander tree. He talked to her easily but in gossiping fashion only, and always with the greatest respect. It was not until the arrival of their coffee that he ventured to become at all personal.

"Will you forgive me if I talk without reserve for a few moments?" he began, leaning a little towards her. "You have your troubles, I know. May I not remind you that you are not alone in your sorrows? Linda, as you know, has no companionship whatever to offer. She does nothing but indulge in fretful regrets over her broken health. When I remember, too, how lonely your days are, and think of your husband and what he might make of them, then I cannot help realising with absolute vividness the supreme irony of fate. Here am I, craving for nothing so much on earth as the sympathy, the affection of — shall I say such a woman as you? And your husband, who might have the best, remains utterly indifferent, content with something far below the second best. And there is so much in life, too," he went on, regretfully. "I cannot tell you how difficult it is for me to sit still and see you worried about such a trifle as money. Fancy the joy of giving you money!"

She awoke a little from her lethargy. She looked at him, startled.

"You haven't told me yet," he added, "how the game went last night?"

"I lost every penny of that thousand pounds," she declared. "That is why I sent for my husband this morning and asked him to take me back to England. I am getting afraid of the place. My luck seems to have gone for ever."

He laughed softly.

"That doesn't sound like you," he observed. "Besides, what does it matter? Write me out some more cheques when we get back. Date them this year or next, or the year after — it really doesn't matter a bit. My fortune is at your disposal. If it amuses you to lose a thousand pounds in the afternoon, and twice as much at night, pray do."

She laughed at him. There was a certain glamour about his words which appealed to her fancy.

"Why, you talk like a prince," she murmured, "and yet you know how impossible it is."

"Is it?" he asked quietly.

She rose abruptly from her place. There was something wrong — she felt it in the atmosphere — something that was almost choking her.

"Let us go back," she insisted.

He ordered the car without another word and they started off homewards. It was not until they were nearing Monte Carlo that he spoke of anything save the slightest topics.

"You must have a little more money," he told her, in a matter-of-fact tone. "That is a necessity. There is no need to worry your husband. I shall

go and bring you a thousand pounds. You can give
me the cheques later."

She sat looking steadfastly ahead of her. She
seemed to see her numbers spread out before her, to
hear the click of the ball, the croupier's voice, the
thrill of victory.

" I have taken more money from you than I meant
to, already, Mr. Draconmeyer," she protested.
" Does Linda know how much you have lent me? "

He shrugged his shoulders.

" What is the use of telling her? She does not
understand. She has never felt the gambling fever,
the joy of it, the excitement. She would not be
strong enough. You and I understand. I have felt
it in the money-markets of the world, where one plays
with millions, where a mistake might mean ruin.
That is why the tables seem dull for me, but all the
same it comes home to me."

She felt the fierce stimulus of anxious thought.
She knew very well that notwithstanding his quiet
manner, she had reason to fear the man who sat by
her side. She feared his self-restraint, she feared
the light which sometimes gleamed in his eyes when
he fancied himself unobserved. He gave her no cause
for complaint. All the time his behaviour had been
irreproachable. And yet she felt, somehow or other,
like a bird who is being hunted by a trapper, a trapper who knows his business, who goes about it with
quiet confidence, with absolute certainty. There
was something like despair in her heart.

" Well, I suppose I shall have to stay here," she
said, " and I can't stay here without playing. I will
take a thousand more, if you will lend it to me."

"You shall have it directly we get to the hotel," he told her. "Don't hurry with the cheques, and don't date them too soon. Remember that you must have something to live on when you get back."

"I am going to win," she declared confidently. "I am going to win enough to pay you back every penny."

"I won't say that I hope not," he observed, "for your sake, but it will certainly give me no pleasure to have the money back again. You are such a wonderful person," he added, dropping his voice, "that I rather like to feel that I can be a little useful to you."

They had neared the end of their journey and Mr. Draconmeyer touched her arm. A faint smile was playing about his lips. Certainly the fates were befriending him! He said nothing, but her eyes followed the slight motion of his head. Coming down the steps from Ciro's were her husband and Felicia Roche. Violet looked at them for a moment. Then she turned her head away.

"Most inopportune," she sighed, with a little attempt at gaiety. "Shall we meet later at the Club?"

"Assuredly," Mr. Draconmeyer replied. "I will send the money to your room."

"Thank you once more," she said, "and thank you, too, for my drive. I have enjoyed it very much. I am very glad indeed that I had the courage to make you tell me the truth."

"I hope," he whispered, as he handed her out, "that you will never lack the courage to ask me anything."

CHAPTER XXI

ASSASSINATION!

Selingman, a large cigar between his lips and a happy smile upon his face, stood in the square before the Casino, watching the pigeons. He had just enjoyed an excellent lunch, he was exceedingly pleased with a new light grey suit which he was wearing, and his one unsatisfied desire was for companionship. Draconmeyer was away motoring with Lady Hunterleys, Mr. Grex was spending the early part of the day in conclave with their visitor from France, and Mademoiselle Nipon had gone to Nice for the day. Selingman had been left to his own devices and was beginning to find time hang upon his hands. Conversation and companionship were almost as great necessities with him as wine. He beamed upon the pigeons and looked around at the people dotted about in chairs outside the Café de Paris, hoping to find an acquaintance. It chanced, however, that he saw nothing but strangers. Then his eyes fell upon a man who was seated with folded arms a short distance away, a man of respectable but somewhat gloomy appearance, dressed in dark clothes, with pale cheeks and cavernous eyes. Selingman strolled towards him.

"How go things, friend Allen?" he enquired, dropping his voice a little.

The man glanced uneasily around. There was, however, no one in his immediate vicinity.

" Badly," he admitted.

" Still no success, eh? " Selingman asked, drawing up a chair and seating himself.

" The man is secretive by nature," was the gloomy reply. " One would imagine that he knew he was being watched. Everything which he receives in the way of a written communication is at once torn up. He is the most difficult order of person to deal with — he is methodical. He has only the hotel valet to look after his things but everything is always in its place. Yesterday I went through his waste-paper basket. I took home the contents but the pieces were no larger than sixpences. I was able to put together one envelope which he received yesterday morning, which was franked ' On His Majesty's Service,' and the post-mark of which was Downing Street."

Selingman shook his head ponderously and then replied seriously:

" You must do better than that, my Sherlock Holmes — much better."

" I can't make bricks without straw," Allen retorted sullenly.

" There is always straw if one looks in the right place," Selingman insisted, puffing away at his cigar. " What we want to discover is, exactly how much does Hunterleys know of certain operations of ours which are going on here? He is on the watch — that I am sure of. There is one known agent in the place, and another suspected one, and I am pretty certain that they are both working at his instigation.

What we want to get hold of is one of his letters to London."

" I have been in and out of his rooms at all hours," the other said. " I have gone into the matter thoroughly, so thoroughly that I have taken a situation with a firm of English tailors here, and I am supposed to go out and tout for orders. That gives me a free entrée to the hotel. I have even had a commission from Sir Henry himself. He gave me a coat to get some buttons sewn on. I am practically free of his room but what's the good? He doesn't even lead the Monte Carlo life. He doesn't give one a chance of getting at him through a third person. No notes from ladies, no flower or jewelry bills, not the shadow of an assignation. The only photograph upon his table is a photograph of Lady Hunterleys."

" Better not tell our friend Draconmeyer that," Selingman observed, smiling to himself. " Well, well, you can do nothing but persevere, Allen. We are not niggardly masters. If a man fails through no fault of his own, well, we don't throw him into the street. Nothing parsimonious about us. No need for you to sit about with a face as long as a fiddle because you can't succeed all at once. We are the people to kick at it, not you. Drink a little more wine, my friend. Give yourself a liqueur after luncheon. Stick a cigar in your mouth and go and sit in the sunshine. Make friends with some of the ladies. Remember, the sun will still shine and the music play in fifty years' time, but not for you. Come and see me when you want some more money."

" You are very kind, sir," the man replied. " I am going across to the hotel now. Sir Henry has been about there most of the morning but he has just gone in to Ciro's to lunch, so I shall have at least half-an-hour."

" Good luck to you! " Selingman exclaimed heartily. " Who knows but that the big things may come, even this afternoon? Cheer up, and try and make yourself believe that a letter may be lying on the table, a letter he forgot to post, or one sent round from the bank since he left. I am hopeful for you this afternoon, Allen. I believe you are going to do well. Come up and see me afterwards, if you will. I am going to my hotel to lie down for half-an-hour. I am not really tired but I have no friend here to talk with or anything to do, and it is a wise economy of the human frame. To-night, mademoiselle will have returned. Just now every one has deserted me. I will rest until six o'clock. Au revoir, friend Allen! Au revoir! "

Selingman climbed the hill and entered the hotel where he was staying. He mounted to his room, took off his coat, at which he glanced admiringly for a moment and then hung up behind the door. Finally he pulled down the blinds and lay down to rest. Very soon he was asleep. . . .

The drowsy afternoon wore on. Through the open windows came the sound of carriages driven along the dusty way, the shouts of the coachmen to their horses, the jingling of bells, the hooting of motor horns. A lime tree, whose leaves were stirred by the languorous breeze, kept tapping against the window. From a further distance came the faint, muffled voices of promenaders, and the echo of the guns from the Tir du Pigeons. But through it all,

Selingman, lying on his back and snoring loudly, slept. He was awakened at last by the feeling that some one had entered the room. He sat up and blinked.

"Hullo!" he exclaimed.

A man in the weird disguise of a motor-cyclist was standing at the foot of the bed. Selingman continued to blink. He was not wholly awake and his visitor's appearance was unpleasant.

"Who the devil are you?" he enquired.

The visitor took off his disfiguring spectacles.

"Jean Coulois — behold!" was the soft reply.

Selingman raised himself and slid off the bed. It had seemed rather like a dream. He was wide-awake now, however.

"What do you want?" he asked. "What are you here for?"

Jean Coulois said nothing. Then very slowly from the inside pocket of his coat he drew a newspaper parcel. It was long and narrow, and in places there was a stain upon the paper. Selingman stared at it and stared back at Jean Coulois.

"What the mischief have you got there?" he demanded.

Coulois touched the parcel with his yellow forefinger. Selingman saw then that the stains were of blood.

"Give me a towel," his visitor directed. "I do not want this upon my clothes."

Selingman took a towel from the stand and threw it across the room.

"You mean," he asked, dropping his voice a little, "that it is finished?"

"A quarter of an hour ago," Jean Coulois answered triumphantly. "He had just come in from luncheon and was sitting at his writing-table. It was cleverly done — wonderfully. It was all over in a moment — not a cry. You came to the right place, indeed! And now I go to the country," Coulois continued. "I have a motor-bicycle outside. I make my way up into the hills to bury this little memento. There is a farmhouse up in the mountains, a lonely spot enough, and a girl there who says what I tell her. It may be as well to be able to say that I have been there for déjeuner. These little things, monsieur — ah, well! we who understand think of them. And since I am here," he added, holding out his hand —

Selingman nodded and took out his pocket-book. He counted out the notes in silence and passed them over. The assassin dropped them into his pocket.

"Au revoir, Monsieur le Gros!" he exclaimed, waving his hand. "We meet to-night, I trust. I will show you a new dance — the Dance of Death, I shall call it. I seem calm, but I am on fire with excitement. To-night I shall dance as though quicksilver were in my feet. You must not miss it. You must come, monsieur."

He closed the door behind him and swaggered off down the passage. Selingman stood, for a moment, perfectly still. It was a strange thing, but two big tears were in his eyes. Then he heaved a great sigh and shook his head.

"It is part of the game," he said softly to himself, "all part of the game."

CHAPTER XXII

THE WRONG MAN

Selingman came out into the sunlit streets very much as a man who leaves a dark and shrouded room. The shock of tragedy was still upon him. There was a little choke in his throat as he mingled with the careless, pleasure-loving throng, mostly wending their way now towards the Rooms or the Terrace. As he crossed the square towards the Hotel de Paris, his steps grew slower and slower. He looked at the building half-fearfully. Beautifully dressed women, men of every nationality, were passing in and out all the time. The commissionaire, with his little group of satellites, stood sunning himself on the lowest step, a splendid, complacent figure. There was no sign there of the horror that was hidden within. Even while he looked up at the windows he felt a hand upon his arm. Draconmeyer had caught him up and had fallen into step with him.

"Well, dear philosopher," he exclaimed, "why this subdued aspect? Has your solitary day depressed you?"

Selingman turned slowly around. Draconmeyer's eyes beneath his gold-rimmed spectacles were bright. He was carrying himself with less than his usual stoop, he wore a red carnation in his buttonhole.

He was in spirits which for him were almost boister-
ous.

" Have you been in there? " Selingman asked, in a
low tone.

Draconmeyer glanced at the hotel and back again
at his companion.

" In where? " he demanded. " In the hotel? I
left Lady Hunterleys there a short time ago. I have
been up to the bank since."

" You don't know yet, then? "

" Know what? "

There was a momentary silence. Draconmeyer
suddenly gripped his companion by the arm.

" Go on," he insisted. " Tell me? "

" It's all over! " Selingman exclaimed hoarsely.
" Jean Coulois came to me a quarter of an hour ago.
It is finished. Damnation, Draconmeyer, let go my
arm! "

Draconmeyer withdrew his fingers. There was no
longer any stoop about him at all. He stood tall
and straight, his lips parted, his face turned upwards, upwards as though he would gaze over the
roof of the hotel before which they were standing,
up to the skies.

" My God, Selingman! " he cried. " My God! "

The seconds passed. Then Draconmeyer suddenly took his companion by the arm.

" Come," he said, " let us take that first seat in the
gardens there. Let us talk. Somehow or other, although I half counted upon this, I scarcely believed.
. . . Let us sit down. Do you think it is known
yet? "

" Very likely not," Selingman answered, as they

crossed the road and entered the gardens. "Coulois found him in his rooms, seated at the writing-table. It was all over, he declares, in ten seconds. He came to me — with the knife. He was on his way to the mountains to hide it."

They found a seat under a drooping lime tree. They could still see the hotel and the level stretch of road that led past the post-office and the Club to Monaco. Draconmeyer sat with his eyes fixed upon the hotel, through which streams of people were still passing. One of the under-managers was welcoming the newcomers from a recently arrived train.

"You are right," he murmured. "Nothing is known yet. Very likely they will not know until the valet goes to lay out his clothes for dinner. . . . Dead!"

Selingman, with one hand gripping the iron arm of the seat, watched his companion's face with a sort of fascinated curiosity. There were beads of perspiration upon Draconmeyer's forehead, but his expression, in its way, was curious. There was no horror in his face, no fear, no shadow of remorse. Some wholly different sentiment seemed to have transformed the man. He was younger, more virile. He seemed as though he could scarcely sit still.

"My friend," Selingman said, "I know that you are one of our children, that you are one of those who have seen the truth and worked steadfastly for the great cause with the heart of a patriot and the unswerving fidelity of a strong man. But tell me the honest truth. There is something else in your life — you have some other feeling about this man Hunterleys' death?"

Draconmeyer removed his eyes from the front of
the hotel and turned slowly towards his companion.
There was a transfiguring smile upon his lips.
Again he gave Selingman the impression of complete
rejuvenation, of an elderly man suddenly transformed into something young and vigorous.

"There is something else, Selingman," he confessed. "This is the moment when I dare speak of
it. I will tell you first of any living person. There
is a woman over there whom I have set up as an idol,
and before whose shrine I have worshipped. There
is a woman over there who has turned the dull paths
of my life into a flowery way. I am a patriot, and I
have worked for my country, Selingman, as you have
worked. But I have worked, also, that I might
taste for once before I die the great passion. Don't
stare at me, man! Remember I am not like you.
You can laugh your way through the world, with a
kiss here and a bow there, a ribbon to your lips at
night, thrown to the winds in the morning. I
haven't that sort of philosophy. Love doesn't come
to me like that. It's set in my heart amongst the
great things. It's set there side by side with the
greatest of all."

"His wife!" Selingman muttered.

"Are you so colossal a fool as only to have guessed
it at this moment?" Draconmeyer continued contemptuously. "If he hadn't blundered across our
path here, if he hadn't been my political enemy, I
should still some day have taken him by the throat
and killed him. You don't know what risks I have
been running," he went on, with a sudden hoarseness.
"In her heart she half loves him still. If he hadn't

been a fool, a prejudiced, over-conscientious, stiff-
necked fool, I should have lost her within the last
twenty-four hours. I have had to fight and scheme
as I have never fought and schemed before, to keep
them apart. I have had to pick my way through
shoals innumerable, hold myself down when I have
been burning to grip her by the wrists and tell
her that all that a man could offer a woman was
hers. Selingman, this sounds like nonsense, I suppose."

"No," Selingman murmured, "not nonsense, but
it doesn't sound like Draconmeyer."

"Well, it's finished," Draconmeyer declared, with
a great sigh of content. "You know now. I enter
upon the final stage. I had only one fear. Jean
Coulois has settled that for me. I wonder whether
they know. It seems peaceful enough. No! Look
over there," he added, gripping his companion's arm.
"Peter, the concierge, is whispering with the others.
That is one of the managers there, out on the pavement, talking to them."

Selingman pointed down the road towards Monaco.

"See!" he exclaimed. "There is a motor-car
coming in a hurry. I fancy that the alarm must
have been given."

A grey, heavily-built car came along at a great
pace and swung round in front of the Hotel de Paris.
The two men stood on the pavement and watched.
A tall, official-looking person, with black, upturned
moustache, in somber uniform and a peaked cap, descended.

"The Commissioner of Police," Selingman whispered, " and that is a doctor who has just gone in. He has been found! "

They crossed the road to the hotel. The concierge removed his hat as they turned to enter. To all appearances he was unchanged — fat, florid, splendid. Draconmeyer stepped close to him.

" Has anything happened here, Peter? " he asked. " I saw the Commissioner of Police arrive in a great hurry."

The man hesitated. It was obvious then that he was disturbed. He looked to the right and to the left. Finally, with a sigh of resignation, he seemed to make up his mind to tell the truth.

" It is the English gentleman, Sir Henry Hunterleys," he whispered. " He has been found stabbed to death in his room."

" Dead? " Draconmeyer demanded, insistently.

" Stone dead, sir," the concierge replied. " He was stabbed by some one who stole in through the bathroom — they say that he couldn't ever have moved again. The Commissioner of Police is upstairs. The ambulance is round at the back to take him off to the Mortuary."

Selingman suddenly seized the man by the arm. His eyes were fixed upon the topmost step. Violet stood there, smiling down upon them. She was wearing a black and white gown, and a black hat with white ospreys. It was the hour of five o'clock tea and many people were passing in and out. She came gracefully down the steps. The two men remained speechless.

" I have been waiting for you, Mr. Draconmeyer," she remarked, smiling.

Draconmeyer remembered suddenly the packet of notes which he had been to fetch from the bank. He tried to speak but only faltered. Selingman had removed his hat but he, too, seemed incapable of coherent speech. She looked at them both, astonished.

" Whatever is the matter with you both? " she exclaimed. " Who is coming with me to the Club? I decided to come this way round to see if I could change my luck. That underground passage depresses me."

Draconmeyer moved up a couple of steps. He was quite himself now, grave but solicitous.

" Lady Hunterleys," he said, " I am sorry, but there has been a little accident. I am afraid that your husband has been hurt. If you will come back to your room for a minute I will tell you about it."

All the colour died slowly from her face. She swayed a little, but when Draconmeyer would have supported her she pushed him away.

" An accident? " she muttered. " I must go and see for myself."

She turned and re-entered the hotel swiftly. Draconmeyer caught her up in the hall.

" Lady Hunterleys," he begged earnestly, " please take my advice. I am your friend, you know. I want you to go straight to your room. I will come with you. I will explain to you then —"

" I am going to Henry," she interrupted, without even a glance towards him. " I am going to my husband at once. I must see what has happened."

She rang the bell for the lift, which appeared almost immediately. Draconmeyer stepped in with her.

"Lady Hunterleys," he persisted, "I beg of you to do as I ask. Let me take you to your rooms. I will tell you all that has happened. Your husband will not be able to see you or speak with you."

"I shall not get out," she declared, when the lift boy, in obedience to Draconmeyer's imperative order, stopped at her floor. "If I may not go on in the lift, I shall walk up the stairs. I am going to my husband."

"He will not recognise you," Draconmeyer warned her. "I am very sorry indeed, Lady Hunterleys — I would spare you this shock if I could — but you must be prepared for very serious things."

They had reached the next floor now. The boy opened the gate of the lift and she stepped out. She looked pitifully at Draconmeyer.

"You aren't going to tell me that he is dead?" she moaned.

"I am afraid he is," Draconmeyer assented.

She staggered across the landing, pushing him away from her. There were four or five people standing outside the door of Hunterleys' apartment. She appealed to them.

"Let me go in at once," she ordered. "I am Lady Hunterleys."

"The door is locked," one of the men declared.

"Let me go in," she insisted.

She pushed them on one side and hammered at the door. They could hear voices inside. In a moment it was opened. It was the Commissioner of the Police who stood there — tall, severe, official.

" Madame? " he exclaimed.

" I am his wife! " she cried. " Let me in — let me in at once! "

She forced her way into the room. Something was lying on the bed, covered with a sheet. She looked at it and shrieked.

" Madame," the Commissioner begged, " pray compose yourself. A tragedy has happened in this room — but we are not sure. Can you be brave, madame? "

" I can," she answered. " Of what are you not sure? "

The Commissioner turned down the sheet a few inches. A man's face was visible, a ghastly sight. She looked at it and shrieked hysterically.

" Is that your husband, madame? " the Commissioner asked quickly.

" Thank God, no! " she cried. " You are sure this is the man? " she went on, her voice shaking with fierce excitement. " There is no one else — hurt? No one else stabbed? This is the man they told me was my husband? "

" He was found there, sitting at your husband's table, madame," the Commissioner of Police assured her. " There is no one else."

She suddenly began to cry.

" It isn't Henry! " she sobbed, groping her way from the room. " Take me downstairs, please, some one."

CHAPTER XXIII

TROUBLE BREWING

The maître d'hôtel had presented his bill. The little luncheon party was almost over.

" So I take leave," Hunterleys remarked, as he sat down his empty liqueur glass, " of one of my responsibilities in life."

" I think I'd like to remain a sort of half ward, please," Felicia objected, " in case David doesn't treat me properly."

" If he doesn't," Hunterleys declared, " he will have me to answer to. Seriously, I think you young people are very wise and very foolish and very much to be envied. What does Sidney say about it? "

Felicia made a little grimace. She glanced around but the tables near them were unoccupied.

" Sidney is much too engrossed in his mysterious work to concern himself very much about anything," she replied. " Do you know that he has been out all night two nights this week already, and he is making no end of preparations for to-day? "

Hunterleys nodded.

" I know that he is very busy just now," he assented gravely. " I must come up and talk to him this afternoon."

" We left him writing," Felicia said. " Of course, he declares that it is for his beloved newspaper, but I am not sure. He scarcely ever goes out in the day-time. What can he have to write about? David's work is strenuous enough, and I have told him that if he turns war correspondent again, I shall break it off."

"We all have our work to do in life," Hunterleys reminded her. "You have to sing in *Aïda* to-night, and you have to do yourself justice for the sake of a great many people. Your brother has his work to do, also. Whatever the nature of it may be, he has taken it up and he must go through with it. It would be of no use his worrying for fear that you should forget your words or your notes to-night, and there is no purpose in your fretting because there may be danger in what he has to do. I prom-ise you that so far as I can prevent it, he shall take no unnecessary risks. Now, if you like, I will walk home with you young people, if I sha'n't be terribly in the way. I know that Sidney wants to see me."

They left the restaurant, a few minutes later, and strolled up towards the town. Hunterleys paused outside a jeweler's shop.

"And now for the important business of the day!" he declared. "I must buy you an engage-ment present, on behalf of myself and all your guardians. Come in and help me choose, both of you. A girl who carries her gloves in her hand to show her engagement ring, should have a better bag to hang from that little finger."

"You really are the most perfect person that ever breathed!" she sighed. "You know I don't deserve anything of the sort."

They paid their visit to the jeweler and afterwards

drove up to the villa in a little victoria. Sidney Roche was hard at work in his shirt-sleeves. He greeted Hunterleys warmly.

" Glad you've come up! " he exclaimed. " The little girl's told you the news, I suppose? "

" Rather! " Hunterleys replied. " I have been lunching with them on the strength of it."

" And look! " Felicia cried, holding out the gold bag which hung from her finger. " Look how I am being spoiled."

Her brother sighed.

" Awful nuisance for me," he grumbled, " having to live with an engaged couple. .You couldn't clear out for a little time," he suggested, " both of you? I want to talk to Hunterleys."

" We'll go and sit in the garden," Felicia assented. " I suppose I ought to rest. David shall read my score to me."

They passed out and Roche closed the door behind them carefully.

" Anything fresh? " Hunterleys asked.

" Nothing particular," was the somewhat guarded reply. " That fellow Frenhofer has been up here."

" Frenhofer? " Hunterleys repeated, interrogatively.

" He is the only man I can rely upon at the Villa Mimosa," Roche explained. " I am afraid to-night it's going to be rather a difficult job."

" I always feared it would be," Hunterleys agreed.

" Frenhofer tells me," Roche continued, " that for some reason or other their suspicions have been aroused up there. They are all on edge. You know, the house is cram-full of men-servants and there are to be a dozen of them on duty in the grounds. Two or three of these fellows are nothing more or less than private detectives, and they all of them know what they're about or Grex wouldn't have them."

Hunterleys looked grave.

" It sounds awkward," he admitted.

" The general idea of the plot," Roche went on, walking restlessly up and down the room, " you and I have already solved, and by this time they know it in London. But there are two things which I feel they may discuss to-night, which are of vital importance. The first is the date, the second is the terms of the offer to Douaille. Then, of course, more important, perhaps, than either of these, is the matter of Douaille's general attitude towards the scheme."

" So far," Hunterleys remarked reflectively, " we haven't the slightest indication of what that may be. Douaille came pledged to nothing. He may, after all, stand firm."

" For the honour of his country, let us hope so," Roche said solemnly. " Yet I am sure of one thing. They are going to make him a wonderful offer. He may find himself confronted with a problem which some of the greatest statesmen in the world have had to face in their time — shall he study the material benefit of his country, or shall he stand firm for her honour? "

" It's a great ethical question," Hunterleys declared, " too great for us to discuss now, Sidney. Tell me, do you really mean to go on with this attempt of yours to-night? "

" I must," Roche replied. " Frenhofer wants me

to give up the roof idea, but there is nothing else worth trying. He brought a fresh plan of the room with him. There it lies on the table. As you see, the apartment where the meeting will take place is almost isolated from the rest of the house. There is only one approach to it, by a corridor leading from the hall. The east and west sides will be patrolled. On the south there is a little terrace, but the approach to it is absolutely impossible. There is a sheer drop of fifty feet on to the beach."

" You think they have no suspicion about the roof? " Hunterleys asked doubtfully.

" Not yet. The pane of glass is cut out and my entrance to the house is arranged for. Frenhofer will tamper with the electric lights in the kitchen premises and I shall arrive in response to his telephonic message, in the clothes of a working-man and with a bag of tools. Then he smuggles me on to the spiral stairway which leads out on to the roof where the flag-staff is. I can crawl the rest of the way to my place. The trouble is that notwithstanding the ledge around, if it is a perfectly clear night, just a fraction of my body, however flat I lie, might be seen from the ground."

Hunterleys studied the plan for a moment and shook his head.

" It's a terrible risk, this, Roche," he said seriously.

" I know it," the other admitted, " but what am I to do? They keep sending me cipher messages from home to spare no effort to send further news, as you know very well, and two other fellows will be here the day after to-morrow, to relieve me. I must do what I can. There's one thing, Felicia's off my mind now. Briston's a good fellow and he'll look after her."

"In the event of your capture —" Hunterleys began.

"The tools I shall take with me," Roche interrupted, "are common housebreaker's tools. Every shred of clothing I shall be wearing will be in keeping, the ordinary garments of an *ouvrier* of the district. If I am trapped, it will be as a burglar and not as a spy. Of course, if Douaille opens the proceedings by declaring himself against the scheme, I shall make myself scarce as quickly as I can."

"You were quite right when you said just now," Hunterleys observed, "that Douaille will find himself in a difficult position. There is no doubt but that he is an honest man. On the other hand, it is a political axiom that the first duty of any statesman is to his own people. If they can make Douaille believe that he is going to restore her lost provinces to France without the shedding of a drop of French blood, simply at England's expense, he will be confronted with a problem over which any man might hesitate. He has had all day to think it over. What he may decide is simply on the knees of the gods."

Roche sealed up the letter he had been writing, and handed it to Hunterleys.

"Well," he said, "I have left everything in order. If there's any mysterious disappearance from here, it will be the mysterious disappearance of a newspaper correspondent, and nothing else."

"Good luck, then, old chap!" Hunterleys wished

him. "If you pull through this time, I think our job will be done. I'll tell them at headquarters that you deserve a year's holiday."

Roche smiled a little queerly.

"Don't forget," he pointed out, "that it was you who scented out the whole plot. I've simply done the Scotland Yard work. The worst of our job is," he added, as he opened the door, "that we don't want holidays. We are like drugged beings. The thing gets hold of us. I suppose if they gave me a holiday I should spend it in St. Petersburg. That's where we ought to send our best men just now. So long, Sir Henry."

They shook hands once more. Roche's face was set in grim lines. They were both silent for a moment. It was the farewell of men whose eyes are fixed upon the great things.

"Good luck to you!" Hunterleys repeated fervently, as he turned and walked down the tiled way.

CHAPTER XXIV

HUNTERLEYS SCENTS MURDER

The concierge of the Hotel de Paris was a man of great stature and imposing appearance. Nevertheless, when Hunterleys crossed the road and climbed the steps to the hotel, he seemed for a moment like a man reduced to pulp. He absolutely forgot his usual dignified but courteous greeting. With mouth a little open and knees which seemed to have collapsed, he stared at this unexpected apparition as he came into sight and stared at him as he entered the hotel. Hunterleys glanced behind with a slight frown. The incident, inexplicable though it was, would have passed at once from his memory, but that directly he entered the hotel he was conscious of the very similar behaviour and attitude towards him of the chief reception clerk. He paused on his way, a little bewildered, and called the man to him. The clerk, however, was already rushing towards the office with his coat-tails flying behind him. Hunterleys crossed the floor and rang the bell for the lift. Directly he stepped in, the lift man vacated his place, and with his eyes nearly starting out of his head, seemed about to make a rush for his life.

" Come back here," Hunterleys ordered sternly. " Take me up to my room at once."

The man returned unsteadily and with marked reluctance. He closed the gate, touched the handle and the lift commenced to ascend.

"What's the matter with you all here?" Hunterleys demanded, irritably. "Is there anything wrong with my appearance? Has anything happened?"

The man made a gesture but said absolutely nothing. The lift had stopped. He pushed open the door.

"Monsieur's floor," he faltered.

Hunterleys stepped out and made his way towards his room. Arrived there, he was brought to a sudden standstill. A gendarme was stationed outside.

"What the mischief are you doing here?" Hunterleys demanded.

The man saluted.

"By orders of the Director of Police, monsieur."

"But that is my room," Hunterleys protested. "I wish to enter."

"No one is permitted to enter, monsieur," the man replied.

Hunterleys stared blankly at the gendarme.

"Can't you tell me at least what has happened?" he persisted. "I am Sir Henry Hunterleys. That is my apartment. Why do I find it locked against me?"

"By order of the Director of the Police, monsieur," was the parrot-like reply.

Hunterleys turned away impatiently. At that moment the reception clerk who downstairs had fled at his approach, returned, bringing with him the manager of the hotel. Hunterleys welcomed the latter with an air of relief.

"Monsieur Picard," he exclaimed, "what on earth

is the meaning of this? Why do I find my room
closed and this gendarme outside? "

Monsieur Picard was a tall man, black-bearded,
immaculate in appearance and deportment, with
manners and voice of velvet. Yet he, too, had lost
his wonderful imperturbability. He waved away the
floor waiter, who had drawn near. His manner was
almost agitated.

" Monsieur Sir Henry," he explained, " an affair
the most regrettable has happened in your room. I
have allotted to you another apartment upon the
same floor. Your things have been removed there.
If you will come with me I will show it to you. It is
an apartment better by far than the one you have
been occupying, and the price is the same."

" But what on earth has happened in my room? "
Hunterleys demanded.

" Monsieur," the hotel manager replied, " some
poor demented creature who has doubtless lost his
all, in your absence found his way there and committed suicide."

" Found his way into my room? " Hunterleys repeated. " But I locked the door before I went out.
I have the key in my pocket."

" He entered possibly through the bathroom," the
manager went on, soothingly. " I am deeply grieved
that monsieur should be inconvenienced in any way.
This is the apartment I have reserved for monsieur,"
he added, throwing open the door of a room at the
end of the corridor. " It is more spacious and in
every way more desirable. Monsieur's clothes are
already being put away."

Hunterleys glanced around the apartment. It

was certainly of a far better type than the one he had been occupying, and two of the floor valets were already busy with his clothes.

"Monsieur will be well satisfied here, I am sure," the hotel manager continued. "May I be permitted to offer my felicitations and to assure you of my immense relief. There was a rumour — the affair occurring in monsieur's apartment — that the unfortunate man was yourself, Sir Henry."

Hunterleys was thoughtful for a moment. He began to understand the sensation which his appearance had caused. Other ideas, too, were crowding into his brain.

"Look here, Monsieur Picard," he said, "of course, I have no objection to the change of rooms — that's all right — but I should like to know a little more about the man who you say committed suicide in my apartment. I should like to see him."

Monsieur Picard shook his head.

"It would be a very difficult matter, that, monsieur," he declared. "The laws of Monaco are stringent in such affairs."

"That is all very well," Hunterleys protested, "but I cannot understand what he was doing in my apartment. Can't I go in just for a moment?"

"Impossible, monsieur! Without the permission of the Commissioner of Police no one can enter that room."

"Then I should like," Hunterleys persisted, "to see the Commissioner of Police."

Monsieur Picard bowed.

"Monsieur the Commissioner is on the premises,

without a doubt. I will instruct him of Monsieur Sir Henry's desire."

" I shall be glad if you will do so at once," Hunterleys said firmly. " I will wait for him here."

The manager made his escape and his relief was obvious. Hunterleys sat on the edge of the bed.

" Do you know anything about this affair? " he asked the nearer of the two valets.

The man shook his head.

" Nothing at all, monsieur," he answered, without pausing from his labours.

" How did the fellow get into my room? "

" One knows nothing," the other man muttered.

Hunterleys watched them for a few minutes at their labours.

" A nice, intelligent couple of fellows you are," he remarked pleasantly. " Come, here's a louis each. Now can't you tell me something about the affair? "

They came forward. Both looked longingly at the coins.

" Monsieur," the one he had first addressed regretted, " there is indeed nothing to be known. At this hotel the wages are good. It is the finest situation a man may gain in Monte Carlo or elsewhere, but if anything like this happens, there is to be silence. One dares not break the rule."

Hunterleys shrugged his shoulders.

" All right," he said. " I shall find out what I want to know, in time."

The men returned unwillingly to their tasks. In a moment or two there was a knock at the door. The Commissioner of Police entered, accompanied by the hotel manager, who at once introduced him.

" The Commissioner of Police is here, Sir Henry,"
he announced. " He will speak with you immediately."

The official saluted.

" Monsieur desires some information? "

" I do," Hunterleys admitted. " I am told that
a man has committed suicide in my room, and I have
heard no plausible explanation as to how he got
there. I want to see him. It is possible that I may
recognise him."

" The fellow is already identified," the Director of
Police declared. " I can satisfy monsieur's curiosity. He was connected with a firm of English tailors here, who sought business from the gentlemen in
the hotel. He had accordingly sometimes the entrée to their apartments. The fellow is reported
to have saved a little money and to have visited the
tables. He lost everything. He came this morning
about his business as usual, but, overcome by despair,
stabbed himself, most regrettably in the apartments
of monsieur."

" Since you know all about him, perhaps you can
tell me his name? " Hunterleys asked.

" James Allen. Monsieur may recall him to his
memory. He was tall and of pale complexion, re-
spectable-looking, but a man of discontented appearance. The intention had probably been in his
mind for some time."

" Is there any objection to my seeing the body? "
Hunterleys enquired.

The official shrugged his shoulders.

" But, monsieur, all is finished with the poor fellow. The doctor has given his certificate. He is

to be removed at once. He will be buried at night-fall."

" A very admirable arrangement, without a doubt," Hunterleys observed, " and yet, I should like, as I remarked before, to see the body. You know who I am — Sir Henry Hunterleys. I had a message from your department a day or two ago which I thought a little unfair."

The Commissioner sighed. He ignored altogether the conclusion of Hunterleys' sentence.

" It is against the rules, monsieur," he regret-ted.

" Then to whom shall I apply? " Hunterleys asked, " because I may as well tell you at once that I am going to insist upon my request being granted. I will tell you frankly my reason. It is not a mat-ter of curiosity at all. I should like to feel assured of the fact that this man Allen really committed sui-cide."

" But he is dead, monsieur," the Commissioner protested.

" Doubtless," Hunterleys agreed, " but there is also the chance that he was murdered, isn't there? "

" Murdered! "

Monsieur Picard held up his hands in horror. The Commissioner of Police smiled in derision.

" But, monsieur," the latter pointed out, " who would take the trouble to murder a poverty-stricken tailor's assistant! "

" And in my hotel, too! " Monsieur Picard inter-vened.

" The thing is impossible," the Commissioner de-clared.

"Beyond which it is ridiculous!" Monsieur Picard added.

Hunterleys sat quite silent for a moment.

"Monsieur the Commissioner," he said presently, "and Monsieur Picard, I recognise your point of view. Believe me that I appreciate it and that I am willing, to a certain extent, to acquiesce in it. At the same time, there are considerations in this matter which I cannot ignore. I do not wish to create any disturbance or to make any statements likely to militate against the popularity of your wonderful hotel, Monsieur Picard. Nevertheless, for personal reasons only, notwithstanding the verdict of your doctor, I should like for one moment to examine the body."

The Commissioner of Police was thoughtful for a moment.

"It shall be as monsieur desires," he consented gravely, "bearing in mind what monsieur has said," he added with emphasis.

The three men left the room and passed down the corridor. The gendarme in front of the closed door stood on one side. The Commissioner produced a key. They all three entered the room and Monsieur Picard closed the door behind them. Underneath a sheet upon the bed was stretched the figure of a man. Hunterleys stepped up to it, turned down the sheet and examined the prostrate figure. Then he replaced the covering reverently.

"Yes," he said, "that is the man who has called upon me for orders from the English tailors. His name, I believe, was, as you say, Allen. But can you tell me, Monsieur the Commissioner, how it was possible for a man to stab himself from the shoulder downwards through the heart? "

The Official extended his hands.

" Monsieur," he declared, " it is not for us. The doctor has given his certificate."

Hunterleys smiled a little grimly.

" I have always understood," he observed, " that things were managed like this. You may have confidence in me, Monsieur the Commissioner, and you, Monsieur Picard. I shall not tell the world what I suspect. But for your private information I will tell you that this man was probably murdered by an assassin who sought my life. You observe that there is a certain resemblance."

The hotel proprietor turned pale.

" Murdered! " he exclaimed. " Impossible! A murder here — unheard of! "

The Commissioner dismissed the whole thing airily with a wave of his hand.

" The doctor has signed the certificate," he repeated.

" And I," Hunterleys added, as he led the way out of the room, " am more than satisfied — I am grateful. So there is nothing more to be said."

CHAPTER XXV

DRACONMEYER IS DESPERATE

Draconmeyer stood before the window of his room, looking out over the Mediterranean. There was no finer view to be obtained from any suite in the hotel, and Monte Carlo had revelled all that day in the golden, transfiguring sunshine. Yet he looked as a blind man. His eyes saw nothing of the blue sea or the brown-sailed fishing boats, nor did he once glance towards the picturesque harbour. He saw only his own future, the shattered pieces of his carefully-thought-out scheme. The first fury had passed. His brain was working now. In her room below, Lady Hunterleys was lying on the couch, half hysterical. Three times she had sent for her husband. If he should return at that moment, Draconmeyer knew that the game was up. There would be no bandying words between them, no involved explanations, no possibility of any further misunderstanding. All his little tissue of lies and misrepresentations would crumble hopelessly to pieces. The one feeling in her heart would be thankfulness. She would open her arms. He saw the end with fatal, unerring truthfulness.

His servant returned. Draconmeyer waited eagerly for his message.

"Lady Hunterleys is lying down, sir," the man

announced. "She is very much upset and begs you to excuse her."

Draconmeyer waved the man away and walked up and down the apartment, his hands behind his back, his lips hard-set. He was face to face with a crisis which baffled him completely, and yet which he felt to be wholly unworthy of his powers. His brain had never been keener, his sense of power more inspiring. Yet he had never felt more impotent. It was woman's hysteria against which he had to fight. The ordinary weapons were useless. He realised quite well her condition and the dangers resulting from it. The heart of the woman was once more beating to its own natural tune. If Hunterleys should present himself within the next few minutes, not all his ingenuity nor the power of his millions could save the situation.

Plans shaped themselves almost automatically in his mind. He passed from his own apartments, through a connecting door into a large and beautifully-furnished salon. A woman with grey hair and white face was lying on a couch by the window. She turned her head as he entered and looked at him questioningly. Her face was fragile and her features were sharpened by suffering. She looked at her husband almost as a cowed but still affectionate animal might look towards a stern master.

"Do you feel well enough to walk as far as Lady Hunterleys' apartment with the aid of my arm?" he asked.

"Of course," she replied. "Does Violet want me?"

"She is still feeling the shock," Draconmeyer

said. " I think that she is inclined to be hysterical.
It would do her good to have you talk with her."

The nurse, who had been sitting by her side, as-
sisted her patient to rise. She leaned on her husband's arm. In her other hand she carried a black
ebony walking-stick. They traversed the corridor,
knocked at the door of Lady Hunterleys' apartment,
and in response to a somewhat hesitating invitation,
entered. Violet was lying upon the sofa. She
looked up eagerly at their coming.

" Linda ! " she exclaimed. " How dear of you! I
thought that it might have been Henry," she added,
as though to explain the disappointment in her tone.

Draconmeyer turned away to hide his expression.

" Talk to her as lightly as possible," he whispered
to his wife, " but don't leave her alone. I will come
back for you in ten minutes."

He left the two women together and descended
into the hall. He found several of the reception
clerks whispering together. The concierge had only
just recovered himself, but the place was beginning
to wear its normal aspect. He whispered an enquiry at the desk. Sir Henry Hunterleys had just
come in and had gone upstairs, he was told. His
new room was number 148.

" There was a note from his wife," Draconmeyer
said, trying hard to control his voice. " Has he
had it ? "

" It is here still, sir," the clerk replied. " I tried
to catch Sir Henry as he passed through, but he was
too quick for me. To tell you the truth," he went
on, " there has been a rumour through the hotel that
it was Sir Henry himself who had been found dead

in his room, and seeing him come in was rather a shock for all of us."

" Naturally," Draconmeyer agreed. " If you will give me the note I will take it up to him."

The clerk handed it over without hesitation. Draconmeyer returned immediately to his own apartments and torn open the envelope. There were only a few words scrawled across the half-sheet of note-paper:

Henry, come to me, dear, at once. I have had such a shock. I want to see you.

VI.

He tore the note viciously into small pieces. Then he went back to Lady Hunterleys' apartments. She was sitting up now in an easy-chair. Once more, at the sound of the knock, she looked towards the door eagerly. Her face fell when Draconmeyer entered.

" Have you heard anything about Henry? " she asked anxiously.

" He came back a few minutes ago," Draconmeyer replied, " and has gone out again."

" Gone out again? "

Draconmeyer nodded.

" I think that he has gone round to the Club. He is a man of splendid nerve, your husband. He seemed to treat the whole affair as an excellent joke."

" A joke! " she repeated blankly.

" This sort of thing happens so often in Monte Carlo," he observed, in a matter-of-fact tone. " The hotel people seem all to look upon it as in the day's work."

" I wonder if Henry had my note? " she faltered.

" He was reading one in the hall when I saw him," Draconmeyer told her. " That would be yours, I should think. He left a message at the desk which was doubtless meant for you. He has gone on to the Sporting Club for an hour and will probably be back in time to change for dinner."

Violet sat quite still for several moments. Something seemed to die slowly out of her face. Presently she rose to her feet.

" I suppose," she said, " that I am very foolish to allow myself to be upset like this."

" It is quite natural," Draconmeyer assured her soothingly. " What you should try to do is to forget the whole circumstance. You sit here brooding about it until it becomes a tragedy. Let us go down to the Club together. We shall probably see your husband there."

She hesitated. She seemed still perplexed.

" I wonder," she murmured, " could I send another message to him? Perhaps he didn't quite understand."

" Much better come along to the Club," Draconmeyer advised, good-humouredly. " You can be there yourself before a message could reach him."

" Very well," she assented. " I will be ready in ten minutes." . . .

Draconmeyer took his wife back to her room.

" Did I do as you wished, dear? " she asked him anxiously.

" Absolutely," he replied.

He helped her back to her couch and stooped and kissed her. She leaned back wearily. It was obvious that she had found the exertion of moving even so far exhausting. Then he returned to his own apartments. Rapidly he unlocked his dispatch box and took out one or two notes from Violet. They were all of no importance — answers to invitations, or appointments. He spread them out, took a sheet of paper and a broad pen. Without hesitation he wrote:

Congratulations on your escape, but why do you run such risks! I wish you would go back to England.

VIOLET.

He held the sheet of notepaper a little away from him and looked at it critically. The imitation was excellent. He thrust the few lines into an envelope, addressed them to Hunterleys and descended to the hall. He left the note at the office.

"Send this up to Sir Henry, will you?" he instructed. "Let him have it as quickly as possible."

Once more he crossed the hall and waited close to the lift by which she would descend. All the time he kept on glancing nervously around. Things were going his way, but the great danger remained — if they should meet first by chance in the corridor, or in the lift! Hunterleys might think it his duty to go at once to his wife's apartment in case she had heard the rumour of his death. The minutes dragged by. He had climbed the great ladder slowly. More than once he had felt it sway beneath his feet. Yet to him those moments seemed almost the longest of his life. Then at last she came. She was looking very pale, but to his relief he saw that she was dressed for the Club. She was wearing a grey dress and black hat. He remembered with a pang of fury that grey was her husband's favourite colour.

"I suppose there is no doubt that Henry is at the Club?" she asked, looking eagerly around the hall.

"Not the slightest," he assured her. "We can have some tea there and we are certain to come across him somewhere."

She made no further difficulty. As they turned into the long passage he gave a sigh of relief. Every step they took meant safety. He talked to her as lightly as possible, ignoring the fact that she scarcely replied to him. They mounted the stairs and entered the Club. She looked anxiously up and down the crowded rooms.

"I shall stroll about and look for Henry," she announced.

"Very well," he agreed. "I will go over to your place and see how the numbers are going."

He stood by the roulette table, but he watched her covertly. She passed through the baccarat room, came out again and walked the whole length of the larger apartment. She even looked into the restaurant beyond. Then she came slowly back to where Draconmeyer was standing. She seemed tired. She scarcely even glanced at the table.

"Lady Hunterleys," he exclaimed impressively, "this is positively wicked! Your twenty-nine has turned up twice within the last few minutes. Do sit down and try your luck and I will go and see if I can find your husband."

He pushed a handful of plaques and a bundle of

notes into her hand. At that moment the croupier's voice was heard.

" *Quatorze rouge, pair et manque.*"

" Another of my numbers! " she murmured, with a faint show of interest. " I don't think I want to play, though."

" Try just a few coups," he begged. " You see, there is a chair here. You may not have a chance again for hours."

He was using all his will power. Somehow or other, she found herself seated in front of the table. The sight of the pile of plaques and the roll of notes was inspiring. She leaned across and with trembling fingers backed number fourteen *en plein*, with all the *carrés* and *chevaux*. She was playing the game at which she had lost so persistently. He walked slowly away. Every now and then from a distance he watched her. She was winning and losing alternately, but she had settled down now in earnest. He breathed a great sigh of relief and took a seat upon a divan, whence he could see if she moved. Richard Lane, who had been standing at the other side of the table, crossed the room and came over to him.

" Say, do you know where Sir Henry is? " he enquired.

Draconmeyer shook his head.

" I have scarcely seen him all day."

" I think I'll go round to the hotel and look him up," Lane decided carelessly. " I'm fed up with this —"

He stopped short. He was no longer an exceedingly bored and discontented-looking young man.

Draconmeyer glanced at him curiously. He felt a
thrill of sympathy. This stolid young man, then,
was capable of feeling something of the same emo-
tion as was tearing at his own heartstrings. Lane
was gazing with transfigured face towards the open
doorway.

CHAPTER XXVI

EXTRAORDINARY LOVE-MAKING

Fedora sauntered slowly around the rooms, leaning over and staking a gold plaque here and there. She was dressed as usual in white, with an ermine turban hat and stole and an enormous muff. Her hair seemed more golden than ever beneath its snow-white setting, and her complexion more dazzling. She seemed utterly unconscious of the admiration which her appearance evoked, and she passed Lane without apparently observing him. A moment afterwards, however, he moved to her side and addressed her.

" Quite a lucky coup of yours, that last, Miss Grex. Are you used to winning *en plein* like that? "

She turned her head and looked at him. Her eyebrows were ever so slightly uplifted. Her expression was chilling. He remained, however, absolutely unconscious of any impending trouble.

" I was sorry not to find you at home this morning," he continued. " I brought my little racing car round for you to see. I thought you might have liked to try her."

" How absurd you are ! " she murmured. " You must know perfectly well that it would have been quite impossible for me to come out with you alone."

" But why ? "

She sighed.

" You are quite hopeless, or you pretend to be ! "

" If I am," he replied, " it is because you won't explain things to me properly. The tables are much too crowded to play comfortably. Won't you come and sit down for a few minutes? "

She hesitated. Lane watched her anxiously. He felt, somehow, that a great deal depended upon her reply. Presently, with the slightest possible shrug of the shoulders, she turned around and suffered him to walk by her side to the little antechamber which divided the gambling rooms from the restaurant.

" Very well," she decided, " I suppose, after all, one must remember that you did save us from a great deal of inconvenience the other night. I will talk to you for a few minutes."

He found her an easy-chair and he sat by her side.

" This is bully," he declared.

" Is what? " she asked, once more raising her eyebrows.

" American slang," he explained penitently. " I am sorry. I meant that it was very pleasant to be here alone with you for a few minutes."

" You may not find it so, after all," she said severely. " I feel that I have a duty to perform."

" Well, don't let's bother about that yet, if it means a lecture," he begged. " You shall tell me how much better the young women of your country behave than the young women of mine."

" Thank you," she replied, " I am never interested in the doings of a democracy. Your country makes no appeal to me at all."

"Come," he protested, "that's a little too bad. Why, Russia may be a democracy some day, you know. You very nearly had a republic foisted upon you after the Japanese war."

"You are quite mistaken," she assured him. "Russia would never tolerate a republic."

"Russia will some day have to do like many other countries," he answered firmly,—"obey the will of the people."

"Russia has nothing in common with other countries," she asserted. "There was never a nation yet in which the aristocracy was so powerful."

"It's only a matter of time," he declared, nonchalantly.

She shrugged her shoulders.

"You represent ideas of which I do not approve," she told him.

"I don't care a fig about any ideas," he replied. "I don't care much about anything in the world except you."

She turned her head slowly and looked at him. Its angle was supercilious, her tone frigid.

"That sort of a speech may pass for polite conversation in your country, Mr. Lane. We do not understand it in mine."

"Don't your men ever tell your women that they love them?" he asked bluntly.

"If they are of the same order," she said, "if the thing is at all possible, it may sometimes be done. Marriage, however, is more a matter of alliance with us. Our servants, I believe, are quite promiscuous in their love-making."

He was silent for a moment. She may, perhaps,

have felt some compunction. She spoke to him a little more kindly.

"We cannot help the ideas of the country in which we are brought up, you know, Mr. Lane."

"Of course not," he agreed. "I understand that perfectly. I was just thinking, though, what a lot I shall have to teach you."

She was momentarily aghast. She recovered herself quickly, however.

"Are all the men of your nation so self-confident?"

"We have to be," he told her. "It's the only way we can get what we want."

"And do you always succeed in getting what you want?"

"Always!"

"Then unless you wish to be an exception," she advised, "let me beg you not to try for anything beyond your reach."

"There is nothing," he declared firmly, "beyond my reach. You are trying to discourage me. It isn't any use. I am not a prince or a duke or anything like that, although my ancestors were honest enough, I believe. I haven't any trappings of that sort to offer you. If you are as sensible as I think you are, you won't mind that when you come to think it over. The only thing I am ashamed of is my money, because I didn't earn it for myself. You can live in palaces still, if you want to, and if you want to be a queen I'll ferret out a kingdom somewhere and buy it, but I am afraid you'll have to be Mrs. Lane behind it all, you know."

"You really are the most intolerable person," she

exclaimed, biting her lip. " How can I get these absurd ideas out of your mind? "

" By telling me honestly, looking in my eyes all the time, that you could never care for me a little bit, however devoted I was," he answered promptly. " You won't be able to do it. I've only one belief in life about these things, and that is that when any one cares for a girl as I care for you, it's absolutely impossible for her to be wholly indifferent. It isn't much to start with, I know, but the rest will come. Be honest with me. Is there any one of the men of your country whom you have met, whom you want to marry? "

She frowned slightly. She found herself, at that moment, comparing him with certain young men of her acquaintance. She was astonished to realise that the comparison was all in his favour. It was for her an extraordinary moment. She had indeed been brought up in palaces and the men whom she had known had been reckoned the salt of the earth. Yet, at that crisis, she was most profoundly conscious that not all the glamour of those high-sounding names, the picturesque interest of those gorgeous uniforms, nor the men themselves, magnificent in their way, were able to make the slightest appeal to her. She remembered some of her own bitter words when an alliance with one of them had been suggested to her. It was she, then, who had been the first to ignore the divine heritage of birth, who had spoken of their drinking habits, pointed to their life of idle luxury and worse than luxury. The man who was at the present moment her suitor forced himself upon her recollection. She knew quite well that he represented a type. They were of the nobility, and they seemed to her in that one poignant but unwelcome moment, hatefully degenerate, men no self-respecting girl could ever think of. Family influence, stern parental words, the call of her order, had half crushed these thoughts. They came back now, however, with persistent force.

" You see," Richard Lane went on, " it mayn't be much that I have to offer you, but in your heart I know you feel what it means to be offered the love of a man who doesn't want you just because you are of his order, or because you are the daughter of a Personage, or for any other reason than because he cares for you as he has cared for no other woman on earth, and because, without knowing it, he has waited for you."

She moved restlessly in her chair. Their conversation was not going in the least along the lines which she had intended. She suddenly remembered her own disquiet of the day before, her curious longing to steal off on some excuse to-day. A week ago she would have been content to have dawdled away the afternoon in the grounds of the villa. Something different had come. From the moment she had entered the rooms, although she had never acknowledged it, she had been conscious, pleasurably conscious of his presence. She was suddenly uneasy.

" I am afraid," she murmured, " that you are quite hopeless."

" If you mean that I am without hope, you are wrong," he answered sturdily. " From the moment I met you I have had but one thought, and until the last day of my life I shall have but one thought, and

that thought is of you. There may be no end of difficulties, but I come of an obstinate race. I have patience as well as other things."

She was avoiding looking at him now. She looked
instead at her clasped hands.

"I wish I could make you understand," she said,
in a low tone, "how impossible all this is. In England and America I know that it is different. There,
marriages of a certain sort are freely made between
different classes. But in Russia these things are not
thought of. Supposing that all you said were true.
Supposing, even, that I had the slightest disposition
to listen to you. Do you realise that there isn't one
of my family who wouldn't cry out in horror at the
thought of my marrying — forgive me — marrying
a commoner of your rank in life?"

"They can cry themselves hoarse, as they'll have
to some day," he replied cheerfully. "As for you,
Miss Fedora — you don't mind my calling you Miss
Fedora, do you? — you'll be glad some day that you
were born at the beginning of a new era. You may
be a pioneer in the new ways, but you may take
my word for it that you won't be the last. Please
have courage. Please try and be yourself, won't
you?"

"But how do you know what I am?" she protested. "Or even what I am like? We have spoken
only a few words. Nothing has passed between us
which could possibly have inspired you with such
feelings as you speak of," she added, colouring
slightly. "It is a fancy of yours, quite too absurd
a fancy. Now that I find myself discussing it with
you as though, indeed, we were talking of it seri-

ously, I am inclined to laugh. You are just a very foolish young man, Mr. Lane."

He shook his head.

"Look here," he said, "I am very good at meaning things, but it's awfully hard for me to put my thoughts into words. I can't explain how it's all come about. I don't know why, amongst all the girls I've seen in my own country, or England, or Paris, or anywhere, there hasn't been one who could bring me the things which you bring, who could fill my mind with the thoughts you fill it with, who could make my days stand still and start again, who could upset the whole machinery of my life so that when you come I want to dance with happiness, and when you go the day is over with me. There is no chance of my being able to explain this to you, because other fellows, much cleverer than I, have been in the same box, and they've had to come to the conclusion, too, that there isn't any explanation. I have accepted it. I want you to. I love you, Fedora, and I will be faithful to you all my life. You shall live where you choose and how you choose, but you must be my wife. There isn't any way out of it for either of us."

She sat quite still for several moments. They were a little behind the curtain and it chanced that there was no one in their immediate vicinity. She felt her fingers suddenly gripped. They were released again almost at once, but a queer sensation of something overmastering seemed to creep through her whole being at the touch of his hand. She rose to her feet.

"I am going away," she declared.

"I haven't offended you?" he begged. "Please

sit down. We haven't half talked over things yet."

"We have talked too much," she answered. "I don't know really what has come over me that I have let you — that I listen to you —"

"It is because you feel the truth of what I say," he insisted. "Don't get up, Fedora. Don't go away, dear. Let us have at least these few minutes together. I'll do exactly as you tell me. I'll come to your father or I'll carry you off. I have a sister here. She'll be your friend —"

"Don't!" the girl stopped him. "Please don't!"

She sat down in her chair again. Her fingers were twisted together, her slim form was tense with stifled emotions.

"Have I been a brute?" he asked softly. "You must forgive me, Fedora. I am not much used to girls and I am sort of carried away myself, only I want you to believe that there's the real thing in my heart. I'll make you just as happy as a woman can be. Don't shake your head, dear. I want you to trust me and believe in me."

"I think you're a most extraordinary person," she said at last. "Do you know, I'm beginning to be really afraid of you."

"You're not," he insisted. "You're afraid of yourself. You're afraid because you see the downfall of the old ideas. You're afraid because you know that you're going to be a renegade. You can see nothing but trouble ahead just now. I'll take you right away from that."

There was the rustle of skirts, a soft little laugh. Richard rose to his feet promptly. He had never been so pleased in all his life to welcome his sister.

"Flossie," he exclaimed, "I'm ever so glad you came along! I want to present Miss Grex to you. This is my sister, Miss Fedora — Lady Weybourne. I was just going to ask Miss Grex to have some tea with me," he went on, "but I am not sure that she would have considered it proper. Do come along and be chaperone."

Lady Weybourne laughed.

"I shall be delighted," she declared. "I have seen you here once or twice before, haven't I, Miss Grex, and some one told me that you were Russian. I suppose you are not in the least used to the free and easy ways of us Westerners, but you'll come and have some tea with us, won't you?"

The girl hesitated. Fate was too strong for her.

"I shall be very pleased," she agreed.

They found a window table and Lane ordered tea. Fedora was inclined to be silent at first, but Lady Weybourne was quite content to chatter. By degrees Fedora, too, came back to earth and they had a very gay little tea-party. At the end of it they all strolled back into the rooms together. Fedora glanced at the watch upon her wrist and held out her hand to Lady Weybourne.

"I am sorry," she said, "but I must hurry away now. It is very kind of you to ask me to come and see you, Lady Weybourne. I shall be charmed."

Richard ignored her fingers.

"I am going to see you down to your car, if I may," he begged.

They left the room together. She looked at him as they descended the stairs, almost tremulously.

" This doesn't mean, you know," she said, " that I
— that I agree to all you have been saying."

" It needn't mean anything at all, dear," he replied. " This is only the beginning. I don't expect
you to realise all that I have realised quite so
quickly, but I do want you to keep it in your mind
that this thing has come and that it can't be got rid
of. I won't do anything foolish. If it is necessary
I will wait, but I am your lover now, as I always
must be."

He handed her into the car, the footman, in his
long white livery, standing somberly on one side.
As they drove off she gave him her fingers, and he
walked back up the steps with the smile upon his lips
that comes to a man only once or twice in his lifetime.

CHAPTER XXVII

Violet glanced at her watch with an exclamation of dismayed annoyance. She leaned appealingly towards the croupier.

" But one coup more, monsieur," she pleaded. " Indeed your clock is fast."

The croupier shook his head. He was a man of gallantry so far as his profession permitted, and he was a great admirer of the beautiful Englishwoman, but the rules of the Club were strict.

" Madame," he pointed out, " it is already five minutes past eight. It is absolutely prohibited that we start another coup after eight o'clock. If madame will return at ten o'clock, the good fortune will without doubt be hers."

She looked up at Draconmeyer, who was standing at her elbow.

" Did you ever know anything more hatefully provoking!" she complained. " For two hours the luck has been dead against me. But for a few of my *carrés* turning up, I don't know what would have happened. And now at last my numbers arrive. I win *en plein* and with all the *carrés* and *chevaux*. This time it was twenty-seven. I win two *carrés* and I move to twenty, and he will not go on."

" It is the rule," Draconmeyer reminded her. " It is bad fortune, though. I have been watching the run of the table. Things have been coming more your way all the time. I think that the end of your ill-luck has arrived. Tell me, are you hungry? "

" Not in the least," she answered pettishly. " I hate the very thought of dinner."

" Then why do we not go on to the Casino? " Draconmeyer suggested. " We can have a sandwich and a glass of wine there, and you can continue your vein."

She rose to her feet with alacrity. Her face was beaming.

" My friend," she exclaimed, " you are inspired! It is a brilliant idea. I know that it will bring me fortune. To the Cercle Privé, by all means. I am so glad that you are one of those men who are not dependent upon dinner. But what about Linda? "

" She is not expecting me, as it happens," Draconmeyer lied smoothly. " I told her that I might be dining at the Villa Mimosa. I have to be there later on."

Violet gathered up her money, stuffed it into her gold bag and hurried off for her cloak. She reappeared in a few moments and smiled very graciously at Draconmeyer.

" It is quite a wonderful idea of yours, this," she declared. " I am looking forward immensely to my next few coups. I feel in a winning vein. Very soon," she added, as they stepped out on to the pavement and she gathered up her skirts, " very soon I am quite sure that I shall be asking you for my cheques back again."

He laughed, as though she had been a child speaking of playthings.

"I am not sure that I shall wish you luck," he said. "I think that I like to feel that you are a little — just a very little in my debt. Do you think that I should be a severe creditor?"

Something in his voice disturbed her vaguely, but she brushed the thought away. Of course he admired her, but then every woman must have admirers. It only remained for her to be clever enough to keep him at arm's length. She had no fear for herself.

"I haven't thought about the matter at all," she answered carelessly, "but to me all creditors would be the same, whether they were kind or unkind. I hate the feeling of owing anything."

"It is a question," he observed, "how far one can be said to owe anything to those who are really friends. A husband, for instance. One can't keep a ledger account with him."

"A husband is a different matter altogether," she asserted coldly. "Now I wonder whether we shall find my favourite table full. Anyhow, I am going to play at the one nearest the entrance on the right-hand side. There is a little croupier there whom I like."

They passed up through the entrance and across the floor of the first suite of rooms to the Cercle Privé. Violet looked eagerly towards the table of which she had spoken. To her joy there was plenty of room.

"My favourite seat is empty!" she exclaimed. "I know that I am going to be lucky."

"I think that I shall play myself, for a change,"

Draconmeyer announced, producing a great roll of notes.

"Whenever you feel that you would like to go down and have something, don't mind me, will you?" she begged. "You can come back and talk to me at any time. I am not in the least hungry yet."

"Very well," he agreed. "Good luck to you!"

They played at opposite sides of the table. For an hour she won and he lost. Once she called him over to her side.

"I scarcely dare to tell you," she whispered, her eyes gleaming, "but I have won back the first thousand pounds. I shall give it to you to-night. Here, take it now."

He shook his head and waved it away.

"I haven't the cheques with me," he protested. "Besides, it is bad luck to part with any of your winnings while you are still playing."

He watched her for a minute or two. She still won.

"Take my advice," he said earnestly. "Play higher. You have had a most unusual run of bad luck. The tide has turned. Make the most of it. I have lost ten mille. I am going to have a try your side of the table."

He found a vacant chair a few places lower down, and commenced playing in maximums. From the moment of his arrival he began to win, and simultaneously Violet began to lose. Her good-fortune deserted her absolutely, and for the first time she showed signs of losing her self-control. She gave vent to little exclamations of disgust as stake after stake was swept away. Her eyes were much too bright, there was a spot of colour in her cheeks. She spoke angrily to a croupier who delayed handing her some change. Draconmeyer, although he knew perfectly well what was happening, never seemed to glance in her direction. He played with absolute recklessness for half-an-hour. When at last he rose from his seat and joined her, his hands were full of notes. He smiled ever so faintly as he saw the covetous gleam in her eyes.

"I'm nearly broken," she gasped. "Leave off playing, please, for a little time. "You've changed my luck."

He obeyed, standing behind her chair. Three more coups she played and lost. Then she thrust her hand into her bag and drew it out, empty. She was suddenly pale.

"I have lost my last louis," she declared. "I don't understand it. It seemed as though I must win here."

"So you will in time," he assured her confidently. "How much will you have — ten mille or twenty?"

She shrank back, but the sight of the notes in his hand fascinated her. She glanced up at him. His pallor was unchanged, there was no sign of exultation in his face. Only his eyes seemed a little brighter than usual beneath his gold-rimmed spectacles.

"No, give me ten," she said.

She took them from his hand and changed them quickly into plaques. Her first coup was partially successful. He leaned closer over her.

"Remember," he pointed out, "that you only

need to win once in a dozen times and you do well. Don't be in such a hurry."

"Of course," she murmured. "Of course! One forgets that. It is all a matter of capital."

He strolled away to another table. When he came back, she was sitting idle in her place, restless and excited, but still full of confidence.

"I am a little to the good," she told him, "but I have left off for a few minutes. The very low numbers are turning up and they are no use to me."

"Come and have that sandwich," he begged. "You really ought to take something."

"The place shall be kept for madame," the croupier whispered. "I shall be here for another two hours."

She nodded and rose. They made their way out of the Rooms and down into the restaurant on the ground-floor. They found a little table near the wall and he ordered some pâté sandwiches and champagne. Whilst they waited she counted up her money, making calculations on a slip of paper. Draconmeyer leaned back in his chair, watching her. His back was towards the door and they were at the end table. He permitted himself the luxury of looking at her almost greedily; of dropping, for a few moments, the mask which he placed always upon his features in her presence. In his way the man was an artist, a great collector of pictures and bronzes, a real lover and seeker after perfection. Often he found himself wandering towards his little gallery, content to stand about and gloat over some of his most treasured possessions. Yet the man's personality clashed often with his artistic preten-

sions. He scarcely ever found himself amongst his
belongings without realising the existence of a curious feeling, wholly removed from the pure artistic
pleasure of their contemplation. It was the sense
of ownership which thrilled him. Something of the
same sensation was upon him now. She was the sort
of woman he had craved for always — slim, elegant,
and what to him, with his quick powers of observation, counted for so much, she was modish, reflecting
in her presence, her dress and carriage, even her
speech, the best type of the prevailing fashion. She
excited comment wherever she appeared. People, as
he knew very well even now, were envying him his
companion. And beneath it all — she, the woman,
was there. All his life he had fought for the big
things — political power, immense wealth, the confidence of his great master — all these had come to him
easily. And at that moment they were like bau-
bles!

She looked up at last and there was a slight frown
upon her forehead.

" I am still a little down, starting from where I
had the ten mille," she sighed. " I thought —"

She stopped short. There was a curious change
in her face. Her eyes were fixed upon some person
approaching. Draconmeyer turned quickly in his
chair. Almost as he did so, Hunterleys paused before their table. Violet looked up at him with quivering lips. For a moment it seemed as though she
were stepping out of her sordid surroundings.

" Henry! " she exclaimed. " Did you come to
look for me? Did you know that we were here? "

" How should I? " he answered calmly. " I was

strolling around with David Briston. We are at the Opera."

" At the Opera," she repeated.

" My little protégée, Felicia Roche, is singing," he went on, " in *Aïda*. If she does as well in the next act as she has done in this, her future is made."

He was on the point of adding the news of Felicia's engagement to the young man who had momentarily deserted him. Some evil chance changed his intention.

" Why do you call her your little protégée? " she demanded.

" It isn't quite correct, is it? " he answered, a little absently. " There are three or four of us who are doing what we can to look after her. Her father was a prominent member of the Wigwam Club. The girl won the musical scholarship we have there. She has more than repaid us for our trouble, I am glad to say."

" I have no doubt that she has," Violet replied, lifting her eyes.

There was a moment's silence. The significance of her words was entirely lost upon Hunterleys.

" Isn't this rather a new departure of yours? " he asked, glancing disdainfully towards Draconmeyer. " I thought that you so much preferred to play at the Club."

" So I do," she assented, " but I was just beginning to win when the Club closed at eight o'clock, and so we came on here."

" Your good fortune continues, I hope? "

" It varies," she answered hurriedly, " but it will

come, I am sure. I have been very near a big win more than once."

He seemed on the point of departure. She leaned a little forward.

" You had my note, Henry? "

Her tone was almost beseeching. Draconmeyer, who was listening with stony face, shivered imperceptibly.

" Thank you, yes," Hunterleys replied, frowning slightly. " I am sorry, but I am not at liberty to do what you suggest just at present. I wish you good fortune."

He turned around and walked back to the other end of the room, where Briston was standing at the bar. She looked after him for a moment as though she failed to understand his words. Then her face hardened. Draconmeyer leaned towards her.

" Shall we go? " he suggested.

She rose with alacrity. Side by side they strolled through the rooms towards the Cercle Privé.

" I am sorry," Draconmeyer said regretfully, " but I am forced to leave you now. I will take you back to your place and after that I must go to the hotel and change. I have a reception to attend. I wish you would take the rest of my winnings and see what you can do with them."

She shook her head vigorously.

" No, thank you," she declared. " I have enough."

He shrugged his shoulders.

" I have twenty-five mille here in my pocket," he continued, " besides some smaller change. I don't think it is quite fair to leave so much money about in one's room or to carry it out into the country. Keep it for me. You won't need to play with it — I can see that your luck is in — but it always gives one confidence to feel that one has a reserve stock, something to fall back upon if necessary."

He drew the notes from his pocket and held them towards her. Her eyes were fixed upon them covetously. The thought of all that money actually in her possession was wildly exhilarating.

" I will take care of them for you, if you like," she said. " I shall not play with them, though. I owe you quite enough already and my losing days are over."

He stuffed the notes carelessly into her bag.

" Twenty-five mille," he told her. " Remember my advice. If the luck stays with you, stake maximums. Go for the big things."

She looked at him curiously as she closed her gold bag with a snap.

" After all," she declared, with a little laugh, " I am not sure that you are not the greater gambler of the two to trust me with all this money !"

CHAPTER XXVIII

TO THE VILLA MIMOSA

With feet that seemed to touch nothing more substantial than air, her eyes brilliant, a wonderful colour in her cheeks, Violet passed through the heavy, dingy rooms and out through the motley crowd into the portico of the Casino. She was right! She knew that she had been right! How wise she had been to borrow that money from Mr. Draconmeyer instead of sitting down and confessing herself vanquished! The last few hours had been hours of ecstatic happiness. With calm confidence she had sat in her place and watched her numbers coming up with marvellous persistence. It was the most wonderful thing in the world, this. She had had no time to count her winnings, but at least she knew that she could pay back every penny she owed. Her little gold satchel was stuffed with notes and plaques. She felt suddenly younger, curiously lighthearted; hungry, too, and thirsty. She was, in short, experiencing almost a delirium of pleasure. And just then, on the steps of the Casino, she came face to face with her husband.

" Henry! " she called out. " Henry! "

He turned abruptly around. He was looking troubled, and in his hand were the fragments of a crushed up note.

" Come across to the hotel with me," she begged,
forgetful of everything except her own immense relief. " Come and help me count. I have been winning. I have won back everything."

He accepted the information with only a polite
show of interest. After all, as she reflected afterwards, he had no idea upon what scale she had been
gambling!

" I am delighted to hear it," he answered. " I'll
see you across the road, if I may, but I have only a
few minutes to spare. I have an appointment."

She was acutely disappointed; unreasonably, furiously angry.

" An appointment!" she exclaimed. " At half-
past eleven o'clock at night! Are you waiting for
Felicia Roche?"

" Is there any reason why I should not?" he asked
her gravely.

She bit her lips hard. They were crossing the
road now. After all, it was only a few months since
she had bidden him go his own way and leave her to
regulate her own friendships.

" No reason at all," she admitted, " only I cannot
see why you choose to advertise yourself with an
opera singer — you, an ambitious politician, who
moves with his head in the clouds, and to whom women
are no more than a pastime. Why have you waited
all these years to commence a flirtation under my
very nose!"

He looked at her sternly.

" I think that you are a little excited, Violet," he
said. " You surely don't realise what you are saying."

"Excited! Tell me once more — you got my note, the one I wrote this evening?"

"Certainly."

His brief reply was convincing. She remembered the few impulsive lines which she had written from her heart in that moment of glad relief. There was no sign in his face that he had been touched. Even at that moment he had drawn out his watch and was looking at it.

"Thank you for bringing me here," she said, as they stood upon the steps of the hotel. "Don't let me keep you."

"After all," he decided, "I think that I shall go up to my room for a minute. Good night!"

She looked after him, a little amazed. She was conscious of a feeling of slow anger. His aloofness repelled her, was utterly inexplicable. For once it was she who was being badly treated. Her moment of exhilaration had passed. She sat down in the lounge; her satchel, filled with mille franc notes, lay upon her lap unheeded. She sat there thinking, seeing nothing of the crowds of fashionably dressed women and men passing in and out of the hotel; of the gaily-lit square outside, the cool green of the gardens, the café opposite, the brilliantly-lit Casino. She was back again for a moment in England. The strain of all this life, whipped into an artificial froth of pleasure by the constant excitement of the one accepted vice of the world, had suddenly lost its hold upon her. The inevitable question had presented itself. She was counting values and realising. . . .

When at last she rose wearily to her feet, Hunterleys was passing through the hall of the hotel, on his way out. She looked at him with aching heart but she made no effort to stop him. He had changed his clothes for a dark suit and he was also wearing a long travelling coat and tweed cap. She watched him wistfully until he had disappeared. Then she turned away, summoned the lift and went up to her rooms. She rang at once for her maid. She would take a bath, she decided, and go to bed early. She would wash all the dust of these places away from her, abjure all manner of excitement and for once sleep peacefully. In the morning she would see Henry once more. Deep in her heart there still lingered some faint shadow of doubt as to Draconmeyer and his attitude towards her. It was scarcely possible that he could have interfered in any way, and yet. . . . She would talk to her husband face to face, she would tell him the things that were in her heart.

She rang the bell for the second time. Only the *femme de chambre* answered the summons. Madame's maid was not to be found. Madame had not once retired so early. It was possible that Susanne had gone out. Could she be of any service? Violet looked at her and hesitated. The woman was clumsy-fingered and none too tidy. She shook her head and sent her away. For a moment she thought of undressing herself. Then instead she opened her satchel and counted the notes. Her breath came more quickly as she looked at the shower of gold and counted the many oblong strips of paper with their magic lettering. At last she had it all in heaps. There were the twenty-five mille he had left with her, and the seventy-five mille she had borrowed from him. Then towards her own losses there was another mille, and a matter of five hundred francs in gold. And all this success, her wonderful recovery, had been done so easily! It was just because she had had the pluck to go on, because she had followed her vein. She looked at the money and she walked to the window. Somewhere a band was playing in the distance. Little parties of men and women in evening dress were strolling by on their way to the Club. A woman was laughing as she clung to her escort on the opposite side of the road, by the gardens. Across at the Café de Paris the people were going in to supper. The spirit of enjoyment seemed to be in the air — the light-hearted, fascinating, devil-may-care atmosphere she knew so well. Violet looked back into the bedroom and she no longer had the impulse to sleep. Her face had hardened a little. Every one was so happy and she was so lonely. She stuffed the notes and gold back into her bag, looked at her hat in the glass and touched her face for a moment with a powder-puff. Then she left the room, rang for the lift and descended.

"I am going into the Club for an hour or so, if I am wanted," she told the concierge as she passed out.

Hunterleys, on leaving the hotel, walked rapidly across the square and found David waiting for him on the opposite side.

"Felicia will be late," the latter explained. "She has to get all that beastly black stuff off her face. She is horribly nervous about Sidney and she doesn't want you to wait. I think perhaps she is right, too. She told me to tell you that Monsieur Lafont himself came to her room and congratulated her after the curtain had gone down. She is almost hysterical between happiness and anxiety about Sidney. Where's your man?"

"I asked him to be a little higher up," Hunterleys replied. "There he is."

They walked a few steps up the hill and found Richard Lane waiting for them in his car. The long, grey racer looked almost like some submarine monster, with its flaring head-lights and torpedo-shaped body which scarcely cleared the ground.

"Ready for orders, sir," the young man annouced, touching his cap.

"Is there room for three of us, in case of an emergency?" Hunterleys asked.

"The third man has to sit on the floor," Richard pointed out, "but it isn't so comfortable as it looks."

Hunterleys clambered in and took the vacant place. David Briston lingered by a little wistfully.

"I feel rather a skunk," he grumbled. "I don't see why I shouldn't come along."

Hunterleys shook his head.

"There isn't the slightest need for it," he declared firmly. "You go back and look after Felicia. Tell her we'll get Sidney out of this all right. Get away with you, Lane, now."

"Where to?"

"To the Villa Mimosa!"

Richard whistled as he thrust in his clutch.

"So that's the game, is it?" he murmured, as they glided off.

Hunterleys leaned towards him.

" Lane," he said, " don't forget that I warned you there might be a little trouble about to-night. If you feel the slightest hesitation about involving yourself —"

" Shut up!" Richard interrupted. " Whatever trouble you're ready to face, I'm all for it, too. Darned queer thing that we should be going to the Villa Mimosa, though! I am not exactly a popular person with Mr. Grex, I think."

Hunterleys smiled.

" I saw your sister this afternoon," he remarked. " You are rather a wonderful young man."

" I knew it was all up with me," Richard replied simply, " when I first saw that girl. Now look here, Hunterleys, we are almost there. Tell me exactly what it is you want me to do? "

" I want you," Hunterleys explained, " to risk a smash, if you don't mind. I want you to run up to the boundaries of the villa gardens, head your car back for Monte Carlo, and while you are waiting there turn out all your lights."

" That's easy enough," Richard assented. " I'll turn out the search-light altogether, and my others are electric, worked by a button. Is this an elopement act or what? "

" There's a meeting going on in that villa," Hunterleys told him, " between prominent politicians of three countries. You don't have to bother much about Secret Service over in the States, although there's more goes on than you know of in that direction. But over here we have to make regular use of Secret Service men — spies, if you like to call them so. The meeting to-night is inimical to England. It is part of a conspiracy against which I am working. Sidney Roche — Felicia Roche's brother — who lives here as a newspaper correspondent, is in reality one of our best Secret Service men. He is taking terrible chances to-night to learn a little more about the plans which these fellows are discussing. We are here in case he needs our help to get away. We've cleared the shrubs away, close to the spot at which I am going to ask you to wait, and taken the spikes off the fence. It's just a thousand to one chance that if he's hard pressed for it and heads this way, they may think that they have him in a trap and take it quietly. That is to say, they'll wait to capture him instead of shooting."

" Say, you don't mean this seriously? " Richard exclaimed. " They can't do more than arrest him as a trespasser, or something of that sort, surely? "

Hunterleys laughed grimly.

" These men wouldn't stick at much," he told his companion. " They're hand in glove with the authorities here. Anything they did would be hushed up in the name of the law. These things are never allowed to come out. It doesn't do any one any good to have them gossiped about. If they caught Sidney and shot him, we should never make a protest. It's all part of the game, you know. Now that is the spot I want you to stop at, exactly where the mimosa tree leans over the path. But first of all, I'd turn out your head-light."

They slowed down and stopped. Richard extinguished the acetylene gas-lamp and mounted again to his place. Then he swung the car round and crawled back upon the reverse until he reached the spot to which Hunterleys had pointed.

"You're a good fellow, Richard," Hunterleys said softly. "We may have to wait an hour or two, and it may be that nothing will happen, but it's giving the fellow a chance, and it gives him confidence, too, to know that friends are at hand."

"I'm in the game for all it's worth, anyway," Lane declared heartily.

He touched a button and the lights faded away. The two men sat in silence, both turned a little in their seats towards the villa.

The minutes glided by as the two men sat together in the perfumed, shadowy darkness. From their feet the glittering canopy of lights swept upwards to the mountain-sides, even to the stars, but a chain of slowly drifting black clouds hung down in front of the moon, and until their eyes became accustomed to their surroundings it seemed to both of them as though they were sitting in a very pit of darkness.

" It is possible," Hunterleys whispered, after some time, " that we may have to wait for another hour yet."

Richard was suddenly tense. He sat up, and his foot reached for the self-starter.

" I don't think you will," he muttered. " Listen ! "

Almost immediately they were conscious of some commotion in the direction of the villa, followed by a shot and then a cry.

" Start the engine," Hunterleys directed hoarsely, standing up in his place. " I'm afraid they've got him."

There were two more shots but no further cry. Then they heard the sound of excited voices and immediately afterwards rapidly approaching footsteps. A man came crashing through the shrubbery, but when he reached the fence over which, for a moment, his white face gleamed, he sank down as though powerless to climb. Hunterleys leapt to the ground and rushed to the fence.

"Hold up, Sidney, old fellow," he called softly. "We're here all right. Hold up for a moment and let me lift you."

Roche struggled to his feet. His face was ghastly white, the sweat stood out upon his forehead, his lips moved but no words came. Hunterleys got him by the arms, set his teeth and lifted. The task would have been too much for him, but Richard, springing from the car, came to his help. With an effort they hoisted him over the fence. Almost as they did so there was the sound of footsteps dashing through the shrubs, and a shot, the bullet of which tore the bark from the trunk of a tree close at hand. The car leapt off in fourth speed, Sidney supported in Hunterleys' arms. A loud shout from behind only brought Richard's foot down upon the accelerator.

"Stoop low!" he cried to Hunterleys. "Get your legs in, if you can."

A bullet struck the back of the car and another whistled over their heads. Then they dashed around the corner, and Richard, turning on the lights, jammed down his accelerator.

"Gee whiz! that's a bloodthirsty crew!" the young man exclaimed, his eyes fixed upon the road. "Is he hurt?"

Roche was lying back on the seat. Hunterleys was on his knees, holding on to the framework of the car.

"They've got me all right, Hunterleys," Roche

faltered. "Listen. Everything went well with me at first. I could hear — nearly everything. The Frenchman kept his mouth shut — tight as wax. Grex did most of the talking. Russia sees nothing in the entente — England has nothing to offer her. She'd rather keep friends with Germany. Russia wants to move eastward — all Persia — India. She's only lukewarm, any way, about the French alliance as things stand at present, and dead off any truck with England. There's talk of Constantinople, and Germany to march three army corps through a weak French resistance to Calais. They talked of France acting to her pledges, putting her recruits in the front, taking a slight defeat, making a peace on her own account, with Alsace and Lorraine restored. She can pay. Germany wants the money. Germany — Germany —"

The words died away in a little groan. The wounded man's head fell back. Hunterleys passed his arm around the limp figure.

"Take the first turn to the right and second to the left, Richard," he directed. "We'll drive straight to the hospital. I made friends with the English doctor last night. He promised to be there till three. I paid him a fee on purpose."

"First to the right," Richard muttered, swinging around. "Second to the left, eh?"

Hunterleys was holding his brandy flask to Roche's lips as they swung through the white gates and pulled up outside the hospital. The doctor was faithful to his promise, and Roche, who was now unconscious, was carried in. In the hall he was laid upon an ambulance and borne off by two attendants. Hunterleys and Lane sat down to wait in the hall. After what seemed to them an interminable half-hour, the doctor reappeared. He came over to them at once.

" Your friend may live," he announced, " but in any case he will be unconscious for the next twenty-four hours. There is no need for you to stay, or for you to fetch the young lady you spoke of, at present. If he dies, he will die unconscious. I can tell you nothing more until the afternoon."

Hunterleys rose slowly to his feet.

" You'll do everything you can, doctor? " he begged. " Money doesn't count."

" Money never counts here," the doctor replied gravely. " We shall save him if it is possible. You've nothing to tell me, I suppose, as to how he met with his wound? "

" Nothing."

They walked out together into the night. The bank of clouds had drifted away now and the moon was shining. Below them, barely a quarter of a mile away, they could see the flare of lights from the Casino. A woman was laughing hysterically through the open windows of a house on the other side of the way. Some one was playing a violin in a café at the corner of the street.

" Richard," Hunterleys said, " will you see me through? I have to get to Cannes as fast as I can to send a cable. I daren't send it from here, even in code."

" I'll drive you to Cannes like a shot," Richard assented heartily. " Just a brandy and soda on our way out, and I'll show you some pretty driving."

They stopped at the Café de Paris and left the car under the trees. Both men took a long drink and Richard filled his pocket with cigarettes. Then they re-entered the car, lit up, and glided off on the road for Cannes. Richard had become more serious. His boyish manner and appearance had temporarily gone. He drove, even, with less than his usual recklessness.

" That was a fine fellow," he remarked enthusiastically, after a long pause, " that fellow Roche ! "

" And we've many more like him," Hunterleys declared. " We've men in every part of the world doing what seems like dirty work, ill-paid work, too, doing it partly, perhaps, because the excitement grows on them and they love it, but always they have to start in cold blood. The papers don't always tell the truth, you know. There's many a death in foreign cities you read of as a suicide, or the result of an accident, when it's really the sacrifice of a hero for his country. It's great work, Richard."

" Makes me feel kind of ashamed," Richard muttered. " I've never done anything but play around all my life. Anyway, those sort of things don't come to us in our country. America's too powerful and too isolated to need help of that description. We shouldn't have any use for politicians of your class, or for Secret Service men."

" If you're in earnest," Hunterleys advised, " you go to Washington and ask them about it some day. The time's coming, if it hasn't already arrived, when your country will have to develop a different class of politicians. You see, whether she wants it or not, she is coming into touch, through Asia and South America, with European interests, and if she does, she'll have to adopt their methods more or less. Poor old Roche! There was something more he wanted to say, and if it's what I've been expecting, your country was in it."

"I guess I'll take Fedora over for our honeymoon," Richard decided softly. "Don't see why I shouldn't come into one of the Embassies. I'm a bit of a hulk to go about the world doing nothing."

Hunterleys laughed quietly.

"My young friend," he said, "aren't you taking your marriage prospects a little for granted? May I be there when you ask Augustus Nicholas Ivan Peter, Grand Duke of Vassura, Prince of Melinkoff, cousin of His Imperial Majesty the Czar, for the hand of his daughter in marriage!"

"So that's it, is it?" Lane murmured. "Why didn't you tell me before?"

Hunterleys shook his head. He gazed steadfastly along the road in front of him.

"It wasn't to my interest to have it known too generally," he said, "and I am afraid your little love affair didn't strike me as being of much importance by the side of the other things. But you've earned the truth, if it's any use to you."

"Well," Richard observed, "I wasn't counting on having any witnesses, but you can come along if you like. I suppose," he added, "I shall have to do him the courtesy of asking his permission, but —"

"But what?" Hunterleys asked curiously.

They were on a long stretch of straight, white road. Richard looked for a moment up to the sky, and Hunterleys, watching him, was amazed at the transformation.

" There isn't a Grand Duke or a Prince or an Imperial Majesty alive," he said, " who could rob me of Fedora ! "

CHAPTER XXX

" SUPPOSING I TAKE THIS MONEY "

There was a momentary commotion in the Club.
A woman had fainted at one of the roulette tables.
Her chair was quickly drawn back. She was helped
out to the open space at the top of the stairs and
placed in an easy-chair there. Lady Weyborne, who
was on the point of leaving with her husband, hastened back. She stood there while the usual restora-
tives were being administered, fanning the unconscious woman with a white ostrich fan which hung
from her waist. Presently Violet opened her eyes.
She recognised Lady Weybourne and smiled weakly.

" I am so sorry," she murmured. " It was silly
of me to stay in here so long. I went without my
dinner, too, which was rather idiotic."

A man who had announced himself a doctor, bent
over her pulse and turned away.

" The lady will be quite all right now," he said.
" You can give her brandy and soda if she feels like
it. Pardon! "

He hastened back to his place at the baccarat
table. Lady Hunterleys sat up.

" It was quite absurd of me," she declared. " I
don't know what —"

She stopped suddenly. The weight was once more

upon her heart, the blankness before her eyes. She
remembered!

"I am quite able to go home now," she added.

Her gold bag lay upon her lap. It was almost
empty. She looked at it vacantly and then closed
the snap.

"We'll see you back to the hotel," Lady Weybourne said soothingly. "Here comes Harry with
the brandy and soda."

Lord Weybourne came hurrying from the bar, a
tumbler in his hand.

"How nice of you!" Violet exclaimed gratefully.
"Really, I feel that this is just what I need. I wonder what time it is?"

"Half past four," Lord Weybourne announced,
glancing at his watch.

She laughed weakly.

"How stupid of me! I have been between here
and the Casino for nearly twelve hours, and had
nothing to eat. No, I won't have anything here,
thanks," she added, as Lord Weybourne started back
again for the bar, muttering something about a sandwich. "I'll have something in my room. If you
are going back to the hotel, perhaps I could come
with you."

They all three left the place together, passing
along the private way.

"I haven't seen your brother all day," Violet remarked to Lady Weybourne.

"Richard's gone off somewhere in the car to-night,
a most mysterious expedition," his sister declared.
"I began to think that it must be an elopement, but
I see the yacht's there still, and he would surely

choose the yacht in preference to a motor-car, if he were running off with anybody! Your husband doesn't come into the rooms much? "

Violet shook her head.

" He hasn't the gambling instinct," she said quietly. " Perhaps he is just as well without it. One gets a lot of amusement out of this playing for small stakes, but it is irritating to lose. Thank you so much for looking after me," she added, as they reached the hall of the hotel. " I am quite all right now and my woman will be sitting up for me."

She passed into the lift. Lady Weybourne looked after her admiringly.

" Say, she's got some pluck, Harry! " she murmured. " They say she lost nearly a hundred mille to-night and she never even mentioned her losings. Irritating, indeed! I wonder what Sir Henry thinks of it. They are only moderately well off."

Her husband shrugged his shoulders, after the fashion of his sex.

" Let us hope," he said, " that it is Sir Henry who suffers."

Violet slipped out of her gown and dismissed her maid. In her dressing-gown she sat before the open window. Everywhere the place seemed steeped in the faint violet and purple light preceding the dawn. Away eastwards she could catch a glimpse of the mountains, their peaks cut sharply against the soft, deep sky; a crystalline glow, the first herald of the hidden sunrise, hanging about their summits. The gentle breeze from the Mediterranean was cool and sweet. There were many lights still gleaming upon the sea, but their effect now seemed tawdry. She sat there, her head resting upon her hands. She had the feeling of being somehow detached from the whole world of visible objects, as though, indeed, she were on her death-bed. Surely it was not possible to pass any further through life than this! In her thoughts she went back to the first days of estrangement between her husband and herself. Almost before she realised it, she found herself struggling against the tenderness which still survived, which seemed at that moment to be tearing at her heart-strings. He had ceased to care, she told herself. It was all too apparent that he had ceased to care. He was amusing himself elsewhere. Her little impulsive note had not won even a kind word from him. Her appeals, on one excuse or another, had been disregarded. She had lost her place in his life, thrown it away, she told herself bitterly. And in its stead — what! A new fear of Draconmeyer was stealing over her. He presented himself suddenly as an evil genius. She went back through the last few days. Her brain seemed unexpectedly clear, her perceptions unerring. She saw with hateful distinctness how he had forced this money upon her, how he had encouraged her all the time to play beyond her means. She realised the cunning with which he had left that last bundle of notes in her keeping. Well, there the facts were. She owed him now four thousand pounds. She had no money of her own, she was already overdrawn with her allowance. There was no chance of paying him. She realised, with a little shudder, that he did not want payment, a realisation which had come to her dimly from the first, but which she had pushed away simply because she had felt sure of winning. Now there was the price to be paid! She leaned further out of the window. Away to her left the glow over the mountains was becoming stained with the faintest of pinks. She looked at it long, with mute and critical appreciation. She swept with her eyes the line of violet shadows from the mountain-tops to the sea-board, where the pale lights of Bordighera still flickered. She looked up again from the dark blue sea to the paling stars. It was all wonderful — theatrical, perhaps, but wonderful — and how she hated it! She stood up before the window and with her clenched fists she beat against the sills. Those long days and feverish nights through which she had passed slowly unfolded themselves. In those few moments she seemed to taste again the dull pain of constant disappointment, the hectic thrills of occasional winnings, the strange, dull inertia which had taken the place of resignation. She looked into the street below. How long would she live afterwards, she wondered, if she threw herself down! She began even to realise the state of mind which breeds suicides, the brooding over a morrow too hateful to be faced.

As she still stood there, the silence of the street below was broken. A motor-car swung round the corner and swept past the side of the hotel. She caught at the curtain as she recognised its occupants. Richard Lane was driving, and by his side sat her husband. The car was covered with dust, both men seemed weary as though they had been out all night. She gazed after them with fast-beat-

ing heart. She had pictured her husband at the
villa on the hill! Where had he been with Richard
Lane? Perhaps, after all, the things which she had
imagined were not true. The car had stopped now
at the front door. It returned a moment later on
its way to the garage, with only Lane driving. She
opened her door and stood there silently. Hunterleys would have to pass the end of the corridor if
he came up by the main lift. She waited with fast
beating heart. The seconds passed. Then she
heard the rattle of the lift ascending, its click as it
stopped, and soon afterwards the footsteps of a man.
He was coming — coming past the corner! At that
moment she felt that the sound of his footsteps was
like the beating of fate. They came nearer and she
shrank a little back. There was something unfamiliar about them. Whoever it might be, it was not
Henry! And then suddenly Draconmeyer came into
sight. He saw her standing there and stopped short.
Then he came rapidly near.

"Lady Hunterleys!" he exclaimed softly. "You
still up?"

She hesitated. Then she stood on one side, still
grasping the handle of the door.

"Do you want to come in?" she asked. "You
may. I have something to say to you. Perhaps I
shall sleep better if I say it now."

He stepped quickly past her.

"Close the door," he whispered cautiously.

She obeyed him deliberately.

"There is no hurry," she said. "This is my sitting-room. I receive whom I choose here."

"But it is nearly six o'clock!" he exclaimed.

" That does not affect me," she answered, shrugging her shoulders. " Sit down."

He obeyed. There was something changed about her, something which he did not recognise. She thrust her hands into a box of cigarettes, took one out and lit it. She leaned against the table, facing him.

" Listen," she continued, " I have borrowed from you three thousand pounds. You left with me to-night — I don't know whether you meant to lend it to me or whether I had it on trust, but you left it in my charge — another thousand pounds. I have lost it all — all, you understand — the four thousand pounds and every penny I have of my own."

He sat quite still. He was watching her through his gold-rimmed spectacles. There was the slightest possible frown upon his forehead. The time for talking of money as though it were a trifle had passed.

" That is a great deal," he said.

" It is a great deal," she admitted. " I owe it to you and I cannot pay. What are you going to do? "

He watched her eagerly. There was a new note in her voice. He paused to consider what it might mean. A single false step now and he might lose all that he had striven for.

" How am I to answer that? " he asked softly. " I will answer it first in the way that seems most natural. I will beg you to accept your losings as a little gift from me — as a proof, if you will, of my friendship."

He had saved the situation. If he had obeyed his

first impulse, the affair would have been finished. He realised it as he watched her face, and he shuddered at the thought of his escape. His words obviously disturbed her.

"It is not possible for me," she protested, " to accept money from you."

"Not from Linda's husband?"

She threw her cigarette into the grate and stood looking at him.

"Do you offer it to me as Linda's husband?" she demanded.

It was a crisis for which Draconmeyer was scarcely prepared. He was driven out of his pusillanimous compromise. She was pressing him hard for the truth. Again the fear of losing her altogether terrified him.

"If I have other feelings of which I have not spoken," he said quietly, "have I not kept them to myself? Do I obtrude them upon you even now? I am content to wait."

"To wait for what?" she insisted.

All that had been in his mind seemed suddenly miraged before him — the removal of Hunterleys, his own wife's failing health. The way had seemed so clear only a little time ago, and now the clouds were back again.

"Until you appreciate the fact," he told her, " that you have no more sincere friend, that there is no one who values your happiness more than I do."

"Supposing I take this money from you," she asked, after a moment's pause. "Are there any conditions?"

"None whatever," he answered.

She turned away with a little sigh. The tragedy which a few minutes ago she had seen looming up, eluded her. She had courted a dénouement in vain. He was too clever.

"You are very generous," she said. "We will speak of this to-morrow. I called you in because I could not bear the uncertainty of it all. Please go now."

He rose slowly to his feet. She gave him her hand lifelessly. He kept it for a moment. She drew it away and looked at the place where his lips had touched it, wonderingly. It was as though her fingers had been scorched with fire.

"It shall be to-morrow," he whispered, as he passed out.

CHAPTER XXXI

NEARING A CRISIS

From the wilds of Scotland to Monte Carlo, as fast as motor-cars and train de luxe could bring him, came the right Honourable Meredith Simpson, a very distinguished member of His Majesty's Government. Hunterleys, advised of his coming by telegram from Marseilles, met him at the station, and together the two men made their way at once to Hunterleys' room across at the Hotel de Paris. Behind locked doors they spoke for the first time of important matters.

"It's a great find, this of yours, Hunterleys," the Minister acknowledged, "and it is corroborated, too, by what we know is happening around us. We have had all the warning in the world just lately. The Russian Ambassador is in St. Petersburg on leave of absence — in fact for the last six months he has been taking his duties remarkably lightly. Tell me how you first heard of the affair?"

"I got wind of it in Sofia," Hunterleys explained. "I travelled from there quite quietly, loitered about the Italian Riviera, and came on here as a tourist. The only help I could get hold of here was from Sidney Roche, who, as you know, is one of our Secret Service men. Roche, I am sorry to say, was shot last night. He may live but he won't be well enough to take any further hand in the game here, and I have no one to take his place."

"Roche shot!" Mr. Simpson exclaimed, in a shocked tone. "How did it happen?"

"They found him lying on the roof of the Villa Mimosa, just over the room where the meeting was taking place," Hunterleys replied. "They chased him round the grounds and we just got him off in a motor-car, but not before he'd been hit twice. He was just able to tell me a little. The first meeting was quite informal and very guarded. Douaille was most cautious — he was there only to listen. The second meeting was last night. Grex was in the chair, representing Russia."

"You mean the Grand Duke Augustus?" Mr. Simpson interrupted.

Hunterleys nodded.

"Grex is the name he is living under here. He explained Russia's position. Poor Roche was only able to falter a few words, but what he said was enough to give us the key-note to the whole thing. The long and short of it all is that Russia turned her face westward so long as Constantinople was possible. Now that this war has come about and ended as it has done, Russia's chance has gone. There is no longer any *quid pro quo* for her alliance with France. There is no friendship, of course, between Russia and Germany, but at any rate Russia has nothing to fear from Germany, and she knows it. Grex is quite frank. They must look eastward, he said, and when he says eastward, he means Manchuria, China, Persia, even India. At the same time,

Russia has a conscience, even though it be a diplomatic conscience. Hence this conference. She doesn't want France crushed. Germany has a proposition. It has been enunciated up to a certain point. She confers Alsace and Lorraine and possibly Egypt upon France, for her neutrality whilst she destroys the British Fleet. Or failing her neutrality, she wants her to place a weak army on the frontier, which can fall back without much loss before a German advance. Germany's objective then will be Calais and not Paris, and from there she will command the Straits and deal with the British Fleet at her leisure. Meanwhile, she will conclude peace with France on highly advantageous terms. Don't you see what it means, Simpson? The elementary part of the thing is as simple as A B C. Germany has nothing to gain from Russia, she has nothing to gain from France. England is the only country who can give her what she wants. That is about as far as they have got, up to now, but there is something further behind it all. That, Selingman is to tell them to-night."

" The most important point about the whole matter, so far as we are concerned," Mr. Simpson declared, " is Douaille's attitude. You have received no indication of that, I suppose? "

" None whatever," Hunterleys answered. " I thought of paying my respects, but after all, you know, I have no official standing, and personally we are almost strangers."

The Minister nodded.

" It's a difficult position," he confessed. " Have you copies of your reports to London? "

" I have copies of them, and full notes of every-thing that has transpired so far, in a strong box up at the bank," Hunterleys assented. " We can stroll up there after lunch and I will place all the documents in your hands. You can look them through then and decide what is best to be done."

The Minister rose to his feet.

" I shall go round to my rooms, change my clothes," he announced, " and meet you presently. We'll lunch across at Ciro's, eh? I didn't mean to come to Monte Carlo this year, but so long as I am here, I may as well make the best of it. You are not looking as though the change had done you much good, Hunterleys."

" The last few days," Hunterleys remarked, a little drily, " have not been exactly in the nature of a holiday."

" Are you here alone? "

" I came alone. I found my wife here by accident. She came through with the Draconmeyers. They were supposed to stay at Cannes, but altered their plans. Of course, Draconmeyer meant to come here all the time."

The Minister frowned.

" Draconmeyer's one man I should be glad to see out of London," he declared. " Under the pretext of fostering good-will, and that sort of thing, between the mercantile classes of our two countries. I think that that fellow has done about as much mischief as it is possible for any single man to have accomplished. We'll meet in an hour, Hunterleys. My man is putting out some things for me and I must have a bath."

Hunterleys walked up to the hospital, and to his surprise met Selingman coming away. The latter saluted him with a wave of the hat and a genial smile.

" Calling to see our poor invalid? " he enquired blandly.

Hunterleys, although he knew his man, was a little taken aback.

" What share in him do you claim? " he asked.

Selingman sighed.

" Alas! " he confessed, " I fear that my claim would sound a little cold-blooded. I think that I was the only man who held his gun straight. Yet, after all, Roche would be the last to bear me any grudge. He was playing the game, taking his risks. Uncommonly bad marksmen Grex's private police were, or he'd be in the morgue instead of the hospital."

" I gather that our friend is still alive? " Hunterleys remarked.

" Going on as well as could be expected," Selingman replied.

" Conscious? "

Selingman smiled.

" You see through my little visit of sympathy at once! " he exclaimed. " Unable to converse, I am assured, and unable to share with his friends any little information he may have picked up last night. By the way, whom shall you send to report our little conference to-night? You wouldn't care to come yourself, would you? "

" I should like to exceedingly," Hunterleys assured him, " if you'd give me a safe conduct."

Selingman withdrew his cigar from his mouth and laid his hand upon the other's shoulder.

"My dear friend," he said earnestly, "your safe conduct, if ever I signed it, would be to the other world. Frankly, we find you rather a nuisance. We would be better pleased if your Party were in office, and you with your knees tucked under a desk at Downing Street, attending to your official business in your official place. Who gave you this roving commission, eh? Who sent you to talk common sense to the Balkan States, and how the mischief did you get wind of our little meeting here?"

"Ah!" Hunterleys replied, "I expect you really know all these things."

Selingman, with his feet planted firmly upon the pavement, took a fresh cigar from his waistcoat pocket, bit off the end and lit it.

"My friend Hunterleys," he continued, "I am enjoying this brief interchange of confidences. Circumstances have made me, as you see, a politician, a schemer if you like. Nature meant me to be one of the frankest, the most truthful, the best-hearted of men. I detest the tortuous ways of the old diplomacy. The spoken word pleases me best. That is why I like a few minutes' conversation with the enemy, why I love to stand here and talk to you with the buttons off our foils. We are scheming against you and your country, and you know it, and we shall win. We can't help but win — if not to-day, to-morrow. Your country has had a marvellously long run of good luck, but it can't last for ever."

Hunterleys smiled.

"Well," he observed, "there's nothing like confidence. If you are so sure of success, why couldn't you choose a cleaner way to it than by tampering with our ally?"

Selingman patted his companion on the shoulder. "Listen, my friend," he said, "there are no such things as allies. An alliance between two countries is a dead letter so soon as their interests cease to be identical. Now Austria is our ally because she is practically Germany. We are both mid-Continental Powers. We both need the same protection. But England and France! Go back only fifty years, my dear Hunterleys, and ask yourself — would any living person, living now and alive then, believe in the lasting nature of such an unnatural alliance? Wherever you look, in every quarter of the globe, your interests are opposed. You robbed France of Egypt. She can't have wholly forgotten. You dominate the Mediterranean through Gibraltar, Malta, and Cyprus. What does she think of that, I wonder? Isn't a humiliation for her when she does stop to think of it? You've a thousand years of quarrels, of fighting and rapine behind you. You can't call yourselves allies because the thing isn't natural. It never could be. It was only your mutual, hysterical fear of Germany which drove you into one another's arms. We fought France once to prove ourselves, and for money. Just now we don't want either money or territory from France. Perhaps we don't even want, my dear Englishman, what you think we want, but all the same, don't blame us for trying to dissolve an unnatural alliance. Was that Simpson who came by the Luxe this morning?"

"It was," Hunterleys admitted.

" The Right Honourable John William Meredith Simpson! " Selingman recited, waving his cigar. " Well, well, we certainly have made a stir with our little meetings here. An inspired English Cabinet Minister, travel-stained and dusty, arrives with his valet and a black dispatch-box, to foil our schemes. Send him along, my friend. We are not at all afraid of Mr. Simpson. Perhaps we may even ask him to join us this evening."

" I fancy," Hunterleys remarked grimly, " that the Englishman who joins you this evening will find a home up on the hill here."

" Or down in the morgue there," Selingman grunted, pointing down to Monaco. " Take care, Hunterleys — take care, man. One of us hates you. It isn't I. You are fighting a brave fight and a losing fight, but you are good metal. Try and remember, when you find that you are beaten, that life has many consolations for the philosopher."

He passed on and Hunterleys entered the hospital. Whilst he was waiting in the little reception-room, Felicia came in. Her face showed signs of her night's anxiety.

" Sidney is still unconscious," she announced, her voice shaking a little. " The doctors seem hopeful — but oh! Sir Henry, it is terrible to see him lying there just as though he were dead! "

" Sidney will pull through all right," Hunterleys declared, encouragingly. " He has a wonderful constitution and he is the luckiest fellow born. He always gets out of trouble, somehow or other."

She came slowly up to him.

" Sir Henry," she said piteously, " I know quite

well that Sidney was willing to take his risks. He
went into this thing, knowing it was dangerous. I
want to be brave. What happens must be. But
listen. You won't — you won't rob me of everything
in life, will you? You won't send David after him? "

Hunterleys smiled reassuringly.

" I can promise you that," he told her. " This
isn't David's job at all. He has to stick to his post
and help out the bluff as a press correspondent.
Don't be afraid, Felicia. You shall have your
David."

She seized his hand and kissed it.

" You have been so kind to me always, Sir Henry,"
she sighed. " I can't tell you how thankful I am to
think that you don't want David to go and run
these horrible risks."

" No fear of that, I promise you," he assured her
once more. " David will be busy enough pulling the
strings another way."

The doctor entered the room and shook hands with
Hunterleys. There was no news, he declared, nothing to be done. The patient must continue in his
present condition for several more hours at least.
The symptoms were, in their way, favourable. Beyond that, nothing could be said. Felicia and
Hunterleys left the hospital together.

" I wonder," she began, as they turned out of the
white gates, " whether you would mind very much if
I told you something? "

" Of course not! "

" Yesterday," she continued slowly, " I met Lady
Hunterleys. You know, I have seen her twice when
I have been to your house to sing for your guests.

She recognised me, I feel sure, but she didn't seem to want to see me. She looked surprised when I bowed. I worried about it at first and then I wondered. You are so very, very secretive just now. Whatever this affair may be in which you three are all concerned, you never open your lips about it. Lady Hunterleys probably doesn't know that you have had to come up to the villa at all hours of the night just to see Sidney. You don't suppose that by any chance she imagined — that you came to see me? "

Hunterleys was struck by the thought. He remembered several chance remarks of his wife. He remembered, too, the coincidence of his recent visits to the villa having prevented him in each case from acceding to some request of Violet's.

" I am glad you've mentioned this, child," he said frankly. " Now I come to think of it, my wife certainly did know that I came up to the villa very late one night, and she seemed upset about it. Of course, she hasn't the faintest idea about your brother."

" Well," Felicia declared, with a sigh of relief, " I felt that I had to tell you. It sounded horribly conceited, in a way, but then she wouldn't know that you came to see Sidney, or that I was engaged to David. Misunderstandings do come about so easily, you know, sometimes."

" This one shall be put right, at any rate," he promised her. " Now, if you will take my advice, you will go home and lie down until the evening. You are going to sing again, aren't you? "

" If there is no change," she replied. " I know that he would like me to. You haven't minded — what I've said? "

"Not a bit, child," he assured her; "in fact I think it was very good of you. Now I'll put you in this carriage and send you home. Think of nothing except that Sidney is getting better every hour, and sing to-night as though your voice could reach his bedside. Au revoir!"

He waved his hand to her as she drove off, and returned to the Hotel de Paris. He found a refreshed and rejuvenated Simpson smoking a cigarette upon the steps.

"To lunch!" the latter exclaimed. "Afterwards I will tell you my plans."

CHAPTER XXXII

AN INTERESTING MEETING

Hunterleys leaned suddenly forward across the little round table.

"The question of whether or no you shall pay your respects to Monsieur Douaille," he remarked, "is solved. Unless I am very much mistaken, we are going to have an exceedingly interesting luncheon-party on our right."

"Monsieur Douaille —" Mr. Simpson began, a little eagerly.

"And the others," Hunterleys interrupted. "Don't look around for a moment. This is almost historical."

Monsieur Ciro himself, bowing and smiling, was ushering a party of guests to a round table upon the terrace, in the immediate vicinity of the two men. Mr. Grex, with his daughter and Lady Hunterleys on one side and Monsieur Douaille on the other, were in the van. Draconmeyer followed with Lady Weybourne, and Selingman brought up the rear with the Comtesse d'Hausson, one of the most prominent leaders of the French colony in Monte Carlo, and a connection by marriage of Monsieur Douaille.

"A luncheon-party for Douaille," Hunterleys murmured, as he bowed to his wife and exchanged greetings with some of the others. "I wonder what they think of their neighbours! A little embarrassing for the chief guest, I am afraid."

" I see your wife is in the enemy's camp," his companion observed. " Draconmeyer is coming to speak to me. This promises to be interesting."

Draconmeyer and Selingman both came over to greet the English Minister. Selingman's blue eyes were twinkling with humour, his smile was broad and irresistible.

" This should send funds up in every capital of Europe," he declared, as he shook hands. " When Mr. Meredith Simpson takes a holiday, then the political barometer points to ' set fair '! "

" A tribute to my conscientiousness," the Minister replied, smiling. " I am glad to see that I am not the only hard-worked statesman who feels able to take a few days' holiday."

Selingman glanced at the round table and beamed.

" It is true," he admitted. " Every country seems to have sent its statesmen holiday-making. And what a playground, too! " he added, glancing towards Hunterleys with something which was almost a wink. " Here, political crises seem of little account by the side of the turning wheel. This is where the world unbends and it is well that there should be such a place. Shall we see you at the Club or in the rooms later? "

" Without a doubt," Mr. Simpson assented. " For what else does one live in Monte Carlo? "

" How did you leave things in town? " Mr. Draconmeyer enquired.

" So-so! " the Minister answered. " A little flat, but then it is a dull season of the year."

" Markets about the same, I suppose? " Mr. Draconmeyer asked.

" I am afraid," Mr. Simpson confessed, " that I only study the city column from the point of view of what Herr Selingman has just called the political barometer. Things were a little unsteady when I left. Consols fell several points yesterday."

Mr. Draconmeyer frowned.

" It is incomprehensible," he declared. " A few months ago there was real danger, one is forced to believe, of a European war. To-day the crisis is passed, yet the money-markets which bore up so well through the critical period seem now all the time on the point of collapse. It is hard for a banker to know how to operate these days. I wish you gentlemen in Downing Street, Mr. Simpson, would make it easier for us."

Mr. Simpson shrugged his shoulders.

" The real truth of the matter is," he said, " that you allow your money-market to become too sensitive an affair. A whisper will depress it. A threatening word spoken in the Reichstag or in the House of Parliament, magnified a hundred-fold before it reaches its destination, has sometimes a most unwarranted effect upon markets. You mustn't blame us so much, Mr. Draconmeyer. You jump at conclusions too easily in the city."

" Sound common sense," Mr. Draconmeyer agreed. " You are perfectly right when you say that we are over-sensitive. The banker deplores it as much as the politician. It's the money-kings, I suppose, who find it profitable."

They returned to their table a moment later. As

he passed Douaille, Selingman whispered in his ear.
Monsieur Douaille turned around at once and bowed
to Simpson. As he caught the latter's eye he, too,
left his place and came across. Mr. Simpson rose
to his feet. The two men bowed formally before
shaking hands.

"Monsieur Simpson," the Frenchman exclaimed,
"it is a pleasure to find that I am remembered!"

"Without a doubt, monsieur," was the prompt
reply. "Your last visit to London, on the occasion
when we had the pleasure of entertaining you at the
Guildhall, is too recent, and was too memorable an
event altogether for us to have forgotten. Permit
me to assure you that your speech on that occasion
was one which no patriotic Englishman is likely to
forget."

Monsieur Douaille inclined his head in thanks.
His manner was not altogether free from embarrassment.

"I trust that you are enjoying your holiday
here?" he asked.

"I have only this moment arrived," Mr. Simpson
explained. "I am looking forward to a few days'
rest immensely. I trust that I shall have the
pleasure of seeing something of you, Monsieur
Douaille. A little conversation would be most agreeable."

"In Monte Carlo one meets one's friends all the
time," Monsieur Douaille replied. "I lunch to-day
with my friend — our mutual friend, without a doubt
— who calls himself here Mr. Grex."

Mr. Simpson nodded.

"If it is permitted," he suggested, "I should like

to do myself the honour of paying my respects to you."

Monsieur Douaille was flattered.

" My stay here is short," he regretted, " but your visit will be most acceptable. I am at the Riviera Palace Hotel."

" It is one of my theories," Mr. Simpson remarked, " that politicians are at a serious disadvantage compared with business men, inasmuch as, with important affairs under their control, they have few opportunities of meeting those with whom they have dealings. It would be a great pleasure to me to discuss one or two matters with you."

Monsieur Douaille departed, with a few charming words of assent. Simpson looked after him with kindling eyes.

" This," he murmured, leaning across the table, " is a most extraordinary meeting. There they sit, those very men whom you suspect of this devilish scheme, within a few feet of us! Positively thrilling, Hunterleys! "

Hunterleys, too, seemed to feel the stimulating effect of a situation so dramatic. As the meal progressed, he drew his chair a little closer to the table and leaned over towards his companion.

" I think," he said, " that we shall both of us remember the coincidence of this meeting as long as we live. At that luncheon-table, within a few yards of us, sits Russia, the new Russia, raising his head after a thousand years' sleep, watching the times, weighing them, realising his own immeasurable strength, pointing his inevitable finger along the road which the Russia of to-morrow must tread.

There isn't a man in that great country so much to be feared to-day, from our point of view, as the Grand Duke Augustus. And look, too, at the same table, within a few feet, Simpson, of you and of me — Selingman, Selingman who represents the real Germany; not the war party alone, intoxicated with the clash of arms, filled with bombastic desires for German triumphs on sea and land, ever ready to spout in flowery and grandiloquent phrases the glory of Germany and the Heaven-sent genius of her leaders. I tell you, Simpson, Selingman is a more dangerous man than that. He sits with folded arms, in realms of thought above these people. He sits with a map of the world before him, and he places his finger upon the inevitable spots which Germany must possess to keep time with the march of the world, to find new homes for her overflowing millions. He has no military fervour, no tinselly patriotism. He knows what Germany needs and he will carve her way towards it. Look at him with his napkin tucked under his chin, broad-visaged, podgy, a slave, you might think, to the joys of the table and the grosser things of life. You should see his eyes sometimes when the right note is struck, watch his mouth when he sits and thinks. He uses words for an ambush and a barricade. He talks often like a gay fool, a flood of empty verbiage streams from his lips, and behind, all the time his brain works."

" You seem to have studied these people, Hunterleys," Simpson remarked appreciatively.

Hunterleys smiled as he continued his luncheon.

" Forgive me if I was a little prolix," he said, " but, after all, what would you have? I am out of office but I remain a servant of my country. My interest is just as keen as though I were in a responsible position."

"You are well out of it," Simpson sighed. "If half what you suspect is true, it's the worst fix we've been in for some time."

"I am afraid there isn't any doubt about it," Hunterleys declared. "Of course, we've been at a fearful disadvantage. Roche was the only man out here upon whom I could rely. Now they've accounted for him, we've scarcely a chance of getting at the truth."

Mr. Simpson was gloomily silent for some moments. He was thinking of the time when he had struck his pencil through a recent Secret Service estimate.

"Anyhow," Hunterleys went on, "it will be all over in twenty-four hours. Something will be decided upon — what, I am afraid there is very little chance of our getting to know. These men will separate — Grex to St. Petersburg, Selingman to Berlin, Douaille to Paris. Then I think we shall begin to hear the mutterings of the storm."

"I think," Mr. Simpson intervened, his eyes fixed upon an approaching figure, "that there is a young lady talking to the maître d'hôtel, who is trying to attract your attention."

Hunterleys turned around in his chair. It was Felicia who was making her way towards him. He rose at once to his feet. There was a little murmur of interest amongst the lunchers as she threaded her way past the tables. It was not often that an English singer in opera had met with so great a success. Lady Hunterleys, recognising her as she passed, paused in the middle of a sentence. Her face hardened. Hunterleys had risen from his place and was watching Felicia's approach anxiously.

" Is there any news of Sidney? " he asked quickly, as he took her hand.

" Nothing fresh," she answered in a low voice. " I have brought you a message — from some one else."

He held his chair for her but she shook her head.

" I mustn't stay," she continued. " This is what I wanted to tell you. As I was crossing the square just now, I recognised the man Frenhofer, from the Villa Mimosa. Directly he saw me he came across the road. He was looking for one of us. He dared not come to the villa, he declares, for fear of being watched. He has something to tell you."

" Where can I find him? " Hunterleys asked.

" He has gone to a little bar in the Rue de Chaussures, the Bar de Montmartre it is called. He is waiting there for you now."

" You must stay and have some lunch," Hunterleys begged. " I will come back."

She shook her head.

" I have just been across to the Opera House," she explained, " to enquire about some properties for to-night. I have had all the lunch I want and I am on my way to the hospital now again. I came here on the chance of finding you. They told me at the Hotel de Paris that you were lunching out."

Hunterleys turned and whispered to Simpson.

" This is very important," he said. " It concerns the affair in which we are interested. Linger over your coffee and I will return."

Mr. Simpson nodded and Hunterleys left the restaurant with Felicia.   His wife, at whom he glanced for a moment, kept her head averted.   She was whispering in the ear of the gallant Monsieur Douaille.   Selingman, catching Draconmeyer's eye, winked at him solemnly.

"You have all the luck, my silent friend," he murmured.

CHAPTER XXXIII

THE FATES ARE KIND

The Bar de Montmartre was many steps under the level of the street, dark, smelly, and dilapidated. Its only occupants were a handful of drivers from the carriage-stand opposite, who stared at Hunterleys in amazement as he entered, and then rushed forward, almost in a body, to offer their services. The man behind the bar, however, who had evidently been forewarned, intervened with a few sharp words, and, lifting the flap of the counter, ushered Hunterleys into a little room beyond. Frenhofer was engaged there in amiable badinage with a young lady who promptly disappeared at Hunterleys' entrance. Frenhofer bowed respectfully.

" I must apologise," he said, " for bringing monsieur to such a place. It is near the end now, and with Monsieur Roche in the hospital I ventured to address myself to monsieur direct. Here I have the right to enter. I make my suit to the daughter of the proprietor in order to have a safe rendezvous when necessary. It is well that monsieur has come quickly. I have tidings. I can disclose to monsieur the meeting-place for to-night. If monsieur has fortune and the wit to make use of it, the opportunity I shall give him is a great one. But pardon me. Before we talk business we must order something."

He touched the bell. The proprietor himself thrust in his head, bullet-shaped, with black moustache and unshaven chin. He wore no collar, and the remainder of his apparel was negligible.

"A bottle of your best brandy," Frenhofer ordered. "The best, mind, Père Hanaut."

The man's acquiescence was as amiable as nature would permit.

"Monsieur will excuse me," Frenhofer went on, as the door was once more closed, "but these people have their little ways. To sell a whole bottle of brandy at five times its value, is to Monsieur le Propriétaire more agreeable than to offer him rent for the hire of his room. He is outside all the things in which we are concerned. He believes — pardon me, monsieur — that we are engaged in a little smuggling transaction. Monsieur Roche and I have used this place frequently."

"He can believe what he likes," Hunterleys replied, "so long as he keeps his mouth shut."

The brandy was brought — and three glasses. Frenhofer promptly took the hint and, filling one to the brim, held it out to the landlord.

"You will drink our health, Père Henaut — my health and the health of monsieur here, and the health of the fair Annette. Incidentally, you will drink also to the success of the little scheme which monsieur and I are planning."

"In such brandy," the proprietor declared hoarsely, "I would drink to the devil himself!"

He threw back his head and the contents of his

glass vanished. He set it down with a little smack of the lips. Once more he looked at the bottle. Frenhofer filled up his glass, but motioned to the door with his head.

" You will excuse us, dear friend," he begged, laying his hand persuasively upon the other's shoulder. " Monsieur and I have little enough of time."

The landlord withdrew. Frenhofer walked around the little apartment. Their privacy was certainly assured.

" Monsieur," he announced, turning to Hunterleys, " there has been a great discussion as to the next meeting-place between our friends — the next, which will be also the last. They are safe enough in reality at the villa, but Monsieur Douaille is nervous. The affair of last night terrified him. The reason for these things I, of course, know nothing of, but it seems that Monsieur Douaille is very anxious indeed to keep his association with my august master and Herr Selingman as secret as possible. He has declined most positively to set foot again within the Villa Mimosa. Many plans have been suggested. This is the one adopted. For some weeks a German down in Monaco, a shipping agent, has had a yacht in the harbour for hire. He has approached Mr. Grex several times, not knowing his identity; ignorant, indeed, of the fact that the Grand Duke himself possesses one of the finest yachts afloat. However, that is nothing. Mr. Grex thought suddenly of the yacht. He suggested it to the others. They were enthusiastic. The yacht is to be hired for a week, or longer if necessary, and used only to-night. Behold the wonderful good-fortune of the affair!

It is I who have been selected by my master to proceed to Monaco to make arrangements with the German, Herr Schwann. I am on my way there at the moment."

" A yacht? " Hunterleys repeated.

" There are wonderful things to be thought of," Frenhofer asserted eagerly. " Consider, monsieur! The yacht of this man Schwann has never been seen by my master. Consider, too, that aboard her there must be a dozen hiding-places. The crew has been brought together from anywhere. They can be bought to a man. There is only one point, monsieur, which should be arranged before I enter upon this last and, for me, most troublesome and dangerous enterprise."

" And that? " Hunterleys enquired.

" My own position," Frenhofer declared solemnly. " I am not greedy or covetous. My ambitions have long been fixed. To serve an Imperial Russian nobleman has been no pleasure for me. St. Petersburg has been a prison. I have been moved to the right or to the left as a machine. It is as a machine only I have lived. Always I have longed for Paris. So month by month I have saved. After to-night I must leave my master's employ. The risk will be too great if monsieur indeed accepts my proposition and carries it out. I need but a matter of ten thousand francs to complete my savings."

The man's white face shone eagerly in the dim light of the gloomy little apartment. His eyes glittered. He waited almost breathlessly.

" Frenhofer," Hunterleys said slowly, " so far as I have been concerned indirectly in these negotiations with you, my instructions to my agent have been simple and definite. We have never haggled. Your name was known to me eight years ago, when you served us in St. Petersburg and served us well. You have done the same thing now and you have behaved with rare intelligence. Within the course of an hour I shall transfer ten thousand francs to the account of François Frenhofer at the English Bank here."

The eyes of the man seemed suddenly like pinpricks of fire.

" Monsieur is a prince," he murmured. " And now for the further details. If monsieur would run the risk, I would suggest that he accompanies me to the office of this man Schwann."

Hunterleys made no immediate reply. He was walking up and down the narrow apartment. A brilliant idea had taken possession of him. The more he thought of it, the more feasible it became.

" Frenhofer," he said at last, " I have a scheme of my own. You are sure that Mr. Grex has never seen this yacht? "

" He has never set eyes upon it, monsieur, save to try and single it out with his field-glasses from the balcony of the villa."

" And he is to board it to-night? "

" At ten o'clock to-night, monsieur, it is to lie off the Villa Mimosa. A pinnace is to fetch Mr. Grex and his friends on board from the private landing-stage of the Villa Mimosa."

Hunterleys nodded thoughtfully.

" Frenhofer," he explained, " my scheme is this. A friend of mine has a yacht in the harbour. I believe that he would lend it to me. Why should we not substitute it for the yacht your master imagines that he is hiring? If so, all difficulties as to placing whom I desire on board and secreting them are over."

" It is a great scheme," Frenhofer assented, " but supposing my master should choose to telephone some small detail to the office of the man Schwann? "

" You must hire the yacht of Schwann, just as you were instructed," Hunterleys pointed out. " You must give orders, though, that it is not to leave the harbour until telephoned for. Then it will be the yacht which I shall borrow which will lie off the Villa Mimosa to-night."

" It is admirable," Frenhofer declared. " The more one thinks of it, the more one appreciates. This yacht of Schwann's — the *Christable*, he calls it — was fitted out by a millionaire. My master will be surprised at nothing in the way of luxury."

" Tell me again," Hunterleys asked, " at what hour is it to be off the Villa Mimosa? "

" At ten o'clock," Frenhofer replied. " A pinnace is to be at the landing-stage of the villa at that time. Mr. Grex, Monsieur Douaille, Herr Selingman, and Mr. Draconmeyer will come on board."

" Very good! Now go on your errand to the man Schwann. You had better meet me here later in the afternoon — say at four o'clock — and let me know that all is in order. I will bring you some particulars about my friend's boat, so that you will know how to answer any questions your master may put to you."

" It is admirable," Frenhofer repeated enthusiastically. " Monsieur had better, perhaps, precede me."

Hunterleys walked through the streets back to Ciro's Restaurant, filled with a new exhilaration. His eyes were bright, his brain was working all the time. The luncheon-party at the next table were still in the midst of their meal. Mr. Simpson was smoking a meditative cigarette with his coffee. Hunterleys resumed his place and ordered coffee for himself.

" I have been to see a poor friend who met with an accident last night," he announced, speaking as clearly as possible. " I fear that he is very ill. That was his sister who fetched me away."

Mr. Simpson nodded sympathetically. Their conversation for a few minutes was desultory. Then Hunterleys asked for the bill and rose.

" I will take you round to the Club and get your *carte*," he suggested. " Afterwards, we can spend the afternoon as you choose."

The two men strolled out of the place. It was not until after they had left the arcade and were actually in the street, that Hunterleys gripped his companion's arm.

" Simpson," he declared, " the fates have been kind to us. Douaille has a fit of the nerves. He will go no more to the Villa Mimosa. Seeking about for the safest meeting-place, Grex has given us a chance. The only one of his servants who belongs to us is commissioned to hire a yacht on which they meet to-night."

" A yacht," Mr. Simpson replied, emptily.

" I have a friend," Hunterleys continued, " an American. I am convinced that he will lend me his yacht, which is lying in the harbour here. We are going to try and exchange. If we succeed, I shall have the run of the boat. The crew will be at our command, and I shall get to that conference myself, somehow or other."

Mr. Simpson felt himself left behind. He could only stare at his companion.

" Tell me, Sir Henry," he begged, almost pathetically, " have I walked into an artificial world? Do you mean to tell me seriously that you, a Member of Parliament, an ex-Minister, are engaged upon a scheme to get the Grand Duke Augustus and Douaille and Selingman on board a yacht, and that you are going to be there, concealed, turned into a spy? I can't keep up with it. As fiction it seems to me to be in the clouds. As truth, why, my understanding turns and mocks me. You are talking fairy-tales."

Hunterleys smiled tolerantly.

" The man in the street knows very little of the real happenings in life," he pronounced. " The truth has a queer way sometimes of spreading itself out into the realms of fiction. Come across here with me to the hotel. I have got to move heaven and earth to find my friend."

" Do with me as you like," Mr. Simpson sighed resignedly. " In a plain political discussion, or an argument with Monsieur Douaille — well, I am ready to bear my part. But this sort of thing lifts me off my feet. I can only trot along at your heels."

They entered the Hotel de Paris. Hunterleys made a few breathless enquiries. Nothing, alas ! was known of Mr. Richard Lane. He came back, frowning, to the steps of the hotel.

" If he is up playing golf at La Turbie," Hunterleys muttered, " we shall barely have time."

A reception clerk tapped him on the shoulder. He turned abruptly around.

" I have just made an enquiry of the floor waiter," the clerk announced. " He believes that Mr. Lane is still in his room."

Hunterleys thanked the man and hurried to the lift. In a few moments he was knocking at the door of Lane's rooms. His heart gave a great jump as a familiar voice bade him enter. He stepped inside and closed the door behind him. Richard, in light blue pyjamas, sat up in bed and looked at his visitor with a huge yawn.

" Say, old chap, are you in a hurry or anything? " he demanded.

" Do you know the time? " Hunterleys asked.

" No idea," the other replied. " The valet called me at eight. I told him I'd shoot him if he disturbed me again."

" It's nearly three o'clock! " Hunterleys declared impressively.

" Can't help it," Richard yawned, throwing off the bed-clothes and sitting on the edge of the bed. " I am young and delicate and I need my rest. Seriously, Hunterleys," he added, " you take a chap out and make him drive you at sixty miles an hour all through the night, you keep him at it till nearly six in the morning, and you seem to think it a tragedy to find him in bed at three o'clock in the afternoon. Hang it, I've only had eight hours' sleep! "

" I don't care how long you've had," Hunterleys rejoined. " I am only too thankful to find you.

Now listen.   Is your brain working?   Can you talk seriously? "

" I guess so."

" You remember our talk last night? "

" Every word of it."

" The time has come," Hunterleys continued,— " your time, I mean.   You said that if you could take a hand, you'd do it.   I am here to beg for your help."

" You needn't waste your breath doing that," Richard answered firmly.   " I'm your man.   Go on."

" Listen," Hunterleys proceeded.   " Is your yacht in commission? "

" Ready to sail at ten minutes' notice," the young man assured him emphatically, " victualled and coaled to the eyelids.   To tell you the truth, I have some idea of abducting Fedora to-day or to-morrow."

" You'll have to postpone that," Hunterleys told him.   " I want to borrow the yacht."

" She's yours," Richard assented promptly.   " I'll give you a note to the captain."

" Look here, I want you to understand this clearly," Hunterleys went on.   " If you lend me the *Minnehaha*, well, you commit yourself a bit.   You see, it's like this.   I've one man of my own in Grex's household.   He came to me this morning.   Monsieur Douaille objects to cross again the threshold of the Villa Mimosa.   He fears the English newspapers. There has been a long discussion as to the next meeting-place.   Grex suggested a yacht.   To that they all agreed.   There is a man named Schwann down in

Monaco has a yacht for hire. Mr. Grex knows about
it and he has sent the man I spoke of into Monaco
this afternoon to hire it. They are all going to em-
bark at ten o'clock to-night. They are going to
hold their meeting in the cabin."

Lane whistled softly. He was wide awake now.

" Go on," he murmured. " Go on. Say, this is
great ! "

" I want," Hunterleys explained, " your yacht to
take the place of the other. I want it to be off the
Villa Mimosa at ten o'clock to-night, your pinnace
to be at the landing-stage of the villa to bring Mr.
Grex and his friends on board. I want you to haul
down your American flag, keep your American sailors
out of sight, cover up the Stars and Stripes in your
cabin, have only your foreign stewards on show.
Schwann's yacht is a costly one. No one will know
the difference. You must get up now and show me
over the boat. I have to scheme, somehow or other,
how we can hide ourselves on it so that I can over-
hear the end of this plot."

The face of Richard Lane was like the face of an
ingenuous boy who sees suddenly a Paradise of sport
stretched out before him. His mouth was open, his
eyes gleaming.

" Gee, but this is glorious ! " he exclaimed. " I'm
with you all the way. Why, it's wonderful, man !
It's a chapter from the Arabian Nights over again ! "

He leapt to his feet and rang the bell furiously.
Then he rushed to the telephone.

" Blue serge clothes," he ordered the valet. " Get
my bath ready."

" Any breakfast, monsieur ? "

"Oh, breakfast be hanged! No, wait a moment. Get me some coffee and a roll. I'll take it while I dress. Hurry up! . . . Yes, is that the enquiry office? This is Mr. Lane. Send round to my chauffeur at the garage at once and tell him that I want the car at the door in a quarter of an hour. Righto! . . . Sit down, Hunterleys. Smoke or do whatever you want to. We'll be off to the yacht in no time."

Hunterleys clapped the young giant on the shoulders as he rushed through to the bathroom.

"You're a brick, Richard," he declared. "I'll wait for you down in the hall. I've a pal there."

"I'll be down in twenty minutes or earlier," Lane promised. "What a lark!"

CHAPTER XXXIV

COFFEE FOR ONE ONLY

The breaking up of Mr. Grex's luncheon-party was the signal for a certain amount of manœuvring on the part of one or two of his guests. Monsieur Douaille, for instance, was anxious to remain the escort of Lady Hunterleys, whose plans for the afternoon he had ascertained were unformed. Mr. Grex was anxious to keep apart his daughter and Lady Weybourne, whose relationship to Richard Lane he had only just apprehended; while he himself desired a little quiet conversation with Monsieur Douaille before they paid the visit which had been arranged for to the Club and the Casino. In the end, Mr. Grex was both successful and unsuccessful. He carried off Monsieur Douaille for a short ride in his automobile, but was forced to leave his daughter and Lady Weybourne alone. Draconmeyer, who had been awaiting his opportunity, remained by Lady Hunterleys' side.

"I wonder," he asked, "whether you would step in for a few minutes and see Linda?"

She had been looking at the table where her husband and his companion had been seated. Draconmeyer's voice seemed to bring her back to a present not altogether agreeable.

"I am going back to my room for a little time," she replied. "I will call in and see Linda first, if you like."

They left the restaurant together and strolled across the Square to the Hotel de Paris, ascended in the lift, and made their way to Draconmeyer's suite of rooms in a silence which was almost unbroken. When they entered the large salon with its French-windows and balcony, they found the apartment deserted. Violet looked questioningly at her companion. He closed the door behind him and nodded.

"Yes," he admitted, "my message was a subterfuge. I have sent Linda over to Mentone with her nurse. She will not be back until late in the afternoon. This is the opportunity for which I have been waiting."

She showed no signs of anger or, indeed, disturbance of any sort. She laid her tiny white silk parasol upon the table and glanced at him coolly.

"Well," she said, "you have your way, then. I am here."

Draconmeyer looked at her long and anxiously. Skilled though he was in physiognomy, closely though he had watched, for many months, the lights and shades, the emotional changes in her expression, he was yet, at that moment, completely puzzled. She was not angry. Her attitude seemed to be, in a sense, passive. Yet what did passivity mean? Was it resignation, consent, or was it simply the armour of normal resistance in which she had clothed herself? Was he wise, after all, to risk everything? Then, as he looked at her, as he realised her close and wonderful presence, he suddenly told himself that it was worth while risking even Heaven in the future for the joy of holding her for once in his arms. She had never seemed to him so maddeningly beautiful as at that moment. It was one of the hottest days of the season and she was wearing a gown of white muslin, curiously simple, enhancing, somehow or other, her fascinating slimness, a slimness which had nothing to do with angularity but possessed its own soft and graceful curves. Her eyes were bluer even than her turquoise brooch or the gentians in her hat. And while his heart was aching and throbbing with doubts and hopes, she suddenly smiled at him.

"I am going to sit down," she announced carelessly. "Please say to me just what is in your mind, without reserve. It will be better."

She threw herself into a low chair near the window. Her hands were folded in her lap. Her eyes, for some reason, were fixed upon her wedding ring. Swift to notice even her slightest action, he frowned as he discerned the direction of her gaze.

"Violet," he said, "I think that you are right. I think that the time has come when I must tell you what is in my mind."

She raised her eyebrows slightly at the sound of her Christian name. He moved over and stood by her chair.

"For a good many years," he began slowly, "I have been a man with a purpose. When it first came into my mind — not willingly — its accomplishment seemed utterly hopeless. Still, it was there. Strong man though I am, I could not root it out. I waited. There was nothing else to do but wait. From that moment my life was divided. My whole-soul devotion to worldly affairs was severed. I had one dream that was more wonderful to me, even, than complete success in the great undertaking which brought me to London. That dream was connected with you, Violet."

She moved a little uneasily, as though the repetition of her Christian name grated. This time, however, he was rapt in his subject.

" I won't make excuses," he went on. " You know what Linda is — what she has been for ten years. I have tried to be kind to her. As to love, I never had any. Ours was an alliance between two great monied families, arranged for us, acquiesced in by both of us as a matter of course. It seemed to me in those days the most natural and satisfactory form of marriage. I looked upon myself as others have thought me — a cold, bloodless man of figures and ambition. It is you who have taught me that I have as much sentiment and more than other men, a heart and desires which have made life sometimes hell and sometimes paradise. For two years I have struggled. Life with me has been a sort of passionate compromise. For the joy of seeing you sometimes, of listening to you and watching you, I have borne the agony of having you leave me to take your place with another man. You don't quite know what that meant, and I am not going to tell you, but always I have hoped and hoped."

" And now," she said, looking at him, " I owe you four thousand pounds and you think, perhaps, that your time has come to speak? "

He shivered as though she had struck him a blow.

" You think," he exclaimed, " that I am a man of

pounds, shillings, and pence! Is it my fault that you owe me money?"

He snatched her cheques from his inner pocket and ripped them in pieces, lit a match and watched them while they smouldered away. She, too, watched with emotionless face.

"Do you think that I want to buy you?" he demanded. "There! You are free from your money claims. You can leave my room this moment, if you will, and owe me nothing."

She made no movement, yet he was vaguely disturbed by a sense of having made but little progress, a terrible sense of impending failure. His fingers began to tremble, his face was the face of a man stretched upon the rack.

"Perhaps those words of mine were false," he went on. "Perhaps, in a sense, I do want to buy you, buy the little kindnesses that go with affection, buy your kind words, the touch sometimes of your fingers, the pleasant sense of companionship I feel when I am with you. I know how proud you are. I know how virtuous you are. I know that it's there in your blood, the Puritan instinct, the craving for the one man to whom you have given yourself, the involuntary shrinking from the touch of any other. Good women are like that — wives or mistresses. Mind, in a sense it's narrow; in a sense it's splendid. Listen to me. I don't want to declare war against that instinct — yet. I can't. Perhaps, even now, I have spoken too soon, craved too soon for the little I do ask. Yet God knows I can keep the seal upon my lips no longer! Don't let us misunderstand one another for the sake of using plain words. I am not asking you to be my mistress. I ask you, on my knees, to take from me what makes life brighter for you. I ask you for the other things only — for your confidence, for your affection, your companionship. I ask to see you every day that it is possible, to know that you are wearing my gifts, surrounded by my flowers, the rough places in your life made smooth by my efforts. I am your suppliant, Violet. I ask only for the crumbs that fall from your table, so long as no other man sits by your side. Violet, can't you give me as much as this? "

His hand, hot and trembling, sought hers, touched and gripped it. She drew her fingers away. It was curious how in those few moments she seemed to be gifted with an immense clear-sightedness. She knew very well that nothing about the man was honest save the passion of which he did not speak. She rose to her feet.

" Well," she said, " I have listened to you very patiently. If I owe you any excuse for having appeared to encourage any one of those thoughts of which you speak, here it is. I am like thousands of other women. I absolutely don't know until the time comes what sort of a creature I am, how I shall be moved to act under certain circumstances. I tried to think last night. I couldn't. I felt that I had gone half-way. I had taken your money. I had taken it, too, understanding what it means to be in a man's debt. And still I waited. And now I know. I won't even question your sincerity. I won't even suggest that you would not be content with what you ask for —"

" I have sworn it! " he interrupted hoarsely. " To

be your favoured friend, to be allowed near you —
your guardian, if you will —"

The words failed him. Something in her face
checked his eloquence.

" I can tell you this now and for always," she continued. "I have nothing to give you. What you
ask for is just as impossible as though you were to
walk in your picture gallery and kneel before your
great masterpiece and beg Beatrice herself to step
down from the canvas. I began to wonder yesterday," she went on, rising abruptly and moving
across the room, " whether I really was that sort
of woman. With your money in my pocket and the
gambling fever in my pulses, I began even to believe
it. And now I know that I am not. Good-bye,
Mr. Draconmeyer. I don't blame you. On the
whole, perhaps, you have behaved quite well. I think
that you have chosen to behave well because that
wonderful brain of yours told you that it gave you
the best chance. That doesn't really matter,
though."

He took a quick, almost a threatening step towards her. His face was dark with all the pas-
sions which had preyed upon the man.

" There is a man's last resource," he muttered
thickly.

" And there is a woman's answer to it," she replied,
her finger suddenly resting upon an unsuspected bell
in the wall.

They both heard its summons. Footsteps came
hurrying along the corridor. Draconmeyer turned
his head away, struggling to compose himself. A
waiter entered. Lady Hunterleys picked up her par-

asol and moved towards the door. The man stood on one side with a bow.

" Here is the waiter you rang for, Mr. Draconmeyer," she remarked, looking over his shoulder. " Wasn't it coffee you wanted? Tell Linda I'll hope to see her sometime this evening."

She strolled away. The waiter remained patiently upon the threshold.

" Coffee for one or two, sir? " he enquired.

Mr. Draconmeyer struggled for a moment against a torrent of words which scorched his lips. In the end, however, he triumphed.

" For one, with cream," he ordered.

CHAPTER XXXV

A NEW MAP OF THE EARTH

Selingman, who was leaning back in a leather-padded chair and smoking a very excellent cigar, looked around at his companions with a smile of complete approval.

"Our host," he declared, bowing to Mr. Grex, "has surpassed himself. For a hired yacht I have seen nothing more magnificent. A Cabinet Moselle, Flor de Cuba cigars, the best of company, and an isolation beyond all question. What place could suit us better?"

There was a little murmur of assent. The four men were seated together in the wonderfully decorated saloon of what was, beyond doubt, a most luxurious yacht. Through the open porthole were visible, every few moments, as the yacht rose and sank on the swell, the long line of lights which fringed the shore between Monte Carlo and Mentone; the mountains beyond, with tiny lights flickering like spangles in a black mantle of darkness; and further round still, the stream of light from the Casino, reflected far and wide upon the black waters.

"None," Mr. Grex asserted confidently. "We are at least beyond reach of these bungling English spies. There is no further fear of eavesdroppers. We are entirely alone. Each may speak his own mind.   There is nothing to be feared in the way of interruption.   I trust, Monsieur Douaille, that you appreciate the altered circumstances."

Monsieur Douaille, who was looking very much more at his ease, assented without hesitation.

"I must confess," he agreed, "that the isolation we now enjoy is, to a certain extent, reassuring. Here we need no longer whisper.   One may listen carefully.   One may weigh well what is said.   Sooner or later we must come to the crucial point.   This, if you like, is a game of make-believe.   Then, in make-believe, Germany has offered to restore Alsace and Lorraine, has offered to hold all French territory as sacred, provided France allows her to occupy Calais for one year.   What is your object, Herr Selingman?   Do you indeed wish to invade England?"

Selingman poured himself out a glass of wine from the bottle which stood at his elbow.

"Good!" he said.   "We have come to plain questions.   I answer in plain speech.   I will tell you now, in a few words, all that remains to be told.   Germany has no desire to invade Great Britain.   If one may believe the newspapers, there is scarcely an Englishman alive who would credit this simple fact, but it is nevertheless true.   Commercially, England, and a certain measure of English prosperity, are necessary to Germany.   Geographically, there are certain risks to be run in an invasion of that country, which we do not consider worth while.   Besides, an invasion, even a successful one, would result in making an everlasting and a bitter enemy of Great Britain.   We learnt our lesson when we took territory from France.   We do not need to repeat it.   Several hundred thousands of our most worthy citizens are finding an honest and prosperous living in London. Several thousands of our merchants are in business there, and prospering. Several hundreds of our shrewdest men of affairs are making fortunes upon the London Stock Exchange. Therefore, we do not wish to conquer England. Commercially, that conquest is already affected. I want you, Monsieur Douaille, to absolutely understand this, because it may affect your views. What we do require is to strike a long and lasting blow at the navy of Great Britain. As a somewhat larger Holland, Great Britain is welcome to a peaceful existence. When she lords it over the world, talks of an Empire upon which the sun never sets, then the time arrives when we are forced to interfere. Great Britain has possessions which she is not strong enough to hold. Germany is strong enough to wrest them from her, and means to do so. The English fleet must be destroyed. South Africa, then, will come to Germany, India to Russia, Egypt to France. The rest follows as a matter of course."

"And what is the rest?" Monsieur Douaille asked.

Herr Selingman was content no longer to sit in his place. He rose to his feet. His face had fallen into different lines. His eyes flashed, his words were inspired.

"The rest," he declared, "is the crux of the whole matter. It is the one great and settled goal towards which we who have understood have schemed and fought our way. With the British Navy destroyed, the Monroe Doctrine is not worth a sheet of writing-paper. South America is Germany's natural heritage, by every right worth considering. It is our people's gold which founded the Argentine Republic, the brains of our people which control its destinies. Our Eldorado is there, Monsieur Douaille. That is the country which, sooner or later, Germany must possess. We look nowhere else. We covet no other of our neighbours' possessions. Only I say that the sooner America makes up her mind to the sacrifice, the better. Her Monroe Doctrine is all very well for the Northern States. When she presumes to quote it as a pretext for keeping Germany from her natural place in South America, she crosses swords with us. Now you know the truth, and the whole truth. You know, Monsieur Douaille, what we require from you, and you know your reward. Our host has already told you, and will tell you again as often as you like, the feeling of his own country. The Franco-Russian alliance is already doomed. It falls to pieces through sheer lack of common interests. The entente cordiale is simply a fetter and a dead weight upon you. Monsieur Douaille, I put it to you as a man of common sense. Do you think that you, as a statesman — you see, I will put the burden upon your shoulders, because, if you choose, you can speak for your country — do you think that you have a right to refuse from Germany the return of Alsace and Lorraine? Do you think that you can look your country in the face if you refuse on her behalf the greatest gift which has ever yet been offered to any nation — the gift of Egypt? The old alliances are out of date. The balance of power has shifted. I ask you, Monsieur

Douaille, as you value the prosperity and welfare of your country, to weigh what I have said and what our great Russian friend has said, word by word. England has made no sacrifices for you. Why should you sacrifice yourself for her? "

Monsieur Douaille stroked his little grey imperial.

" That is well enough," he muttered, " but without the English Navy the balance of power upon the Continent is entirely upset."

" The balance of power only according to the present grouping of interests," Mr. Grex pointed out. " Selingman has shown us how these must change. Frankly, although no one can fail to realise the immense importance of South America as a colonising centre, it is my honest opinion that the nation who scores most by my friend Selingman's plans, is not Germany but France. Think what it means to her. Instead of being a secondary Power, she will of her own might absolutely control the Mediterranean. Egypt, with its vast possibilities, its ever-elastic boundary, falls to her hand. Malta and Cyprus follow. It is a great price that Germany is prepared to pay."

Monsieur Douaille was silent for several moments. It was obvious that he was deeply impressed.

" This is a matter," he said, " which must be considered from many points of view. Supposing that France were willing to bury the hatchet with Germany, to remain neutral or to place Calais at Germany's disposal. Even then, do you suppose, Herr Selingman, that it would be an easy matter to destroy the British Navy? "

" We have our plans," Selingman declared solemnly. "We know very well that they can be carried out only at a great loss both of men and ships. It is a gloomy and terrible task that lies before us, but at the other end of it is the glory that never fades."

"If America," Douaille remarked, "were to have an inkling of your real objective, her own fleet would come to the rescue."

"Why should America know of our ultimate aims?" Selingman rejoined. "Her politicians to-day choose to play the part of the ostrich in the desert. They take no account, or profess to take no account of European happenings. They have no Secret Service. Their country is governed from within for herself only. As for the rest, the bogey of a German invasion has been flaunted so long in England that few people stop to realise the absolute futility of such a course. London is already colonised by Germans — colonised, that is to say, in urban and money-making fashion. English gold is flowing in a never-ending stream into our country. It would be the most foolish dream an ambitious statesman could conceive to lay violent hands upon a land teeming with one's own children. Germany sees further than this. There are richer prizes across the Atlantic, richer prizes from every point of view."

"You mentioned South Africa," Monsieur Douaille murmured.

Selingman shrugged his shoulders.

"South Africa will make no nation rich," he replied. "Her own people are too stubborn and powerful, too rooted to the soil."

Monsieur Douaille for the first time stretched out his hand and drank some of the wine which stood by his side. His cheeks were very pale. He had the appearance of a man tortured by conflicting thoughts.

" I should like to ask you, Selingman," he said, " whether you have made any definite plans for your conflict with the British Navy? I admit that the days of England's unique greatness are over. She may not be in a position to-day, as she has been in former years, to fight the world. At the same time, her one indomitable power is still, whatever people may say or think, her navy. Only last month the Cabinet of my country were considering reports from their secret agents and placing them side by side with known facts, as to the relative strength of your navy and the navy of Great Britain. On paper it would seem that a German success was impossible."

Selingman smiled — the convincing smile of a man who sees further than most men.

" Not under the terms I should propose to you, Monsieur Douaille," he declared. " Remember that we should hold Calais, and we should be assured at least of the amiable neutrality of your fleet. We have spoken of matters so intimate that I do not know whether in this absolute privacy I should not be justified in going further and disclosing to you our whole scheme for an attack upon the English Navy. It would need only an expression of your sympathy with those views which we have discussed, to induce me to do so."

Monsieur Douaille hesitated for several moments before he replied.

"I am a citizen of France," he said, "an envoy without powers to treat. My own province is to listen."

"But your personal sympathies?" Selingman persisted.

"I have sometimes thought," Monsieur Douaille confessed, "that the present grouping of European Powers must gradually change. If your country, for instance," he added, turning to Mr. Grex, "indeed embraces the proposals of Herr Selingman, France must of necessity be driven to reconsider her position towards England. The Anglo-Saxon race may have to battle then for her very existence. Yet it is always to be remembered that in the background are the United States of America, possessing resources and wealth greater than any other country in the universe."

"And it must also be remembered," Selingman proclaimed, in a tone of ponderous conviction, "that she possesses no adequate means of guarding them, that she is not a military nation, that she has not the strength to enforce the carrying out of the Monroe Doctrine. Things were all very well for her before the days of wireless telegraphy, of aeroplanes and airships, of super-dreadnoughts, and cruisers with the speed of express trains. She was too far away to be concerned in European turmoils. To-day science is annihilating distance. America, leaving out of account altogether her military impotence, would need a fleet three times her present strength to enforce the Monroe Doctrine for the remainder — not of this century but of this decade."

Then the bombshell fell. A strange voice suddenly intervened, a voice whose American accent seemed more marked than usual. The four men turned their heads. Selingman sprang to his feet. Mr. Grex's face was marble in its whiteness. Monsieur Douaille, with a nervous sweep of his right arm, sent his glass crashing to the floor. They all looked in the same direction, up to the little music gallery. Leaning over in a careless attitude, with his arms folded upon the rail, was Richard Lane.

"Say," he begged, "can I take a hand in this little discussion?"

CHAPTER XXXVI

CHECKMATE!

Of the four men, Selingman was the first to recover himself.

"Who the hell are you, and how did you get up there?" he roared.

"I am Richard Lane," the young man explained affably, "and there's a way up from the music-room. You probably didn't notice it. And there's a way down, as you may perceive," he added, pointing to the spiral staircase. "I'll join you, if I may."

There was a dead silence as for a moment Richard disappeared and was seen immediately afterwards descending the round staircase. Mr. Grex touched Selingman on the arm and whispered in his ear. Selingman nodded. There were evil things in the faces of both men as Lane approached them.

"Will you kindly explain your presence here at once, sir?" Mr. Grex ordered.

"I say!" Richard protested. "A joke's a joke, but when you ask a man to explain his presence on his own boat, you're coming it just a little thick, eh? To tell you the truth, I had some sort of an idea of asking you the same question."

"What do you mean — your own boat?" Draconmeyer demanded.

He was, perhaps, the first to realise the situation. Richard thrust his hands into his pockets and sat upon the edge of the table.

" Seems to me," he remarked, " that you gentlemen have made some sort of a mistake. Where do you think you are, anyway? "

" On board Schwann's yacht, the *Christabel*," Selingman replied.

Richard shook his head.

" Not a bit of it," he assured them. " This is the steam-yacht, *Minnehaha*, which brought me over from New York, and of which I am most assuredly the owner. Now I come to think of it," he went on, " there was another yacht leaving the harbour at the same time. Can't have happened that you boarded the wrong boat, eh? "

Mr. Grex was icily calm, but there was menace of the most dangerous sort in his look and manner.

" Nothing of that sort was possible," he declared, " as you are, without doubt, perfectly well aware. It appears to me that this is a deliberate plut. The yacht which I and my friends thought that we were boarding to-night was the *Christabel*, which my servant had instructions to hire from Schwann of Monaco. I await some explanation from you, sir, as to your purpose in sending your pinnace to the landing-stage of the Villa Mimosa and deliberately misleading us as to our destination? "

" Well, I don't know that I've got much to say about that," Richard replied easily.

" You are offering us no explanation? " Selingman demanded.

" None," Richard assented coolly.

Selingman suddenly struck the table with his clenched fist.

" You were not alone up in that gallery ! "

" Getting warm, aren't you? " Richard murmured. Selingman turned to Grex.

" This young man is Hunterleys' friend. They've fixed this up between them. Listen! "

A door slammed above their heads. Some one had left the music gallery.

" Hunterleys himself! " Selingman cried.

" Sure! " Richard assented. " Bright fellow, Selingman," he continued amiably. " I wouldn't try that on, if I were you," he added, turning to Mr. Grex, whose hand was slowly stealing from the back of his coat. " That sort of thing doesn't do, nowadays. Revolvers belong to the last decade of intrigue. You're a bit out of date with that little weapon. Don't be foolish. I am not angry with any of you. I am willing to take this little joke pleasantly, but —"

He raised a whistle to his lips and blew it. The door at the further end of the saloon was opened as though by magic. A steward in the yacht's uniform appeared. From outside was visible a very formidable line of sailors. Grex, with a swift gesture, slipped something back into his pocket, something which glittered like silver.

" Serve some champagne, Reynolds," Richard ordered the steward who had come hurrying in, " and bring some cigars."

The man withdrew. Richard seated himself once more upon the table, clasping one knee.

" Look here," he said, " I'll be frank with you. I

came into this little affair for the sake of a pal. It was only by accident that I found my way up yonder — more to look after him than anything. I never imagined that you would have anything to say that was interesting to me. Seems I was wrong, though. You've got things very nicely worked out, Mr. Selingman."

Selingman glared at the young man but said nothing. The others, too, were all remarkably bereft of words.

"Don't mind my staying for a little chat, do you?" Richard continued pleasantly. "You see, I am an American and I am kind of interested in the latter portion of what you had to say. I dare say you're quite right in some respects. We are a trifle too commercial and a trifle too cocksure. You see, things have always gone our way. All the same, we've got the stuff, you know. Just consider this. If I thought there was any real need for it, and I begin to think that perhaps there may be, I should be ready to present the United States with a Dreadnought to-morrow, and I don't know that I should need to spend very much less myself. And," he went on, " there are thirty or forty others who could and would do the same. Tidy little fleet we should soon have, you see, without a penny of taxation. Of course, I know we would need the men, but we've a grand reserve to draw upon in the West. They are not bothering about the navy in times of peace, but they'd stream into it fast enough if there were any real need."

The chief steward appeared, followed by two or three of his subordinates. A tray of wine was placed upon the table. Bottles were opened, but no one made any attempt to drink. Richard filled his own glass and motioned the men to withdraw.

"Prefer your own wine?" he remarked. "Well, now, that's too bad. Hope I'm not boring you?"

No one spoke or moved. Richard settled himself a little more comfortably upon the table.

"I can't tell you all," he proceeded, "how interested I have been, listening up there. Quite a gift of putting things clearly, if I may be allowed to say so, you seem to possess, Mr. Selingman. Now here's my reply as one of the poor Anglo-Saxons from the West who've got to make room in the best parts of the world for your lubberly German colonists. If you make a move in the game you've been talking so glibly about, if my word counts for anything, if my persuasions count for anything — and I've facts to go on, you know — you'll have the American fleet to deal with at the same time as the English, and I fancy that will be a trifle more than you can chew up, eh? I'm going back to America a little earlier than I anticipated. Of course, they'll laugh at me at first in Washington. They don't believe much in these round-table conferences and European plots. But all the same I've got some friends there. We'll try and remember this amiable little statement of policy of yours, Mr. Selingman. Nothing like being warned, you know."

Mr. Grex rose from his place.

"Sir," he said, "since we have been and are your unwilling guests, will you be so good as to arrange for us at once to relieve you of our presence?"

"Well, I'm not so sure about that," Richard remarked, meditatively. "I think I'd contribute a good deal to the comfort and happiness of this generation if I took you all out to sea and dropped you overboard, one by one."

"As I presume you have no such intention," Mr. Grex persisted, "I repeat that we should be glad to be allowed to land."

Richard abandoned his indolent posture and stood facing them.

"You came on board, gentlemen, without my invitation," he reminded them. "You will leave my ship when I choose — and that," he added, "is not just at present."

"Do you mean that we are to consider ourselves your prisoners?" Draconmeyer asked, with an acid smile.

"Certainly not — my guests," Richard replied, with a bow. "I can assure you that it will only be a matter of a few hours."

Monsieur Douaille hammered the table with his fist.

"Young man," he exclaimed, "I leave with you! I insist upon it that I am permitted to leave. l am not a party to this conference. I am merely a guest, a listener, here wholly in my private capacity. I will not be associated with whatever political scandal may arise from this affair. I demand permission to leave at once."

"Seems to me there's something in what you say," Richard admitted. "Very well, you can come along. I dare say Hunterleys will be glad to have a chat with you. As for the rest of you," he concluded, as Monsieur Douaille rose promptly to his feet, "I have a little business to arrange on land which I think I could manage better whilst you are at sea. I shall therefore, gentlemen, wish you good evening. Pray consider my yacht entirely at your disposal. My stewards will be only too happy to execute any orders — supper, breakfast, or dinner. You have merely to say the word."

He turned towards the door, closely followed by Douaille, who, in a state of great excitement, refused to listen to Selingman's entreaties.

" No, no! " the former objected, shaking his head. " I will not stay. I will not be associated with this meeting. You are bunglers, all of you. I came only to listen, on your solemn assurance of entire secrecy. We are spied upon at the Villa Mimosa, we are made fools of on board this yacht. No more unofficial meetings for me! "

" Quite right, old fellow," Richard declared, as they passed out and on to the deck. " Set of wrong 'uns, those chaps, even though Mr. Grex is a Grand Duke. You know Sir Henry Hunterleys, don't you ? "

Hunterleys came forward from the gangway, at the foot of which the pinnace was waiting.

" We are taking Monsieur Douaille ashore," Richard explained, as the two men shook hands. " He really doesn't belong to that gang and he wants to cut adrift. You understand my orders exactly, captain? " he asked, as they stepped down the iron gangway.

" Perfectly, sir," was the prompt reply. " You may rely upon me. I am afraid they are beginning to make a noise downstairs already! "

The little pinnace shot out a stream of light across the dark, placid sea. Douaille was talking earnestly to Hunterleys.

"Pleasantest few minutes I ever spent in my life," Richard murmured, as he took out his cigarette case.

CHAPTER XXXVII

AN AMAZING ELOPEMENT

The sun was shining brilliantly and the sky was cloudless as Richard turned his automobile into the grounds of the Villa Mimosa, soon after nine o'clock on the following morning. The yellow-blossomed trees, slightly stirred by the west wind, formed a golden arch across the winding avenue. The air was sweet, almost faint with perfume. On the terrace, holding a pair of field-glasses in her hand and gazing intently out to sea, was Fedora. At the sound of the motor-horn she turned quickly. She looked at the visitor in surprise. A shade of pink was in her face. Lane brought the car to a standstill, jumped out and climbed the steps of the terrace.

" What has brought you here? " she asked, in surprise.

" I have just come to pay you a little visit," he remarked easily. " I was only afraid you mightn't be up so early."

She bit her lip.

" You have no right to come here at all," she said severely, " and to present yourself at this hour is unheard of."

" I came early entirely out of consideration for your father," he assured her.

She frowned.

" My father? " she repeated. " Please explain at once what you mean. My father is on that yacht and I cannot imagine why he does not return."

" I can tell you," he answered, standing by her side and looking out seawards. " They are waiting for my orders before they let him off."

She turned her head and looked at him incredulously.

" Explain yourself, please," she insisted.

" With pleasure," he assented. " You see, I just had to make sure of being allowed to have a few minutes' conversation with you, free from any interruption. Somehow or other," he added thoughtfully, " I don't believe your father likes me."

" I do not think," she replied coldly, " that my father has any feelings about you at all, except that he thinks you are abominably presumptuous."

" Because I want to marry you? "

She stamped with her foot upon the ground.

" Please do not say such absurd things! Explain to me at once what you mean by saying that my father is being kept there by your orders."

" I'll try," Lane answered. " He boarded that yacht last night in mistake. He thought that it was a hired one, but it isn't. It's mine. I found him there last night, entertaining a little party of his friends in the saloon. They seemed quite comfortable, so I begged them to remain on as my guests for a short time."

" To remain? " she murmured, bewildered. " For how long? "

" Until you've just read this through and thought it over."

He passed her a document which he had drawn from his pocket. She took it from him wonderingly. When she had read a few lines, the colour came streaming into her cheeks. She threw it to the ground. He picked it up and replaced it in his pocket.

" But it is preposterous! " she cried. " That is a marriage license! "

" That's precisely what it is," he admitted. " I thought we'd be married at Nice. My sister is waiting to go along with us. I said we'd pick her up at the Hotel de Paris."

Severe critics of her undoubted beauty had ventured at times to say that Fedora's face lacked expression. There was, at that moment, no room for any such criticism. Amazement struggled with indignation in her eyes. Her lips were quivering, her breath was coming quickly.

" Do you mean — have you given her or any one to understand that there was any likelihood of my consenting to such an absurd scheme? "

" I only told her what I hoped," he said quietly. " That is all I dared say even to myself. But I want you to listen to me."

His voice had grown softer. She turned her head and looked at him. He was much taller than she was, and in his grey tweed suit, his head a little thrown back, his straw hat clasped in his hands behind him, his clear grey eyes full of serious purpose, he was certainly not an unattractive figure to look upon. Unconsciously she found herself comparing him once more with the men of her world, found herself realising, even against her will, the charm of his naïve and dogged honesty, his youth, his tenacity of purpose. She had never been made love to like this before.

"Please listen," he begged. "I am afraid that your father must be in a tearing rage by now, but it can't be helped. He is out there and he hasn't got an earthly chance of getting back until I give the word. We've got plenty of time to reach Nice before he can land. I just want you to realise, Fedora, that you are your own mistress. You can make or spoil your own life. No one else has any right to interfere. Have you ever seen any one yet, back in your own country, amongst your own people, whom you really felt that you cared for — who you really believed would be willing to lay down his life to make you happy?"

"No," she confessed simply, "I do not know that I have. Our men are not like that."

"It is because," he went on, "there is no one back there who cares as I do. I have spent some years of my life looking — quite unconsciously, but looking all the same — for some one like you. Now I have found you I am glad I have waited. There couldn't be any one else. There never could be, Fedora. I love you just in the way a man does love once in his life, if he's lucky. It's a queer sort of feeling, you know," he continued, leaning a little towards her. "It makes me quite sure that I could make you happy. It makes me quite sure that if you'll give me your hand and trust me, and leave everything to me, you'll have just the things in life that women want. Won't you be brave, Fedora? There are some things to break through, I know, but they don't amount to much — they don't, really. And I love you, you know. You can't imagine yet what a wonderful difference that makes. You'll find out and you'll be glad."

She stood quite still. Her eyes were still fixed seawards, but she was looking beyond the yacht, now, to the dim line where sky and sea seemed to meet. The vision of her past days seemed to be drawn out before her, a little monotonous, a little wearisome even in their splendour, more than a little empty. And underneath it all she was listening to the new music, and her heart was telling her the truth.

"You don't need to make any plans," he said softly. "Go and put on your hat and something to wear motoring. Bring a dressing-bag, if you like. Flossie is waiting for us and she is rather a dear. You can leave everything else to me."

She looked timidly into his eyes. A new feeling was upon her. She gave him her hand almost shyly. Her voice trembled.

"If I come," she whispered, "you are quite sure that you mean it all? You are quite sure that you will not change?"

He raised her hand to his lips.

"Not in this world, dear," he answered, with sublime confidence, "nor any other!"

She stole away from him. He was left alone upon the terrace, alone, but with the exquisite conviction of her return, promised in that last half-tremulous, half-smiling look over her shoulder. Then suddenly life seemed to come to him with a rush, a new life, filled with a new splendour. He was almost humbly conscious of bigger things than he had ever realised, a nearness to the clouds, a wonderful, thrilling sense of complete and absolute happiness. . . . Reluctantly he came back to earth. His thoughts became practical. He went to the back of his car, drew out a rocket on a stick and thrust it firmly into the lawn. Then he started his engine and almost immediately afterwards she came. She was wearing a white silk motor-coat and a thick veil. Behind her came a bewildered French maid, carrying wraps, and a man-servant with a heavy dressing-case. In silence these things were stowed away. She took her place in the car. Lane struck a match and stepped on to the lawn.

" Don't be frightened," he said. " Here goes! "

A rocket soared up into the sky. Then he seated himself beside her and they glided off.

" That means," he explained, " that they'll let your father and the others off in two hours. Give us plenty of time to get to Nice. Have you — left any word for him? "

" I have left a very short message," she answered, " to say that I was going to marry you. He will never forgive me, and I feel very wicked and very ungrateful."

" Anything else? " he whispered, leaning a little towards her.

She sighed.

" And very happy," she murmured.

CHAPTER XXXVIII

HONEYMOONING

Hunterleys saw the Right Honourable Meredith Simpson and Monsieur Douaille off to Paris early that morning. Then he called round at the hospital to find that Sidney Roche was out of danger, and went on to the villa with the good news. On his way back he stayed chatting with the bank manager until rather later than usual, and afterwards strolled on to the Terrace, where he looked with some eagerness towards a certain point in the bay. The *Minnehaha* had departed. Mr. Grex and his friends, then, had been set free. Hunterleys returned to the hotel thoughtfully. At the entrance he came across two or three trunks being wheeled out, which seemed to him somehow familiar. He stopped to look at the initials. They were his wife's.

" Is Lady Hunterleys leaving to-day? " he asked the luggage-porter.

" By the evening train, sir," the man announced. " She would have caught the *Côte d'Azur* this morning but there was no place on the train."

Hunterleys was perplexed. Some time after luncheon he enquired for Lady Hunterleys and found that she was not in the hotel. A reception clerk thought that he had seen her go through on her way to the Sporting Club. Hunterleys, after some mo-

ments of indecision, followed her. He was puzzled
at her impending departure, unable to account for
it. The Draconmeyers, he knew, proposed to stay
for another month. He walked thoughtfully along
the private way and climbed the stairs into the Club.
He looked for his wife in her usual place. She was
not there. He made a little promenade of the rooms
and eventually he found her amongst the spectators
around the baccarat table. He approached her at
once.

" You are not playing? "

She started at the sound of his voice. She was
dressed very simply in travelling clothes, and there
were lines under her eyes, as though she were fa-
tigued.

" No," she admitted, " I am not playing."

" I understood in the hotel," he continued, " that
you were leaving to-day."

" I am going back to England," she announced.
" It does not amuse me here any longer."

He realised at once that something had happened.
A curious sense of excitement stole into his blood.

" If you are not playing here, will you come and
sit down for a few moments? " he invited. " I should
like to talk to you."

She followed him without a word. He led the way
to one of the divans in the roulette room.

" Your favourite place," he remarked, " is occu-
pied."

She nodded.

" I have given up playing," she told him.

He looked at her in some surprise. She drew a
little breath and kept her eyes steadily averted.

"You will probably know sometime or other," she continued, "so I will tell you now. I have lost four thousand pounds to Mr. Draconmeyer. I am going back to England to realise my own money, so as to be able to pay him at once."

"You borrowed four thousand pounds from Mr. Draconmeyer?" he repeated incredulously.

"Yes! It was very foolish, I know, and I have lost every penny of it. I am not the first woman, I suppose, who has lost her head at Monte Carlo," she added, a little defiantly.

"Does Mr. Draconmeyer know that you are leaving?" he asked.

"Not yet," she answered, after a moment's hesitation. "I had an interview with him yesterday and I realised at once that the money must be paid, and without delay. I realised, too, that it was better I should leave Monte Carlo and break off my association with these people for the present."

In a sense it was a sordid story, yet to Hunterleys her words sounded like music.

"I am very pleased indeed," he said quietly, "that you feel like that. Draconmeyer is not a man to whom I should like my wife to owe money for a moment longer than was absolutely necessary."

"Your estimate of him was correct," she confessed slowly. "I am sorry, Henry."

He rose suddenly to his feet. An inspiration had seized him.

"Come," he declared, "we will pay Draconmeyer back without sending you home to sell your securities. Come and stand with me."

She looked at him in amazement.

" Henry ! " she exclaimed. " You are not going to play? Don't! Take my advice and don't ! "

He laughed.

" We'll see," he replied confidently. " You wouldn't believe that I was a fatalist, would you? I am, though. Everything that I had hoped for seems to be happening to-day. You have found out Draconmeyer, we have checkmated Mr. Grex, I have drunk the health of Felicia and David Briston —"

" Felicia and David Briston? " she interrupted quickly. " What do you mean? "

" You knew, of course, that they were engaged? " he explained. " I called round at the villa this morning, after I had been to the hospital, and found them busy fixing the wedding day."

She looked at him vaguely.

" Engaged? " she murmured. " Why, I thought —"

A spot of colour suddenly burned in her cheeks. She was beginning to understand. It was Draconmeyer who had put those ideas into her head. Her heart gave a little leap.

" Henry ! " she whispered.

He was already at the table, however. He changed five mille notes deliberately, counted his plaques and turned to her.

" I am going to play on your principle," he declared. " I have always thought it an interesting one. See, the last number was twenty-two. I am going to back twenty and all the *carrés*."

He covered the board around number twenty. There were a few minutes of suspense, then the click as the ball fell into the little space.

" *Vingt-huit, noir, passe et pair!* " the croupier announced.

Hunterleys' stake was swept away. He only smiled.

" Our numbers are going to turn up," he insisted cheerfully. " I am certain of it now. Do you know that this is the first time I have played since I have been in Monte Carlo? "

She watched him half in fear. This time he staked on twenty-nine, with the maximum *en plein* and all the *carrés* and *chevaux*. Again the few moments of suspense, the click of the ball, the croupier's voice.

" *Vingt-neuf, noir, impair et passe!* "

She clutched at his arm.

" Henry ! " she gasped.

He laughed.

" Open your bag," he directed. " We'll soon fill it."

He left his stake untouched. Thirty-one turned up. He won two *carrés* and let the table go once without staking. Ten was the next number. Immediately he placed the maximum on number fourteen, *carrés* and *chevaux*. Again the pause, again the croupier's voice.

" *Quatorze rouge, pair et manque!* "

Hunterleys showed no exultation and scarcely any surprise. He gathered in his winnings and repeated his stake. This time he won one of his *carrés*. The next time *quatorze* turned up again. For half-an-hour he continued, following his few chosen numbers according to the run of the table. At the end of that time Violet's satchel was full and he was beginning to collect mille notes for his plaques. He made

a little calculation in his mind and decided that he·
must already have won more than the necessary
amount.

" Our last stake," he remarked coolly.

The preceding number had been twenty-six. He
placed the maximum on twenty-nine, the *carrés*,
chevaux, the column, colour and last dozen. He felt
Violet's fingers clutching his arm. There was a little buzz of excitement all round the table as the
croupier announced the number.

" *Vingt-neuf noir, impair et passe!* " . . .

They took their winnings into the anteroom beyond, where Hunterleys ordered tea. There was a
little flush in Violet's cheeks. They counted the
money. There was nearly five thousand pounds.

" Henry ! " she exclaimed. " I think that that
last coup was the most marvellous win I ever saw ! "

" A most opportune one, at any rate," he replied
grimly. " Look who is coming."

Draconmeyer had entered the room, and was peer-
ing everywhere as though in search of some one. He
suddenly caught sight of them, hesitated for a moment and then approached. He addressed himself
to Violet.

" I have just seen Linda," he said. " She is bro-
ken-hearted at the thought of your departure."

" I am sorry to leave her," Violet replied, " but I
feel that I have stayed quite long enough in Monte
Carlo. By the bye, Mr. Draconmeyer, there is that
little affair of the money you were kind enough to
advance to me."

Draconmeyer stood quite still. He looked from
husband to wife.

"Four thousand pounds, my wife tells me," Hunterleys remarked coolly, as he began to count out the notes. "It is very good of you indeed to have acted as my wife's banker. Do you mind being paid now? Our movements are a little uncertain and it will save the trouble of sending you a cheque."

Draconmeyer laughed. It was not a pleasant laugh, nor was it in the least mirthful.

"Dear me!" he exclaimed. "I had forgotten that little matter. As you will, certainly."

He accepted the notes and stuffed them into his pocket.

"By the bye," he continued, "I think that I ought to congratulate you, Sir Henry. That last little affair of yours was wonderfully stage-managed. Your country owes you more than it is ever likely to pay. You have succeeded, at any rate, in delaying the inevitable."

"I trust," Hunterleys enquired politely, "that you were not detained upon the yacht for very long?"

"We landed at the Villa at twelve o'clock this morning," Draconmeyer replied. "You know, of course, of the little surprise our young American friend had prepared for Mr. Grex?"

Hunterleys shook his head.

"I have heard nothing definite."

"He was married to the daughter of the Grand Duke Augustus at midday at Nice," Draconmeyer announced. "His Serene Highness received a telephone message only a short time ago."

Violet gave a little cry. She leaned across the table eagerly.

"You mean that they have eloped?"

Draconmeyer assented.

" All Monte Carlo will be talking about it to-morrow," he declared. " The Grand Duke has been doing all he can to get it hushed up, but it is useless. I will not detain you any longer. I see that you are about to have tea."

" We shall meet, perhaps, in London? " Hunterleys remarked, as Draconmeyer prepared to depart.

Draconmeyer shook his head.

" I think not," he replied. " The doctors have advised me that the climate of England is bad for my wife's health, and I feel that my own work there is finished. I have received an offer to go out to South America for a time. Very likely I shall accept."

He passed on with a final bow. Violet looked across their table and her eyes shone.

" It seems like a fairy tale, Henry," she whispered. " You don't know what a load on my mind that money has been, and how I was growing to detest Mr. Draconmeyer."

He smiled.

" I was rather hating the beast myself," he admitted. " Tell me, what are your plans, really? "

" I hadn't made any," she confessed, " except to get away as quickly as I could."

He leaned a little across the table.

" Elopements are rather in the fashion," he said. " What do you think? Couldn't we have a little dinner at Ciro's and catch the last train to Nice; have a look at Richard and his wife and then go on to Cannes, and make our way back to England later? "

She looked at him and his face grew younger.

There was something in her eyes which reminded him of the days which for so many weary months he had been striving to forget.

"Henry," she murmured, "I have been very foolish. If you can trust me once more, I think I can promise that I'll never be half so idiotic again."

He rose to his feet blithely.

"It has been my fault just as much," he declared, "and the fault of circumstances. I couldn't tell you the whole truth, but there has been a villainous conspiracy going on here. Draconmeyer, Selingman, and the Grand Duke were all in it and I have been working like a slave. Now it's all over, finished this morning on Richard's yacht. We've done what we could. I'm a free lance now and we'll spend the holidays together."

She gave him her fingers across the table and he held them firmly in his. Then she, too, rose and they passed out together. There was a wonderful change in Hunterleys. He seemed to have grown years younger.

"Come," he exclaimed, "they call this the City of Pleasure, but these are the first happy moments I have spent in it. We'll gamble in five-franc pieces for an hour or so. Then we'll go back to the hotel and have our trunks sent down to the station, dine at Ciro's and wire Richard. Where are you going to stake your money?"

"I think I shall begin with number twenty-nine," she laughed.

They lunched with Richard and his wife, a few days later, at the Casino at Cannes. The change in the two young people was most impressive. Fedora had lost the dignified aloofness of Monte Carlo. She seemed as though she had found her girlhood. She was brilliantly, supremely happy. Richard, on the other hand, was more serious. He took Hunterleys on one side as they waited for the cars.

"We are on our way to Biarritz," he said, "by easy stages. The yacht will meet us there and we are going to sail at once for America."

"Fedora doesn't mind?" Hunterleys asked.

"Not in the least," Richard declared exultantly. "She knows what my duty is, and, Hunterleys, I am going to try and do it. The people over there may need a lot of convincing, but they are going to hear the truth from me and have it drummed into them. It's going to be 'Wake up, America!' as well as 'Wake up, England!'"

"Stick at it, Richard," Hunterleys advised. "Don't mind a little discouragement. Men who see the truth and aren't afraid to keep on calling attention to it, get laughed at a great deal. People speak of them tolerantly, listen to what they say, doubt its reasonableness and put it at the back of their heads, but in the end it does good. Your people and mine are slow to believe and slow to understand, but the truth sinks in if one proclaims it often enough and loudly enough. We are going through it in our own country just now, with regard to National Service, for one thing. Here come your cars. You travel in state, Richard."

The young man laughed good-naturedly.

"There's nothing in life which I could give her that Fedora sha'n't have," he asserted. "We spent the first two days absolutely alone. Now her maid and my man come along with the luggage in the heavy car, and we take the little racer. Jolly hard work they have to keep anywhere near us, I can tell you. Say, may I make a rather impertinent remark, Sir Henry?"

"You have earned the right to say anything to me you choose," Hunterleys replied. "Go ahead."

"Why, it's only this," Richard continued, a little awkwardly. "I have never seen Lady Hunterleys look half so ripping, and you seem years younger."

Hunterleys smiled.

"To tell you the truth, I feel it. You see, years ago, when we started out for our honeymoon, there was a crisis after the first week and we had to rush back to England. We seem to have forgotten to ever finish that honeymoon of ours. We are doing it now."

The two women came down the steps, the cynosure of a good many eyes, the two most beautiful women in the Casino. Richard helped his wife into her place, wrapped her up and took the steering wheel.

"Hyères to-night and Marseilles to-morrow," he announced, "Biarritz on Saturday. We shall stay there for a week, and then — 'Wake up, America!'"

The cars glided off. Hunterleys and his wife stood on the steps, waving their hands.

"Something about those children," Hunterleys declared, as they vanished, "makes me feel absurdly young. Let's go shopping, Violet. I want to buy you some flowers and chocolates."

She smiled happily as she took his arm for a moment.

" And then? "

" What would you like to do afterwards? " he asked.

" I think," she replied, leaning towards him, " that I should like to go to that nice Englishman who lets villas, and find one right at the edge of the sea, quite hidden, and lock the gates, and give no one our address, and have you forget for just one month that there was any work to do in the world, or any one else in it except me."

" Just to make up," he laughed softly.

" Women are like that, you know," she murmured.

" The man's office is this way," Hunterleys said, turning off the main street.

THE END